"Prepare to burn the midnight oil. I couldn't put this book down. *The Veil* revealed a shocking early Mormon practice that chills the blood, but makes it much easier to understand the grip of fear that still holds Mormons today."

—***Francine Rivers,*** author

"Diane Noble's thoughtfully paced, can't-put-down narrative is filled with characters I cheered for, cried for, grieved for. Historical research and spiritual insights underpin this stunning work by one of Christian fiction's finest writers."

—***Liz Curtis Higgs,*** author

"*The Veil* is a tender, yet fascinating novel that reveals the truth about a little known part of American history—the early years of Mormonism in Utah. Diane Noble has written a beautiful story about God's unconditional love and the way he shows himself to those who earnestly seek his face."

—***Robin Lee Hatcher,*** author

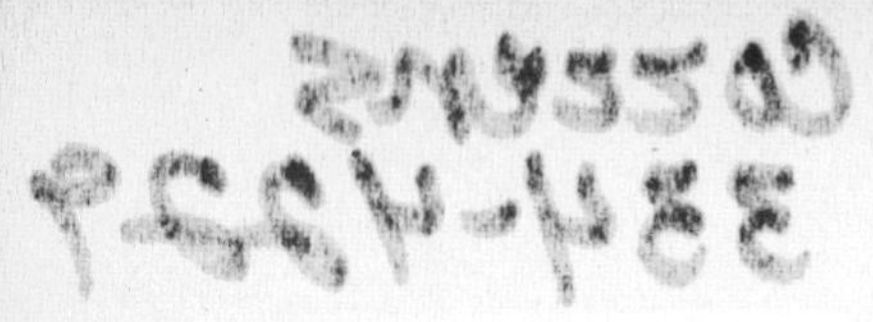

"Diane Noble has done her part to shine light through the veil of secrecy and misunderstanding surrounding the early days of the Mormon movement. I was spellbound as I read—you will be too!"

—***Angela Elwell Hunt,*** author

"From the moment Lucas Knight battles the downstream creek, the reader is plunged into a maelstrom of deceit and man-made edicts. I couldn't put it down."

—***Don Pape,*** president, Canadian Signature Group

"*The Veil* is . . . a fine piece of writing that tells a foreboding and compelling story of power and spiritual searching within the lives of ordinary people."

—***Jane Kirkpatrick,*** author

"Noble's work is a tour de force, a compelling story of romance, courage, and enduring love set against a tumultuous backdrop of prejudice and fear on the Mormon frontier."

—***Ronald Woolsey,*** author/historian

THE VEIL

Other Books by Diane Noble

Tangled Vines

(written as Amanda MacLean)

Westward

Stonehaven

Everlasting

Promise Me the Dawn

Kingdom Come

The Veil

Diane Noble

WaterBrook
Press
Colorado Springs

THE VEIL
PUBLISHED BY WATERBROOK PRESS
5446 North Academy Boulevard, Suite 200
Colorado Springs, Colorado 80918
A division of Bantam Doubleday Dell Publishing Group, Inc.

The characters and events in this book are largely fictional. For further information see the Preface and Author's Notes.

ISBN 1-57856-014-4

Printed in the United States of America
1998—First Edition

1 3 5 7 9 10 8 6 4 2

To Tom
With all my love

"This hope we have as an anchor of the soul,
both sure and steadfast, and which enters
the Presence behind the veil . . ."

Hebrews 6:19, NKJV

ACKNOWLEDGMENTS

I would like to offer thanks to the following people for their support during the writing of *The Veil.*

My husband, Tom, a historian, was my partner in the intensive research that provided the foundation for this project. Together we visited the Mountain Meadows Massacre site and traveled much of the Utah portion of the trail taken by the wagon company. Early on, we had the opportunity to interview descendants of those involved in the massacre as well as descendants of relatives of the wagon train families. My husband's belief in this story and in my writing prodded me along even when other projects threatened to interfere. His love and encouragement never wavered.

A decade ago Carolyn Coker, writing teacher extraordinaire and friend, took my first storytelling attempts seriously—long before I did. It was in her class that the first seeds of *The Veil's* story took root. I am grateful for her belief in me and for her always well-placed words of wisdom. Other past-and-present members of what has become Carolyn's lively literary critique group also provided wonderful insights: Jim Brown, Paul Hawley, Barbara Hoffman, Billie Johnson, Donna Sanders, Kim Sarchet, and Anna Waterhouse.

If one person could qualify as *The Veil's* midwife, that person is Liz Curtis Higgs. Liz provided much of the day-to-day prayer and loving support—mostly long distance by e-mail—that brought forth this work. Through my final months of intense writing, rewriting, and editing, she "listened" thoughtfully and gave generously of her time to encourage and advise. Her own keen sense of the art of fiction writing provided me an invaluable sounding board for characters and plot.

Several years ago, when I first met Lisa Bergren, I had no idea what an impact this chance meeting would have on my life. Yet God knew, and he knit us together as editor-author and also as friends. Lisa's astute, enthusiastic, and sensitive editing direction significantly helped define *The Veil.*

I am happily in debt to each.

PREFACE

The events that provide the historical backdrop for *The Veil* are true. But to understand their unfolding, the reader must be aware of the emotional and political climate that existed in Utah Territory in the mid-nineteenth century. Prior to 1857, the Mormons had been persecuted and evicted from Kirkland, Ohio; Far West, Missouri; and Nauvoo, Illinois. They suffered terrible atrocities in all these places but none worse than in Far West in the late 1830s. A few years later, their founder and leader, Joseph Smith, was murdered as part of the Mormon exodus from Nauvoo. In the mid 1840s, their new Prophet, Brigham Young, led the beleaguered Saints west to the Salt Lake Valley, where they fervently determined never again to be chased from their promised land. But in 1857, word reached the Saints that U.S. government troops were heading west to take over the Territory and replace Young as governor. The result was a frenzy of outrage and fear that spread like wildfire throughout the Territory.

It was no coincidence that the same year Brigham Young stepped up preaching his theology of blood atonement—the necessity of killing one's enemies in order to save their eternal lives. If anyone—apostate or enemy—could hope to reach heaven, Young and his elders taught, it could be only through the spilling of that person's blood. Therefore, killing one's enemies became a sacred duty. It also became a license to kill. Non-Mormons were obvious targets. Such was the mood when an innocent wagon company, known in this work as the Farrington Train, headed west . . . straight into the heart of the brutal, warlike atmosphere of Utah Territory.

The characters in *The Veil* are largely fictional, although many are based on participants on both sides of the events at Mountain Meadows. Quotes attributed to Brigham Young and other Mormon leaders are taken from actual sermons, writings, and Mormon newspaper accounts of the period.

PROLOGUE

Lucas

Haun's Mill, Missouri
October 1838

Lucas Knight fled through the woods, his breath coming in short, painful pants. The boy was too scared to think, too numbed by what he had just witnessed, to consider anything but shoving through the tangle of wild berry vines and scratchy brambles.

From a ways down the trace, from the compound that had been his home, the terrifying shouts of the hunters carried toward him. Lucas stopped and cocked his head, listening carefully, his chest heaving.

The hunters were still after him. He could hear their horses crashing through the brush and their hounds howling as they followed his trail.

Sobs of fear caught in his throat. His heart pounded as he waited. He knew the woods better than anyone. Since he and his ma and pa and baby brother had moved to Haun's Mill a year ago, he had roamed the hillsides. He knew every secret hiding place, every cave, every lookout, every oak best for climbing.

He set his lips in a straight, stubborn line and lifted his chin, gulping back his sobs. They wouldn't catch him. He was smarter than they were. He would get to safety. Somehow.

He remembered a cave just beyond the creek up ahead. If he made it to the water, the hounds might lose his scent. Then he could climb up the steep trail on the other side to the point of rocks.

The horses and hounds and hunters drew nearer. Lucas could feel the vibrations from pounding hooves beneath his feet, and his ears ached from listening to the dogs trailing his scent. He imagined their bared teeth, their panting breath. The image made his knees weak with fear.

He was the lone witness to what the hunters had done. They wouldn't let him live if they caught him. He ran faster.

Lucas spotted the creek, barely visible through a stand of alders, and stopped to catch his breath. The soft neigh of a horse followed by a rustling in the brush caused the hair on the back of Lucas's neck to stand tall. Halting cautiously, he squinted into the dense wood. No one was in sight, and he breathed easier.

He crouched low in a thicket of ferns then moved silently toward the water, gingerly making his way across its moss-covered stones. His gaze skimmed the brush for the presence he had earlier felt, but again he saw no one.

Lucas pushed off from a rock, and half-swimming, half-crawling over the slick and muddy creek bottom, he slowly made his way upstream. The current was swift in some places, so he figured the men would suppose he'd headed downstream because it was safer and easier.

Behind him, the hunting dogs were howling at the water's edge, yipping, crying, braying, digging, snorting where they had lost his scent.

But Lucas, now beyond a deep bend in the creek bed, didn't stop, figuring it wouldn't be long until the hunters reckoned his direction. He had just reached a small waterfall beyond another bend when he heard a rider coming through the brush directly ahead.

His heart caught in his throat. He couldn't return downstream. The brush on the far side of the creek was too sparse for hiding. He was trapped.

As he considered his plight, a tall, black horse broke into the clearing and halted abruptly in a patch of late-afternoon sunlight. It struck the burly rider across the face, making his dark hair gleam and his ice blue eyes look startlingly pale against his swarthy skin. The rider didn't seem at all surprised to see Lucas.

The boy stood, water streaming from his clothes. Around him the shin-high water bubbled and swirled. He felt like crying but kept himself from it, thinking how ashamed his pa would be if he let even one tear fall. Biting his lip, he mutely acknowledged the man with a nod.

"Lucas," the man said gently, "you did right by coming this way. I hoped you'd pick the creek."

Lucas tried to keep the tremble out of his voice. "You been the one watchin' me?"

"Yes, son. I've never been far. I was just waiting until you put more distance between you and the posse."

The boy waded through the water to the creek bank. "They're still comin', Brother Steele," he said. The cool air struck his wet clothes and his thin body, and he shivered.

"You lost them, at least for now, boy. You did it better than most men I know."

In spite of what he had been through, Lucas felt proud. "You know, then, what's happened?"

"Yes, son, I know," John Steele said, his voice grim. "I know."

The hounds bawled again from someplace downstream. Steele narrowed his eyes, squinting in that direction. Still astride his mount, he removed his wool coat and tossed it to Lucas. "Here. Put this on and climb up. We've got to get out of here."

Lucas slipped his arms into the sleeves, reached up to take Steele's big, callous hand, then swung onto the horse behind the saddle. A few minutes later, as the black mare carried them deep into the woods, the boy leaned his cheek against Steele's broad back.

Before long, dusk settled around them like a shroud, and fog laced among the alders and pines and oaks, dripping a heavy mist from the branches. The woods seemed filled with the smell of damp, loamy soil and decaying leaves. The mare thundered along the trace for hours, it seemed to Lucas. He clung to John Steele, his arms circling the man, afraid to let go.

At last Steele halted the horse in front of a log house, and Lucas rubbed his sleepy eyes with the back of his fists. Several horses were tied to hitching posts, and the glow of lantern light spilled through the windows out into the darkness. John Steele dismounted then reached up to take the boy from the horse.

The big man strode to the house, Lucas in his arms. He didn't stop until he reached a worn horsehair chair near the fireplace. After he had kicked the chair closer to the crackling fire, he placed the boy on its cushion, his manner gentler than his size bespoke.

"Get some blankets," Steele ordered one of the men who had trailed after them into the room. "And he needs food. What this boy's been through . . ." His voice faltered, and he didn't go on.

Lucas could hear the sound of voices from an adjoining room. Then the first man returned with two heavy, faded quilts. He handed them to Steele, who then knelt before the boy, enclosing him in the covers, tucking them around him as gently as if Lucas were his own son. By now several other men had moved into the room and stood nearby. One of them drew closer, holding out a crockery bowl with steam curling into the air above it.

Lucas reached for the bowl and dipped in the tin spoon that had been brought with it. Squirrel stew. It reminded him of his ma's cooking, and quick tears stung his eyes. He pushed the crock back toward the man, who exchanged glances with Steele then withdrew it.

"What's happened?" A tall man with an angular face and shoulder-length silver hair stepped forward. The others—seven all together—moved aside for him. His name was Porter Roe. Lucas had heard him speak at a Sunday meeting once. He remembered his pa saying that Brother Roe was a holy man, maybe nearly as holy as the Prophet himself. Holy and dangerous. A man you would want to have on your side. Those were Pa's exact words, he remembered.

"What's happened, John?" Porter Roe said again to Steele. His voice was flat, as if containing some hidden anger. Lucas figured he knew what had happened back at the mill. Roe glanced at the boy; their eyes met briefly before he turned again to John Steele.

"Another settlement attack?" he asked Steele.

John nodded. "The worst you can imagine, Porter. Out at Haun's Mill. We lost at least seventeen—children . . . women . . . babies.

Some of our best men." He hesitated. "The boy here is the only survivor. At least the only one I could find."

"There's no one else," Lucas whispered. "I saw what happened 'cause I played dead . . . until they got busy with the rest of the killin'. Then I—" He squeezed his eyes shut, unable to go on.

Porter Roe pulled up a ladder-back chair and swung a leg over it to sit. The others sat as well, some on the rough-hewn pine floor, others on various stools or chairs. "Do you feel like talking about it, son?" Brother Roe asked.

The boy felt his eyes fill again and his chin tremble. He fought acting like a baby in front of these men.

"It might help us find those who did this to you—to your family, son. We need to act fast."

Lucas nodded. He understood. Maybe he could help. At least then he wouldn't feel like such a baby. Swallowing hard, he said, "They were on horseback, the killers, I mean. Maybe a hundred. Or more. They came fast. Seemed like out of nowhere. When I heard the horses, I ran to the blacksmith's shop with my ma and little brother." He paused. It had happened only a few hours ago, and already it didn't seem real.

Ma. He pictured her soft, pretty face. The sound of her laughter, low and bubbly. It seemed he could still hear her voice telling him to get out of bed that morning, telling him his plate of warm bread and jam was on the table. And coffee with some sugar and cream, just the way she knew he liked. Now she was dead, along with his pa and all the others. And in place of her pretty face, he saw only blood. Her blood mingled with that of his little brother, Eli.

John Steele patted his shoulder. "Maybe tomorrow would be better."

"It'll never be better, Brother Steele," Lucas said. "Never."

"Did you hear any names? Did the killers say anything you remember?" Roe asked.

Lucas closed his eyes. Oh yes. He remembered their voices. Clearly. Too clearly. He looked at Brother Roe. "They were laughing, calling out to each other as they hacked up the people and shot their guns."

In the room, the men had fallen silent. The only sound was that of the fire crackling and popping.

"I heard the killers shouting above the screams."

John Steele's hand still rested on Lucas's shoulder. He was glad it was there. It reminded him of warmth and life, not death. He swallowed again. "They were laughing about being the Missouri Wildcats."

"Wildcats?" Porter Roe repeated, frowning.

"Yes sir. I didn't hear any names other than that. Just laughing and talking loud about being Missouri Wildcats—like it was something to be proud of."

"Any of you heard anything about wildcats?" Porter Roe turned to the others, but they were shaking their heads. "Wildcats," he said, as if savoring the sound of the word in his mouth. "We'll see how wild they are once we finish with them. And I tell you the honest truth, young man, we'll find someone who'll talk, someone who'll tell us who killed your kin. And we'll not stop until they've paid for their sins."

There was fire in his eyes as he spoke, and Lucas couldn't pull his gaze away from the powerful, angular face. Then he saw that the others' expressions held the same burning fervor. These men would take care of him.

As they continued making plans to find the killers, John Steele pulled his chair closer. "I knew your pa well," he said. "He was a good man, and you'll grow up to bring him honor among the Saints."

Lucas drew in a shuddering breath, feeling strangely calmed by the words.

"You're not without family, Lucas Knight," John Steele continued. "You're one of us. You'll mourn your ma and pa and little brother. The friends you saw die today. But you're part of a bigger family. I'm sure your ma and pa told you that."

"Yes sir. They did."

"From the Prophet on down to the youngest baby, we care for our own."

"Yes sir," Lucas whispered. "I know."

"From this day forward, you will be my son, though I know I'll never take the place of your flesh-and-blood father."

Lucas nodded. No one ever could.

"But tomorrow morning I'm taking you home. My wife, Harriet, will welcome another youngun. And I'll be happy to finally have a son."

Lucas stared into the fire, watching its flames lick high. Finally he whispered, "Thank you, Brother Steele."

John Steele smiled gently, and Lucas again noticed his ice blue eyes.

"Calling me Brother Steele is fine for now. But when it feels right, I want you to call me Father."

"Yes sir." Lucas said. A few minutes later he let his weary body slump against the back of his chair. It was long after midnight, and as hard as he tried to keep them open, his eyes threatened to close.

"It's all right to sleep. Rest will bring you strength."

Lucas nodded, but he already knew the images that would come to him when he closed his eyes. The nightmares that would terrify him in his sleep.

As if reading his thoughts, John Steele said, "We'll watch over you, just as Brother Roe said. You sleep, son, and we'll keep watch."

"Just like angels watchin' over you," one of the men said, and the others spoke up in agreement.

"I'd say more like avenging angels," Porter Roe said. "We're soon to be the Saints' army of avenging angels."

As he drifted to that shadowy place between wakefulness and sleep, Lucas heard the men's voices drone on through the night.

"It is time to act," said Porter Roe. "We have the Prophet's mandate. From this day and this hour forward, we will suffer no more. As God and all the holy angels are our witnesses, our rights shall no more be trampled. We declare this now is a war of extermination.

"We will act until the last drop of our enemies' blood is spilled. We will carry this vow with our swords to each and every house until each inhabitant shall be utterly destroyed." The room was quiet as he added, "From this day forward, let those who have dared to rise against us take heed. There will be no mercy."

Shivering, Lucas burrowed deeper into the warm blankets. His eyes flicked open once more, and he met John Steele's gaze. He quickly turned away, not knowing if it was strength or vengeance that glowed in the man's face. Finally the child drifted into a dark and troubled sleep.

Much later, instead of the brutality he had witnessed, Lucas was visited in his dreams by powerful angelic figures looking strangely like the men who had rescued him. They carried silver swords. Glinting swords that dripped crimson blood.

One angelic being held his sword higher than the rest, letting it turn to reflect the sun with diamondlike brilliance, and he looked at Lucas with eyes the color of blue ice.

Hannah

Wolf Pen Creek, Kentucky
November 1838

Seven-year-old Mattie McClary hid himself in the darkness at the corner of the room, as was his habit when his pa was in one of his bouts. *Bouts,* that's what Ma always called them. They happened when food was scarce and there were no rabbits for the cooking pot. It was then that Pa got to drinking. Yesterday, Pa had come home with only a scrawny rabbit then set to drinking through the night. Mattie worried that tonight it would be worse because his pa had taken a flask with him when he left for the hunt.

Now the day was moving into the half-light of late afternoon, and the sun was about to hide itself behind the hills of the hollow. Mattie watched his mother rocking little Hannah, who slept on her lap.

"Sleep, baby mine, I'm gonna sing you a heaven song. I'm gonna make you an angel's harp, baby mine, oh, sweet baby mine," his mother whispered softly. She stroked the little girl's yellow curls with the back of her finger then smiled and looked over at Mattie as if a new idea had just struck her.

"Mattie, fetch me Pa's cup. Over there by his jug." She nodded toward his pa's whiskey mug on the sideboard. "Then fill it with water from the bucket, son."

Mattie grabbed the mug and filled it, then, being careful to hold it level, walked across the room to his mother. He set it on a small table beside the rocking chair then drew back again, something inside telling him things might not be safe when his pa came through the door. All he could do was wait and watch over pretty Hannah and their ma.

Ma's eyes were squeezed closed now, and she was whispering soft words to the child. He didn't remember her doing that with his brothers. But he had been younger then—maybe he just couldn't remember. Since she was born two years ago, Hannah had seemed too small and rose-petal pale to be real, Mattie thought. They all had wiry, wheat-colored hair, but the boys' hair stuck out instead of lying in pretty curls the way baby Hannah's did.

The mountain's shadow was about to cross the house, and Mattie knew it was time for Pa to come home. The boy shivered in the thin light. To rid his mind of the fright, he concentrated on the child in his ma's arms; he had decided long ago that Hannah must be an angel, just like the picture in his ma's old Bible.

His ma was still rocking Hannah and humming with her face lifted to heaven. When she stopped, the little girl opened her eyes and stared up at her mother.

"Father in heaven, this here's Hannah," said Claire. "I'm bringin' her before you today to ask a blessing. I been a-waitin' the circuit preacher for two years, now, and he's never darkened the door once't. So I reckon it's up to me." She was silent a minute then looked over to where the McClary family Bible lay dusty on a shelf. "Son, bring me the Book," she said.

Mattie didn't have to ask which book she meant: It was the only one in the house. He rose and carried the heavy Holy Bible to his mother then sat again in the dark corner.

Claire shifted Hannah to the crook of her arm then laid the Holy Bible on her lap. She read silently for a moment, her lips moving with each word. When she looked up at her son, her eyes glistened with tears. "Listen to this, Mattie," she finally said, her forehead creasing into a frown as she struggled to read the words aloud.

"For this child I prayed; and the Lord hath given me my petition which I asked of him. Therefore also I have lent him to the Lord; as long as he liveth he shall be lent to the Lord."

"What does it mean, Ma?"

She smiled gently. "It means I prayed hard for this little girl, Hannah. And God answered my prayer. And now I'm givin' her back to him. For as long as she lives, she belongs to him."

Mattie puckered his face into a thoughtful frown. "But will Hannah always know she belongs to God?"

"My lands, you've got a curious mind, child," his mother answered. "All I know is life's too hard to predict how Hannah'll end up, especially bein' a girl in these dark hills . . ."

"But will she know what you did, givin' her away and all?"

"God doesn't grow weary like I do or discouraged like unto death itself. She's safe in his care. Better'n mine." She let out a deep and troubled sigh. "But will Hannah ever know what I done?" She looked down at the pretty little girl in her lap. "Sometimes folks never know they belong to God," she said finally, shaking her head slowly. "Even though they're plumb in the middle of his big hand . . . where even their names're written."

Mattie said no more, and after a minute Claire looked back to the big family Bible. "Listen here," she murmured and began to read again.

"My heart rejoiceth in the Lord, mine horn is exalted in the Lord; my mouth is enlarged over mine enemies; because I rejoice in thy salvation." She read on, and Mattie listened to the sweetness of his mother's voice. Even though she stumbled over words and hesitated while sounding them out, her awe made him listen as if God himself were speaking. Finally she concluded, "He will keep the feet of his saints, and the wicked shall be silent in darkness; for by strength shall no man prevail. The adversaries of the Lord shall be broken to pieces; out of heaven shall he thunder upon them: the Lord shall judge the ends of the earth; and he shall give strength unto his king, and exalt the horn of his anointed."

She looked back to Mattie. "You asked if Hannah will ever know—?"

He nodded.

"Maybe someday you'll tell her, Mattie."

He frowned, trying to figure out why his ma couldn't tell Hannah herself. He didn't answer.

"I want you to promise me, if need be, you'll tell our Hannah when she's old enough."

He thought about it, and it seemed an easy enough promise to make. "I'll tell her," he said. "I promise."

"You remember what I read. You remember it all, you hear?"

"I will, Ma," he said solemnly.

Then Claire bowed her head, and Mattie did the same. He waited for several long seconds then peeked through squinted eyes, watching his mother dip her thin fingers into the cup.

Just then, the room darkened with the shadow of his father standing in the doorway. After a moment's hesitation, Angus McClary strode unevenly into the room. He halted, swaying a bit, and let his eyes adjust to the dim light. His shoulders were slumped, his face lined and tired. No game hung from his belt.

With a frightened expression, Claire quickly wiped her fingers on Hannah's faded dress.

"What's this?" Angus asked loudly, his words slurred. The little girl whimpered then put her thumb in her mouth and watched her father with large, round eyes.

"Hush, Angus. You're scarin' her." Claire's voice was soft, and she gathered the child closer.

Angus strode to the rocker and stood, towering over Claire. "What are you doin' with this?" he asked, looking at his whiskey cup, not at Hannah.

No one answered.

"I said, what are you doin'?" Angus swayed a bit as he spoke. He blinked, trying to focus.

Mattie wanted to fly in a rage toward his father. But he knew that would only make things worse for his ma and Hannah, so he clamped his lips together and tightened his fists.

Claire stared mutely at her husband. Mattie wondered if his ma didn't want to say what she was doing for fear of Pa, or if it was because she'd done something holy and wished to keep it to herself.

"Answer me, woman," he muttered.

Still, Claire was silent.

"I said, speak to me!" Angus's face was dark with unreasonable anger. His stare suddenly lit on the Holy Bible, now lying on the table. In one swift, sure movement, he lifted it and hurled it at the fireplace. The worn, beloved Book smashed against a log then fell into the coals.

Sparks and ashes rose, and Mattie watched as the pages began to curl and turn golden in the intense heat.

"Oh, Angus," Claire moaned, her eyes now wet with tears. She brought her hand to her mouth then shook her head. "That belonged to my ma. It's all I had left of her."

Angus seemed momentarily confused, and he tried to focus his bleary eyes. When he did, his gaze lit on Mattie hiding in the corner. "What're you lookin' at?" he demanded.

Biting his lip, Mattie uncurled his little body, brushed himself off, then walked boldly to stand before his father.

"Ma meant no harm," he said.

"What do you mean?"

"She was blessin' our Hannah." The boy spoke reverently. "'Cause no one else was here to do it."

Angus looked from Mattie to Claire, who stared defiantly back at him with eyes like wet granite. He sighed as the smell of burning paper and leather filled the room.

"Can we get it out, Pa?" Mattie said bravely. "Please?" He tried to keep from crying, knowing his tears would only further anger his pa.

"It's too late," Angus said. But his shoulders slouched, whether in despair or sadness, Mattie didn't know. The two stood mutely watching what was left of the Bible turn to embers, gray ashes, then dust.

When it was done, Mattie glanced back across the room. Hannah was gazing up into her mother's eyes. Tears trailed down Claire's cheeks, and her lips moved slowly in prayer.

Claire looked up to meet her son's gaze. Then she gently touched Hannah's forehead where it was wet with her mother's tears. Slowly, carefully, she traced the sign of a cross.

Ellie and Alexander

Drake's Creek, Arkansas
December 1838

Seventeen-year-old Ellie Ingram looked up as Alexander Farrington approached on horseback from across the snow-dusted meadow. She stood in the small rock shelter, the thin winter sun barely warming her shoulders. Ellie gathered her heavy woolen cloak close, stamped her feet to rid them of their numbness, and shivered, partly in nervousness, partly because of the chill.

"Alexander," she said softly as he drew closer. His gray eyes met hers, and he nodded with a smile as he swung off the tall sorrel. With a fiery spirit and hair the color of creek sand, he was more rugged in appearance than handsome, but there was something about the intensity of his gaze that caused Ellie's heart to melt whenever she saw him.

"I wasn't sure you'd meet me," he said.

"You piqued my curiosity, Alexander, nearly leaving me no choice."

He grinned. "I hoped it would, Ellie. I also hoped you'd not think me too forward or disrespectful by asking you to hear me out today."

"We live on the frontier," she stated, repeating the same argument she'd heard her older sisters use with their ma. "Things are necessarily different here. I take no offense."

"We been courting for some weeks now, Ellie, and I have a serious question to ask."

Ellie bit her bottom lip and nodded shyly. "You mentioned such." For days now she'd pondered what he might say, and her heart thudded hard beneath her ribs as she considered it again.

Alexander took her hand and led her to a stone bench by the creek. He laid his coat upon it then waited as she settled onto the seat. He knelt before her, taking her hand once more.

"Ellie," he said, looking into her eyes. "Will you do me the honor of becoming my wife?" Before she could answer, he rushed on, "I love you, but if you say no, dearest, I truly will understand. It's a heavy burden I'm asking you to take on."

Ellie swallowed hard and nodded, knowing full well his meaning. She had already pondered it in her heart. By marrying Alexander, she would become a ready-made mother. Charity Anne Farrington, Alexander's first wife, had died of the consumption years before, leaving five stairstep children, the eldest being Hampton, who was fourteen, and the youngest, Amanda Roseanne, who was eight. Handsome children with hair of the darkest mahogany, they were known throughout the county as a lively handful, especially Amanda Roseanne.

Alexander touched her cheek. "I love you so, Ellie. If you need more time—"

Ellie reached up and took his hand, turned it over, and kissed his palm. "Alexander, I love you. And I would be honored to become your wife . . ." Her voice faltered.

He smiled gently. "Then why do I suspect you're about to politely say no?"

She turned away from him, looking across the brown grasses of the meadow. The clouds were thickening with dark moisture, and a cold breeze had kicked up. The cold sliced through flesh and muscle to her bones. "It's not what you think, Alexander," she whispered, almost as if to herself. "It's not fear of mothering. I've been minding my own little sisters practically since I could walk. And I love your children because they're part of you. No, it's not that." She turned to meet his troubled gaze.

"Then, what is it?"

"You're a wanderer, Alexander, by your own admission. You've traveled the continent, scouting trails and trading furs. When I marry, I don't want a husband who'll be away from home more than not. I want to be with you. Not two thousand miles away."

For a long time Alexander didn't speak. "What if we went west together?" he finally said. "I don't mean now. Sometime in the future. We could go together. Take the little ones with us. My brother's been speaking of it lately. Taking the whole family." He grinned. "Aunts, uncles, cousins, our ma and pa, the whole kit and caboodle of us." His eyes were shining as he considered her.

Ellie had to laugh. In his excitement, he looked more like a schoolboy than an experienced trailmaster and scout. "I might think about it," she agreed.

"It wouldn't be for some years," he said. "Treks like this take planning. And money."

"You'd be the captain?" she asked, lifting one brow and tilting her chin upward.

"And you'd be the captain's wife," he said, again lifting her fingertips to his lips and kissing them lightly. "We'd be starting a new life. Maybe in Oregon Territory. Or California."

"I do like the sound of that, Captain Farrington," Ellie said, her smile widening. "I do indeed."

He was still on bended knee. "I promise to cherish you, no matter where life's journey takes us," he said, his voice husky, "until the day I die."

"And I, you," Ellie whispered. "Yes, my dear captain, I will marry you!"

As Alexander stood to fold Ellie into his arms, the sound of hoofbeats carried across the meadow. A moment later, a pony's whinny announced the arrival of another rider. They turned to watch as Amanda Roseanne rode into sight, long, dark hair flying from underneath her gray woolen bonnet.

Her eyes were bright, and her cheeks were pink from the cold as she slid from the saddle. "There you are!" she declared, racing toward them. "I've been looking everywhere."

"Is something wrong—?" Alexander began, his face reflecting a father's worry.

By now the eight-year-old was standing in front of them, hands on her hips. "Hampton said we're marrying Miss Ellie."

Ellie and Alexander exchanged glances. "Your big brother is correct," Alexander said. "We were just about ready to come tell you ourselves."

"That part's fine. I'm glad about the weddin'," she said without hesitation. "But Billy says we're going west in a wagon." Her lower lip trembled. "He said we're going far, far away. And we're never coming back."

"It's true; we may be leaving," said Alexander, kneeling in front of Amanda Roseanne. It tugged at Ellie's heart the way he touched his daughter's dark hair with his fingertips. "But not for a long time. You'll be a big girl by then."

"I'm glad about havin' a new ma," said the little girl, looking up shyly at Ellie. "But I don't know if I want to go so far away from home."

Ellie knelt beside Alexander, and she reached for the little girl's hands.

"Wherever we go," she said, "it's God who will be leading us. Just like a shepherd takes care of his flock, he's leading us. And he's holding you—just like he holds his little lambs—in his arms. The Holy Bible tells us he's holding you and all your brothers and sisters near his heart. That's what makes us feel at home, no matter where we are."

Amanda Roseanne suddenly giggled. "Hampton's nearly as big as a horse. And Billy too. God's holdin' them like lambs?"

Alexander laughed. "They're both healthy, strapping boys, but they're still in need of God's leading. The same is true for you—even after you're as big as that pony over there." She followed his gaze and giggled again.

Ellie stood, and the little girl took her hand. "Miss Ellie," she said, her face tilted upward. "Can I be in the weddin'?"

She gently touched the child's cheek. "I was hoping you'd want to be," she said. "You and your sisters too."

"I want to hold your veil," Amanda Roseanne said, her face now all smiles, "and throw posies." She danced about happily. "And I want to call you Ma."

"I'd like nothing better," said Ellie.

Alexander's loving gaze met Ellie's, and she smiled into his eyes. "Shall we go home to tell the others about the wedding?" he asked.

"Yes," Ellie said, her joy so deep she could scarcely breathe. "Let's do."

"But *I* want to tell Hampton and Billie and everyone about goin' west," said Amanda Roseanne. "*I* want to be the one to tell about that." She seemed to have forgotten that the trek west might be years away.

"Then tell you will!" said Alexander, taking his daughter's hand.

The sun had now slipped behind darkening clouds, and a light snow was falling. Alexander and Ellie, with little Amanda Roseanne dancing between them, walked toward the waiting horses. Ellie shivered in the cold.

One

Wolf Pen Creek, Kentucky
September 1846

Ten-year-old Hannah McClary crept along the trace leading from the creek to the crest of Pine Mountain. Farther on, the trail wound into the lavender hills, through the pass, and far beyond where the eye could see, to Kentucky's tall silver grass country.

With every step Hannah looked for evidence that her brother Mattie had taken this path when he disappeared. She stopped, brushed her hair back from her face, and inspected the broken twig of a mountain laurel, turning it in her fingers. He'd gone looking for some old Daniel Boone trail, she was sure. Hannah figured her brother left Indian signs for her to follow, just as he had done in play when she was but a wee tike.

Hannah examined the bent twig for shreds of buckskin, perhaps caught as Mattie hurried by. But there were none. She frowned, turning the tender shoot in her hand. It was a recent break, maybe caused by a lone Cherokee hunter, or maybe by Mattie. She moved farther up the trace, deeper into the dark forest of birches, oaks, hickories, and maples.

Her brother had always said he would take her with him when he left—that was the part about his leaving that saddened her the most. Her other six siblings were mostly sullen, like their pa, or unnaturally quiet. Since their ma died, only Mattie seemed to have the same curiosity for life that Hannah had. He was her protector, her champion, just like knights of old they read about in the primers and fairy-tale books some distant cousin had sent from Virginia. And he told her stories he'd heard from their Irish grandma'am. Stories about God and his care for them all. Mattie said he knew for certain that Hannah was someone special in the eyes of her Creator.

Mattie had taught himself to read and write, then he'd taught Hannah as well, opening a world of notions and longings to them both. The rest of the family, with the exception of their ma, couldn't be bothered with book-learning. The others mocked them, calling Mattie and Hannah dreamers, scoffing at the very word.

But now Mattie had left without Hannah, without a hint telling her where he was going. And every day when her chores were done, Hannah searched for his trail, thinking surely he meant for her to follow.

Today, as usual, there was no sign of Mattie, and Hannah let out a short sigh of frustration. Little Shepherd Creek lay just over the hill, and she hurried through the thick rhododendron bushes to reach it, flopping down on her stomach when she did and splashing its cool, clear water on her hot face.

Hannah squinted at her reflection as she scooped up a swallow of water and gulped it down. One time Mattie had told her that, although she should be careful of vainglory, her eyes were like some bright Indian stones he'd seen once at a trading post. The thought of such a hue, of course, had pleased Hannah hugely. But now, looking into the rippling water, she could see nothing except the hint of a sad and somewhat curious expression. The creek water was too dark to see the freckles that Mattie always teased her about or the wild curls that he told her were exactly the color of sunlight on wheat.

It was Mattie who had called her Fae, saying the name was better suited for such a sprite as she. When Hannah asked what a fae was, he just smiled and said it was a cross between a fairy and an angel, only a bit different, since any faes around there were wee Kentucky mountain folk and strong as oxen. Mattie was the only one to call her by that name. She wished she could hear him say it now.

Still lying on her stomach staring into the creek, Hannah rested her chin in her palms, thinking of all she missed about her brother. The scent of decaying leaves and damp earth filled her nostrils. She preferred that scent to any other she could think of, from wild lilacs to baking bread. The only scent that came close was a sprinkle of rain on a warm, summer day.

As she lay there, Hannah was struck by a thought she couldn't put from her mind. What if she followed this trail to its end, looking for her brother? Mattie himself had told her about the Cherokee trading post just to the west of Pine Mountain. If she could follow the trace up the mountain beside Little Shepherd Creek, she hoped it would lead her to the outpost. After all, it was an Indian trail from centuries ago. Once there, she was certain someone would tell her if Mattie had traveled through. The thoughts tumbled through her mind, growing until she finally concluded that it was exactly what she needed to do.

Feeling immensely better, Hannah sat up and wiped her hands on her homespun skirt. Of course, she'd need provisions, and that would take some planning. Victuals for days, perhaps weeks, of traveling. She would make pemmican out of berries, cornmeal, and lard, just like Mattie had said the Indians made. And she would borrow Pa's rifle. That might take some doing, because she knew how upset Pa would be when he found it missing. She didn't like to consider that he would miss his rifle more than he would miss her, but she knew it to be true.

A few years earlier, Pa had taught the older boys to shoot. Hannah, knowing better than to ask Pa to teach her too, had badgered Mattie into setting up a target at the top of the hollow, out of earshot of the house, and teaching Hannah everything he knew about the old mountain-man rifle. She had learned to load the powder, place the ball, and ram it down the barrel, and soon she could outshoot the rest of the boys.

Hannah headed back down the trace toward the house at Wolf Pen Creek, skipping and humming as she went. With all Mattie had taught her about survival in these mountains, she knew she could find her brother. Of course, that was figuring Mattie wanted to be found.

Barely two weeks later, Angus McClary hauled his defiant runaway daughter back down the trace from where he had found her hiding in a clump of sweet-smelling rhododendron at the crest of Pine Mountain.

"I was just looking for Mattie," she wailed.

Angus tightened his grip on her shoulder. "I'll not put up with you one day longer," he muttered. Clomping noisily down the trail behind their father, Hannah's six brothers snickered in agreement.

She clamped her lips together, determined to keep her dismay to herself. Her first attempt to follow Mattie had failed, but that did not mean she would not try again. She would just be smarter next time. She lifted her chin, staring dead ahead as her father pulled her rapidly along the trail.

As soon as they reached the house, Angus dismissed the boys so he could talk to his daughter alone. Bees droning in the background were more pleasant to Hannah than the mean sound of her father's voice as he laid out his plan. A cottontail hopped from behind a clump of ferns, and the family's big yellow dog barked sharply, sending the little animal skittering out of sight.

"I'll have no argument from you," he told her. "You have no say in this. You're going to Sophronia's."

"Who's Sophronia?"

"Your mother's aunt."

"But I don't know her," she said. "How can you send me to someone I don't even know?"

Her brothers, who were now lolling on the porch, howled with delight at the word of her coming departure. Hannah didn't give them the satisfaction of acknowledging their hoots and hollers.

"Why?" she asked again. By now there was a knot in her stomach.

"This here is no place for a girl," Angus finally admitted, his voice unnaturally gruff. "And Sophronia is the only one I can think of who might be willin' to take you in."

Hannah swallowed hard. It was one thing to run away trying to find Mattie. It was another to be sent away from home as if she were no more useful to the family than some old worn-out pack mule. Hannah didn't cry easily, but her father's words caused a sting in the back of her eyes.

"You're set on sending me away to this . . . this stranger?" she finally managed.

"It's a sight better than marrying you off, Hannah Grace," her father said. Behind him, the boys guffawed.

Hannah looked up at her pa. But he didn't meet her eyes. He was still holding the rifle, rubbing the barrel carefully with his shirttail.

Hannah tried again. "But, Pa—" she began. "You can't really mean it. You don't mean for me to go . . . do you?"

Her father's face seemed to soften for an instant, then immediately became hard set again. "I mean it with every bone in my body, child," he said. "It's high time you left these hills."

"But what about Mattie? What if I'm gone when he comes back? What if I miss him?" she cried, hardly able to bear the thought. "What then?" Her father knew nothing of the kinship deeper than blood that ran between them, and she knew her words fell on a hardened heart.

"He ain't never comin' back," one of her brothers taunted from the porch. "He's still a-lookin' fer ol' Dan'l." The other boys joined in the gruff laughter. "And he's got a lot of country to cover before he finds ol' Dan Boone," one of the others added. "'Specially since Dan'l died some years ago."

Hannah ignored them. "I know he meant for me to follow him. I just know it. Please, don't send me to Sophronia. Just let me try one more time to find Mattie. Please, Pa?"

"You quit your whining, Hannah," her father demanded. "You'll do as I say. You forget Mattie. You run away again, you'll just get yourself caught by Indians. You're lucky we found you before they did. We'll leave first thing in the morning. And I don't want to hear any back talk."

"Tomorrow?" That definitely would not give her time to try once more to find Mattie. "At least let's wait till the end of the week. Or maybe till after harvest. You'll need help with the corn. I'm always a big help. You've said so yourself."

"We leave tomorrow for Illinois. And that's that!" her pa said as he turned to walk toward the porch full of boys.

"Illinois?" Hannah whispered, looking up at her pa. That was a long way off. She'd seen it on a map.

"That's the last place I heard your great-aunt Sophronia was living."

Great-aunt Sophronia. Hannah drew in a deep sigh of resignation, trying to imagine life with some tottering ancient woman who could do nothing more than sit in a rocking chair, covered by a lap robe.

Her gaze moved to the distant Kentucky hills with their cloak of pines, birches, oaks, and maples, soon to turn flame red and burnished gold. Then she focused on the late-summer wildflowers scattered among the pale meadow grasses. She would be gone by the time the blossoms were spent; she would be forgotten by the time spring brought new life.

She blinked back her tears and watched as her pa entered the house and slammed the door behind him. "All right," she finally muttered to herself. "Tomorrow."

Barely a month later, Angus McClary, with Hannah at his side, drove the buckboard through the thriving town of Nauvoo, Illinois. They stopped only once, to ask the whereabouts of Sophronia Shannon. A smiling, apple-cheeked woman in a poke bonnet pointed out the way, and within the hour, Angus clucked the horses to the top of a rise near the river.

He reined the horses onto a winding dirt road that led through a wide picket gate to a modest two-story house painted gray and white. A friendly looking place, Hannah had to admit, set right in the middle of a countryside filled with breathtaking beauty. The house was framed by a great stretch of grassland, dotted by apple trees heavy with bright red fruit. Wildflowers bloomed in patches of yellow and purple across the summer green pasture that was crisscrossed with trails winding into the woods beyond. A small wood-slatted barn stood just beyond the house, and two horses grazed in a corral to its side.

Angus halted the horses, but before they could step from the wagon a white-haired woman opened the door, gave them a quizzical look, then moved toward them with a surprisingly spry gait.

Great-aunt Sophronia was anything but what Hannah had imagined. This was no shriveled old woman sitting under a lap blanket. Instead, Sophronia seemed to glow like the evening star. She had wild, curly hair that she didn't bother to tie down. Hannah's had the same unruly curl, but whereas Hannah's was the color of the morning sun, Sophronia's was white as fresh-fallen snow. Her skin was tanned, and her eyes were the color of a purple sky, with squint lines that turned up as if from decades of pleasing thoughts. She was tall and broad shouldered, her big hands callous like a man's.

Sophronia held Hannah by the shoulders with her wide hands, looking her up and down. "You're a fine work. A fine work." Then she smiled and hugged her close. "My, it's going to be good to have young blood in the household again," she said after the circumstances had been explained.

"It's female manners she needs, Sophie." Angus was standing behind Hannah. "Growin' up with a house full of brothers and no ma, she's turned out more boy than girl. Hannah needs some settling. I figured bein' here, close to town and all, you could see to it she gets the best life has to offer."

Hannah was stunned. It was the first time she had considered her pa might be sending her away for her own good, not simply getting her out from under foot or keeping her from running off with his rifle.

Then Hannah noticed that Sophronia didn't seem to be paying any attention whatsoever to Angus's words. Instead, the older woman had fixed her gaze on Hannah and was studying her with a look of admiration. Hannah smiled, feeling something deep inside unfold the same way a blossom opened to the sun, and she basked unabashedly in the love and warmth she found there.

She barely noticed when her pa prepared to leave for Wolf Pen Creek the following morning. She was too busy listening to Sophronia tell how she'd seen Mattie. He'd been by to visit her twice in Nauvoo and had promised to come back for a third visit sometime soon.

"Of course," she laughed, as Hannah's pa headed the buckboard back down the road. "*Soon* to our Mattie might be years from now."

Hannah couldn't stop asking questions about her brother. Though Sophronia had no answers for most of them, Hannah held close the knowledge that Mattie had been seen and that he was alive and well.

"And I declare, I think he's happy!" Sophronia added as if reading her thoughts. "The boy's a natural wanderer, and though last he said he was heading south because he'd met a girl he planned to woo, I have no doubt he'll return someday. Maybe with his new bride."

"Did he say if she's pretty?"

"Pretty as a picture," Sophronia said, and Hannah sighed with happiness.

"What's her name?"

"He called her his sweet Mandy."

"I always wanted a sister. Maybe Mandy will be the one."

The first week of Hannah's stay, Sophronia said she wanted to hear all about the girl's life in Kentucky. She listened attentively as they worked side by side in the garden, tilling the soil around the autumn crop of squash and gourds. Hannah hadn't had anyone so interested in her words since Mattie, and she talked nonstop, answering all of her aunt's questions and asking hundreds of her own.

They rode Sophronia's mares, Berry and Foxfire, along the rusty-red trails, the elderly woman surprising the girl with her spirited yet gentle way with horses. She taught Hannah to brush and comb Foxfire, the horse she said was now Hannah's own, and Hannah learned to clean out the stalls and pitch fresh hay from the loft.

By the end of the third week, the first frost of winter covered the flat, bleak land, and Sophronia taught her niece the art of laying a fire in the fireplace, keeping the coals hot so the fire would last all day long.

In the dark of late afternoon they often sat near the large stone fireplace in Sophronia's front living room, the older woman in a tapestry-covered rocker, her yarn basket at her side, Hannah in a slender oak rocker, scarred from years of use. Bookcases lined the roughhewn walls, and framed prints that appeared to be from some faraway country like England, Scotland, or maybe Ireland, Hannah thought, were scattered around the entire room. An oak secretary fit squarely against the wall opposite the fireplace, a pewter lamp glowing from its gleaming top. A worn horsehair sofa with two well-used overstuffed chairs completed the sitting area around the fire, a flat trunk with an embroidered lace doily serving as a tabletop. Two large windows draped with Irish lace flanked the heavy door leading to a wide front porch with its sweeping view of the fenced pasture and the small woods beyond the barn.

Hannah loved this cozy room when the day's chores were done and she and Sophronia could sit and talk and laugh. She especially loved the sound of Sophronia's voice when she said Hannah's name, making the word sound full of love.

Her aunt showed Hannah how to pop dried corn in a wire basket over the flames, and they spent hours telling tales as they munched on the corn's fragrant, snow white goodness.

"You'll see soon enough that here in Nauvoo we're part of a big family," Sophronia said one afternoon.

"We've got other relatives?" Hannah asked, reaching for another fistful of popcorn. "Pa only told me about you."

Her aunt chuckled. "No, child. That's not what I mean." She hesitated, for a moment merely watching the licking flames in the fireplace. Then she looked back to Hannah and smiled, her eyes bright. "I've found religion."

"You have?" She crunched on another bite of popcorn. "You're not a Holy Roller, are you?" She had heard about them from her brothers, who would imitate the wild gyrations of a snake-handling group that gathered not far from Wolf Pen Creek.

Sophronia laughed. "Oh, goodness no, child. Nothing like that!"

"What then?"

Her aunt chuckled again. "We're called Saints." Then, noticing her niece's quizzical look, she patted her wild curls and grinned. "I don't look much like a saint, do I?"

"You do to me—though I don't reckon I know what one looks like." She hesitated, thinking. "These Saints . . . they're the ones who are your family?"

"*Our* family now. Yours and mine. For all eternity. Our Prophet will rejoice to add another to our fold."

Hannah wrinkled her nose at all the new words. "They care about me?"

Again, Sophronia laughed. "Our Prophet is holy and ordained of God. Our first was Joseph Smith, who was killed last year, and now we follow God's second Prophet and the president of our Church, Brigham Young."

"And we're all family? How many?" Hannah didn't much like the idea of sharing Sophronia with anyone else. Her aunt was plenty enough family for her.

Sophronia seemed to sense her confusion. "We take care of each other, Hannah. Live in harmony, sharing our worldly goods. Everyone—from the smallest baby to the feeblest widow—is cared for. We want to merely live in peace." A shadow crossed her aunt's face. "I need to be honest, child. It hasn't always been peaceful. And it isn't now."

Hannah frowned as she noticed her aunt's expression.

"Mobs from the outside—we call them Gentiles—have attacked our families, sometimes entire settlements. There have been beatings and killings. Things I can't even speak of have been done to our women and children."

Hannah leaned back and rocked her chair in thoughtful silence. She wanted to ask what things couldn't be spoken of. Her aunt's words caused frightening images to whirl through her mind. Her stomach felt sick. But she didn't want her aunt to stop talking.

"Why?" she finally asked. "Why did these people—the Gentiles—do these things?"

"People are always afraid of what they don't understand. They were just afraid of the ideas."

"What ideas?"

"Well, for one, the idea that God was once a man and that through good works he worked his way up to becoming God."

"That doesn't sound so awful."

"Others thought it was blasphemy. Then they found out that the Prophet said God had revealed that every man can be a god. If he lives right—obeys the revelations of our leaders, does good work throughout his life—after he reaches heaven, he'll someday be the god of his own world."

Neither one spoke for several minutes. Hannah bit her lip. People becoming gods. This would require more thought later. She suddenly wished Mattie could be there with her, hearing Sophronia's words, mulling them over and deciding what they meant.

Sophronia noticed her confusion. "It was all the talk about men becoming gods and our God having been a man—and other ideas—that made people afraid."

"But just because they don't understand, just because they are afraid, they didn't have to hurt people."

"I know, dear. The people who hurt and killed probably would never have done such things on their own. But they got together and became riled up, talking and carrying on. Mobs are like one person, strong and meanspirited, a giant that doesn't know right from wrong. A mob'll do things a man would never think of doing alone."

Sophronia reached again for the poker. Sparks sprayed up the chimney as she stoked the fire a few times then placed another log on the coals.

"Why didn't the Saints fight back?" Hannah asked, feeling angry about anyone trying to hurt someone like Sophronia. "Did they ever fight back?"

Sophronia looked at her with a pleased expression. "Well, yes. They did—finally. And I'll be getting to that. But first I want to tell you now about what happened in Missouri." She settled back into the chair. "And I want you to pay close attention. It will explain a lot of things you'll find out about later. But for now, let me tell you about what happened there."

Sophronia stared into the fire then went on, her voice low. "This is the part that's hardest for me to tell." She took a deep breath. "Two hundred men attacked some families at Haun's Mill. Some of the Saints, seeing the militiamen coming, ran into the blacksmith shop, but it had so many gaps in the wood sides that the Gentiles just shot right through it. The Gentiles hid behind trees. Just took their time picking off the Saints one by one.

"An old man named Thomas Jones decided to surrender. He handed the Gentiles his gun, and they hacked him to pieces with a corn cutter." Sophronia's voice was a whisper now. Hannah reached over and took her aunt's big, callous hand in hers. Sophronia didn't seem to notice. Her voice went on without emotion. "When the women ran toward the brush, the Missouri Wildcats shot at them like it was a sport, calling out scores depending on how quickly they felled each one. They laughed while they did it."

Hannah shuddered. She imagined the women running like deer through the thicket. Wounded. Getting up. Trying to run again. She knew the thrill of hunting, the joy of making a direct hit with a musket. It made her sick to think of men taking that kind of joy in killing women.

"After shooting every Saint they could see, the mob entered the blacksmith's shop to finish off the wounded. They found two children—brothers named Lucas and Eli—hiding under the bellows. Lucas Knight pretended to be dead. He heard the men drag little Eli from his hiding place. 'Don't shoot,' said one Gentile. 'It's just a boy.'

" 'Nits make lice,' said the other. Then he placed his rifle near the boy's head and fired."

Hannah caught her breath. She had never heard anything so terrible.

"Seventeen people died at Haun's Mill that day." Sophronia's voice broke. Hannah squeezed her aunt's big, rough hand. "And one of them was a very special man named Jacob." It seemed the room was filled with Sophronia's sadness. Her aunt quickly brushed away her tears with her fingers, her wet cheeks glistening in the firelight.

"Jacob had asked me to be his wife just a few weeks before. I hadn't decided whether or not to take that step—it meant coming into the Church, and I wasn't sure I wanted to do that. I had my doubts . . ." She hesitated, peering into Hannah's face as if wondering how much more to say. She must have decided Hannah was kin, trusted kin, and she could say most anything she wanted, because a faint smile lifted the lines around her eyes and mouth.

She nodded and patted her grandniece's hand. "I still have those doubts, child. Even now. Someday I'll tell you why."

Hannah waited for her to continue, but her aunt seemed set to tell the rest of the Haun's Mill story instead.

"Mostly, when Jacob asked for my hand, I was thinking that I'd lived all those years alone, and I wasn't sure I was ready to be someone's wife. I wish now I hadn't been so stubborn. Jacob had wanted us to be sealed in the temple as soon as it was built. We would've been sealed for all eternity. But I waited too long. If I hadn't put it off, I would've died right there with him and all the others. I would've lived with him forever in eternity."

"Oh no! I'm so glad you didn't. Die, I mean. I'm so glad you're here now. With me." Hannah paused, thinking about her aunt's life, then she added quietly, "But you decided to be a Saint anyway?"

"Oh yes, child. I did." The color returned to Sophronia's cheeks. "Oh yes. I was taken in among the others like I was blood kin. Cared for and loved. My Jacob—and all of them who died that day—became martyrs. The Church grew by the thousands when word spread of Haun's Mill."

"What happened to the child—the boy named Lucas Knight?"

"He's nearly a grown man now. Seventeen, his last birthday." Sophronia's voice took on a happier tone. "He's a fine work. And you've probably guessed that I don't say that about many people. He lives near here. You'll meet him one day soon.

"If he hadn't already been taken in by John Steele, I would've adopted him myself." She chuckled. "Lucas knows I still claim him as my own. He comes by here as often as he can. Busy as he is, he still finds time to bring me fresh rabbit or venison after he's been hunting. This little house was built because of Lucas. Did most of it himself. A fine boy, that one."

Sophronia went on. "Our leaders have their eye on him. Everyone knows Lucas Knight might someday lead the Danites, our Avenging Angels, to victory over all our enemies."

She frowned, then stood and stoked the fire. "Though I wonder about the boy's suitability—if he's of the right temperament."

Hannah swallowed hard, trying to follow her aunt's meaning. "I don't understand."

"The Danites are our secret army. What they do is secret. But I do know—just as all the Saints do—that they atone for the great and terrible sins committed against us. Lucas, of all people, knows the reasons behind the angels' vengeance. But as to whether he could ever lead the group . . ." Her voice fell off, and she shook her head slowly.

Hannah stared into the fire, watching the flames lick higher, sending up a sizzling spray of glowing pinpoints of light. She tried to comprehend all she'd just been told.

She might be only ten years old, but she was aware that there was no turning back from where she'd just landed. She wondered about the people who had taken in her aunt. What was it about them that made them the hunted? And now had turned them into hunters?

Whatever it was—whether she liked it or not—she was now one of them. They would care for her, protect her, feed and clothe her.

A loud rapping at the heavy wooden door interrupted her thoughts, and Sophronia rose and moved toward the entry. Moments later, she returned.

"Hannah," she said, "what did I tell you? Our boy Lucas is here!" Then she looked at Lucas. "This is Hannah McClary."

Standing beside her aunt was the most extraordinary young man Hannah had ever seen. He was lean and wiry with thick black hair and light eyes that stood out against his angular, tanned face. Sophronia had been right. He was a fine work. Hannah, tongue-tied for the moment, stared wordlessly. Finally she stuck her hand out and shook his hand the way Mattie had taught her. But when she'd finished, Lucas didn't release her hand. Instead, he held it lightly by the fingertips.

"It's a pleasure to make your acquaintance, Hannah McClary," he said with a grin. Then he bowed formally and kissed her hand.

Suddenly all of her bashfulness disappeared, and Hannah looked into Aunt Sophie's and Lucas Knight's smiling faces. All her life she'd longed for a family to wrap her in their arms. And now it was hers for the taking. If she needed to be a Saint, then so be it.

"I'm glad to meet you, Lucas," she said, matching his grin and standing as tall as her years allowed. After all, she was in the presence of an angel, an Avenging Angel.

Two

Two weeks later Hannah sat in a clump of grass on a bluff overlooking the river. As had become her pattern after she groomed Foxfire and Berry and cleaned their stalls, Hannah had climbed the hill just beyond Sophronia's frame house to sit and think about her new life.

Below the grassy precipice lay the small settlement of Nauvoo, serenely protected by the river's bend. From here, it seemed to Hannah a little corner of an enchanted toy paradise—patchwork gardens near miniature cottages, horses and carriages moving along the dusty streets, people hurrying about like little tin soldiers.

She rested her gaze on the temple at the heart of Nauvoo. Its steeple gleamed in the sun, so high that even from here it seemed to touch heaven. She sighed contentedly at the thought. *Heaven.* Maybe she'd found it after all.

Hannah was lost in thought, wondering about Sophronia and her Saints and what the future held for Hannah among them, when the sound of horse's hooves pulled her from her reverie.

She shaded her eyes against the sun and watched as a man on horseback climbed the bluff along the winding road to Sophronia's house. The horse was in a full gallop, its rider bent over the saddle, riding as if one with the horse. Hannah grinned in delight as the rider drew closer.

Lifting her long skirts over her knees, Hannah raced down the hill toward the house.

"A rider's coming!" Hannah called out to Sophronia halfway to her destination. "I think it's Lucas Knight!"

Sophronia was kneeling, picking squash from their vines in the garden. She smiled up at Hannah, her long, white apron smudged with soil, her wild hair shining in the autumn sun. "What color's the horse?"

"Black." Hannah now stood beside her aunt, gulping air to catch her breath. "And he was riding like the wind."

"That'd be Lucas, then. On Black Star." Sophronia nodded and, still smiling, snapped off another squash and placed it in the basket at her side. "It's about time he paid us another visit," she said, standing and wiping her hands on her apron.

"Hey!" The rider had rounded the last curve and was now in full view.

"Hey, yourself!" Sophronia shouted back with a laugh. "Is that any way to greet your elder?"

The young man, hat low over his eyes, swung from his horse and walked to where Sophronia stood, hands on hips. She lifted a white brow. "I say, young man, is that any way to greet an old lady?"

He stepped closer and, gently holding Sophronia's shoulders, studied her face. "And calling yourself old doesn't deserve an answer, Sophie. You're as young and spry as anyone I ever laid eyes on."

Then he turned to look at Hannah, examining her from underneath the curled brim of his hat.

She squinted up at him in the bright sun, her nose wrinkled. This young Lucas Knight suddenly reminded her of Mattie. Maybe it was his voice. Maybe the light in his eyes. Sudden tears threatened to rise up from that saddest of all places inside. She bit her lip to stem the flow.

Lucas stepped closer. "Standing here in the sunshine, Hannah, you sure favor your aunt. Anyone ever tell you that before?"

His comment took Hannah's mind off Mattie, and she gave him a grateful smile. "I think I'd rather favor her than anyone else in the world."

"Go on, now, both of you," Sophronia said and wiped her hands again on the apron. "Fact is," she went on, "I've got work to do in the garden. Why don't you two take Foxfire and Berry out for a ride? Turn Black Star out to pasture. I'm sure he needs a rest."

Lucas grinned. "Yes ma'am."

"Just be back in time for supper. Lucas, it's your turn to make the biscuits."

Hannah glanced up at him in admiration. "Biscuits?"

"Don't tell anyone ever." He said, pretending to scowl. "Only Sophie knows I like to cook. And she's taught me how to make just about everything—from flapjacks to roast venison."

"I had him standing on a crate in my kitchen to reach the stove long before he was your age, Hannah. Fact is, this boy of mine makes better piecrust than most brides."

Lucas threw back his head and laughed. "Now, that's going a little too far, Sophie."

Sophronia winked at Hannah. "He's just worried about what the other angels in that army of his might think!"

Suddenly, the young man's demeanor changed, and Hannah watched, fascinated, as Lucas moved away from them. He hadn't physically backed away. No, it was as if his mind or his heart had taken a step backward. He lifted his jaw, and a shadow veiled his eyes.

If Sophronia noticed, she said nothing. After a moment, she gave Lucas a quick hug. "You two go riding now. You're going to be surprised, young man. This little girl will give you a run for your money. She's a natural on Foxfire."

Lucas smiled, the earlier hard look gone. He nodded with a grin. "Then let's go. Want to race to the barn?"

Before the words were out of his mouth, Hannah had lifted her skirts and was racing ahead of him, her face to the brisk wind, her yellow curls flying behind her.

She slammed into the barn door with her hands, breathless and laughing. Seconds later, Lucas touched the door. "Don't let it go to your head," he panted. "I'll beat you next time!"

"Don't count on it," she declared. "I've got seven brothers, and I could beat any one of them in a footrace." She lifted her chin triumphantly. "Even Mattie."

Lucas held the door open to let Hannah step into the barn ahead of him. “Tell me about your brothers,” he said as they walked to the horses.

“There’s not much to tell, except about—”

“Mattie?” Lucas finished for her with a grin.

She gave him a quizzical look, wondering how he knew.

“He’s the only one you mentioned by name. Is he your favorite?”

Hannah slipped a halter over Foxfire’s head and led her from her stall. She patted the mare’s sleek neck as she looped the lead rope over the hitching rail and then turned and paused before getting the saddle off its rack. “Yes,” she sad sadly. “But he ran off. I don’t know where he is or if I’ll ever see him again.” Reddening, she caught herself. Sophronia had told her the horror that Lucas survived. The killing of his baby brother, Eli. She bit her lip. “Oh, I’m sorry, Lucas. Your little brother . . . what you went through . . .”

Lucas swung a saddle onto Berry then gave Hannah an understanding look. “Sophie told you, then.” He took the saddle from her hands and lifted it onto Foxfire.

Hannah nodded. Moments later they both mounted up and walked the horses down the length of the barn, hoofbeats clacking dully on the wood-plank floor.

Once in the sunlight, the horses’ hides gleamed, and the scent of their sun-warmed bodies filled Hannah’s nostrils. Lucas led the way along the fence to one of the worn, rust-colored trails that headed toward the woods. He kicked Berry into a trot, and Hannah followed on Foxfire. After several yards they picked up an easy canter. Hannah breathed in the scent of the wildflowers and grassy fields, closing her eyes, enjoying Foxfire’s smooth rhythm and the soft summer breeze against her face.

Lucas headed Berry through the trees to where the forest thinned out a little, then up a slight incline to the bluff overlooking the river. They rode along the bluff for a time before Lucas reined in Berry and signaled for Hannah to do the same. She gently reined her horse to a standstill. Both horses shook their heads, causing their manes to lift in the breeze and their bridles to jingle.

He nodded toward the river. "There's a place just below where you can see nearly a hundred miles west. But we can't take the horses." He grinned at her from beneath his hat brim, his eyes teasing. "You up for a hike?"

"Another race?"

He laughed. "No. This is much too dangerous. I just want to show you what it looks like. But you'll have to be careful."

Hannah slid from her saddle. "Let's go." Then she watched as Lucas dismounted and led the horse to a clump of birch trees where he tethered their reins.

"Ready?" He asked, reaching for her hand to help her scramble over an outcropping of rocks.

The gesture reminded her of Mattie, and Hannah swallowed hard, quickly pulling her hand away so she wouldn't disgrace herself with watery eyes.

They climbed down the side of the cliff, over another group of rocks, around some pines and live oaks, and through some brush to the lookout point Lucas had mentioned. The sun, already on its downward slant, struck the place, turning the reddish soil and sandy rocks to burnished gold. Below them, the river wound in a ribbon of silver-green, stretching until it disappeared into the horizon. Gentle hills turned into flat prairie, melting into a sea of yellow and pale green, stretching out, it seemed to Hannah, into forever.

"Oh, my," she breathed. "So that's the West."

"Wait till you see the sunset over it," Lucas murmured, his eyes still on the horizon. "It's even better than this."

"How could it be?" she asked, not expecting an answer. "I've never seen so far before. How could anything be better than this?"

Lucas laughed, removed his hat, and ran his fingers through his dark hair. "Just wait, Hannah. Just wait." He was quiet a minute then turned to face her. "We're going west, you know."

"Who is?"

"The Saints." He curled his hat brim then placed the hat back on his head, low over his eyes.

"Not Sophronia. You don't mean Sophronia too."

He nodded. "She doesn't want to go. But she must."

"Why?"

"It wouldn't be safe for her to stay alone."

"I'll be with her."

His face softened, and for a moment Hannah thought Lucas might laugh at her bold statement, but he didn't. She admired him for that.

"Does my aunt know she must leave?"

"I've tried to tell her, but she won't listen. She won't even listen to Brigham Young himself."

"Why does everyone have to leave?" Hannah settled onto a nearby rock, keeping her eyes on Lucas, who was standing in the direct light of the setting sun, one foot propped on a large stone. In the orange glow, his eyes looked lighter than ever against his tanned skin.

"Sophie told me she let you know about the persecution we've been getting from the Gentiles."

Hannah nodded. "She told me."

"The Church has been told to get out of Nauvoo by the end of winter. Those who disobey will be persecuted."

"Persecuted?"

"Punished."

Hannah knew he spoke of the bad things that Sophronia had told her about. "But why? I thought Nauvoo was built by the Saints. That it belongs to them."

Instead of answering, Lucas turned the conversation to the future in the West. "Our leaders have told us about a wide-open land, more colorful and spread out than even this, Hannah," he said. "We're going to set up our kingdom there—God's kingdom—in a land that no one can take from us again."

"Is it far away?"

He nodded solemnly. "Yes. And Sophie needs to come with us, not lag behind. We'll be safer traveling together."

"We'll go by covered wagon?"

Suddenly, Lucas threw back his head and laughed in the way that Hannah was coming to love. Then he gazed at her, admiration in his eyes. "My goodness, girl, but you're a curious one. So many questions."

Hannah clamped her lips together in a straight line and lifted her chin. "You're about to ask me to help you convince Sophronia to go west. You want me to tell her that I want to go."

He laughed again, a sound that was merrier than the rushing waters of Little Shepherd Creek in the springtime. "You read minds too?"

"Well, isn't that why you're telling me about the Saints' trip west?"

"Not entirely. But yes, I was intending to ask you to help me convince her."

"If I'm going to do that, I need to know exactly why."

"I thought your aunt told you about the persecution."

"She did. Sort of. She also told me about the Avenging Angels. The Danites."

For a moment Lucas didn't speak. Then he asked, "Are you sure you're only ten?"

"I'm almost eleven. Besides, what does that have to do with it?"

"You seem to be thinking this through the way most adults would."

"I want to know about the Danites and what you're doing to protect us until we leave—if we leave." Hannah watched Lucas carefully, reading his expression to see if he would tell her the truth.

"We protect our own, Hannah. And even by telling you that, I've told you too much."

She considered him for a moment as the sun sank deeper into the horizon.

"There's something else bothering you, isn't there?" Lucas asked.

Hannah nodded. "My pa always said you can't believe everything you hear."

"What part don't you believe?"

"That people can do such bad things to each other. Cruel things."

Lucas's face turned to granite. At first Hannah thought he was angry that she doubted him, doubted her aunt. Then she noticed his eyes. He seemed to be fighting something inside, maybe crying.

She reached for his hand. "I'm sorry," she said. "I didn't mean that what happened in Haun's Mill never happened, about your brother and all . . . Oh," she cried, "I'm sorry."

He turned away from her, pulling back his hand at the same time. For several minutes he gazed at the sunset without speaking. The sky had now turned orange and red and purple. Even the thin ribbon of the river had turned crimson.

When Lucas turned again to Hannah, he seemed to have settled some question only he knew. "What would you think if I showed you how folks feel about us?" he asked.

"Showed me? You mean I could go with you to see firsthand?"

He nodded.

"Go with you on a raid?" Hannah's heart began to thud in her chest as she pictured herself on Foxfire alongside Lucas on Black Star, fighting with the Lord's mighty army of angels, avenging his favored people.

"A raid?" Lucas repeated, laughing. "No, that's not what I have in mind."

Hannah was disappointed, but she didn't say so. "If not a raid, what then?"

"You'll find out tonight after supper." He reached for Hannah's hand to help her stand, and they started back up the hillside.

"You mean after you ask Sophronia if I can go?"

He nodded. "Yes, we'll need to ask her," he agreed. "But I think she'll say yes." He smiled. "I'll protect you with my life, if necessary, Hannah. She knows that."

"Will I need to wear black?" she inquired, still thinking of the raid as they made their way over some sandstone boulders.

Lucas stopped, looking over his shoulder at her. Then he grinned. "Might be a good idea. But there's something else."

"What?"

"You need to dress like a boy."

"A boy?"

He nodded. "You'll need to play like you're my little brother."

Hannah wrinkled her nose then broke into a wide grin. She liked the sound of that. Lucas's little brother. "All right," she said. "I'd like that." Then she scrambled ahead of him as fast as she could. "Last one to reach the horses is possum scat!"

The sound of Lucas's laughter behind her made Hannah want to sing and dance and turn cartwheels all at the same time. She was suddenly happier than she had been in months. Oh yes, she would convince Sophronia to go west with the Saints. She and Lucas and Sophronia were family. Hannah would have it no other way.

By the time supper was over that night, a light rain had begun to fall. Hannah pulled on some old trousers and a deerskin shirt of Lucas's then donned a wide-brimmed felt hat, being careful to poke her light curls tightly inside.

Lucas walked to the window and looked out at the rain. "I'll take good care of our Hannah," Lucas said gently, turning to Sophronia. "Don't worry."

"You're not going to a raid, now, are you, Lucas?"

He shook his head. "Only a gathering," he said simply.

Sophronia still seemed worried, and Hannah gave her a quick hug as they left the house. "I've been chased by bears and mountain cats back home in Kentucky," she said. "Nothing could be more dangerous than that." She didn't add that Mattie had always been the one to shoo them off with their pa's rifle.

Her aunt smiled and patted Hannah's cheek. "You just take care, Hannah, child."

Finally, Lucas and Hannah made their way to the barn and saddled the horses. Minutes later, they mounted, Hannah on Foxfire, Lucas on Black Star.

Shivering more from excitement than cold, Hannah yanked her hat closer to her ears and peered through the darkness. This was going to be a night to remember. She could feel it in her bones.

They rode for several minutes without talking. The trail narrowed, and Lucas took the lead. Hannah nudged Foxfire with her heels, following Lucas and Black Star into a small stand of nearly bare trees.

He reined his horse to a standstill, and Hannah pulled up beside him, Foxfire dancing sideways and shaking her head, her mane flopping. The night was eerily quiet. Now that the rain had stopped, only the dripping mist from the cottonwood branches broke the silence.

"We're heading to a meeting," Lucas said. "These people are not our friends, as you'll soon see. While we're there, you can't say anything. No matter what you hear or see, you mustn't speak." His voice was earnest. "You've got to promise me."

"I promise." Hannah's voice sounded small in the darkness. "But why?"

"You'll find out when we get there. I just want you to listen."

"Is it a Danite meeting?"

Lucas sighed. "No. Far from it."

"But it's a secret meeting."

"The meeting's no secret. It's who we are that's the secret. We don't want anyone to identify us. And remember, as far as anyone at the meeting knows, we're brothers."

"I'll remember," she said.

"You may be hearing things said that will make your blood boil. You may find it hard to sit still and not say anything back. But Hannah—" Lucas put his hand on her arm. "Your life may depend on your keeping quiet."

"I'll not say anything. I promise."

"All right, then. You ready?"

"Let's go," Hannah said as she relaxed the reins and let Foxfire follow Black Star.

Soon Hannah could see the glow of lantern light flickering through some trees in the distance. The path forked onto a muddy road and down a hill where the light was lost momentarily. After they had followed the winding road a distance longer, Lucas turned off onto another, smaller road leading through a field to a sprawling two-story farmhouse.

Torches lined the barnyard, and the smell of burning pitch was strong. Men—Hannah thought maybe thirty-five or so—lolled about on makeshift chairs of barrels or logs. Others were standing in small groups, talking and laughing. No one seemed to notice when she and Lucas tethered their horses to a post and sat on a log toward the back of the group.

Hannah pulled her hat further down on her head and checked to make sure no unruly curls had sprung from beneath it.

"Don't fuss," Lucas whispered.

"I wasn't."

"Put your hands in your pockets."

Hannah jammed her hands in her trousers and let out a sigh.

Someone rolled a small farm wagon to the front of the group, and a man climbed up to stand on the bed of it. He was a big man, and in the torchlight, his broad face was covered with a beard, full and long, whiter than chalk. He reminded Hannah of a big white ox.

"If you're new to our meetings and don't know me, my name's Jared Boggs," he began in a gravel-edged voice. "I live down the road, next farm over. Some of the boys and me been talking about gettin' rid of our problems. I'm sure you know what problems I'm talking about."

There was a spattering of laughter throughout the group.

"Well, we're meeting here tonight to make plans for riddin' ourselves of them forever." He gazed around the group, nodding as some of the men bobbed their heads in agreement. "I'm talking about the Mormons. Now it's true, we've gotten rid of some—one way or another."

From behind Hannah and Lucas, more laughter rose into the damp night air.

Jared Boggs went on, "I hear there's some who're talking about staying put instead've moving on. And we can't let that happen, can we?"

Shouts of "No! We can't!" rose from the back of the mob.

Boggs glanced around the group. "Saints." He practically spat the word. "They call themselves Saints, followers of a man who said he was a Prophet. I'm here to tell you this was no man of God. He was kin with the devil hisself. And I'm glad he's dead. Fryin' in hell. Roasting on a spit across God's fire. Anybody who'd say that Jesus Christ and the devil are brothers must be kin with the devil hisself. And he said it. Oh yes, he said it all right."

The crowd murmured in response. Hannah noticed that Lucas's expression was hard, and he worked his jaw as he stared at the speaker.

"If we let any of 'em stay, they'll multiply," Jared Boggs continued. "Multiply like maggots on a corpse. Them and their ideas that they can take more'n one wife. Why, it's been said Joseph Smith himself had more'n thirty."

Thirty wives? Hannah fought to keep from asking Lucas about it right then.

Jared Boggs raised his voice even louder, now yelling at the ruffians before him. "We don't want one Mormon devil livin' within a thousand miles of here! In this county. In this state!"

The crowd shouted in agreement.

"We've taken enough! We've tolerated enough! Now it's time to burn them out." Jared Boggs raised a fist into the air. "And when we're through, they'll stay out! The ones who live through it'll never want to see this state again."

Hannah's breath came in small quick stabs. What if she and Lucas were found out? She shuddered to think what might happen. But beside her, Lucas seemed calm. He surprised her by nodding his head and shouting out as if agreeing with the man on the wagon. Maybe that was wise. Hannah nodded her head, then glanced around to see if anyone noticed. No one did. They were too busy agreeing with Jared Boggs. She nodded right along with Lucas just to be safe.

When the crowd quieted down, Boggs continued. "I'll tell you what me and some of the others have planned," he said. "Then you all tell me who wants to join us."

Hannah listened in horror as he described in detail what the mob would do, farm by farm, house by house, person by person, until the last Saint was forced to leave. Hannah felt her cheeks getting hot, and she thought she might be sick. They were talking about Sophronia. The horrid things they were saying they'd do would be done to

Sophronia, and maybe to Hannah herself. She reached to touch Lucas's hand then thought better of it and shoved her hand back in her pocket.

The men broke into smaller groups and began planning how and when they would strike. As their voices rose in agitation and anticipation, Lucas nodded toward the horses, and after a moment they stood and sidled to the back of the gathering. Lucas spoke to a few of the men as they moved past, telling them he needed to get his little brother home before their ma found out he was gone. "I'll try to come back later," he said with a grin and a mock salute.

Lucas and Hannah rode in silence for a long while, Lucas's horse taking the lead. Then the girl pulled Foxfire alongside Black Star.

"What they said . . . they won't do all those things, will they?" she asked, looking across at Lucas.

"I'm sorry you had to hear it, Hannah. The only reason I wanted you to was so you can help me convince Sophronia to leave."

"What if she won't listen? You won't let anything happen to her, will you, Lucas? You won't leave without us, will you?"

Lucas didn't answer, and in the silence that had fallen between them, Hannah could hear the dripping of the trees and, a distance away, the sad cry of a screech owl. Then Lucas halted the black and reached for her hand. He held it between his, rubbing it till it warmed. "You've got to help me convince Sophronia. There is no other way."

"Why will she listen to me if she won't listen to you?"

Lucas smiled. "I have a feeling you could talk a snake into giving up its rattles if you set your mind to it."

Hannah couldn't help smiling. In her thinking, that was better than being called pretty. "Yes, of course," she said. "You know I'll try."

"Good," Lucas said and let go of her hand.

"But she's stubborn," Hannah said after they had begun riding again.

"I know she is," Lucas agreed with a slow nod.

A heavy mist laced in and out of the trees, still dripping noisily. Once in a while, a half-moon floated overhead, only to disappear again as they rode. Hannah nudged Foxfire to keep up with the black as they moved over the crest of the bluff near Sophronia's.

The moon again slid from behind thin clouds in time for Hannah to see the little frame house that she'd come to love. She understood, at least in part, why Sophronia could not leave. Lucas watched her as if he knew her thoughts, and she gave him a small smile as they rode silently toward the house.

Hours later, the moon had begun its slow arch downward as Lucas dismounted and tethered the black's reins to the branch of a cottonwood. He took a deep breath and sat on a stump, awaiting the arrival of the others.

"That you, boy?" a voice called out minutes later.

"I'm here," Lucas answered.

"Good boy." John Steele dismounted and strode to where Lucas sat. "You were there tonight?"

"Yes sir."

"I thought I spotted you. I was in front."

"I saw you."

"Who was the lad with you?"

Lucas smiled. "No lad, that one. Her name's Hannah McClary. She's Sophronia's niece, actually, her grandniece."

"She's not here with you now?" Steele glanced around as if half-expecting to see the child jump out from the stand of cottonwoods.

Lucas chuckled. "I'm sure she'd have come if I'd asked. But no, I took her to the meeting for one purpose alone—to get her to help convince Sophronia to leave. I know it scared the daylights out of her, but I figured it was worth it to save Sophronia's life."

"And the girl's life, too, if she's living with Sophronia."

"That she is. She's now Sophie's ward."

Just then three other horsemen arrived, and the discussion turned to the mob scene they had witnessed earlier in the evening. After a few minutes, Steele went into detail about the night's mission, giving the men their assignments with military precision.

Steele cleared his throat. "All right, men. We'll strike simultaneously." He glanced at his pocket watch. "At midnight—that's exactly seventeen minutes from now. You know what to do."

They nodded, then Steele said it was time to ask God's blessing on their mission. All five men knelt in a circle, facing each other, arms held upward with elbows bent to form the shape of a box over their heads.

"We are your servants, Lord, here at your bidding through your revelation as spoken to the Prophet," Steele intoned. "We ask your blessing upon our deeds. We ask for your divine protection as we avenge the death of your beloved servant Joseph Smith, our highest priest and Prophet. We ask your divine sanctification upon our acts as we avenge the deaths of all the martyrs who have perished at the hands of these, our enemies."

The men murmured "amen" in chorus then turned to Steele, whose eyes were filled with passion and godly fervor. "God be with you all," he said as he stood and gave each a salute.

"And he with you," they repeated, saluting their commanding officer.

The three latecomers received a holy kiss from Steele then mounted and rode into the night.

"You ready?" Steele asked Lucas.

The young man nodded. "You know how I feel."

John Steele draped his arm around Lucas's shoulders. "Remember what I told you. It will help to keep Eli's face before you. Think about what they did that day. The martyrs whose deaths we avenge aren't just those who died in the Carthage jail."

"I know."

"They are also your mother and father and brother."

"Yes sir."

"Remember how Eli died in your arms."

Lucas swallowed hard and nodded again. "Yes, sir," he said. But he didn't want to remember his little brother lying in a sea of crimson blood.

John Steele checked his pocket watch again, turning it toward the light of the moon. "It's time," he murmured, and the two men moved silently down the path that led to Jared Boggs's farmhouse. At the back door they paused only a moment then silently turned the knob and entered.

Jared Boggs and his wife lay sleeping in an upstairs bedroom, just off a long hallway. The two men stood silently in the doorway, letting their eyes adjust to the dark of the room.

The woman seemed to sense something was amiss. She opened her eyes and raised her head slightly, looking sleepily around the room, her eyes unfocused. After a moment, she sighed deeply, fell back against her pillow, and closed her eyes.

John Steele moved to the foot of the bed, studying the positions of the bodies that lay sprawled in sleep before him. When he acted, his movements were swift and sure. And utterly without sound.

Steele finished the deed, wiping his knife on the bedclothes and giving Lucas a quick nod. A coldness settled deep into the pit of Lucas's stomach, and he tried to bring little Eli's face to mind, hoping as always to make sense of these acts. But all he could see was blood, as dark as midnight, seeping from under a well-trimmed silver beard and Jared Boggs staring upward with sightless eyes.

John Steele and Lucas Knight left the room as silently as they had entered. They had nearly reached their horses when a woman's scream pierced the silence of the night.

In the distance a screech owl answered.

Three

The following night after supper, Lucas carried in an armload of dry wood for the fireplace as Sophronia settled into her rocking chair and reached for her knitting basket. Seated in her own high-back rocker, Hannah watched the slump of Lucas's shoulders as he worked at the hearth, setting the logs in the fireplace. Through the evening she had noticed that he was unusually quiet. She herself had been lost in thought after the previous night's outing, and she figured it was the same with Lucas. They needed to talk about moving west and, knowing Sophronia, it was not going to be an agreeable conversation. So she accepted Lucas's dark manner, thinking she understood.

Settling onto the horsehair sofa, Lucas picked up a needlepoint pillow that Sophronia had made years ago, seemed to study the design for a moment, then looked up. "Sophie, it's time to make your decision about leaving," he finally said quietly. The elderly woman started to protest, but Lucas held up his hand. "Consider it, Sophie. When the rest of us leave, you won't be safe. I know on good authority that the vigilantes will do anything to make sure you go. Please, come with us." His voice held a passion that Hannah hadn't noticed before.

Lucas sensed Hannah's gaze and glanced at her with a sad, half-smile. She thought maybe it was her cue to speak. "Where I went with Lucas last night," she said to her aunt, "there were some men who said terrible things about Mormons. Awful things," she added with a whisper.

Her aunt gave Lucas a sharp look then turned back to Hannah. "What did they say, child?"

Hannah bit her lip, remembering. "They called us names. Said we were devils and the like. Said they were going to burn the house of every Saint in Nauvoo, burn us dead or alive to be rid of us."

"You let her hear such things, Lucas? I thought you had better judgment than that." Her tone was sharp, laced with disappointment in the young man. "You had no call to take her to such a place. I thought you were going to a gathering of other Saints."

"I did it to convince you, Sophronia. I thought you might listen to Hannah."

"You thought wrong, Lucas. You shouldn't have taken her to such a place." She stood and stoked the fire, generating a burst of sparks. "I trusted you. If I didn't consider you as close a kin as my son, I wouldn't have let her go."

Lucas sat forward. "Your life—and Hannah's—are in danger. Can't you see?" He let out a deep sigh of exasperation, shaking his head slowly. "I had to do what I did."

Sophronia settled back into her rocker. "It's only the result that counts, Lucas, not your method?"

He looked away, staring into the fire for a moment. "You must come with us," he murmured, almost as if to himself. "We leave in two weeks for winter quarters. The temple will be closed here in Nauvoo. There will be no one left to protect you."

"God is with me."

"I won't be here, Sophie."

"You've been ordered to go, then? You said you would be."

"Yes."

Sophronia frowned. "That's the one thing I don't understand about the Saints."

"What do you mean?"

"Tell me what would happen to you if you disobeyed those in command."

"They speak for God, Sophie. You know that."

"You didn't answer my question, Lucas."

He stared at the elderly woman, and Hannah watched them both, fascinated. Her aunt loved the Church and its people, of that Hannah had no doubt. But it was the first time she had seen Sophronia question its authority, question Lucas's blind obedience.

When he didn't answer, Sophronia went on, "If we keep running, Lucas, when will it ever stop? I'm tired of running." Her eyes reflected the flames in the fireplace. "And I have my doubts about the reasons given for doing so."

"Sophie, we're being forced out. And aside from that, we're going to a new Promised Land. We'll be marching as God's chosen people to *our* Promised Land. Tragedy will turn into triumph. You'll see."

"Balderdash," she muttered.

Lucas sat without moving, studying the fire. "Don't ever become an apostate, Sophie. Promise me that." His voice was low and passionate, almost too quiet. "Sometimes I worry about the things you tell me. Your thoughts, your ideas . . ." His voice trailed off.

"We all have a right to our ideas, son. You know that as well as I do."

Lucas didn't answer right away. He just watched the fire thoughtfully. "You sometimes speak without thinking," he said at last. "Some of the things you've said have been noticed. And now that you're thinking of staying here there's been talk. That's all. Just talk."

"Talk about what? Having a mind of my own?" Sophronia's voice was indignant.

"I know where your heart is. But others have heard you criticize Brigham Young for leaving Nauvoo. Just be careful, Sophie. Put those things out of your mind." Lucas looked at her kindly. "If you'd just go with us, people would no longer doubt your sincerity. Please think about it."

"What will they do if I don't? Tell me, son, just what will they do?" Sophronia laughed heartily. Lucas didn't laugh.

Hannah shivered. It was obvious Sophronia did not plan to leave this place. She had to admire her aunt's determined independence, but she also feared for them both.

"How about you, Hannah?" Lucas suddenly asked. "Do you want to go with us?" She knew he still counted on her to try and convince Sophronia.

"Yes sir. I do."

Even Sophronia laughed at her quick response.

Grinning, Lucas went on, "I promise you, there's no greater adventure to be had in this lifetime than to join with the Saints. You'll see the kingdom of God being built right before your eyes. You'll be with us when Christ returns to rule through all eternity. You'll be there working side by side with the Saints. Working to build God's kingdom on earth!"

Sophronia had told her that Christ would return as king of heaven and earth. Of that, she had no doubt. She had said Jesus had eyes like burning coal and he would ride from heaven on his glorious horse.

Hannah wondered what it would be like to be there in person—there in Utah Territory or wherever the Saints landed—watching Christ ride on the winds through the sky. She would be one of God's elect, waiting for the king to come.

Lucas went on to describe the journey west. They would form a line, each family in a farm wagon covered with canvas, he said. He promised to stick close to Sophronia and Hannah if they would agree to come, protecting and helping out as he could. He spoke of the importance of staying together, and of Brigham Young and his revelations, of their duty to obey him, and of their rewards, here and in heaven, if they did.

Then Lucas smiled gently. "Please don't say no quite yet, Sophronia. Come with us. Please!"

Later, when Lucas had gone, Sophronia and Hannah climbed the stairs to the girl's bedroom. Hannah pulled on her nightclothes, and after her aunt folded down the comforter on the big iron bedstead, she slipped between the covers.

"I know you; you're wondering why I can't agree with Lucas." Sophronia fluffed the pillow, plopped it into place at the headboard, then sat on the edge of the bed. "You're so much like I was at your age, Hannah. The spitting image." Pride shined in her eyes, warming Hannah through to the soul. "I want to give you a good home for the time you'll be with me."

"I want to be with you forever, Aunt Sophie."

Sophronia smiled softly as she pulled up the comforter and settled onto the other side of the bed again. She took Hannah's hand in hers. "I've never had family before, Hannah, at least that I'm responsible for. And now that I do, I want to stay put. No more persecution. No more being run out of my home."

"But Lucas said we'll be heading to a new Promised Land. God has given it to us, and no one will ever take it away."

"That's what was said about this place, child. The same words. This was to be our Promised Land too."

"God changed his mind?"

Sophronia chuckled. "No, child. Man came up against his will. Maybe this was his first choice for us. Moving west is his second. But I'm thinking he'll bless us whether we stay or go."

"So we're not going?"

"No, honey. We're staying put."

"But what about the awful things the mob said they'd do?"

Sophronia bent to kiss her niece on the cheek. "I know firsthand what they can do to people. Believe me I do. But it's those who seem weak that they pick on. Not the strong." She was quiet as if lost in thought, or memories, for a moment. "We're the strong ones, Hannah. Don't ever forget that."

Hannah nodded sleepily, and Sophronia reached to turn out the light on the bedside table.

Before closing the door, Sophronia turned. "I love Lucas and will miss him," she said. "Don't think for a minute I won't. He's as close to me as my own son. I'm hoping the boy will see fit to stay, but I'm afraid he's right about his duty. He dare not, child. He dare not stay." A moment later, Sophronia closed the door and left Hannah to her own thoughts of Lucas heading to the Promised Land without them. She squeezed her eyes shut and prayed that Lucas and Sophronia's God would bring about a miracle causing them to go.

Two weeks passed before Hannah saw Lucas again.

"I've come to say good-bye," he said as he lolled against the kitchen sideboard, munching on one of Sophronia's biscuits.

Sophronia looked at him with sad eyes, nodding slowly. "When do you leave, son?"

"Tomorrow."

"Everyone?"

"Some have already left. Those still here are meeting by the river at sunrise to ferry across. I've got an empty wagon for you if you change your mind."

"We're staying, son. I'm sorry."

"So am I, Sophie." Then he glanced at Hannah. "How about taking a ride on Foxfire? Black Star's in need of a race."

She nodded and let out a deep sigh. "Yes, I'd like that." It would be their last ride together. "But you'll be disappointed."

"Disappointed?"

Hannah grinned. "Because Foxfire can beat Black Star any day of the week."

"Is that right?" He lifted a dark brow.

"Any day," she repeated emphatically.

"Then let's do it!"

Moments later they raced to the barn, saddled up, and galloped wildly into the wind, steamy vapor trailing back from the horses' nostrils in the bitter cold. A half-hour later, they climbed the bluff overlooking the river and the road west. Hannah admitted, laughing breathlessly, that the race was a draw.

"I liked being your little brother," she said, looking across the bleak winter landscape. "Even for just a while." She shoved her hands into her pockets, wishing she could say something more about what Lucas's friendship meant to her.

He tousled her curls affectionately. "Yeah, me too," he said in a husky voice. "But I'll be back someday. I'm sure that some of my missions will head me this direction. Besides, Sophronia means too much to me. I can't stay away for long."

"How long?"

He chuckled. "Are you always this direct?" But before she could answer, his expression sobered. "I don't know, Hannah. I can't promise anything."

Hannah nodded sadly.

To the west, the winter sun began to drop behind a long strand of clouds in the western sky. The vivid sunset colors of their first visit were gone, replaced by a deep and dark violet-gray. A wind kicked up, blowing through the barren trees with a mournful sound, lifting the hair around Hannah's face and stinging her cheeks.

She shivered, and Lucas put his arm around her thin shoulders. "We'd better get you home," he said. "Sophie'll have my hide if you take a chill."

Hannah agreed. Yet the truth was it was simply too sad to stay in the place much longer. A short time later, they rode into Sophronia's yard and dismounted. Lucas gave Sophronia a bear hug as she wiped her hands on her apron. Then he chucked Hannah under the chin. Without another word, he swung a leg over Black Star's saddle and rode into the gathering dusk.

Sophronia clutched Hannah close to her side as they stood at her front door and watched Lucas disappear into the darkness.

That night Hannah could not sleep; her mind whirled with thoughts of losing Mattie . . . and now Lucas. Sophronia was family, and she loved her. But Lucas had convinced her that the Saints belonged together. They were all family, a sacred family. No matter what Aunt Sophie said, Hannah could not shake the feeling that they should be lined up at the river with the others.

Finally, she pulled back her covers and padded to the window. She drew back the lace curtains and peered out. Sighing, she wondered how long it would take to pack Sophronia's belongings. Maybe if she woke her aunt now and tried once more to convince her, they could still pack their essentials in a farm wagon and meet the others by sunup.

Hannah was still arguing with herself about waking Sophronia when she noticed a movement at the side of the barn. The moon had disappeared behind the clouds, so she squinted and stepped closer to the glass, rubbed off the moisture with her flannel sleeve, and looked again.

There it was. A figure as black as midnight, slipping around the building. Silently. So silently.

Then Hannah spotted another. And another. But they seemed more shadow than reality. She rubbed her eyes, then rubbed the cold window again.

There was a sudden burst of a flickering light. Then another. Men were lighting torches! They quickly formed a circle around the house.

Hannah caught her breath and stepped away from the window.

"Aunt Sophie!" she screamed, running from the room. "Aunt Sophie, wake up! Oh, please, wake up!"

She ran down the hallway, half-sobbing, half-screaming in fear. "Aunt Sophie, they're here! The mob is here! They've got torches—"

Her aunt met her in the hallway. "Calm down, child," she said evenly. "Hush, now. Do you hear me?"

Hannah stifled a sob and nodded. "What're we going to do?" she finally whispered. Then she noticed her aunt was carrying a Hawken just like her pa's.

"You know how to shoot this?" Sophronia asked in a matter-of-fact voice.

"Yes ma'am, I do," Hannah said quietly. "Where's the powder and balls?"

"It's loaded, honey. You take this one. I've got another."

Hannah accepted the rifle, noticing how the feel of heavy metal and wood quieted her hands. By the time Sophronia returned, Hannah was breathing normally. She calmly followed her aunt down the stairs.

The acrid smell of burning tar and wood filled Hannah's nostrils as they descended. Her eyes stung and began to water. "The house," she cried. "They've already torched it."

"No, only the barn," Sophronia said. "I saw it from my window. Now, stay behind me, child."

"I'm here," she whispered. She reached for her aunt's free hand. Sophronia squeezed it and held it fast.

They reached the door, and Sophronia turned. "No matter what happens, I want you to stay behind me."

"I can't hide behind you when it comes time to shoot," Hannah said.

"Before we go out there, I need to tell you something." Her voice was urgent.

"Yes ma'am?"

"First I'm going to find out which one's the leader, then I'm going to shoot him."

Hannah nodded.

"I'm counting on the confusion that will follow to give you time to get away." Her aunt coughed as the smoke from the barn thickened, drifting toward the house. Outside, the taunting yells grew closer.

"Me? What about you?" Hannah cried.

"Don't worry about me. I'll catch up with you later."

"What do you want me to do?"

"As soon as I fire, I want you to run into the woods. Don't stop, just keep running."

"What about the horses? Shouldn't I get them for us?" Hannah's voice was a ragged whisper. She coughed and wiped her stinging eyes with her fists.

"It's too late for them, child," Sophronia said gently.

"Oh no!" Hannah caught her hand to her mouth. "Maybe they're in the woods. Aunt Sophie! They've got to be. Oh, Berry and Foxfire . . ."

Sophronia grabbed her hand in urgency. "Don't think about them, Hannah. Only think about getting away when I shoot. Do you understand?"

Hannah tried to calm herself. "Yes ma'am."

"All right, then, it's time," her aunt said and squared her shoulders as she reached for the door handle. "We'll go out of our own accord," she muttered to herself, "not be picked off like rabbits after they torch the house." Then she stepped outside, and Hannah followed, standing to one side and slightly behind her aunt. Hannah knew Sophronia hid the Hawken in the generous folds of her nightdress on the opposite side.

The air was filled with smoke from the barn, its flames shooting into the night sky, crackling like a thousand rifle reports. The smoke was thicker here than it had been inside the house, and Hannah coughed again, swiping at her nose. With her other hand, she clutched the rifle behind her nightdress.

The men, still in a circle around the house, gathered closer. Their faces were covered with handkerchief triangles, and she could see only their eyes, dark and mean. Then Hannah noticed that a hedge of dried brush and rags that smelled of pinewood turpentine had been built around the front of the house, between the mob and the wide front porch where she and Sophronia stood.

"Well, now. What have we here?" called one muffled voice.

"An old lady Saint and a little girl Saint," taunted another. "My, my, my! Puny little things, ain't they?"

"Where's your protector?" called a deep, hoarse voice from one side. "I hear tell you most always got some kind of angel here watchin' over you. Avenging Angel I've heard he's called." He laughed and spat on the ground. "Ain't that always the way with angels? They're never around when you need 'em most."

Sophronia drew herself up tall, her wild curls reflecting the flames of the barn fire. "You back off, now," she called out. "Shoo, now! Shoo!"

"Shoo," mimicked one of the men in a falsetto voice. "Shoo, she says. Like we was some kind of flies. Shoo-fly, boys! Shoo-fly!" He broke into gales of rude laughter. Several others joined him.

"Just what're you gonna do if we don't shoo?" called a tall, thin man in the center of the group. "Call on your God to help you fight us off?"

"Let's hear you call him! I wanna hear how you Saints pray to your devil-god," someone yelled as the men moved closer.

"Father God!" Sophronia suddenly yelled, stunning the men, who stopped short. "Father God, let your retribution begin."

The men looked at each other cautiously. "Ol' woman's crazy as a loon," one of them muttered.

Sophronia raised her fist high, and Hannah watched her aunt with admiration. "I call upon God to strike down the leader of this mob!" she cried out, shaking her fist at heaven. Her long wild curls shook as she spoke, and her alabaster face glowed with a golden sheen from the fire. She moved her eyes to the mob. "Which of you shall it be?" she shouted. "Which of you should my God strike first?"

No one moved.

"I declare," she said dramatically. "Your leader must be so busy shaking in his boots he can't walk."

Finally, the tall, thin man who'd spoken earlier stepped forward. "I ain't afraid to see your God answer your prayer," he taunted, lifting both arms as if in supplication.

"Well, I have to admit," Sophronia said almost apologetically, "that sometimes my God needs a little help."

The men exchanged glances. "I told you she's crazy," muttered someone from the back, and a few others turned to laugh with him.

At the precise moment their attention was diverted, Sophronia quickly lifted the Hawken to her shoulder and fired. The tall, thin man fell, moaning, to the ground, writhing and grabbing at his knee. Just as Sophronia predicted, there was a moment of confusion.

"Go now, child!" she hissed at Hannah. "But give me your rifle first."

Hannah did as she was told, now understanding that her aunt never intended to let her fire. She was simply holding another loaded firearm for her aunt.

By the time the men had recovered from their surprise, Hannah had raced across the yard and into the woods. And Sophronia was aiming the second rifle at the man who had mimicked her.

"Now, first man moves, you'll find yourself on the ground with your friend there," she said with a smile. "My God helps those who help themselves, as you can plainly see."

The men fell silent and backed away slightly. The man curled on the ground held his knee and moaned again.

At the same time, there was a commotion from the woods. Sophronia's attention was diverted for an instant, and a man at the front of the mob rushed toward her with a triumphant howl.

Four

From her hiding place in the woods, Hannah watched Sophronia glare at the men, dark silhouettes against the orange-flame sky. It was a standoff. She bit her lip as Sophronia waved the loaded Hawken. Both pride and fear made her heart pound hard against her ribs. For several minutes no one spoke or moved.

Then Hannah heard someone near her in the tangle of winter-dead vines and brush. She caught her breath and listened.

It must be a night animal, a raccoon or possum, she finally decided. Or maybe it was just her imagination fueled by fear. Then she heard the sound again. This time there was no denying it, and she shrank back into the brush, afraid to breathe.

A horse whinnied softly and stamped its foot. Hannah squinted into the darkness, but the undergrowth blocked her view.

Just then the horse neighed and reared, and a heartbeat later it crashed through the brush toward the clearing. Now Hannah could clearly see both horse and rider. For all her fear, she grinned, wanting to run out into the clearing and join in the melee.

It was Black Star. And though the rider's face was covered with a dark kerchief and a hat was pulled low on his head, there was no mistaking the man's identity. It was Lucas Knight! The black reared again, its eyes wild with fear of the fire and smoke.

At precisely the same moment, Sophronia looked toward the rider. A large, burly man close to the porch moved quickly toward the elderly woman. She swung the rifle in his direction. But it was too late. He had already reached her and easily wrestled the heavy weapon from her grasp.

But before he could take aim, Lucas spoke. "I wouldn't try that if I were you," he said in a dead-calm voice.

His words were met by silence. Hannah understood why. He held two rifles, one aimed at the mob, the other at the man who had just taken the Hawken from Sophronia.

Black Star skittered sideways, his nostrils flaring, but Lucas's gaze never left the man standing on the porch. "I strongly recommend," he said, his voice quiet but menacing, "that you hand the little lady back her property. Butt first. That's right. Nice and easy." He strung out the words with a menacing tone then waited as the man did as he was told, and soon Sophronia was aiming the Hawken right at his face.

"Now, you go join the rest of your friends," she said, her chin held high.

The man moved toward the mob, stepping over the hedge of kindling and kerosene, hands up, glancing at the others as if asking whether they were going to help him charge Lucas. But no one seemed willing to be the first to move. Hannah shifted her position, waiting to see how one man could possibly keep the mob at bay, even with Sophronia's help.

As Hannah was trying to figure out what Lucas was planning to do next, Sophronia moved down the wide porch stairs and planted herself by Lucas and the black. The young man murmured something Hannah couldn't hear, then her aunt started to move backward toward Hannah's brushy hiding place, the Hawken still trained at the circle of men.

"Now, the rest of you," Lucas shouted. "Up on the porch!" The men glanced at each other then slowly started to move forward. Two of the men helped their injured leader, half carrying, half pulling him along. One or two others started to lay down their still-burning torches. "You'll be needing those," Lucas commanded. "Take them with you."

One by one, the men stepped across the hedge of brush they had built earlier. As they crossed, they held their torches high. The group shuffled and crowded and murmured as they took their places just as Lucas had commanded.

Hannah caught her hand to her mouth. The sight of the men on the porch, holding their torches so they wouldn't set each other on fire, made her certain what Lucas had planned.

"It'll be all right, child," Sophronia said, startling Hannah. She gently touched Hannah's shoulder. She had moved so quietly to the girl's side that Hannah, intent on Lucas's business with the men, hadn't noticed until she spoke.

"But the house," Hannah whispered. "It's—" She couldn't finish.

"It's about to burn, Hannah. I know."

Hannah looked up at Sophronia's face, barely visible in their dark hiding place. "Everything you love is in there." Hannah thought she might cry, knowing how much the place meant to her aunt.

"Not everything, Hannah. Not everything." But her voice was filled with more sadness than Hannah had ever heard in a person.

Hannah looked back through the clearing. "What about the men? Lucas can't mean for them to burn too." She turned back to her aunt, suddenly aware of the power of the Danites. The terrible, swift, unmerciful power that Lucas as one of them held in his hands. "Surely he won't cause them harm. Will he?"

"Think about what they were about to do to us, Hannah." Then she seemed to notice the horror on her grandniece's face. She patted the girl's shoulder again. "I think he means to confuse them, maybe just long enough for us to get away. He's got horses waiting for us back a ways. He told me to find you, then the horses. He'll meet us and show us the way."

"The way?"

"To the river, where the others are waiting to cross. They've had to hide because of the rampage going on in Nauvoo tonight."

"We'll be going with the Saints?"

But before Sophronia could answer, their attention was drawn back to the clearing, where the men stood watching Lucas. They had pulled down their masks at his command, because he said he wanted to know their identities so he could notify their families of their deaths.

The men, some still looking defiant, others filled with stark fear, stared at him. Hannah shuddered, and Sophronia gently pulled her to standing. "We must go, child. Lucas will expect us to be ready when he joins us."

Hannah nodded mutely, and after one last glance at the men with their torches and Lucas on a skittering and dancing Black Star, she followed her aunt as they made their way deeper into the woods.

They had nearly reached the horses, tethered to a small oak near an old stone well, when a shot rang out. A man's shout carried through the woods from Sophronia's house, followed by another. More distant yells filled the air, and the acrid smell of burning brush and kerosene drifted toward them. Then came another shot and more screams.

Sophronia grabbed Hannah's hand, and they ran the rest of the way to the horses. She looked at her aunt in wonder. "It's Foxfire," she whispered. "How—?"

Sophronia shook her head, patting Berry. "I don't know how he got them out of the barn." She shook her head again as she mounted. "Hurry, honey. We can ponder all this later. Hurry into that saddle!"

Seconds later, Lucas broke through the woods, the black flying across the ground.

"Let's go!" he shouted just as Hannah swung her leg over Foxfire's saddle.

She nodded and kicked her heels into her horse's flanks. Lucas took the lead, and Hannah fell in behind him, Sophronia at the rear. They rode along the bluff, finally heading onto a trace that before now had been unknown to Hannah. Though the night was dark except for an eerie orange glow in the sky over Sophronia's house, Lucas and the black seemed to know instinctively which way to go.

Hannah couldn't make out the winding trail, but Black Star was surefooted, and Foxfire, strangely calm for having been rescued from a burning barn, followed with deliberate grace. They rode for nearly an hour before arriving at the river.

"We'll need to wait here," Lucas said as Black Star snorted and kicked the ground. Hannah and Sophronia moved their horses beside him. "It's too dangerous now to make our way through town to join the others." The beach was narrow on this stretch of the river, and now that the earliest gray of dawn had started to light the sky, Hannah could make out a small rocky hollow in the river cliff.

"We can dismount, rest the horses." He nodded to the shallow cave. "There's some bedding and warm clothing inside. If you need anything or just want to rest, make yourself at home. I'll keep watch out here."

"How long until we leave?" Sophronia asked.

"About two hours." He frowned as if not sure how much to tell them. "One of the ferries will head south to pick us up instead of going straight across the river with the others."

"You arranged this ahead of time, then?" Sophronia asked.

Lucas nodded.

"How did you know we'd be here with you?"

For a moment he didn't speak. "I knew, Sophie. That's all. I just knew."

Hannah slid from Foxfire's back and, after Sophronia dismounted, led both horses to the river. Sophronia moved wearily to the cave, but Hannah stayed with Lucas, who had swung from the saddle and was rubbing Black Star's neck as the horse drank.

"What happened to the men, Lucas? Back at Aunt Sophronia's, I mean."

"That's not for you to worry about, Hannah."

"But I want to know."

He cocked his head. "They were bad men. They deserved to die."

"Is that what you do? Kill bad people?"

"I haven't killed anyone."

"So they didn't die."

He shook his head slowly, almost as if he was sorry they hadn't. "No, they didn't die, Hannah. After they threw their torches at the hedge they'd built, I fired a couple of shots above their heads to scare them into the house. As you know, there's another way out the back. I'm sure it didn't take them long to find it."

"So you were just trying to confuse them . . . just long enough for us to get away."

He nodded.

"That's what Aunt Sophie said you were doing."

"Have you ever killed anybody, Lucas?" She absently played with Foxfire's mane, combing the coarse strands with her fingers.

He looked out across the silver-gray river but didn't answer. Hannah knew enough not to pursue the question. Besides, maybe she didn't want to know. In her eyes, Lucas stood taller in stature than even Mattie. Why, hadn't he just saved their lives? Yet if he killed, even for the right reasons, Hannah didn't think she would ever think of him in the same way.

"What if you had to, Lucas?" she asked with sudden insight. "What if God told you to?"

He looked back into her face, a small grin playing at one side of his mouth. "God?"

She nodded vigorously. "Aunt Sophie said that Brigham Young is God's mouthpiece. Words flow right out of God's heart into his mouth." She stared at him evenly. "What then? I mean if the Prophet said God told him you needed to kill someone."

Lucas stared at her for the longest time without speaking. "What you say is true, Hannah. Brigham Young does speak for God."

"And if he tells you to kill?"

"Then I have to obey."

"What if he's wrong? I mean, what if he wasn't really listening when God talked to him? That happens to me sometimes. I'll be thinking hard about why frogs sing only at night or why butterflies look like they're dancing with sunbeams or why stars look like they're on fire sometimes, and Aunt Sophie will say something three, sometimes four times before I hear it." She frowned. "Then I'll pretend I know what she said, because I'm feeling embarrassed about not listening. What if that happens to the Prophet? What if he isn't listening properly when God says something?"

Lucas reached over and affectionately tousled Hannah's curls. After a moment, he moved back, sobering. "Brother Brigham's been anointed by God himself, Hannah. I would think if you were God's only chosen Prophet on earth, you'd listen hard. You'd listen carefully and make sure you didn't make any mistakes."

Hannah nodded. "I hope he never asks you to kill for God, Lucas."

Lucas stared at her without answering, and in the thickening mist of the winter dawn, his eyes seemed to take on the sheen of blue-black gunmetal. Hannah shivered when she could see no emotion showing through.

She reached for her friend's hand. "Lucas," she said, holding it tightly between both of hers. "Are you going to stay with us all the way to the Promised Land?"

He smiled and, pulling his hand free, tousled her hair once more. She was glad to see the warmth had returned to his eyes. "Wouldn't miss it. I'm going to teach you to be the best oxen driver this side of the Pacific Ocean."

"You are?"

He grinned. "Without fail."

"What else?"

"You've got to learn to drive the wagon into a night circle with the others."

Hannah liked the sound of Lucas's plans, and the thought of the adventure ahead made some of the horror of the night begin to fade. She sat on a large, round rock near the water. "What else?" she almost demanded in her enthusiasm.

"You'll need to learn doctoring."

"Doctoring?"

"Setting broken arms or treating snakebites—cutting an X in the flesh then sucking out the poison. Think you can do that?"

"There're lots of snakes along the way?"

He nodded.

"That's nothing. Back home in Kentucky, I've seen more vipers than you can shake a stick at. I'm not afraid of any old snake or its bite. You just show me how, and I'll do it." Hannah felt like saluting. "What else?"

Lucas laughed, and the sound of it lifted her spirits even more. "I can see you're going to make quite a pioneer, Hannah," he said with a wide grin.

"Hannah, come up here and put on some warmer clothes," Sophronia called as she started down the rocky incline from the shelter. Amazingly, her aunt had found a homespun-looking skirt and blouse that fit her tall, broad-shouldered frame perfectly. A woolen shawl covered her shoulders, and she had donned a gingham poke bonnet. Even her heavy leather boots looked suitable.

Hannah was reluctant to leave Lucas's side, but she knew her aunt was right. She started clambering up the hill, but she wasn't out of earshot before she heard Sophronia's words to Lucas. She turned to listen.

"Strikes me as odd, son, that these clothes fit me to perfection. You can't tell me these supplies were left for the benefit of your Danites." She touched the bonnet. "Somehow, I don't think they'd have much need for a poke bonnet. Or the rest of the trunk of clothes, for that matter—all seemingly made to fit my frame."

Lucas didn't answer.

"You knew about this ahead of time, didn't you, son? That's how you got the horses out."

Still the young man remained mute.

"But I want—no, I *need* to know if you planned it." She stared hard at the young man. "Did you pretend to be one of the mob and lead them to my house? Did you do that to have your way? To get me to go west with the others, Lucas? Did you burn me out so there'd be no turning back?"

Hannah caught her breath and stood at the cave's mouth as if made of stone. Could Lucas have done such a thing? She watched his face for signs of guilt, but she couldn't see clearly in the still-gray hours of dawn.

"Sophie," he finally said. "I thought you knew me. I thought you knew my love for you . . . for Hannah."

Sophronia didn't wait for Lucas to go on; she reached out and touched Lucas's arm gently. "Son, oh, my son!" she cried. "I worry that they'll capture your heart!" Then almost fiercely, she gathered him into her embrace. Hannah couldn't be sure, but she thought she saw Lucas weeping.

"It was planned, Lucas. I know it as well as I know my own name. You can't tell me it wasn't."

"I didn't know until they sent me for you, Sophie," Lucas said quietly. "Please believe that. I didn't know."

By the time Hannah had pulled on her own well-fitting clothes and clambered back down the hillside, Lucas and Sophronia were seated, talking about plans for the future as if their exchange had never happened.

A short time later, as a thin sun lifted above the eastern riverbank, a ferry appeared from around a distant bend. The trunks were loaded from the cave, and the horses were penned on board with a dozen or more other teams. Then slowly, very slowly, the flatboat pulled away from shore.

Hannah stood at the railing, staring eastward. She'd been in Illinois for just a short time, and now she was heading hundreds of miles farther away from home. There had been no time to post a letter to her pa, telling him where she was headed.

Would she ever see Mattie again? She felt tears start to well up in her eyes. Sophronia had said he was planning another visit to Nauvoo. How would he ever find them now? Would he think to follow them to their Promised Land? Would any of the Gentiles tell him where they'd gone?

She tried to swallow the lump that had formed in her throat. Suddenly Lucas was beside her. "It'll be all right, Hannah," he said gently, as if understanding her thoughts. "Turn around. Look at the other side."

Hannah turned. The sunlight slanted across the water, creating a shimmering path of rippled light. She smiled up at Lucas. "It's pretty," she said, trying to forget her sadness. He noticed that she'd been weeping and pulled a kerchief from his pocket, the same one he'd worn across his face the night before. Tenderly, he wiped away her tears.

Five

Utah Territory
Spring 1857

The warm sun had risen high when Lucas Knight strode down tree-shaded Main Street toward Sophronia's small, two-story house on the far side of town. Horse-drawn wagons and carriages passed, and he nodded at the friendly faces. Several people called out words of greeting; others merely smiled and waved. Joab and Martha Heber rode by in a fancy carriage newly shipped from Boston, their two unmarried daughters sitting in the half-seat behind them. Both girls flushed and giggled when they saw him. Grinning, Lucas blew them a kiss and tipped his hat. He had watched the girls grow into comely young women from the skinny little waifs they'd been, covered with dirt and clothed in tattered rags, when the family had arrived years before with the first handcart immigration.

Nearly ten years had passed since Lucas arrived in the Great Salt Lake valley, driving his wagon next to Hannah and Sophronia's. Then this land had been nothing but a salt-covered desert; now rows of brightly painted shops flanked the cobbled street where he walked.

He took pleasure in the hard-earned prosperity of the Saints. There could be no harder working, more God-fearing people on earth. How true the Scripture that Brother Brigham was forever quoting from the prophet Isaiah: *Be strong, fear not: behold, your God will come with vengeance, even God with a recompense; he will come and save you. . . . Then shall the lame man leap as an hart, and the tongue of the dumb sing: for in the wilderness shall waters break out, and streams in the desert. And the parched ground shall become a pool, and the thirsty land springs of water: in the habitation of dragons, where each lay, shall be grass with reeds and rushes.*

Lucas turned off Main Street and headed down a small, winding lane that led to Sophronia's cottage just outside of town. For as far as he could see in any direction, in what was once a bleak and empty landscape, elms and sycamores now cast forth their leafy branches, providing welcome shade beneath the desert's vivid sun. Carpets of grass and white picket fences surrounded the small, English-style brick houses with their gaily trimmed shutters.

Flower beds filled with early spring roses, irises, and daisies framed each front yard, and vegetable gardens already showing signs of their coming bounty graced the rear of each cottage. Behind most of the homes, Lucas could see apple orchards, now in full bloom, spreading their slender, blossom-covered branches toward the sun like arms of worship held heavenward.

Yes, it was a good land filled with a good people, he mused as he walked. Good people, many of whom had nearly sacrificed their lives to make this desert bloom. Brother Brigham had been right in bringing the Saints here.

Then Lucas paused, frowning, as he looked back at the well-planned city. He could see the good in the land and in its people, and he tried to consider only the virtue of what the Saints had accomplished. As happened too often nowadays, though, Lucas pushed his doubts, his musings, to the back of his mind, away from the darker side of the beauty before him. Yet those doubts remained in place.

There was no denying the triumph of God's people over the elements, but at what price? As he walked down the lane, he wondered if other Saints reflected on the sacrifices given to build this kingdom. Grumbling wasn't allowed in this place, and perhaps that was proper. Neither was dissension permitted nor any word against Brigham Young or his council, the apostles, the elders, or the bishops.

In keeping with their unspoken promises of optimism and their sworn vows of obedience, most who had suffered when they crossed the Plains wisely kept their own counsel once they arrived in the valley. Those who didn't soon learned to keep quiet, or they suffered the consequences.

When he and Sophronia and Hannah crossed, they had known hardship, but they had crossed during spring and summer after waiting out a severe winter. But hundreds who'd crossed in the bitter cold, following the elders' orders, had perished—from starvation, from exposure, or from the stubborn ignorance of those who led them.

He took a deep breath, trying to push the indictment of the elders, the apostles, the president's council—God's elect—from his mind. But he couldn't forget how the new converts, mostly the elderly and infirm, and the families with young children had not been told of the journey's hardships before they were recruited by missionaries in England, Scotland, and the Scandinavian countries. They hadn't been told that they would take turns pulling carts of unseasoned wood, each heavy handcart filled with the belongings of several families.

Lucas had seen one of the early handcart groups when he and a few eastward-traveling missionaries encountered them in Iowa. He would never forget their faces as Apostle Franklin Richards and Elders Webb and Felt—riding fine horses alongside their stout teams of oxen pulling supply wagons outfitted for their own journey—rebuked the converts for grumbling.

The handcart pioneers had wept in repentance, then in joy, as the apostle lifted his hand and gave them a blessing, prophesying in the name of God of Israel:

The Almighty God is making a way for you, his people, to Zion. Though the snow may fall and the storm rage on your right hand and your left, not a hair of your heads will perish.

Yet they *had* perished. Hundreds had frozen to death. Hundreds more had starved. Those who survived were little more than skeletons when they arrived in the valley of the Saints during the following months.

Lucas pushed the memory of the false prophecy from his mind. He especially tried to forget Brigham Young's words as the pitiful, straggling few survivors pulled their broken-down handcarts along the main street of Zion. "A successful experiment," Lucas had overheard him say to John Steele. "A successful experiment indeed."

Lucas picked up his pace now that he could see Sophronia's two-story cottage in the distance. He and some of the other bishops and elders had built the small brick dwelling shortly after their arrival in the valley. Like the others, it was English style with a steep roof that nearly touched the ground. Soon after it was finished, Sophronia and Hannah had planted poplar, mulberry, and maple saplings that some of their neighbors had given them, having had to bring them from the East. Now, of course, the trees had reached full growth and provided a luxurious canopy of shade.

Sophronia had also planted grapevines after Lucas had built an arbor at the side of the house and an apple orchard in the back. The young plants and seedlings thrived with an abundance of fresh water brought from the nearby mountains by the irrigation system built by the Church.

Hannah had planted ivy in a bed at the front of the house, and now it twined up the posts that flanked the entrance, creating a lacy cover over the porch. She'd pleaded with Lucas to build a porch swing, and unable to resist her sweet smile, he'd of course built her the finest swing to be found anywhere in the valley. She spent every spare moment of her day there. Every day after her chores were finished, after the horses were exercised and the cows milked, she would settle into the swing and read.

She read every book she could get hold of, most of them several times. Everyone knew that if they wanted to clear out an attic or trunk of unused books, they had only to go as far as Sophronia's cottage to be rid of them. Each time he visited, Hannah proudly showed Lucas her latest acquisitions ranging from Hawthorne to Emerson, from Browning to Longfellow.

By now he'd reached the little picket fence in front of the cottage, and Hannah, from her usual place in the swing, glanced up, smiling when she saw him. She stood to greet him, then almost shyly leaned against the front porch railing, watching him open the gate.

He grinned at her standing there in the slant of sunlight. The sight of her always lifted his spirits. In the ten years since their wagon train had rumbled into the valley of the Saints, Hannah had grown into a fetching young woman. No longer was she the impetuous, skinny wood sprite he'd first met in Illinois. And he wasn't the only man to notice: Many an elder's head was turned at the sight of her.

Just as the grown-up Hannah hadn't lost one freckle that graced her small nose, neither had she lost one ounce of spirit. Far from it. In many ways, she was more outspoken than ever. Lucas couldn't count the times he'd had to warn the girl to bridle her tongue.

Whereas many of the women wore modest bonnets or hats to cover their heads, Hannah—following Sophronia's lead—let her unruly curls have their own way, without comb or paper flower clip to adorn or tame them.

Now she lifted a brow and considered him solemnly. "You seem especially lost in thought this morning, Lucas."

"It seems to be one of those mornings—one made for thinking deep thoughts and considering God's beauty," Lucas said, bounding up the porch stairs. "And you, dear Hannah, are one of his finest examples."

Hannah reached up to ruffle his hair affectionately. "I think you've just got a case of spring fever, dear boy. Makes one see the world through rose-colored glasses."

He chuckled softly and caught her hand. A brief shadow seemed to cross her face. Sophronia had been feeling poorly of late, so he attributed the uneasiness on Hannah's face to that.

"How is Sophie?" he asked as they moved to the swing.

Hannah frowned. "Not much better. She's resting right now."

"I've been concerned about her." Lucas held the swing still as Hannah settled into it, then, seating himself, he started rocking it gently as they looked out toward the Wasatch Mountains to the east. "In fact, I went by to see Doc Jones on my way here. He gave me an elixir. Said it might strengthen her blood."

Again Hannah looked worried. "It's more than strengthened blood she needs, Lucas. I've been as worried as you are lately, but I'm not sure what's wrong."

"She won't say?"

Hannah shook her head. "She says, although it's in a voice filled with spirit and vigor, that she's got a right to slow down if she declares she wants to." She paused. "I think it's something more serious than a blood ailment, Lucas."

"What do you mean?" He looked at Hannah intently, trying to read her expression.

"There's more that makes up a person than body and soul."

"You've got to be more plainspoken than that, Hannah. What are you talking about?"

"It started when Elder Webb reprimanded her after services at the arbor."

"Sophie's never paid much attention to the chastisement she gets for being outspoken. I've always thought she rather glories in it." Lucas chuckled, enjoying memories of Sophronia's sharp mind and tongue. "Everyone knows she means no harm."

"This was different. He was vicious and minced no words. You weren't there and didn't hear. But others, friends of hers, were. They heard how he spoke—they turned away as if she had some malady they might catch." Hannah met his gaze earnestly. "Elder Webb was downright disrespectful. Meanspirited. He called her a crazy old woman who was touched in the head."

"Did she say anything afterward?" Lucas asked, sitting forward slightly.

"She wouldn't speak of it at all. Said the remembrance of Elder Webb's face as he spoke made her feel she couldn't breathe properly." Hannah pushed the swing to get it rocking again, and a breeze lifted a few strands of her hair.

For a long time Lucas didn't answer. He stared across the fields at farmhouses and cattle, barely noticing the greening of the valley of the Saints in the warm spring air. He fixed his gaze on a rocky point on the distant mountains and considered how much he should tell Hannah.

Through the years she and Sophronia had become closer than blood kin. While he was in the safe haven their home provided, he put aside the stance he usually adopted for John Steele, the man who'd raised him. Even so, there was a line Lucas had drawn because of the danger his disclosures could bring to Sophronia and Hannah.

"The Prophet's received word from God about the need for a great reformation," he finally said, looking back to Hannah. "He's talked to his elders and some of the apostles about it."

"Reformation?" Hannah looked at him with a frown. "What has that got to do with how Brother Webb treated Aunt Sophie?"

"It has everything to do with it, Hannah. Everything. Especially when it comes to speaking out against the Church or against God's Prophet the way Sophie does."

"Sophronia's always had a sharp tongue. For years you yourself have warned her to no avail." Around them the scent of fresh-cut grass and newly blooming roses drifted toward them on a slight breeze. Hannah and Lucas waved to a young man driving a team as the farm wagon rattled down the road.

"The Prophet's worried about disobedience. He wants us purified, our sins atoned for." Lucas hesitated. "The chaff burned away from us all, no matter the cost."

Hannah stood and moved to the porch rail then turned and leaned against it as she studied Lucas, her expression thoughtful. "There's no purer soul among us, I dare say, than Aunt Sophie. She's filled with love for the Church, the Prophet, for this valley."

"I know she is," Lucas said softly. "But it seems that love doesn't matter. It's actions that count, acts of obedience."

"Blind obedience, Lucas?" She swallowed hard and dropped her voice in her earnestness. "Sometimes I wonder about our life here." She studied his face. "We're expected to do as we are told, no matter the consequences. We can't disagree, or we'll be punished. It's a wonderful life—as long as we obey all the rules."

"Any civilized society has laws that must be obeyed, Hannah. You know that as well as I do." Even as he uttered the words, Lucas knew they sounded hollow.

"But Lucas, I worry about our freedom." Her gaze held his, refusing to let go, holding him close with the emotion of her wide, blue eyes. "What if we wanted to leave? The valley, I mean. You and Sophronia and me. What would happen?"

"We'd be welcome to go, just as any Saint is, Hannah."

"Tell me who has left—"

He interrupted, giving her names and dates.

"But none of us have ever heard from them again." Now there was a challenge in those eyes. "How do we know they ever made it farther than the border?"

Lucas didn't answer.

"Tell me the truth, Lucas. Not just what you've been told to say."

"I've told you all I can." A heavy silence fell between them, then Lucas spoke again. "Look around, Hannah. Look at the valley, alive with an abundance of food and grain. And this beautiful city we've built. It's been raised by the toil of us all, by our hard work and discipline.

"Our calling isn't easy. Jesus Christ himself said the way is narrow and few will make it." He sighed and reached for her hand, drawing her closer, and she again sat down beside him on the swing. "I have questions, too, about our faith. But Hannah, I know what life is like on the other side—outside our kingdom here in Utah. I know what the Gentiles did to my family back at Haun's Mill. There is no life for me—for us—anywhere else but here."

Still holding her small hand in his, Lucas went on. "We are preparing for Christ's kingdom on earth, Hannah. Don't forget that. Life in Deseret may seem unfair, narrow, and harsh, but it's for a purpose. We—all of us—are part of God's glorious army. We need to be fit for the job. Discipline and obedience are necessary to make this army great." He smiled gently. "Besides, we're being tested, perfected, for that glorious day to join him in ruling the world."

Hannah pulled her hand away. "But, dear Lucas, you've again hit upon a sore point, something Sophronia noticed long ago."

He frowned. "What is that?"

"This kingdom will be ruled only by men."

He grinned. "Ah, yes. I think you've mentioned that before."

"And I don't like it any better now, Lucas Knight. For instance, I have it on good authority that when we marry, we'll be given secret names."

"Wait a minute. Are you saying 'we,' as in you and me?" His grin widened.

"You know we're meant for each other, Lucas. You might as well admit it." She brightened, giving him a sisterly poke in the ribs. "Now listen to what I'm saying. When we—you and I—say our vows, we will be given secret names."

"You're not supposed to know that, Hannah."

She raised a sly eyebrow and smiled. "The names, I've heard," she continued, "are so that we can be called into heaven when we die."

"You're not supposed to know that either."

She ignored his admonition. "But Lucas, what I don't understand—and Sophronia agrees—is why you as my husband will be the only one who can call me into heaven. You'll be the only one to know my name."

He chuckled. "Don't you trust me?"

But this time Hannah didn't smile. "I trust you, Lucas. I always have, and I always will." She frowned. "But what if I married someone I don't trust?"

The thought sliced through his heart like a knife.

"It seems to me that my husband would have the upper hand. I would have to do as he says, or he wouldn't call me into heaven." She gazed at him evenly, her voice husky as she continued, "That's true, isn't it, Lucas?"

"Yes," he said softly and reached for her hand again. "But, Hannah, you just asked me to marry you. That's the third time now since you were ten years old. It seems to me that there's not much chance I'll get away."

He thought about that first time. Hannah had been sitting on the wood-slat wagon seat, popping a whip above the oxen's backs as they crossed the Plains. Lucas rode beside the wagon on Black Star, and Sophronia rested under the canvas cover of the wagon. The prairie winds had stung Hannah's cheeks red and ruffled her flaxen hair.

She'd looked up at him, nodded her head very seriously, then announced, "I'm going to marry you someday, Lucas Knight."

The second time had been when she was sixteen. They'd been riding Foxfire and Black Star across the fields. Foxfire reared at the sight of a jackrabbit, throwing Hannah. When her horse raced wildly away from them, Lucas had swooped Hannah up and into the saddle in front of him. She'd nestled in his arms as he kicked Black Star into a full gallop, chasing after the runaway mare. When Foxfire finally halted, Hannah looked up at Lucas, telling him not to stop. "I like being here," she said. "I want to stay in your arms forever, Lucas Knight."

"You'll change your mind," he'd said, though he felt the same way. "You're only sixteen. You'll soon have a passel of boys standing in line, waiting to court you."

But Hannah had shaken her head vigorously. "We're meant for each other, Lucas. Don't try to fight it. We *will* marry someday, you know."

Now Lucas smiled warmly at Hannah, more lovely than ever at twenty years old. "This is the third time you've asked, you know," he reminded her again.

She smiled back. "They say the third time's a charm."

"They also say the man should do the asking."

"Then you'd better hurry, Lucas."

"I have some . . ." He hesitated. ". . . things to take care of first, Hannah. So don't yet start sewing your wedding dress." He forced his voice to be light.

"You must ask permission from John Steele?"

"It's only proper. He is my father and my friend."

"He also has the authority to say no on behalf of the Church." She frowned. "This takes us back to obedience, Lucas. What if John Steele says no? Do we blindly obey?"

Lucas drew in a deep breath. He had already struggled with that very question. He nodded. "If the answer is no, there will be good reason."

Hannah stood angrily. "You would just accept that, Lucas? You would let me marry another?"

He stared at her face, realizing what it was he'd noticed that was different about her expression. It was fear he saw there. Hannah was afraid. He stood and moved closer to her. Tenderly, he touched her face and turned it toward his. "Hannah," he said, "what is it? There's something you haven't told me. Something that prompted this whole discussion."

She nodded, and tears welled up in her eyes. "You haven't asked what it was that riled Aunt Sophie so—what caused Elder Webb to rebuke her."

"No, I haven't. What was it?"

"She was spouting off about the practice of plural marriages."

"It's no secret how she feels. She's done that before."

"This time it was different. She was aiming her remarks at one particular Saint."

"Who?"

For a moment, she didn't speak. She looked down at her hands, folded on the porch rail. "John Steele," she finally murmured. But Lucas wasn't surprised. John already had nine wives and, it was said, was looking for another.

"Why did she pick on John? Nearly all of the apostles and elders have more than one wife."

"Because John Steele had come calling here the day before."

"Surely, he's not thinking of taking Sophronia as his tenth wife!" Lucas almost laughed at the thought.

"No, Lucas, he's not."

Lucas felt his heart drop into his stomach. He thought he might be sick. He knew what Hannah was going to say next, even before she uttered a word.

"It's me he wants, Lucas," she whispered. "He's asked Sophronia for my hand in marriage."

SIX

Lucas strode purposefully up the walk and to the front door of John Steele's large, two-story brick house, one of several homes the man maintained. Not all his wives were content to share the same household, and because of the constant bickering, he'd moved the primary troublemakers to a ranch near the ironworks in the south. His town house, however, remained his favorite residence, and because of his position within the Church, he could usually be found in residence with his first wife, Harriet, the woman who'd helped him raise Lucas, and three of his most comely wives.

Harriet answered the door, her round face brightening when she saw Lucas. "Dear boy," she said softly, wiping her hands on her apron before giving him a gentle embrace.

Lucas kissed her plump cheek. "Harriet," he said. "You look well."

She smiled timidly and glanced down at her soiled apron. "Why, thank you, Luke. That's quite a compliment for an old lady like me. Half the time I feel so worn out I figure I look pretty haggard."

Lucas took her hands, turned them over, and rubbed his thumb across her calluses. "With the work you do for the ladies of the Church plus running this house with its small army of wives and children, it's no wonder you're worn out." His voice softened. "You deserve a rest."

A shadow crossed Harriet's face, and she withdrew her hands. "I'm fit as a fiddle, Luke. Don't you be worrying about me." She circled her arm around him as they moved down the long entry hall to the parlor. "Now, what brings you to this part of town? Church business?" She nodded to one of two high-backed chairs that flanked a sturdy settee. "Sit down, son." She settled heavily onto the settee.

Lucas did as he was bidden, glancing around the room, again marveling at the beautiful furnishings. Made by local artisans, they were stylish and functional but not fussy. John Steele liked the finer things in life, and his houses reflected his taste. Lucas looked back to Harriet. "I've come to see John about a personal matter. Is he here?"

"He's out back, showing Sara the right way to weed the corn." She chuckled. "Last week she nearly pulled up every new sprout. Said she thought they were all weeds."

"Maybe she's never seen corn," Lucas said. "Does it grow in Wales?"

Harriet shrugged. "Maybe if John would pick his wives more carefully, he wouldn't have to worry about whether or not they've ever tended corn or cows or cauliflower. All that would be settled ahead of time." Then she narrowed her eyes in thought and said no more.

"Shall I go out back to see John?" Lucas asked gently. "Or wait till he comes in?"

"Oh, law, no. I'll go fetch him." She smiled. "I nearly forgot my manners in my excitement to see you, son. It's been too long."

"I know. And I plan to remedy that. I'll be coming to see you more often. You can count on it."

Harriet looked confused. "That might be a far piece for you to come a-calling, Luke. John said you'd be going to England on a mission by the end of the month."

"He hasn't said anything to me about it."

"Hmm. I thought you were all but packed and ready to go."

Lucas shook his head uncertainly. "He must have meant someone else."

She gazed at him evenly as she pushed herself to standing, her expression telling him there was no doubt who John meant. "I'll go fetch him, Luke," she said finally. "You can ask him yourself."

Lucas nodded and stood politely—just as she'd taught him years ago—as Harriet left the parlor.

He walked to the room's double French doors, opened one, and stepped onto a wide porch. He surveyed the garden below. Finger-sized plants were poking through rich soil in what would soon be a patchwork garden of vegetables and flowers. Brigham Young had ordered the Saints to begin building a complex irrigation system the first year they arrived. Completed several years ago, it now brought an abundance of fresh water rushing from the mountains for crops, cattle, gardens, and people. John Steele had been instrumental in the project, and as the Prophet's Indian agent, he had enlisted the local Utes to do most of the hard labor.

"Luke, my boy!" John Steele, breaking into Lucas's thoughts, strode through the French doors to where Lucas stood. He shook the younger man's hand vigorously. "It's about time you paid your mother and me a visit."

Lucas considered the man who'd raised him. Whether showing his latest wife how to weed a corn patch or leading the Avenging Angels on a mission, he always looked the same: immaculately dressed with every strand of his chin-length silver hair neatly in place, his emotions masked behind piercing blue eyes.

"John," Lucas said pleasantly as he released John's hand. "It's good to see you."

"We've missed you at the meetings. Where've you been?"

Lucas leaned his back against the porch railing, crossing one ankle over the other, considering the Danites. It was true. He avoided meeting with the other Angels as often as possible. "My feelings aren't a secret," he finally said.

John settled into a white iron chair in front of Lucas. "You know, don't you, son, that you really have no choice but to attend? You are a chosen man. Chosen by God to be a priest of the Melchizedek order.

"And as a priest, your obedience is required. You must keep God's commandments as revealed through the Prophet."

"I know that, John. You've taught me well."

"Not well enough, it appears." John Steele's voice had taken on a hard edge. "You are no longer a child."

"I was never a child," Lucas added grimly.

But John Steele ignored his comment. "You know my meaning. You became a priest of the Aaronic order at age twelve. That holy act was an acceptance of your priestly responsibilities. You will suffer the consequences if you shirk your responsibilities."

John had always claimed that Lucas meant more to him than did his own flesh-and-blood children. How many times had they had this conversation? And it always ended the same.

"I've told you before, I've seen too much killing," Lucas said. "I don't care what the reason, whether it be for holiness' sake, atonement's sake, or even the coming Great Reformation."

Lucas fixed his gaze on John Steele's ice blue eyes. "I want to serve the Church. I want to serve God." He walked to the corner of the porch, looking out over the garden. Then he turned back to Steele. "But isn't there another way?"

"God's called you to obedience, son."

"Why does that obedience require killing?"

"It's the obedience that counts, son, whether it's carrying out blood atonement or some other act."

Lucas didn't answer.

"Is that what you came to see me about?"

"No." Lucas shook his head slowly. "No, actually it isn't." He walked back to where John was seated and settled into a chair beside him. "I'm very disturbed about something I just heard. I'm sure there must be some mistake—that it can't possibly be true—but I wanted to find out the truth from you."

John chuckled. "One thing you can always count on among the Saints is making a good tale better." He threw his head back and started to laugh. "Why, just the other day I heard—"

Lucas interrupted, leaning forward in his seat. "This didn't come to me as a tidbit of gossip."

"What is it, then?"

"That you've asked Sophronia for permission to court Hannah."

John fixed his gaze on the younger man. Then a half-smile curved his lips. "Well, yes, son. That's true. I have indeed. It's about time someone took those two under his wing."

"Those *two*?"

John smiled. "They both need looking after, and given the option,

Hannah is certainly more marriageable than Sophronia." He chuckled and settled back into his chair, crossing one booted foot over the other. "Though God's revelation to the Prophet clearly states, 'If any man espouse a virgin and desire to espouse another and the first give her consent, then is he justified; he cannot commit adultery, for they are given him . . . and if he have ten virgins given unto him by this law, he cannot commit adultery, for they belong to him; and they are given unto him—therefore is he justified.' " He grinned. "And they're both virgins. So maybe I'll take them both."

Lucas controlled his growing anger. "And if your other wives do not give their consent?"

"Ah, dear boy, but they will. You surely know about that revelation."

Lucas nodded. "You have the power to condemn any wife to eternal damnation if she refuses to give her consent."

"Yes, yes." Then he sat forward seriously. "But you understand the reason for such justice, don't you?"

"As I said before, John. You've taught me well. Of course I know." And he quoted from God's revelation to Joseph Smith: "'Then shall they be gods . . . from everlasting to everlasting . . . because they have all power, and the angels are subject unto them.'"

John nodded. "'Then shall they be gods,'" he repeated, "and goddesses." Then he paused. "Do you see the seriousness of this, son? I don't look lightly upon the prospect of another marriage—or two. It is a consideration of utter seriousness, of eternal consequence."

Lucas pressed on. "Hannah's barely more than a child. She's only twenty." He wanted to say more, but knew the power of John's quick anger. He needed to appear reasonable yet strong to talk John out of any claim to Hannah.

"Most marry much younger than she is now. You know that." John's unblinking gaze seemed to look right through Lucas. "Is there something else?" When Lucas didn't answer, he continued. "I'm your spiritual father, Luke, and I care for you as if you were my own flesh and blood. I'm here to give you spiritual guidance, give you any help I can. Please tell me what's eating at you."

"It's just that Hannah and I have been close. It's always been assumed, well, that we would marry," Lucas began, then paused. How could he explain Hannah's importance in his life, hers and Sophronia's? He frowned. "That is," he began again, "I had always intended to—"

John sat forward, interrupting. "Hannah McClary. Your intended? Are you courting her? Have you asked for her hand?"

"No, no. Not officially."

"Lucas, Lucas," John said, warmth returning to his voice. "I had no idea you were sweet on that little beauty."

Lucas felt his face flush, and he fought to keep his growing anger in check. "Hannah's much more than 'a little beauty,' John."

"That she is," the older man agreed, raising an eyebrow. "That she is." He paused. "Now, you say that you haven't spoken your intentions to the young woman."

"That's right."

"Am I correct in assuming that you intend to court her?"

"Yes sir."

"And of course that explains your reaction to my intentions toward the little miss." His voice was calm, reasonable. "You'd like for me to leave the courting of Hannah McClary to you."

Lucas stared at the man. He knew John Steele didn't give up easily. He nodded. "Yes. That's correct."

John crossed his legs at the ankles and clasped his hands behind his head. He seemed to be weighing his words carefully when he again spoke. "Think about what I can offer Hannah that you cannot. I plan to build Hannah a fine ranch near Cedar City. She and Sophronia can live there from now till kingdom come, if they like. You live in the barest of circumstances, and with your traveling missions for the Church, you can't offer Hannah much of a permanent home of any kind." He raised an eyebrow. "Or maybe you plan to move into Sophronia's home?"

"A home for them is not the issue, John. Hannah doesn't hold such finery as you have of much account. It doesn't matter to her, or to Sophronia."

"Then let's consider the future." John settled back in his chair again, a smile on his face. "You know what my standing in the Church will bring for Hannah."

Lucas knew only too well. He must keep the commandments to become a god and king of his own world in the hereafter. God, the heavenly Father, had been a mortal at one time, and through good works and keeping the commandments, he'd risen through the hierarchy of heaven to become God the Father over earth. John Steele—and every male Saint—knew the same powers would be theirs if they kept their endowment vows and the vows of their priesthood, Aaronic and Melchizedek. He'd come full circle, back to the issue of the priesthood—the issue of obedience.

He nodded slowly. "Yes, I know what you can offer." He again thought about the celestial marriage. Through her marriage to John, Hannah would be exalted, even someday worshiped as a goddess herself, as long as she obeyed her husband. Together, John's family of wives would populate their own world with spiritual children that would someday be born into the earthly bodies of worthy Mormon women.

Lucas let out a deep sigh. "I know what you can offer Hannah that I cannot," he repeated. "At least not yet."

"Another reason for your obedience, son," he said gently and reached over to pat Lucas on the knee. "Perhaps this is the impetus you need to prove yourself once and for all, to the Prophet, to the apostles, to all the brotherhood of priests. There's nothing like love to spur a man to action."

"What is it you want me to do?"

"I know your aversion to killing, even in the name of blood atonement. Someday you will have to perform that duty, and perhaps you need some additional training before taking the oath and truly becoming one of us. But first I want you to make another journey on behalf of the Church."

"To England?"

John smiled again. "Harriet must have mentioned it."

"She did."

"Actually, Wales and Scotland as well as England. There's a rumor of a coming war with the States. We need more people—strong, young men, as many as you can convert—in this valley to stand against the armed forces that are sure to come." He paused. "It's an important task, son. One might even call it a mission. One of supreme importance. And I want you to lead it."

When Lucas didn't answer, John continued, "While you are gone, I want you to consider your duties as a Mormon. If you feel you are deserving of such a fine young Saint as Hannah when you return, then you can marry at once—with my blessing, son."

Lucas nodded slowly, considering John's words. Maybe this mission would help him decide about his commitment to the Church. He would be away from the growing pressure to participate in the Danites' vengeance against apostates and Gentiles. "I'll agree," he said, "but first I would like to speak to Hannah of my intentions."

"Perhaps it would be wise to first test your devotion to our heavenly Father, Luke. I would advise you to say nothing of your plans until you know that you can fulfill them. What if, upon your return, you still cannot take the Danite oath, become one with us? Would it be fair for dear Hannah to have waited for naught—" He paused, staring into Lucas's face. "—only to have her hopes dashed because you are not worthy, a keeper of your covenant?"

"You are right, sir," Lucas conceded at last, nodding slowly. "You are right." Then he added, "I would also like your word that you will not court Hannah or Sophronia in my absence."

"I give you my word, son."

Lucas nodded and shook John's hand as they both stood.

"It's settled, then," John said, then paused for a moment before continuing. "You'll have one other responsibility on this mission."

"What's that?"

"The Prophet has asked that you bring Emma's niece over from London. A pretty little thing and rather delicate. She'll need special care along the way."

"All right. What's her name?"

"Evangeline Cooper." John gave him instructions on how to find the girl. "The Prophet has handpicked a groom for her. She'll be marrying as soon as she arrives in the valley." And he gave Lucas the date they would be expected back.

Lucas smiled. "I'll see to it that she's here in time for her wedding," he said, chuckling. "Ribbons and bonnets and gowns and all." He knew Emma Young's reputation for finery, and he figured her niece would share the same feminine inclinations. "I'm to take the usual route?"

The older man nodded. "Yes. The Overland Trail to St. Louis, and from there make your way to New York."

"I'll leave in three days." His mind was immediately drawn to Hannah, and he tried not to think about how difficult it would be to say good-bye.

"That's settled, then. I knew I could count on you, son." John led the way across the porch to the wide stairs. "There's something else I want you to do for me."

"Name it." Lucas had reached the stairs and turned again to face John.

"There will be wild rumors on the trail about the coming war. We don't know if troops will be sent this year or next, but if you hear anything significant, find out every detail you can, then ride like the wind back here."

"I will. You can rest assured." Lucas stuck out his hand to shake the older man's.

"I thought so, son. But before you go, there's a meeting I'd like for you to attend after services tomorrow morning."

"Is that an order?"

John didn't smile. "Yes. Actually, it is."

The younger man nodded slowly. "Then I'll be there."

"I knew I could count on you, Lucas." He paused. "I hope I always can."

But Lucas didn't answer. He headed down the stone walkway, let himself through the gate, then mounted the tall black stallion he called Spitfire. Glancing up at the porch where John stood watching him, Lucas raised his hand in a salute.

John Steele gave Lucas a return wave, but his expression was unreadable. Lucas nudged Spitfire in the flanks and headed back through town.

SEVEN

That night in his small cabin at the edge of the grassy hills near the Wasatch Mountains, Lucas agonized over his coming mission. Long past midnight he lay in bed, staring at the ceiling. Harsh moonlight streaked through the room's single window, creating ghostly patterns of shadow and light.

Outside, an owl screeched mournfully from a stand of aspen and was answered by another a distance away. As he listened a thought kept forming from someplace deep inside him: *Take Hannah and Sophronia and escape. Without turning back. Without thought for the present, the future, or even eternity. Flee!*

He pushed the idea from his mind and focused instead on the Church, his calling, his priesthood, those good Saints who had taken him in as an orphan. They had sheltered him. Loved him. Become his family. He'd read the *Book of Mormon* and, on his knees, asked the Spirit for confirmation that the book was true—just as all new seekers were told to do.

When the burning—like so many dancing flames of fire—filled his heart, Lucas had decided the *Book of Mormon* was truth itself. God had restored the gospel to this generation through his chosen one, Joseph Smith.

But Lucas wanted more. He yearned for God, yearned to be a worthy priest of the highest order. He'd done his best to keep the vows of holy priesthood. He'd taken seriously his oath to avenge the blood of the fallen Prophets, Joseph and his brother, Hyrum Smith. His right arm had been anointed to make it strong to avenge the blood of the fallen Saints, to take revenge against the government of the United States.

He had pledged obedience in all things, understanding full well that disobedience would mean that his throat would be cut from ear to ear, his bowels torn out, his heart ripped from his body—those very actions had been acted out symbolically when he said his vows. He had never been given the direct order to kill, yet when the time came—when John thought he was at last ready—he did not think he could obey. Yet to leave the priesthood, to become apostate, invited certain death. That's what the Avenging Angels were all about. Fleeing—as something deep inside him commanded—would bring down vengeance, perhaps even death, on Hannah, Sophronia, and himself.

Could he risk harming those he loved? He had no solid reason for fleeing. It was merely a feeling in the pit of his stomach. If, as he had asked about in prayer, the *Book of Mormon* was true, and if the Prophet spoke words, prophecies, sent from God himself, shouldn't they all stay in the valley of the Saints?

Shouldn't they obey without question so that godhood and the highest place in paradise would be theirs?

Lucas let out a deep sigh and threw off the covers. He swung his legs to the floor and walked to the window to look out at the moonlit night. The sounds of crickets and frogs carried on the breeze from a nearby mountain spring. He wondered if his dark thoughts were a test of some kind. Maybe they were from the devil himself. Or maybe God was testing him to see if he was truly worthy of godhood.

He considered the millions of glowing stars and planets, the heavens that seemed to stretch into eternity. Was God testing his obedience? Or testing his devotion to the Church?

If he blindly obeyed the Prophet's bidding, then Hannah would be his for all eternity once he returned. He would be spending days on the trail and then on a ship, alone. Perhaps John had known Lucas needed time in solitude to contemplate his calling as part of the Avenging Angels, as part of the Melchizedek priesthood.

Lucas fixed his gaze on a distant star and wondered what it would be like to be king of his own planet—his kingdom, with Hannah at his side as his goddess queen.

He suddenly grinned. He could almost hear Sophronia saying, "Hogwash, boy. That's just plain old hogwash."

He turned from the window and lay back on his cornhusk bed, pulling up the covers. But his smile quickly disappeared, and he spent the rest of the night tossing in worry about Hannah and Sophronia. In his dreams he saw them dragged before the apostles, accused of apostasy. He called out to Aunt Sophie, warning her to remain silent, but she didn't hear him.

Instead, she shook her fist at the Prophet. When she spoke, her words were in the language of strange tongues, often spoken by the holiest of Saints. Her wild, white hair reflected the sun, and she was shouting words Lucas couldn't understand. But they held the truth; he knew they did; he just couldn't understand them, not one word.

Sophie's eyes, full of love and compassion, met his, then she and Hannah were dragged away. Hannah cried and reached out to Lucas. But he couldn't move; his limbs were limp. No matter how desperately he wanted to speak on her behalf, he remained mute.

He awoke in a sweat then tossed and turned a while longer, finally arising before first light. For a long time he sat at his small wooden table, his head in his hands. At his elbow was the *Book of Mormon*, but he couldn't bring himself to open the cover.

When the sun had risen high that same morning, Hannah, with Sophronia beside her on the wagon bench, drove the high-stepping bay to Sunday services at the Saints' meetinghouse, the bowery. Tying the horse to the hitching post, she helped her aunt step down from the wagon. Hannah took Sophronia's arm as they moved up the wide stone stairs to the sanctuary entrance, where several people milled about and children skipped and jumped and played.

They had nearly reached the top of the stairs when Lucas stepped through the entrance door to greet them, meeting Hannah's gaze as if he'd been watching for her.

She drew in a deep breath, regarding him as he walked toward them. Hannah wasn't sure exactly when the transformation had taken place, but now, at twenty-seven, Lucas had become a man, weathered and tanned, the light in his eyes reminding her of the reflection of sunlight on deep green water.

She swallowed hard. "Good morning, Lucas."

He nodded, and they exchanged small talk about the weather and the upcoming sermon by the Prophet. As Lucas spoke, Hannah noticed that his expression didn't match his lighthearted words.

Sophronia was the first to mention it. "What is it, son? Is there something else you're about to tell us?"

"Sophie, you know me too well." He grinned and gave her shoulders a squeeze. "And you're right. I do have something I'm reluctant to tell."

"What is it?" Sophronia asked, not being one to wait for bad news.

"I'm going away for a time."

Hannah felt as if her breath had just been squeezed from her lungs. "Going away?" she whispered. "Where?"

"England," he said. "And Wales and Scotland."

"Oh no," Hannah whispered. "Not again."

He nodded. "Yes."

"Another handcart immigration you're bringing across?" Sophronia said, raising an eyebrow.

"You know me better than that, Sophie."

"Do you want to go?" Hannah asked, fighting the urge to gather him into her arms and never let go. "Was it an order, or did you volunteer?"

Lucas didn't answer.

Sophronia broke the silence. "You've got Brigham's ear, son. And John Steele's too. You don't have to do anything you don't want to do." She took hold of Lucas's forearm. "You know as well as I do that the Prophet isn't always right. Just think how wrong he was when he made those poor things cross the Great Plains pulling carts as though they were pack mules." She shook her head, and Hannah was glad to see some of her aunt's spirit had returned. "Sometimes," she continued, lifting her chin, "sometimes the Prophet doesn't know the difference between his nose and a donkey's—"

Lucas held up his hand to silence her. "Sophie! Don't speak such blasphemy! Especially here." His voice was stern.

Hannah considered the change in Lucas's demeanor, the seriousness of his warning. Yet she knew something was troubling him, something more than just his leaving. When he glanced around as if assessing nearby listeners, she knew it was time to get her aunt inside. Hannah took Sophronia's arm. "We need to go in. It's time."

Sophronia nodded reluctantly, and Lucas escorted them up the walkway then held the door open for the two women to enter. As she passed him, Hannah met his eyes. "Will I see you again before you go?" she whispered so no one standing nearby would hear.

"Of course," he said gently.

"Tonight?"

In the foyer, Porter Roe spotted the couple and raised a hand, motioning for Lucas to join him. Lucas merely squeezed Hannah's hand before moving toward Brother Roe.

Hannah settled beside Sophronia on a wooden bench in the long, bare room, facing the Prophet and his council, who sat on a platform in front.

The Saints lifted their voices in song then several of the elders prayed endless, droning prayers. Usually Hannah had to stifle several yawns to make it through the interminably lengthy services, but not today. Her mind whirled with Lucas's news of his departure.

It wasn't until the Prophet stood to speak that her attention was finally captured by the service. Some of the older leaders droned on with voices that Aunt Sophie often said were worse than the monotonous buzzing sound of a beehive, but Brigham Young was different. He spoke with a spirit of inner fire and strength, a voice that made people sit up and take notice. Hannah was fascinated by him.

She watched him move to the pulpit. A person couldn't help being drawn to his presence. It wasn't just because of his dark, ruggedly handsome face or his godly and majestic bearing. No, Hannah thought as she watched him, there was something else. It was as if he could see into a person and know all that was there. Hannah shuddered, dismissing the thought, and gave her attention to his words as he stepped back from the pulpit and stared out at the congregation, first to the men, then to the women, speaking fervently about the Saints' responsibility to keep their covenant with God.

He had been speaking for nearly half an hour when his voice became angry, rising with emotion. "There is not a man or a woman who violates the covenants made with their God who will not be required to pay the debt," he said, leaning on the pulpit.

Behind the Prophet, the elders kept benign gazes on two people—first a man, then a woman. Hannah glanced at the man who had caught their attention, sitting on a bench across the room. She thought she remembered his name was Hambelton. His head was down as if embarrassed.

The woman, sitting on the bench in front of her, was the pretty wife of Brother Brown, the storekeeper. Hannah wondered why these young people would have caught the attention of those on the platform.

There was a long silence in the room. Then the Prophet slammed his fist onto the pulpit. Several people jumped, startled.

"Let me say this again! There is not a man or a woman—not anyone—who violates the covenants made with God who will not be required to pay the debt. The blood of Christ will never wipe that out. YOUR OWN BLOOD MUST ATONE FOR IT!"

The room was deadly silent as the speaker looked out across the congregation, his face fixed in rawboned judgment, his brows knit together. His voice remained loud. "There are sins that men commit for which they cannot receive forgiveness in this world or in that which is to come, and if they had their eyes open to see their true condition, they would be perfectly willing to have their blood spilt upon the ground.

"And furthermore, I know that there are transgressors who, if they could step outside of themselves and see that this is the only condition upon which they can obtain forgiveness, would beg of their brethren to shed their blood." His eyes bored in on individual Saints, first one, then another, then another. Then he lowered his voice so it sounded almost gentle, tearful, when he continued, "I have had men come to me and offer their lives to atone for their sins."

Hannah heard a few people draw in their breath. Then there was silence, and he went on, "It is true that the blood of the Son of God was shed for sins through the Fall. It was shed for those sins committed by men." His gaze again traveled from face to face as if watching for reaction to his words. "There are sins that can be atoned for by an offering upon an altar, as in ancient days."

He suddenly smiled, nodding as if he knew they were all in agreement on that point. A long silence followed, then his voice rose in righteous-sounding anger when he again spoke. "There are sins that the blood of a lamb or of a calf or of turtle doves cannot remit.

"If there is anything that separates you from your God, from your Church, it has to die," he said. "And I read to you the words of the Holy Scripture: 'If thy right eye offend thee, pluck it out, and cast it from thee: for it is profitable for thee that one of thy members should perish, and not that thy whole body should be cast into hell.'

"What is it in your life that offends God, offends the Church? Whatever, whoever, it is an abomination before him and must be plucked out and cast away."

Hannah swallowed hard, thinking the speaker looked directly into her eyes as he spoke.

"And if you can't do it," he continued, his voice growing softer, "if you can't do it . . . those who love you will have to do it for you."

Shivering, Hannah sensed someone watching her and glanced at the elders and apostles seated behind the speaker. John met her gaze. But there was something in his expression that alarmed her. Uncomfortable, she turned quickly away.

A few minutes later the sermon was over, and Hannah sighed in relief as they stood for a final hymn. Then she helped Sophronia move slowly down the center aisle toward the back of the church. Her aunt smiled and nodded to friends and neighbors as they passed, and when they reached the door, Hannah noticed that the apostles and a few of the elders now gathered around the Prophet. Lucas Knight, Porter Roe, and John Steele stood to one side, deep in conversation.

When the rest of the congregation had filed from the meetinghouse and the doors were closed, John Steele stepped to the pulpit. Several elders and apostles filled the first two benches, most of them active Danites. Lucas sat at the end of the second bench.

"You all realize why we're here," John Steele said solemnly.

There were murmurs and nods of agreement.

"Let's get this done, then." Steele nodded to an elder at the center of the first bench. "Bring in the accused."

The elder entered a small room to the right of the podium, and after a few minutes came back with Brother Hambelton. The young man had the fresh-scrubbed look of someone who hadn't known much of life. His cheeks were flushed red as he stood facing John Steele.

"Brother Hambelton, turn and face your accusers." Steele then addressed his words to the council. "Brothers, we have one of our own who has violated his covenant with God. He has sinned." The young man looked at the floor.

Steele went on. "But if we love Brother Hambelton, what should we do? What should he do? Think about the Prophet's sermon. What does God require of him if he wants to be restored into fellowship with God? What does God require of us to save his eternal soul?"

The young accused man, his face now covered with perspiration, still stared at the floor, his shoulders slumped forward. Steele moved closer and circled his arm around the man's shoulder. Brother Hambelton stared dead ahead as if transfixed.

John continued, his voice now a whisper, "Some sins must be atoned for by the blood of the man. Isn't that what we heard today?"

He sighed, giving the words time to soak in, then repeated, "The Prophet has said—and it was from God—that there is forgiveness only through the shed blood of the man himself." The young man nodded, now looking at John as if in some silent agreement.

"What have you to say, Brother Hambelton?"

The young man pulled out a handkerchief and mopped his forehead. His hands were shaking. He took a deep breath and tried to speak but only stammered, as if the words were stuck in his throat.

"What have you to say?" John Steele asked again.

"I, ah, I—" He mopped his face again, looked into his accuser's eyes then toward the council members sitting before him. He took a deep breath. "I wish to die for my sins."

"And what sins are these that you wish to die for? You must confess them—each and every one."

The young man's cheeks were still flushed, his eyes bright. He spoke in a murmur. "I confess the sin of adultery."

Steele shook his head sadly at the younger man. "Adultery is a sin of weakness and depravity." He didn't speak for several minutes as he watched Brother Hambelton carefully. "Is it not true that after committing adultery once before, you were warned by the council—warned that death would be the penalty if you sinned in such a way again? Is this not true?"

Brother Hambelton nodded. "Yes," he said.

"You sold your birthright for a mess of pottage. You sold your soul's salvation for a few moments of carnal pleasure. You knew the consequences—yet you led the adulteress down the same evil path." John looked at the man, his eyes hard. "What have you to say to this?"

"I know I sinned. But please accept my death as atonement for—" He hesitated. "—for us both. Don't punish her. It was my doing. I am the sinner."

"We are here to deal with *your* sins. Yours alone. How we deal with the adulteress is not your concern. Continue now with your confession."

"I confess the sin of pride."

"How so?"

"It was prideful thinking that I could have another man's wife."

"What else?"

Brother Hambelton confessed his sins, one by one, large and small. Then in a clear voice he said he was pleased that the Church was taking a stand against sin—rooting it out before it could spread. Blood atonement was a powerful teaching. How else, but by blood, could a person be cleansed?

But Lucas, seated and watching the proceeding in horrified fascination, wondered how much bloodletting there would be before the reformation that Brigham Young spoke of was complete.

In a flash of remembrance, Lucas saw the old shed at Haun's Mill. He remembered the terror, knowing they were surrounded by men who were trying to kill them. He saw his pa die from the first ball fired. Then the others had died one by one, until there was only Lucas lying facedown on the floor and his little brother, Eli, by his side.

He heard his brother's screams as the Gentiles pulled him, kicking and fighting, from beside Lucas. "Nits make lice," they said. The brutal words roared again in his head. "Nits make lice. Nits make lice." He wanted to run to his baby brother, save him from the monsters. But Lucas couldn't move. He lay flat on the floor, playing dead. Then he heard the screams of his brother calling out for help, calling him by name. Over and over again. He saw in vivid clarity the pink and red of the little boy's head as the ball blew it to pieces. He could still hear his brother calling his name. Through all the years it had never stopped.

Lucas came back to the present as John Steele directed Brother Hambelton to kneel. The council members gathered around him and began to pray. John Steele stood with his hands resting on the bowed head of the young man. All the elders sank to their knees encircling him. They raised their arms above their heads, folding them at the elbows to form the shape of a square.

As Lucas knelt beside John Steele, the older man whispered, "You'll be meeting us later tonight, son. It's expected."

Sick at heart, Lucas nodded mutely then listened as each of the apostles prayed for Brother Hambelton's eternal soul.

Lucas knocked at the cottage door long after Sophronia had retired to her bedroom.

"I can't stay," Lucas said, stepping inside. He took both Hannah's hands in his. "It will make it too difficult to leave if I stay longer."

"You make your journey sound so final. You're coming back, aren't you?"

"Yes, of course." But something about his expression seemed unsure, guarded.

"When?"

"I'm not sure. It depends on the success of my work with the new converts. But I'm hoping it won't be long."

Hannah didn't speak for a moment, just looked at him, already feeling the loneliness of missing him.

Lucas let go of her hands and touched her cheek lightly with the back of his fingers. "I'll miss you, Hannah."

She reached up and took his face in her hands, looking directly into his eyes. "I don't want you to leave," she murmured, her voice dropping to a whisper. "I know I've childishly asked you to marry me, told you how much I think we belong together, but I've never really told you all that's in my soul. Those thoughts that only you would understand."

The stark grief on Lucas's face matched her heart's deep sorrow. But it was a different kind of grief than her own. It was as if he knew something he wasn't telling her. Lucas, seeming to sense her confusion, touched her lips with his fingers. "Don't say anything more, Hannah. I've told you all I can." Pulling her into his arms, he held her close. They stood in the center of Sophronia's parlor, holding each other tightly. "I don't know what I'll do without you," he whispered. Then he pulled back and considered her without speaking, as if memorizing her face.

It came to her suddenly. "Atonement," Hannah suddenly said,

thinking of the morning's sermon. "Am I the eye that offends you? You have to pluck my love from your life and cast it away?" She backed away from him, astonished at the clarity of the meaning of Lucas's mission. "Is that why you're leaving? Is John Steele asking you to give me up as some sign of your devotion to the Church?" She paused, narrowing her eyes as a new thought formed. "Has he asked for my hand in marriage—to test your devotion? To him? To the Church?" Her last words came out as a sob. "That's why your good-bye sounds so final."

"Hannah, no!" he began, but she interrupted.

"It's the Church, isn't it?" She let out a ragged sigh. "And to think this morning I realized I would not die for this—this—" She searched for the word. "—this damnable institution. I decided that you—*you*, Lucas Knight—you and our love for each other—would be the only thing I would die for. Not the Church or its gods. I may be condemned. I don't care. No one can make me stop loving you." Then she covered her face with her hands.

"Please, Hannah," Lucas began again. He moved toward her and tried again to draw her to him.

She pushed him away. "Don't say anything, Lucas. Just listen." She turned to look at him. Tears trailed down her cheeks, and she swiped at them with her fingers. "Have you ever wondered about getting out? I mean all of us—you, Sophronia, and me. Just leaving it all behind."

"Hannah, please. Don't speak of it. That's apostasy. It isn't safe."

She pressed her lips together to keep them from trembling. "Don't you see?" she said after a moment of studying him. "We shouldn't have to worry about speaking our minds." She reached up and touched his jaw, stroking it gently. "Lucas, we shouldn't have to worry about following the Church's orders—you following your mission, me obediently keeping up appearances—before we can be married." She paused, pulling back and looking him straight in the eyes. "And what would you do if an apostle, an elder, or even the Prophet himself, declined to let us wed . . . or wanted me for his own? What would you do? Would your devotion to the Church be stronger than our love?"

Lucas met her troubled gaze with an intensity of emotion that seemed to pull her heart and soul into his safekeeping. There was such caring in his face, such unspoken love, that Hannah caught her breath. "The Church will bless our union; you must believe that, Hannah. I can't tell you any more than that, but please believe it. They aren't out to destroy us. They will bless us on the day we wed."

"The day we wed?" Hannah searched his face. "Wed? Us?"

Lucas smiled, then added. "But, Hannah, you can't say a word to anyone. I wasn't supposed to tell."

"Oh, Lucas!" Hannah cried and circled her arms around his neck.

Grinning, he kissed her once on the tip of her nose then fully on her lips. "My darling," he murmured, "will you wait for my return?" His expression told her he already knew her answer.

"I've waited since the day I met you," she declared. "I'll wait forever to be yours if I have to." Then with a deep and contented sigh, Hannah laid her head on Lucas's chest, relishing the warmth of his rough woolen vest against her cheek. "Oh, Lucas," she murmured. "Just promise you'll come back to me soon."

"A thousand wild, stampeding horses couldn't keep me away," he said, pulling her into a tender embrace.

An hour later, Lucas, with John Steele and Porter Roe at his side, watched Brother Hambelton kneel beside a freshly dug grave, his face buried in his hands. Snatches of mumbled, sobbing utterances filled the midnight silence.

When John Steele finished entreating the Lord's blessing on the atonement, Hambelton looked up and nodded. Then the young man fixed his gaze far into the midnight darkness. His face was grim, but he held himself steady.

"Brother Hambelton, do you understand that you are giving your life in order to save it eternally?" John Steele's voice was gentle yet filled with godly authority.

The young man nodded, still not meeting their eyes.

"It is an honorable thing you are doing, Brother—to willingly shed your blood for remission of your sins."

Brother Hambelton nodded again, slowly. "Just do it, brothers," he whispered raggedly. "Just be done with it, I beg you."

"As you wish, Brother." John Steele pulled a knife from a sheath at his belt and moved quickly toward the kneeling man.

"Do you want a hood?" he asked.

"No."

John Steele now stood directly in front of Brother Hambelton. Placing his palm on the young man's forehead, he raised his other hand upward and began to call out in a booming voice, "May the Father, Son, and Holy Ghost accept this sacrifice and forgive Brother Hambelton's trespasses. Today, may this man be accepted into your kingdom."

Then he moved quickly behind the young man, with one hand yanking his head backward by the hair, exposing the white flesh of his neck. In one swift motion, he slid the razor-sharp blade from ear to ear. Blood, black in the midnight darkness, poured onto the ground.

Without a word, Lucas and John Steele lifted the body into the grave. Porter Roe sat with his back against the trunk of a sycamore, watching the men shovel dirt and tamp it down until there was little more than a slight mound.

It was well known that Porter Roe, or as some called him, Son of Thunder, had personally carried out over one hundred acts of blood atonement. Not even John Steele was his equal in sheer numbers. But as the man sat silently watching in the darkness, Lucas had a chilling thought. Porter Roe was about to pass on his mantle as Son of Thunder to a younger man. And as Roe's piercing eyes met his, he wondered if he'd been chosen.

Lucas rode home alone in the moonlight, and the usual suffocation and stomach sickness that came to him after such a scene hit him full force. He stopped several times to vomit and to attempt to rid his mind of Brother Hambelton's young face.

Atonement. Blood atonement. *Oh, God,* he breathed as he rode, *when will the atonement you require be enough? When will the killing be enough to appease you?*

What kind of a God is this, he wondered, who requires a young man's blood in place of his contrite heart?

Is there not such a thing as forgiveness? The Prophet has said there are those sins that cannot be forgiven by Jesus Christ's atonement on the cross.

He halted his horse and looked up at the moon. A cooling breeze blew off the mountains, rustling the leaves of a nearby grove of quaking aspen.

What if the Prophet is wrong about which sins require such measures? Or, for that matter, what if he's wrong about blood atonement in all cases? If God be God, then wouldn't he be powerful enough to include all sin in Christ's atonement? Why would he choose for some sins—for instance, Brother Hambelton's adultery—to be unforgiven except by the letting of the man's own blood?

Then, instead of ushering the young man into paradise cleansed of his sin, Lucas, alongside John Steele and Porter Roe, had merely committed murder, and poor Brother Hambelton had lost his life due to their folly. And blood atonement, instead of saving his soul, was ending his life.

It was also destroying Lucas's.

"God help me!" he cried into the midnight sky. "God help me!"

Eight

Two days later, in the ashen light of dawn, Lucas saddled Spitfire and headed northeast toward his first destination, Fort Bridger. From there he planned to follow the Mormon Trail east to Independence then make his way to New York Harbor, where he would book passage to England.

As he rode, his thoughts were with Hannah. He tried to think of his mission, the Church, anything but the pain of missing her. But her memory was too overpowering. He would never forget how they had held each other, both knowing it would be months, perhaps a year or longer, before they met again. And he remembered how Hannah had looked when they parted, both strong and vulnerable at the same time.

She was as much a part of him as life itself. He'd watched her grow into womanhood under the purple Utah skies. He remembered how her nose freckled in the blazing sun and how her sunlit curls brushed against her cheek in the breeze, how her laugh rang across the fields when they were riding, and how she looked at him with those wide, clear eyes that spoke of her spirit and her adoration. He would miss her desperately.

Lucas sighed deeply and reined his horse toward a creek that flowed down from Big Mountain about eight miles from Deseret. From there he would head for the Mormon ferry at the Red Fork of the Weber River. The terrain was treacherous, and Lucas was glad for the surefooted young stallion.

By now they had climbed several hundred feet through the pass, and the land was showing patches of snow. When he found the creek, Lucas broke away a thin layer of ice so the horse could drink. He filled his canteen, remounted, and rode on. They soon reached the top of a steep rise, and Lucas turned to look back at the valley of the Saints.

The lake was a jeweled ribbon of blue fading into the horizon, the city an even patchwork of wide roads and green fields. He marveled at the contrast with the arid land around it. The irrigation canals, sparkling in the sun, crisscrossed the land, bringing fresh mountain water to the thirsty valley.

Lucas considered this valley, his home for the past ten years. It wasn't the thought of being thousands of miles away from this place that created a void deep inside him. It was the thought of being away from Hannah and Sophronia that made grief slice like a knife through his heart.

Lucas urged Spitfire onward. The sun was nearly straight up now, and here and there he crossed through shadows of clouds as he rode. The more distance he put between the valley and himself, the easier it was to think of what lay ahead instead of what lay behind. He began thinking about the assignment John Steele had given him.

Lucas's mandate was to convert then identify and evaluate possible recruits from the various groups in the British Isles. He would mingle with them, listen to the conversations of the more energetic and dynamic young men, all the while analyzing their devotion to the Church.

He thought of John Steele's words during one of their recent meetings. "The Church easily appeals to the old, but it's the strength of young men we need. Find them—find those who are strong in body and spirit, single-minded, forthright, bold, and loyal." Then he had added, "And I don't want to see you back in Deseret until you can bring dozens of recruits with you."

Steele was a complicated man, intelligent and cunning. His interests ranged from Church politics to theology, from world history to Indian affairs. He had boundless energy, riding from one end of the territory to the other as the Church's agent to the Utes, Brigham Young's voice to all the Saints in outlying settlements.

It was common knowledge that Steele had a special relationship with Brigham, that in a sacred ceremony the Prophet had sealed John to himself as his adopted son just as John had sealed Lucas to himself. They were sealed as brothers, as father and son, throughout all eternity. In many ways it was a more sacred relationship than that of husband and wife.

Yet Steele could be ruthless, especially when acting against apostates. Lucas had been little more than a boy when he first rode with John against an apostate, a new convert who'd been caught speaking against the Church's teachings. The man, who had been in the territory for less than six months, had publicly denounced the leadership of Brigham Young before deciding to leave the Saints. He had headed for California and was following the Virgin River in the south of the Utah Territory when the Danites struck.

The man had bedded down on a cliff overlooking a deep pool of churning, icy water. His fire had died to glowing embers when they entered his camp, and he had looked up in surprise as John Steele grabbed him.

"Time to feed the fish," the older man had said as he slit open the man's stomach.

Then young Lucas watched mutely as John rolled the apostate over the cliff into the water, the shiny ropelike innards trailing, splashing into the dark water around him.

"We have to stop the spreading of lies," John Steele had said righteously to the boy as they remounted and rode on.

That was the first time Lucas vomited while on a mission for the Angels.

Now, as Lucas rode through a stand of live oaks mixed with pines, he thought about how the Church handled outspoken women, women who might turn apostate. It was true that most women did not speak out against the Church. They were given strict guidance for their behavior from their fathers while still at an impressionable age and from their husbands after marriage. Joseph Smith had begun a group in

Nauvoo, the Mothers of Israel, made up of motherly women who took troublesome younger women in hand, counseled them, and directed them in the ways of the Church.

Lucas suddenly grinned at a memory from long ago. He had been with Sophronia when she was asked to join the Mothers of Israel, sometimes called the Mothers of Zion. She had been agreeable—even flattered to be considered—until she found out the advice-giving would include Church precepts that she passionately disagreed with. "You want me to do what?" she had sputtered. "You want me to counsel young girls to be a willing second, third, or seventeenth wife?" Then she had added, "Balderdash!" as she hurried the ladies out her front door.

Now he had the feeling that if Sophronia continued on her path of blasphemy, she might be placed in a dangerous position. His dream about Sophie and Hannah being accused of apostasy came back full force, and as he nudged the tall, black stallion up a rocky crevasse, he tried to push the haunting image—and his fear—from his mind.

Three days later Lucas reached the ferry at the Red Fork of the Weber.

"Ho there, brother!" Lucas was greeted by Josiah Elkins, a wiry man with weathered skin, darker than that of the nearby Utes. He had called himself Elk for so long it was said he had forgotten his real name.

"Ho, yourself, brother," Lucas answered, grasping the man's hand in the Saints' secret handshake. Elk called himself a Saint, though whenever he claimed it Lucas saw a glint in the old man's eyes, as if a secret joke lurked somewhere inside.

"Got any news?" Lucas asked as he blindfolded Spitfire so Elk could lead him onto the raft that served as a ferry.

Elk smiled, showing more spaces than teeth. Elk was good at a few things: making money for the Saints, telling all he'd heard from other travelers, and fabricating what he hadn't. Elk lived alone in a small house above the river with no one to talk to but a few chickens and some scrawny goats. His ferry, or more accurately, the Church's ferry, was the only raft on the deep and treacherous Weber, and this stretch of the river was the safest. So he got his gossip from folks traveling from Deseret and other parts west, and from folks heading to Utah Territory, California, and Oregon from the East.

"I've gotta git the talk they're carrying before I collect my crossing fee," Elk had told Lucas years before. "They don't talk to me after they find out how much they owe me." Then he had grinned, showing his nearly toothless gums.

Lucas figured there wouldn't be much news today. It was only March. Much too early in the season for the emigrants from either side of the continent to have traveled this far.

"Any travelers by here lately?" Lucas asked after they had started across the river.

"Not many."

"I probably know as much as you do, then," Lucas baited him.

"Probably not." Elk didn't take the bait. He just nodded, a slow smile splitting his leathery face.

"Deseret's going to be adding some to its population again," Lucas said, thinking to get the man started talking with news of his own.

The older man shrugged. "Nearly wore out my raft with the ones who came across last year."

"These are coming from England, Wales . . . Scotland."

Elk wasn't impressed and shrugged again, keeping his gaze on the river. "I've got better news than that," he muttered.

"I thought you might."

"I hear tell Deseret's getting ready for war."

"We're always getting ready for war, old man. That's not anything new."

Elk assessed him with sharp, bright eyes. "That's not what I'm talking about."

"Shoot."

Elk scratched his beard, then his shoulder, then his arm; he yawned loudly before he answered. "Rumor is that the new President—Buchanan—wants to get rid of Brigham Young. I hear tell they want to take away his governorship. Run him out of the territory. Run off the rest of us too."

"That's no great news, Elk. There's always rumors that the Gentiles are getting ready to run us off our land." He waited while Elk poled the ferry across a golden patch of sand just beneath the rippling water.

"The rumor is, emigrants traveling through Deseret report they haven't been treated fair. They tell tall tales about how Brigham has set up his own kingdom. Say he's committing treason agin' the ol' U-S-of-A. Emigrants have taken their stories of mean, cheatin' Saints back to Washington." He chuckled as if glad to be considered part of such a group.

"We always fear we'll be run off again," Lucas said, putting his arm around Elk's thin shoulders. "None of us'll ever forget what's been done to us. We'll always be readying for war. That's nothing new."

Elk turned to look at him. "This time it's different."

"What do you mean?"

The older man raised a bushy brow as he moved the pole. "A government agent's been killed. He'd been sent by Buchanan to take ol' Brigham's place."

Lucas looked hard at the man to see if he was lying. He hadn't heard anything about this. "When did this happen?"

"Oh, going on a couple of weeks now."

"In the territory? He was killed inside the territory?"

"Yessiree."

"Had he reached the Prophet? Talked with him?"

"Haven't heard that fer sure." Elk's leathery face again split into a gum-showing smile.

"How did he die?"

"Rumor has it that he didn't see eye-to-eye with the Utes he met up with on the trail." He chuckled. "Rumor also has it that some of them Utes was white."

"People are always blaming white Utes for every atrocity in the territory. Gentiles enjoy spreading colorful lies about us." Lucas turned away, grimly watching the approaching shoreline. He tried to comprehend what he had just been told. After a few minutes, he turned back to Elk, who was now pulling the raft close to the dock. "Any idea who knows about this? Any of the apostles? Brigham?"

"I hear tell they all do. I hear tell the word for action came to the Utes from John Steele—he's the Indian agent for Brigham—"

Lucas cut him off. "Yes, yes. I know that," he said. "Steele himself gave the orders?"

Elk nodded. "That's what I heard."

"You wouldn't be lying to me, old man, would you? Stretching the truth because you didn't have anything better to tell?"

Elk gave Lucas an unblinking stare. "Deseret's going to war. Whether you believe me or not. The Saints'll be marching as smart as you please against the ol' U-S-of-A. My guess is war'll be here before the year's out. Now, what do you think of that?"

Lucas didn't answer. He was too busy wondering why John Steele hadn't told him any of this before he left. Minutes later as he rode away from the ferry crossing, Lucas's thoughts focused on the old man and whether or not he'd spoken the truth. There was only one way to know for sure: find someone else to verify the facts. He would ask around at Fort Bridger and then at Leavenworth, where he'd heard troops were stationed. If Elk was right and he confirmed that the valley of the Saints was in danger, he would have to ride faster than the wind back to Deseret to warn the Saints.

Lucas kicked the black's flanks, spurring the stallion into a gallop. But he couldn't put from his mind John Steele's deception, or more accurately, his omission of the truth. Why hadn't he told Lucas about the U.S. agent? Was it to get Lucas out of Deseret? And if so, why?

If a U.S. government agent had died—no matter what the cause—the Saints would be blamed. The repercussions could be serious when word reached Washington. There would be no time for gathering new recruits from the Old World, sailing them across the Atlantic, then trekking back across the Great Plains to Deseret. Why then was John so all-fired anxious to send Lucas on his way?

The black continued onward, and Lucas, lost in thought, searched for answers.

Three weeks later, just as Hannah stepped through the back door and into Sophronia's house, a knock sounded at the front door. Hannah had been out for a morning ride on Felicity, or Filly as she was mostly called, the sleek bay mare that Lucas had presented Hannah on her birthday.

Hannah rounded the corner from the kitchen then headed down the entrance hall. Through the leaded glass at the front door, she could see the shadowy figure of a tall, large-shouldered man.

The rapid, light knocking carried through the house again.

Hannah lifted her skirts and hurried to the door, wondering who would be paying her a midweek visit. When Church elders or Mothers of Zion members called, they usually stated their intentions at Sunday services. This past Lord's Day, no one had said anything about calling.

She opened the door.

John Steele removed his hat and gave her a smile. "Good morning, Hannah," he said.

"Why, Brother Steele, what a surprise to see you out this way," Hannah said.

"I have news of Lucas Knight."

"You do?"

Steele nodded, rolling the rim of his hat in his hands.

"Oh, my goodness," Hannah said, embarrassed. "I've completely forgotten my manners." She gestured to the front porch swing. "Would you care to sit a while? Perhaps have a glass of cider?"

He gave her an answering grin. "That would be very pleasant. Thank you. Yes, yes, I would like some apple cider." He chuckled amiably. "I've been out riding most of the morning, and it would be nice to rest a spell."

"Please, then, sit down. I'll be with you in a few minutes." Hannah closed the door and headed to the kitchen. She wished Sophronia hadn't chosen that day for riding into town to visit friends. The thought of entertaining John Steele for even a few minutes was not pleasant. The sole reason she hadn't sent him on his way was because of his news of Lucas.

Once they were settled into the swing with two glasses of cider and a plate of dried fruit-filled cookie bars, they chatted for a few minutes about the unusually warm spring weather, Brigham Young's latest sermon, and finally, about the importance of Lucas's mission to England. Hannah watched John as they talked, noticing his aristocratic profile, his dark, gray-streaked hair, his well-groomed beard. The fine cloth and fit of his clothes spoke of a man who paid careful attention to detail. But there was something about his confident demeanor that also disturbed her. It was as if he had some secret knowledge about his place in the valley, in the Saints' kingdom, that elevated him above all others.

"Thank you for seeing me," he finally said, meeting her gaze with a warm smile.

"You said you have news of Lucas," Hannah said.

He leaned back in the swing, crossing his legs at the ankles. "Yes, yes. I did, and I have much to tell you." He took a sip of apple cider. "But first—while I have you all to myself, Hannah—tell me about yourself."

She frowned and started to protest, but he held up a hand amiably. "It's true. You've always got so many young men buzzing around you at services that I've never had a moment to even say hello." He chuckled softly. "I know how highly Lucas thinks of you. I'd like to find out more." He leaned back, crossing his legs leisurely.

"I'm sorry," she said. "I'm not sure you'd be interested . . . "

"On the contrary, my dear. I'm very interested. I've heard bits and pieces about your home in Kentucky. How you ended up in Deseret by default rather than choice. That you wouldn't have agreed to trekking across the country except that you and Sophronia had to leave Nauvoo so suddenly."

Hannah laughed lightly. "All the Saints still in Nauvoo that winter hightailed it out as fast as we did."

"I heard Sophronia drove off some ruffians single-handedly so the two of you could escape." He shook his head. "Now that's a story I'd like to hear."

And it was a story Hannah loved to tell, despite her apprehensions about John Steele. "I was only ten, but I'll never forget that night as long as I live." And she began telling him about Sophronia in her shining glory, holding the thugs at bay with the Hawken so that Hannah could escape into the woods.

"How did you finally get away?"

"Lucas Knight showed up—" Hannah suddenly stopped, remembering how Lucas had miraculously appeared in the midst of the smoke and flames and terror. She ached with the memory of the sight of him that night, sitting tall on his magnificent black horse.

"You miss him, don't you?" John's voice was soft. It was as if he were reading her thoughts.

"What do you mean?"

"Lucas Knight. Do you miss him?"

"Yes, of course. We all do."

"But it's different for you, isn't it?" He was watching her carefully. "It's different for you both."

Hannah fell silent for a moment. "Are you asking me if we're courting?" She narrowed her eyes, feeling a sense of entrapment as she remembered what Lucas had said about their coming betrothal remaining a secret.

John didn't speak for a moment. "Yes. That's what I'm asking."

Hannah suddenly looked up into his eyes and gave him a dazzling smile. "Why, I'm surprised at you, Brother Steele," she said, forcing her tone to remain light. "Any feelings between Lucas and me really can't be of any interest to someone like you."

John looked surprised, as if he didn't know whether to be pleased or put off by her response. "What do you mean, 'someone like me'?"

"Well, someone of such importance," she said sweetly. "I mean, you're so busy doing Church business and all, running to all ends of the earth for Brother Brigham. People say you speak and act for him, that you are, in fact, his voice. Some call him the 'Lion of the Lord.' One could say you're the voice of the lion."

Steele looked at her with piercing eyes then smiled benignly. "I had no idea you saw me that way."

"I'm not the only one who does, Brother Steele."

"Then you understand why I must keep myself informed of what is happening in the lives of the people in our valley."

"Of course I do," she agreed smoothly. "But why should you care about my life, or Lucas's? After all, he isn't here and, from what I understand, won't be for quite some time."

John Steele let out a deep and troubled sigh. "That's part of the reason I'm here, Hannah. I am Lucas's spiritual adviser, the only father he remembers."

"Yes, I know that."

"He trusts me. Trusts my judgment."

"He's told me as much."

"He asked me for permission to court you before he left."

Hannah remained silent.

John Steele leaned forward earnestly. "I asked him to wait to speak to you about the matter until he returns from England. It would be a test of your love for each other."

Hannah nodded, trying to understand where the conversation was headed. "A test?" she finally murmured. "Why would you suggest that?"

"It's a matter of faith, dear. A matter of following the precepts of our faith as you enter into this sacred union."

"Do you mean taking seriously our wedding vows, our sealing as man and wife?" She frowned, trying to follow his obscure meaning.

"Let me explain," he said patiently. "Lucas received my blessing when he asked for my permission to be betrothed to you upon his return."

Hannah nodded. "Go on."

"I agreed, you see, because . . ." John leaned back and sighed again. " . . . his mission had much more to do with a test of his devotion to the Prophet and to the Church than with the mission itself. He will be returning with a young woman, handpicked, to be married in the endowment house."

"Brother Brigham is taking another wife?"

"Oh no!" John Steele threw back his head and laughed. "Oh, dear me, no."

"Then I don't understand what this young woman—what did you say her name was again?—what she has to do with Lucas."

"Her name is Evangeline, and she has everything to do with Lucas. And with you."

Hannah shook her head uncertainly, a sick feeling beginning to churn somewhere between her heart and her stomach. "Tell me, then," she said, keeping her voice low, measured. "Tell me, what has it to do with me?"

John Steele reached for her hand and held it in a gentle, almost fatherly way, between the two of his. "Celestial marriage is the most honorable state before God. Through it a man reaches his fullest potential, ultimately attaining godhood."

Hannah nodded. "I know this to be true."

"These precious, sacred unions of a man and a woman bound on earth through their sealing ceremony will also be bound in heaven."

"I know this also."

"And you know then that if you agree to marry Lucas, you will be his throughout eternity?"

"Yes," Hannah said solemnly. "I know about the sacredness of these vows."

He squeezed her hand. "What I have to tell you next may be more difficult to understand. But remember, it is part of the test of your faith. The same that will ultimately bring you to Lucas as his wife."

"Go on," she whispered.

"Part of Lucas's progression to godhood is dependent on his belief in celestial marriage."

For a moment she didn't speak. Finally, after swallowing hard, she managed to whisper, "You mean multiple wives, don't you? You're trying to tell me that Lucas has gone to England to bring back a wife."

"Yes, dear. He couldn't bring himself to tell you."

"And he's expecting me to become his second wife?"

"Oh no. He would never agree to that. You are to become his number one wife. Evangeline—whom I told you was handpicked for Lucas—will be his second. You will marry in the same ceremony." He rushed on. "I think you'll like Evangeline, or Evie, as her friends call her. I hear she is a delightful creature, pretty and educated. Since you're close to the same age, I am certain you'll soon be as close as sisters."

Hannah stood abruptly, knocking over the table with the tray of glasses and cookies. The cider spilled, and the glasses shattered. "No!" she cried. "I will not marry Lucas. Not under those circumstances."

By this time, John was standing near her, trying to help with the overturned tray. Hannah stood with her back to the man, covering her face with her hands. Her shoulders trembled, and hot tears filled her eyes.

"Oh, my dear, I'm sorry," said John. "I had hoped you would stand firm through the testing. Satan will try to sway you, overpower what you know is best for Lucas, for you and his celestial brides, for all eternity. Please, give it some thought. Let me counsel you and help you understand the power that will be yours in the kingdom of heaven." He turned her gently by the shoulders to face him. "*Your* kingdom, child," he said earnestly. "Don't you understand? You and Lucas will be creating spirit children throughout all eternity, populating your own world." He lifted her chin, locking his gaze on hers. "You can give Lucas this gift."

She pulled away from him, stepping backward. "The gift of godhood."

"By agreeing to celestial marriage."

"And if I don't agree?"

"If you were already married and did not allow Lucas to take another wife, Lucas would have the right to damn you to hell. It is God's law."

"But if I do not marry him, this . . ." Her voice faltered. ". . . this Evangeline he's gone to fetch, will become his first wife."

"Yes."

"And he will still achieve godhood."

"Yes, probably with many other wives. Again, it is God's law, not man's."

"So my gift has no real meaning. He can achieve godhood without my blessing."

"Yes."

"Then he shall. Because I will have no part of such a marriage."

John Steele held her gaze. "I understand," he said finally.

"I would like to be alone now," Hannah said.

But John stepped closer and reached for her hand. "Hannah," he said, his voice low. "Our leaders are wise and godly men. They listen for our Father's guidance and choose paths for us all that will bless us, not condemn us."

Just then, Sophronia drove up in the carriage and turned into the long driveway at the side of the house. She halted the single horse, looking worried as she stepped from the vehicle.

"Brother Steele," she said as she walked to the porch, "what brings you out our way?"

"Sophronia," he said smoothly, "it's always a pleasure to see you." He took her hand and lifted it to his lips.

Sophronia pulled it away briskly.

"I believe I've outstayed my welcome," he said pointedly to Hannah. He lifted a brow to Sophronia and, after an uncomfortable and silent moment, headed toward the walkway. At the gate he paused, looking back at the two women.

"I would like to continue our discussion, Hannah, about celestial marriage," he said. "I will come to call on Saturday next, and we'll continue where we left off."

John Steele didn't await an answer but strode resolutely to his waiting horse, mounted, and rode toward town. Sitting ramrod straight, reins in hand, he didn't look back.

Nine

Before John Steele had ridden from sight, Sophronia had taken Hannah by the hand and turned her toward the house. "We have some decisions to make," she said, steering her grandniece through the door.

Hannah nodded mutely and followed her aunt to the kitchen table. Sophronia poured them each a cup of fruit tea and settled into a chair across from Hannah. As Hannah lifted hers to take a sip, the cup rattled in its saucer.

Sophronia reached for her hand and squeezed it gently. "Tell me what he said."

Hannah felt fresh tears sting her eyes. "He said that Lucas has been sent to England to fetch a new bride."

"For himself?"

Hannah nodded.

"Do you believe him, child?"

"I don't know what to believe." She let her gaze travel to the window and looked out at the Wasatch Mountains, the same mountains Lucas had traveled through weeks earlier. "The Church is his life. He's sworn to be obedient to death." She turned back to Sophronia.

"But Lucas loves you, child. He knows how you—how we—feel about men taking more than one wife. I can't imagine that he'd ask it of you . . ."

"Unless he had some reason to."

Sophronia let go of Hannah's hands and took a sip of tea. "I wonder," she mused. After a moment she spoke again, her forehead furrowed in thought. "Are you sure that Lucas knows about this bride?"

Hannah considered the question then nodded. "Brother Steele said he did."

Her aunt let out a long breath. "For weeks I've been struggling with how to think of our brother," she said. "And I've concluded we can't trust him, Hannah."

"I know you feel this way, but he's one of Brigham Young's chosen leaders."

"He wants to marry you himself, Hannah. Think what such an aim might cause a man to do."

Hannah gave her a small smile. "Eliminate the competition?"

"Yes. Not only send Lucas away but discredit him as well."

"By telling me the most hurtful thing he could think of—that Lucas is going to take another bride. Young, beautiful, and educated."

Sophronia nodded. "You're in a dangerous position, Hannah. We both are. I've already told John he can't court you. And if you refuse his advances . . ." Her voice trailed off uncertainly. "His pride is at stake if he pursues you and you refuse him the time of day."

Hannah nodded slowly. "Also his standing in the Church. He's already told me that celestial marriage strengthens a man's prospects for godhood."

Sophronia grimaced. "And it's said that virgins are more valuable in that respect than any other bride." She paused thoughtfully. "It's a dangerous spot to be in, child. I've noticed how some of the others watch you. Even if Brother Steele doesn't have his way with you, there will be others waiting."

Hannah leaned forward, taking Sophronia's hand again. Her own pain over Lucas was lessening as she considered her aunt's words. "This isn't easy for you, is it? Doubting the Church and its leaders after all these years."

Quick tears moistened Sophronia's eyes. "That's why I've been poorly, I think. When we started out, following the young Joseph, the Church seemed new and alive. What a wonder it was to consider that God had restored his Church in these latter days! And that I was alive to witness it! I was willing to give my life for our cause, for our people."

Hannah brought Sophronia's frail hand to her cheek. "And now?"

The older woman shook her head slowly. "I feel I don't recognize it anymore. Who ever heard such a thing as a man taking so many wives? Or a man having the ability to condemn a first wife to hell for refusing to let him take a second, or third . . . and on and on?"

"You want to leave, don't you?"

"I've pondered it considerably, dear. But I always wind up back where I started. Where would we go? I broke all my ties to the past when the Mormons took me in after Haun's Mill."

"We are family, Sophronia. The two of us. You're my mother, my friend, all the blood kin I want or need." She smiled. "And I have the feeling we could live anywhere, do anything we set our minds to. If you want to leave, just say the word."

Sophronia met her gaze evenly. "I don't think it's a matter of wanting to, child. I don't think we have a choice, unless you can think of another way to avoid a celestial marriage to John Steele."

Hannah nodded and slowly lifted her cup to take a sip. But as Sophronia stood and reached for the kettle to pour more tea, Hannah's thoughts sobered. What they were about to undertake was more dangerous than she wanted to consider. Her aunt, though strong willed and as tough as nails, was still an old woman, unfit for travel of any great distance. Hannah figured their best chance to get out of the territory would be to head into the mountains by horseback, cross the Weber at the Red Fork, and ride on to Fort Bridger. She'd heard the trail discussed enough that she felt they could find their way. Once at Bridger, they could join up with a wagon company heading west to Oregon or California and disappear in their ranks. The more travelers in the party, the better.

The greatest danger of all would come if it was discovered that she and Sophronia had become apostates and fled . . . She shuddered.

"Child, what are you thinking?" Sophronia looked worried as she poured the tea.

"It's a dangerous thing we're planning," Hannah said gently. "Are you sure you want to risk it?"

Sophronia settled again into her chair. "For the longest time I've felt as though I'm suffocating, Hannah. And now, just thinking about getting away, suddenly I can breathe again." She patted her niece's hand. "It's worth the risk, child. It's worth it."

"Then we'll plan to leave as soon as we can."

"In the dead of night," Sophronia added, a long-absent sparkle returning to her eyes.

"Yes," Hannah agreed. "And we'll ride northeast."

"I thought so," Sophronia said, rising from the table. "Now, I think I'll start packing." She headed slowly down the hallway toward her bedroom.

"Don't forget the Hawken," Hannah called after her. "And the balls and powder."

Sophronia turned and gave her a sly grin. "We've still got two rifles, dear. They're both waiting by the door. I've been planning this getaway for quite some time."

"You have?" Even after ten years together, Sophronia still amazed her. Hannah couldn't help smiling.

"I made good use of my resting time during the past weeks. I've been mapping out every detail of our trip."

Hannah's love for her aunt swelled inside. "You knew then that it would come to this."

Sophronia nodded. "Oh yes. From the minute our dear brother asked to court you, I knew, Hannah. I made up my mind that day." Then without another word she turned to continue down the hall. After a moment, Hannah heard her aunt singing to herself as she packed.

Two weeks and three days later, Sophronia and Hannah saddled their horses and packed a mule with clothing, blankets, a few cooking utensils, and a barrel filled with salt pork, wheat flour, dried fruit, and nuts. Then they headed toward the Wasatch Mountains. A sliver of a moon rose above the dark silhouette of pines, casting dim light on their way as they climbed rapidly along an unused, rock-strewn trappers' trail, far from the main road leading to Fort Bridger.

Hannah worried about Sophronia and watched her carefully, making sure she didn't become too fatigued. But her aunt seemed to relish the adventure and told her to move onward as quickly as possible. Even so, they were well aware of the dangers and stopped often to listen for the sounds of someone following.

But the night was silent except for the yipping of distant coyotes and the occasional hooting of an owl. A sharp breeze stung Hannah's cheeks as they rode, and she breathed in the fragrant mountain air, sometimes closing her eyes and considering that Lucas might have ridden the same trace on his way east, breathing the same air, looking up at the same moon.

The next morning they stopped by a stream, ate some dried venison and cold biscuits, and watered the animals before riding deeper into the forested mountains. The trail disappeared then reappeared as a fainter trace than before. Sophronia rubbed her back and her arms, and Hannah tried to get to her stop and rest. But she stubbornly clamped her lips together and kept riding.

On the third day they reached the Red Fork of the Weber. Gingerly the horses eased down to the ferry crossing, neighing and snorting as they slid in the rocky sand.

"Well, well, well," shouted an old man as he heard the commotion and limped from his house. "What have we here?"

"You must be Elk," Hannah said pleasantly. "Lucas Knight told us about you. We're friends of his."

"That right?" Elk said after he cleared his throat and spat at the dirt, raising a small dust cloud. He narrowed his eyes at Hannah. "Now, what I'd like to know is why two ladies'd be traveling alone on this trail. Two ladies comin' from the valley the way you are—strikes me as unusual." He spat again. "Unusual indeedy."

"We're on our way to meet another pioneering group of Saints," Hannah lied. "They're mostly women and children. We've been sent to help."

Elk gave her a sly, gummy smile. "That right?" He made no move toward the ferry.

She nodded.

"Funny I ain't heard nothing about any incomin' group. Fact is, the only folks I been told might be comin' are soldiers."

Sophronia dismounted then stepped forward slowly and deliberately until she had fixed her gaze straight at his eyes. "Sonny," she said, "the wrath of God will fall upon your shoulders unless you help us across this river." Her wild, white hair glowed in the sunlight, and she raised her fist heavenward, looking up at the purple heavens.

Elk's mouth fell open as if he believed God's wrath might actually be forthcoming any moment. "Git yer horses," he rasped. "Git 'em ready to step on board."

Sophronia smiled and grabbed for her horse's reins. Hannah followed her aunt to the ferry, and within minutes they were floating swiftly across the river. They were halfway to the north side of the Weber when she saw that Elk's gaze was fixed on a distant point. When he noticed her questioning look, he quickly shifted his stare.

Then she spotted a ribbon of smoke where Elk had been looking. It appeared to be from a campfire several hours behind them on the same trail. Her heart leapt to her throat, and she turned to see that Sophronia was watching it too. Their eyes met, and Sophronia set her lips in a thin line then turned to watch the distant shore.

That night Sophronia seemed too tired to continue riding. Hannah found a campsite a short distance from the trail. They didn't dare light a campfire, so after a meal of nuts, jerky, and cold biscuits, they placed their bedding pallets side by side for warmth.

The eerie quiet of the night gave Hannah the feeling they were in danger. When she heard the first wild animal, like the call of an Indian, she was certain.

"Are you awake?" she whispered hoarsely to her aunt.

"Yes, child, I am." Sophronia's voice sounded weak. Hannah reached for her hand and squeezed it. Her aunt's hand was cold.

"I've got the Hawken." Hannah reached for the rifle, which she'd earlier placed by her bedroll.

"It's loaded, child."

"I know." She helped Sophronia find shelter in the brush, tucking the blankets around her shaking body. The journey was taking its toll on her health. She patted her aunt's soft cheek. "It'll be all right," she whispered.

"I wish I could do more."

"No, you just stay here and hold on to this." She placed the second Hawken in her hands. "I know you remember what to do with it."

Sophronia straightened her shoulders and gave her an answering grin. "It's like riding a horse, dear. You never forget how."

Hannah quickly grabbed the other Hawken and the balls and powder horn, then scooted in beside Sophronia to wait. In the distance, another wild call hooted and was answered by another, closer to their camp. It was a long wait until she heard the approach of horses' hooves and some rustling in the brush. She peered into the darkness but could see nothing.

Suddenly all was quiet. The silence was so palpable she could taste it. The forest creatures had halted their nocturnal wanderings, and the night birds had quit their lonely calls.

But Hannah knew they were being watched by living, breathing creatures. Above the loamy scent of soil and decaying leaves, she could smell the sharp, pungent, wild-animal scent of Indians. Probably Utes. She also knew it was their way to await sunrise to attack. She swallowed hard and reached for Sophronia's frail and icy hand.

As Hannah waited through the long night, she wondered if this was where death would overcome her. For the first time in years, she thought about her family back at Wolf Pen Creek. She wondered if they had ever missed her presence after she left.

And Mattie. Sweet Mattie McClary, the only blood kin she thought really loved her until Sophronia had taken her into her heart.

Where was Mattie? Did he ever wonder about his little sister, the one he called Fae, like the sprites and angels? She settled back against the tree trunk and listened again to the silence. Only the moan of a breeze in the pines could be heard.

She remembered Mattie's stories, the sound of his voice telling her about God in his heavens, looking down on them both, holding them in his hands. Mattie had told her that he'd once heard their Irish grandma'am say that God was her friend above all others, that he walked with her and talked with her. The rest of the family thought the old woman was tetched in the head. But Mattie had said he knew for certain she wasn't, because there was a kindness and gentleness and lightness of spirit in her that it seemed could only come from God himself.

And Mattie had said something else about God that until now she'd forgotten. He said, and she couldn't remember why he knew, that God had known about Hannah and loved her since before the beginning of time.

As she sat with the Hawken across her knees and Sophronia by her side, Hannah thought about such a God . . . a God who had known her name and loved her long before she was born.

It seemed like such a simple thing, yet it was profound in its tender simplicity. *A God who knows my name. And loves me.* She looked up at the heavens and considered the brilliant stars in the black velvet sky. Was there a God other than the one who called for revenge and the atonement of spilled blood? Was there really a God of love?

Around her, the eerie silence breathed its fear into her, and Hannah's heart pounded. *God,* she breathed, *are you here?*

Beloved child, I have called you by name. You are mine.

Sophronia suddenly tightened her grasp on Hannah's hand, turning her niece's attention to their present danger. "Did you hear that, child? A twig snapped," she whispered. "There. Again. Did you hear it?"

Hannah did. She squeezed Sophronia's hand in reply and waited as the moccasined footsteps approached. But they moved no closer. She waited again, almost afraid to breathe, for what seemed to be hours.

The sky was turning ashen now, and the faintest hint of dawn outlined the eastern horizon barely visible through the pines. Hannah knew it wouldn't be long before the attack. She only hoped their deaths would be merciful and quick.

Again, the footsteps sounded, and she quickly stood, Hawken to shoulder. Beside her, Sophronia struggled to her feet, holding her own rifle. Almost as if acting on an unspoken order, a circle of savages stepped through the brush in front of them.

"Stay back," Hannah commanded, pointing the Hawken at the one she assumed was their leader. But the Utes continued to move forward. Their wild smell, or maybe it was her own fear, nauseated Hannah.

"That won't be necessary, my dear," a calm and civilized voice said from outside the clearing. "You can lay down your arms."

Surprised, Hannah glanced at Sophronia, then back to the place the voice had come from. "Who is it? Show yourself," she demanded, still holding the Hawken.

"You know who I am," said the voice. A moment later, John Steele stepped into the clearing. John Steele, Mormon agent to the Utes, the man who could command their every move. "And you are outnumbered, so I would suggest you drop your weapons immediately. You never know what might set these savages off."

Mutely, Hannah laid the Hawken at her feet. But Sophronia kept hers trained on John Steele. "Tell your aunt to drop her weapon," he said evenly. "Now."

"Aunt Sophie, do as he says," Hannah said, but Sophronia didn't move. It was as if she didn't hear Hannah's voice. "Please, Sophie, put it down," she said softly.

"I've had enough of this nonsense to last a lifetime," Sophronia muttered. Her arm was now shaking under the weight of the rifle. "And I'm not going back."

"You're coming dangerously close to apostasy," Steele said.

"If I am, then I'm proud of it," Sophronia muttered. "Proud indeed."

"Sophronia, you don't know what you're saying," Hannah pleaded. "Please, put down the Hawken. Let's talk to John and get this all straightened out." Then her eyes met Steele's. "John," she said softly, "this isn't what you think."

He laughed. "I know exactly what it is." His voice was low, threatening.

"It is exactly what he thinks, Hannah," Sophronia said. "I don't care if I have to shoot my way out of this, I'm not going back. And I'm not letting him take you back."

An Indian near to Sophronia drew a bowie knife from a sheath. Fearing for her aunt's life, she grabbed for Sophronia's weapon.

But it was too late. Sophronia pulled the trigger.

John Steele fell backward, a string of foul words spewing from his mouth. Blood spurted from his right shoulder, and he grabbed the place with his left hand, still swearing. He glared at the two women. "You'll pay for this," he breathed. "You'll pay dearly."

Sophronia collapsed in Hannah's arms.

Hannah tended to her aunt then bandaged John's shoulder where the bullet had nicked him. Solemnly the group, all on horseback, made its way back down the mountain to the Red Fork of the Weber.

Sophronia remained silent, but as they rode John described to Hannah the details surrounding an apostate's dishonorable trial.

"You must also understand, dear," he said with a smile, "once an apostate attempts to leave the Church, all property, all belongings, are confiscated. You and your aunt now have nothing to call your own. Nothing."

They rode in silence for several minutes as the information sank into the depths of Hannah's despairing soul. "But don't fear; you'll be well cared for. Saints take care of our own."

When she didn't answer, he laughed lightly. "Now, there is one way you can save your aunt's life." He laughed again. "Perhaps even her home, though never again will it be considered truly hers."

Ten

John Steele asked to make an announcement the next Sunday at the bowery following the morning services. As if aware of the arrangement, the Prophet, smiling his congratulations, nodded his approval as John stepped onto the dais. Hannah caught her breath, wondering how she could possibly get through the ordeal.

A pleased expression graced John's face as he stood before the congregation. After a few words praising Hannah's industrious and giving nature, he smiled and asked her to join him on the platform. Hannah understood very well the role she was required to play. With a smile and a nod, she held her head high and stepped onto the platform, taking her place by his side.

But as she turned to face him, waves of suffocation threatened to overtake her.

John took her hand then turned to the watching crowd. "May I be the first to introduce you to the next soon-to-be Mrs. John Steele," he said in a proud tone. "Our dear Hannah McClary has consented to settle down into the proper life of a Saint, as my wife, as part of the Steele family."

He smiled down at her, his eyes menacing. Her stomach twisted, and she swallowed hard.

"Even the angels in heaven are rejoicing this day," he continued. "Hannah will soon be joining me, her holy husband, as one flesh, one spirit in celestial marriage. Our union, my friends, will be more than the joining of man and wife. It is a necessary step in our journey into eternity, especially Hannah's journey to God. No wonder the angels rejoice!"

There were murmurs of delighted agreement from the crowd. A

scattering of "amens" rose from both the men and the women, along with some light applause.

John turned toward Hannah, taking both her hands. Reluctantly, she again raised her gaze to his and straightened her spine to keep from shuddering. His expression was bright with feeling, but it contained no trace of the holy estate of which he spoke. She drew in a breath to calm herself, but to no avail.

John lifted one of her hands and kissed her slender fingers as sweet sighs rose from the women in the congregation. The Saints loved a betrothal almost as much as they loved a wedding. The men and women assumed this was to be a natural coupling of man and woman, God-ordained, just as Joseph Smith and Brigham Young set forth. A young woman, with no man to care for her well-being, would soon have a close-knit family to care for her every need. And her husband-to-be would gain a higher place in heaven for taking her into his fold.

Hannah turned again to the crowd and nodded, playing the role of John's happy betrothed as best she could. She hoped John wouldn't notice that her knees were trembling or that her hands had turned clammy.

Her gaze swept across the crowd, finally resting on Sophronia, who sat in the back. But Hannah quickly looked away, unable to bear her aunt's sorrowful face. She knew about her aunt's slaughtered dreams, the dead hopes that lay cold in her heart. For they were the same as hers.

But Lucas was at the heart of her desperate dreams.

How different this announcement would have been had he been the one standing at her side. What celebration! What joy!

Lucas! Her beloved. *Oh, Lucas!*

Suddenly, Hannah no longer could find the strength to pretend false happiness or even contentment with her lot. Drawing in a deep breath, she tilted her face upward, as if seeking solace somewhere far distant from this place, this valley and its people.

She pictured Lucas, the love in his eyes when he beheld her, the husky timbre of his voice when he spoke her name.

John Steele was saying a few more words to the congregation, but Hannah heard only the noise of his voice.

She stood mute, completely still, as more applause filled the room and several men called out thanks to God and the prophets for John's good fortune.

Tears filled Hannah's eyes, and the people calling out their congratulations faded into watery, misshapen forms.

The only image she could see clearly was Lucas's face.

"You'll have to do better than that," John Steele said an hour later as he drove Hannah home from services. He was taking the longer route through some verdant orchards and fields to the north of the city. He flicked a whip over the backs of the high-stepping team of grays pulling the carriage.

Hannah didn't answer.

"You brought me disgrace by your actions. Perhaps you don't realize the honor I've bestowed on you, the mercy. You and your aunt could have been punished for your act of attempting to leave the valley. Instead, because of me and my position, doors will open to you." He paused, flicking the reins. "Yet you stood before the congregation this morning like a lamb about to be slaughtered."

"I'm doing my best, Brother Steele," she said. "You have to understand, this is all new to me. It's . . . difficult."

He directed the carriage to the side of the road and halted the horses under a sycamore tree. "I've told you to call me John," he said, facing her.

"All right, John," she said, giving him a tight smile. "Is that better?"

He looked at her as if trying to assess her. "You do understand your position," he said. "You're not out of danger's reach. At least not without my help."

"Of course I understand." She lifted her chin to give him an unblinking assessment of her own. "I'm upholding my end of the bargain," she said. "I've agreed to marry you, but I didn't agree to like it.

You can bully me into this sham of a betrothal, the disgrace of this union you call marriage, but you can't make me like it—or you."

He suddenly threw back his head and laughed out loud. "Ah, my dear," he said finally, "don't you see? The more you resist, the more irresistible you become. It's your spirit that attracted me from the first time I saw you." His words chilled her, and she turned away from him.

John reached across the carriage seat, put his hand on her jaw, and turned her back around to face him. She recoiled, shrinking into the farthest corner of the bench seat. John's hands dropped into his lap, but his fingers wrapped around the whip handle, white-knuckled.

Her tone was heavy with sarcasm when she spoke again. "And when you first considered me . . . as so irresistible . . . it didn't matter to you that my heart was spoken for," she said, "by your adopted son."

A flicker of something, perhaps uncertainty, crossed John's face. "I told you, Lucas is going to marry another." He lifted a brow. "And don't try to tell me you would willingly share Lucas with a pretty young thing who's been chosen by the Prophet himself." He moved closer to her and touched her cheek. Hannah jerked her head away.

"I didn't believe you when you first told me, and I don't believe you now," she said, her voice low. "Lucas will not marry another."

"Lucas Knight belongs to the Church. Not to you, as you seem determined to believe. Lucas will do anything to obey his God and his elders," John said, then he fell quiet for a moment to let his words soak in. "Just as you will, my darling. You *will* obey without question—both the Church, and me, as your spiritual leader, as the head of our home."

"We're not married yet," muttered Hannah, tight-lipped. "I have no reason to accept you as my husband, to obey you without question, until after our . . . our sealing ceremony." Glancing about frantically, she noticed for the first time that he'd driven them to an isolated place. There was not another carriage on the road, not a farmhouse or ranch in sight.

"Ah, but you're wrong about that." He touched her jaw again, letting his fingers slide to her chin. His dark, menacing look told Hannah she'd better not move. She fought to keep from spitting in his face. "You gave yourself into my hands the moment you decided to flee with your apostate aunt," he said, looking deep into her eyes. "You know what happens to apostates, Hannah, don't you?"

She wouldn't give him the satisfaction of an answer.

"Let me tell you. They suffer much for their sins, my darling." He was whispering now, his lips close to her ear, so close that she could feel the heat of his breath. "Their blood must atone for their sins. Otherwise, you see, they will never reach heaven. It is the sworn duty of the Saints to see that blood atonement is carried out on their behalf." He paused, his gaze penetrating any calm Hannah tried to find within herself.

"Let me describe it for you. You need to understand every detail."

Hannah dared not breathe.

"Their hands are bound as they kneel before their fresh-dug graves," he said. "Sometimes the apostate helps dig his or her own grave, shovelful by shovelful, even if it takes all night. No matter what age this apostate might be. No matter how frail."

Hannah bit her lip, trying not to think about the images his words conjured.

"Then the apostate is held fast—like this!" He grabbed her mane of hair. She gasped as he jerked her head backward, held fast at an awkward angle.

She closed her eyes as he drew his finger from one ear to the other slowly across her exposed throat. She swallowed hard and fought to keep from crying out.

"And picture this," he breathed again in her ear. "Let's say the apostate is Aunt Sophronia. Her neck will be grasped just as I am grasping yours." He yanked her head farther back for emphasis. "And her blood will be let, just as I, at this moment, could let yours."

Hannah caught her breath as a piece of thin, cold metal slid with the barest touch across her throat. Its sharp tip pricked the skin just beneath her ear, and she felt a drop of blood slide down her neck.

"Your aunt's blood will pour into her grave," he whispered softly into her ear. "Dark as midnight, the blood will be as it becomes one with the soil and soaks into the earth."

Hannah remained mute, her heart pounding wildly in her chest.

"Sophronia's body will follow the blood into the grave she has helped dig, rolled in without ceremony, covered with shovels full of dirt and rocks.

"We do not mark apostates' graves, my precious Hannah. And sometimes, if the sin is considered especially vile, we leave the grave purposely shallow."

Hannah shuddered, trying to push the image of coyotes and wolves digging in the loose soil from her mind. "Please," she whispered hoarsely, "please, say no more . . ."

But he touched her lips with one finger. "Shhh," he breathed. "I need to know if I've made myself clear."

Hannah tried to nod, but his hand still painfully clutched her hair and she couldn't move her head. "Yes," she finally whispered.

"Good," he said, his breath warm in her ear. "And now, my darling, I need to know if you do indeed understand that you belong to me. Now and throughout all eternity."

She didn't answer. She couldn't say the words or even nod an assent.

"I asked, my darling, if you belong to me. Now is the time to practice your obedience. I do expect you to answer." He let the tip of his knife play against the skin of her throat.

Her eyes still closed, tears squeezed between her lids and traced down her cheeks, dripping onto her still-exposed neck, stinging her flesh as they fell on the wound.

Finally she muttered, "I do."

"I can't hear the words, my darling," he said. "What did you say?"

She swallowed hard and said in a shrill, clear voice. "I do."

But instead of answering, John moved his lips from her ear to her mouth.

"I had hoped I might convince you," he murmured as his lips pressed against hers. Finally he released his hold on her.

Bile rose in her throat, and she shoved him away with such force that the buggy rocked precariously. The horses whinnied and shook their manes, turning their heads to eye the vehicle.

Hannah waited, almost afraid to breathe, to see what great anger she had provoked.

But John surprised her by throwing back his head and laughing loudly, coarsely, a look of triumph on his flushed face. "Ah, yes. You are a spirited little filly," he chuckled as he popped the whip above the team. "Oh yes, indeed."

Hannah didn't speak the rest of the way to Sophronia's house. But John was in high spirits, chuckling as he tried to catch her eye with a knowing look and speaking of his plans for moving her to the south of the territory, where she and Sophronia would live separately from his other wives, separated from all the valley's Saints.

She kept her gaze straight ahead, holding a handkerchief to her neck to stop the drops of blood from staining her clothes.

Sophronia looked up from her rocking chair on the porch as Hannah approached. "Child!" the older woman cried as she stood and leaned against the railing, frowning in worry. "What is wrong?" She put her hand gently over Hannah's, where she still held the handkerchief against her neck. "What's happened?"

Hannah bit her lip, blinking back her tears. She couldn't tell her aunt about the terror of the past hour or what John Steele had said about apostates. "He's a mean-spirited man," she said. "It seems he's used to getting his way."

Sophronia stepped back. "He didn't violate you, did he?" The set of her jaw was suddenly fierce. She looked ready to break his neck, barehanded, this very moment.

"No, Aunt Sophie, no. Nothing like that," she assured her. She laughed weakly. "Though I think he's trying hard to steal something precious from my mind and soul."

Sophronia grabbed both Hannah's hands and drew her to the chair next to the rocker. "Tell me, child, what happened, if you can. Tell me what's ahead for us both."

Hannah settled into her chair gratefully, closing her eyes a moment and letting the summer sounds of sawing cicadas and twittering sparrows envelop her like a protective shroud. From the kitchen wafted the aromas of baking cornbread and roasting venison. Beside her, Sophronia's rocking chair creaked as it moved.

Here, with the familiar, cozy scents and sounds, the nearness of her aunt, Hannah's heart finally quit its violent pounding. Here, she could try to push all thoughts of John Steele from her mind.

She reached for Sophronia's hand. "I don't know what's ahead. The only thing I know for certain is that I refuse to let John Steele invade those places in my heart that don't belong to him."

Sophronia squeezed her hand. "Those places that belong to Lucas?"

Hannah's eyes were open now, and she was gazing out at the familiar countryside, the Wasatch Mountains rising in the distance. It was restful to consider the deep blue of the sky, the wide expanse of the valley. "No, it's more than that, Aunt Sophie. Much more."

"Tell me, child." Sophronia rocked gently, following Hannah's gaze.

"When I first came to stay with you in Nauvoo, you were willing to die for the Church, even though you said you had doubts."

Sophronia nodded slowly. "Maybe I've always been an apostate, though if I'd been asked I probably would've denied it."

"Are you?" She turned to face her aunt.

"There were days long ago when I thought the Saints knew something the rest of the world didn't. But that was before the cruelty and killing—the vengeance.

"Oh, my, but I thought young Joseph had started a fine Church filled with God-fearing people. I thought his was the only way, his Church God's only Church. Now I wonder if there's a church, or a God, at all." There was bitterness and disappointment in her voice when she continued. "If the Saints reflect the kind of God they serve, we're better off without knowing him. Maybe better off without him completely."

"You were shunned this morning, weren't you?" Hannah asked, still holding her aunt's hand.

"Yes, child," she said softly. "But it's not the first time. It probably won't be the last."

When Hannah was a child and had first come to live with her aunt, Sophronia had told her how she was loved by her Church family, the apostles and bishops and elders, all the brothers and sisters. She was ready to die for her Church, for her people, and they for her.

Sophronia went on, "Criticizing the Prophet, John Steele, all the leaders and their teachings, was one thing. But attempting to leave the valley of the Saints is quite another. I can't be trusted, I suppose." There was more defiance than sadness in her voice.

"Many are the same who took you in all those years ago, Sophie. It must hurt."

"They cross the street to avoid speaking to me," she said. "I suppose many are afraid to be seen talking to me, afraid of what others will think." She let out a sigh while she rocked. "A pretty sad bunch," she muttered.

"Fear can be a powerful tool, Sophie."

Suddenly Sophronia turned to her, her eyes piercing Hannah's. "That's what John Steele used against you today, isn't it, child?"

Hannah nodded. "But all it does is make me more determined to find a way out of the territory for us. I don't intend to give up the fight."

Sophronia patted her hand, and there was a proud look in her eyes. "I'll fight by your side, Hannah. We'll get through this together. Fear or not."

"Do you think any of the others feel they're ruled by fear?"

"Depends, I suppose," Sophronia said wisely, "on whether they're happy in their circumstances." Then she added wryly, "Or if they've ever tried to leave the valley."

"So it has nothing to do with God at all. I mean, in the long run, it's man they fear."

Sophronia looked thoughtful, and for a moment she didn't speak. "I would like to think that is true, child. I said a minute ago that the God of the Saints is one we're better off not knowing. But maybe there's a different God than the one we've been taught to serve."

Hannah nodded. "Someone who doesn't require our works, our blood sacrifices, our cruel vengeance." She paused, her gaze again on the deep heavens above the Wasatch. "Sometimes I think *that* God is so real I can almost reach out and touch him. Then an emptiness sets in . . . and a desperate sadness."

Sophronia watched her intently. "And it seems he's beyond your reach?" She was silent a moment before continuing, "Sometimes I feel the presence of this same God, Hannah, a God of light and truth who's calling me to find him. Then I feel a darkness as heavy and thick as a black curtain settle over me, and I fear it's all been just fanciful thoughts."

Hannah nodded. "If this God isn't there, what's left? Just the darkness?"

"I've believed in Joseph Smith and his teachings for so long it's become part of me. Now I see all that's wrong with the Church and this God they profess to serve, but when I think of turning from it forever . . ." Sophronia narrowed her eyes in thought. "I fear I'll find only that curtain of darkness.

"I received my conviction about the Church years ago, and I was sure I had found the way. I read the *Book of Mormon* and prayed for God to tell me the witness was true.

"But child," she went on, "if it *is* true, how can blood atonement, the killing, the vengeance, also be true? Didn't God himself say 'vengeance is *mine*'?"

As a child Hannah had prayed a prayer for wisdom and had received the same answer, a tingling that enveloped her from tip to toe, confirming what the elders and their wives had told her to expect when they invited her to pray. Yet she was as much in the dark now as then about God's truth.

"We'll find a way," she repeated, "a way to truth." She frowned, biting her lip. "That's what I meant a few minutes ago. That part of me that seeks truth and freedom—that's what John will never touch."

Unbidden, the image of John Steele's menacing face crowded other thoughts from her mind. She could almost hear the echo of his earlier words to her: "I asked, my darling, if you belong to me. Now is the time to practice your obedience. I do expect you to answer."

No! She cried to herself. *No!*

"Child, what's the matter?" Sophronia was frowning as she peered into Hannah's face. "There's something you aren't telling me. I can see it in you."

She didn't want to frighten her aunt or cause her any more grief. But Sophronia had long been her confidante, her friend, the mother she'd never known. "I'm afraid, Sophie," she finally said. "I feel so alone. John's only a part of that fear. There's something desperately dark and evil here . . . an enemy larger than the whole of this valley and all its people combined."

Without hesitation, Sophronia stood and gathered her niece into her arms just as she had done when Hannah was a child. The old woman's body felt solid and strong, as always, and Hannah gave up a shuddering sigh as her aunt hugged her fiercely. "Child, child," she crooned, her comforting tone so familiar, so loved. "We're together. We'll make it through this. We'll find a way out. You'll see." She pulled back and looked Hannah in the eye. "Why, we've fought off Saint-haters in Nauvoo and survived the elements during our crossing. I would say there's not much we can't do if we set our minds to it. Isn't that right, child?"

Hannah nodded.

"Now, you just stay right here." She held Hannah close. "You may be a grown woman, but you're not too big for me to comfort," she said softly.

For the longest time, Hannah stood with Sophronia's arms wrapped around her, thinking only that here, this moment, she was safe. "Aunt Sophie," she finally murmured, "you said we'd find a way out."

"That I did."

Hannah stepped back, leaning against the side of the arbor, her arms crossed. "I've thought about it until my brain nearly refuses to think anymore. And I still can't figure how to get us out of this."

"We'll come up with something."

"John's threats are too . . ." Her voice faltered. ". . . too personal. Too dangerous."

"He's using me, isn't he—to keep you from bolting?"

Hannah didn't answer, but her aunt could read her expression.

"I thought so," she said softly. "Don't fret, child, we'll think of something." Her eyes moved from Hannah's face as she looked out at the Wasatch. "We'll find a way." But her face held a sadness deeper than before.

Eleven

Crooked Creek, Arkansas
Spring 1857

Ellie Farrington climbed up the hillside above the wagon company rendezvous. Nearly two decades had passed since she and Alexander had said their marriage vows, pledging to love, honor, and cherish each other until parted by death.

The years now seemed to have melted together as if they were the colors of life on an artist's palette. Colors that brought to Ellie's mind the winter meadow where she had told Alexander she would marry him. Colors of the passing seasons as they sowed seeds, tended the soil, and harvested crops in the field beside their small Arkansas farm. Colors of laughter and tears while they reared Alexander's children and prayed too long for babies of their own. And all the while, they dreamed of California. Dreams that caused the hues on the palette to turn to gold.

The years had not changed how she felt about Alexander, except that now he was dearer to her than even the afternoon they had wed. Oh, how she remembered that day! They had danced to music that seemed straight out of heaven itself. She smiled to herself. Her heart still skittered like a schoolgirl's when she beheld her husband, now captain of the Farrington wagon train. And many of the same neighbors, friends, and blood kin who had celebrated with them on their wedding day were now camped in wagons and tents below, readying for the trek west.

She let out a satisfied sigh. After all these years, their dream was about to be realized. Soon the whole Farrington family would settle in California. Hampton and Billy, Alexander's sons, along with their young wives, Sadie and Bess, were part of their father's company. The others had promised to follow soon, even Amanda Roseanne and her husband.

She turned to move up the trail again and had gone only a few yards when she heard the scramble of footsteps behind her.

"Mommy!" Meg called. "Mommy, wait!" Ellie turned and watched her six-year-old approach, dark braids flying, eyes bright with excitement. The child gave her a disarming smile and reached for her hand. Ellie's heart melted, and instead of the sharp words she'd intended, she gave her daughter a quick embrace.

"I thought you were asleep when I left the wagon, young lady."

"Sarah and I were just pretending. There's too much noise tonight."

Ellie laughed. Her daughter was right. No one in the wagon camp seemed willing to settle down, least of all the children. Riding on the breeze with the smoky fragrance of the cook fires were sounds of laughter and talking, the music of fiddles and mandolins and harmonicas, and the clatter of iron cookware being washed and packed away.

"But if you don't get those eyes closed soon, you'll be too tired to hold them open tomorrow morning."

"Papa said I can ride with him until the trumpet blows." Meg, still holding Ellie's hand, marched up the rocky path with her.

"Your papa's going to be mighty busy. You can't begin to imagine what it'll be like, Meg. When your papa shouts the command, 137 people, 40 wagons, and 900 head of cattle will be leaving this place." No wonder the folks in camp tonight were wild with anticipation, Ellie thought, as she watched her wide-eyed daughter.

Meg skipped over a root in their pathway. "Papa said Sarah and me—"

"Sarah and I," Ellie corrected.

Meg let out an exasperated sigh. "Papa said Sarah and *I* could ride our ponies next to him out front where we can see. He said it'll be a sight he doesn't ever want us to forget."

"All right, then," Ellie said as they stopped on the trail. "But if you're going to have such an exciting morning, you must get back to the wagon and into bed."

"But I want to go with you . . ." Meg started to whine, then her pout turned to a frown. "Where're you going anyway?"

"To find your papa. I think he's up the trail a ways."

"In his thinking spot?"

Ellie chuckled. "Yes, in his thinking spot." Since the families had begun to gather weeks before, Alexander had taken to climbing to the outcropping of boulders up ahead, his place of solitary refuge away from the loud and eager and sometimes complaining voices of the wagon company. It was also the place where she and her husband could speak alone. They'd both come to treasure their quiet moments together at day's end.

"But I want to go too. Papa didn't give me a good-night kiss."

"He'll come give you your kiss when we get back to camp." Meg's lower lip stuck out in a pretty pout, and Ellie gave her another quick hug. "Now you get back to the wagon and into bed, you hear?"

Meg nodded slowly. "Yes ma'am."

"What was Sarah doing when you left?" Ellie sighed, thinking of Meg's sister. Though she wasn't as adventurous, she could be just as mischievous as her twin.

"She's playing with Phoebe in the wagon. Making sure all her clothes are packed." She rolled her eyes.

Ellie smiled. Phoebe was Sarah's wooden doll, one of the two that Alexander had carved for the twins for their first birthday. Meg would rather climb trees or skip stones across the flowing water of a brook while Sarah spent hours playing house and caring for her precious Phoebe. Meg, on the other hand, had never named her doll and kept her in a hatbox, fully dressed in the tiny doll clothes Ellie had sewn. Phoebe's wooden face had been worn smooth with Sarah's kisses;

Meg's doll still showed the whittling marks of Alexander's workmanship.

"Now, you hop back down this trail and into bed. Tell Sarah to put Phoebe to bed and get to sleep herself. Papa and I will be in to kiss you both good night in just a few minutes."

"All right, Mommy," said the little girl, turning with another heavy sigh.

"Meggie?" Love welled up in Ellie's heart. Meg looked back. "Come here for one more hug." Meg's face brightened, and she fell into her mother's arms. "I love you, baby."

"I love you, Mommy." Meg squeezed Ellie around the neck. "But I'm not a baby."

"You'll always be my baby, sweetheart. Even when you're grown and have children of your own. Now, off you go." And after another quick hug, Meg skipped back down the trail. Ellie watched until her daughter safely reached the edge of camp and had once again climbed into the back of the Farrington wagon. Meg turned and waved, then closed the back flap.

Before continuing her ascent to the rocky ledge above, Ellie considered the wagon camp for a few minutes. Tents and wagons stretched out as far as she could see. Tomorrow it all would be gone.

She smiled as she saw a few of her friends—talkative Polly O'Donnell; sweet and sassy Liza Barrett, who, though she was more than a decade older than Ellie, was closer than a sister; and Alexander's widowed sister-in-law, Jane Farrington—all busy with last-minute packing. Hampton and Billy were hurrying to and from their own wagons, with their wives at their sides, readying for the morning's departure.

Nearly all in the company were related; Polly and Jesse O'Donnell were kin to the Mitchell boys, Joel and Lawson, who'd joined as cattlehands. She smiled, thinking of their kindness. Polly and Jesse had five daughters of their own, enough to keep any set of parents busy . . . without the added duties of two gangling, growing boys. But they weren't alone in taking on extra mouths to feed during the trek. Besides caring for their grandchildren, Abe and Liza Barrett were also keeping watch over their nearly grown nephews, William and John Prewitt. The boys—young, green, and feisty—had signed on to help Alexander with the cattle drive.

Ellie hoped the blood kinship of the wagon company would help Alexander keep the folks in line. Mutiny had split apart more than one train before its journey was done. No, these folks were extended families of cousins and aunts and uncles and grandparents, people who loved each other and spoke openly about how they believed God had knit them together for a purpose.

Last month they had come from the four counties in northwest Arkansas, elected Alexander as their captain, purchased farm wagons with tall, arched canvas covers, ordered their supplies, and when all was said and done, pulled into Crooked Creek to await good weather. And while they tarried, they'd practiced hitching and driving their teams and circling their wagons as quickly as possible for the night circle and as a defense against danger.

Even Alexander had been surprised that Ellie had taken to the task so readily. Ellie smiled to herself, remembering the expression on Alexander's face. She had poked and prodded her oxen until her hands were raw from handling the long, sticklike goad. She'd even learned to turn the animals to the right by shouting "Gee!" then left by shouting "Haw!" with only a tap of the goad as a reminder. She'd practiced hard until the beasts obeyed, just to see her husband's eyes shine with pride. She glanced down at her hands, wondering if the calluses would ever disappear.

Ellie turned away from her view of the camp. Tucking an errant strand of dark hair behind one ear, she stopped for a minute to rub the small of her back. The infant she carried in her womb was tiring her with a weariness she hadn't before known. She rubbed her back again and started up the hillside.

She tried to push away any worry about this baby. After all, why wouldn't she be tired? All day she and Alexander and the twins had been readying to go; hefting trunks and Dutch ovens and bags of wheat flour, coffee, and sugar into the supply wagon; packing dishes in barrels of cornmeal; airing quilts and blankets, beating them clean. But now, she thought, satisfied, it was done, and the Farringtons were ready to depart.

Just as Ellie reached the top of the hillside, she stepped on some loose gravel and grabbed on to the low branch of a sycamore tree to keep her balance. Alexander was sitting on a large boulder just beyond the sycamore, and he turned, hearing her footsteps.

"Ellie," he said, smiling a welcome as she moved closer. Ellie loved the way he said her name, and she smiled in return. He reached for her hand as she settled onto a flat boulder beside him.

"Did you get the girls into bed?"

She nodded. "I thought I had, but Meg followed me up the trail, too excited to settle down. I doubt they'll get any sleep tonight." She shook her head slowly. "I promised them we'd be in for good-night kisses before we retire."

A full moon was now rising, so bright it dimmed the stars, and she could see the concern on his face. From the shallows of a slow-moving creek below them rose the night songs of frogs and crickets, a low din that had kept Ellie awake during their first weeks at Crooked Creek.

"And you, Ellie? How are you feeling?"

"More tired than anything else, but that's to be expected," she said, reaching to rub her back again. He moved her hand away and began kneading her tight muscles in the small hollow of her back. His touch was surprisingly gentle for a man with such massive, strong hands, and she closed her eyes, enjoying his touch. "But more important, dearest," she murmured, head down, as he worked, "how are you feeling about our company's readiness?"

At first he didn't answer. "I don't know if we could ever be completely ready," he admitted. "Some of the folks still can't handle their teams." He laughed lightly. "Of course, they'll know a lot more than they do now once we've been on the road a day or two."

"There it is," Ellie said, lifting her head and looking west. Her husband followed her gaze toward the wagon trail on the grassy flatlands to the northwest. Ellie laughed softly. "I can hardly believe tomorrow's the day. The day we've dreamed about. We are going to California, Alexander! Think of it! Tomorrow!"

He nodded. "I think you've caught the California fever even more than I have."

"I know it was your dream first," she said, remembering how he had spoken of it even on the day he asked for her hand in marriage. "But it's mine equally now."

He chuckled. "I think it's that ranch on an ocean cliff I've promised to build. I've described the crashing of the waves and the sounds of sea gulls calling on the wind so many times." He laughed lightly again. "I think, my dearest, it's the ocean that's calling you west."

But Ellie didn't laugh with him. Gazing up at the moon, she said, "Just being with you until the day we die, Alexander, is all I want." Then she turned to him again. "Whether it's a little house tucked away in Arkansas, a soddy on the prairie, or a ranch in California." She touched his cheek. "It's just you I want to be with. You and our babies all wrapped in God's arms."

Alexander touched her cheek.

She felt a flutter of life deep in her womb and raised her face to Alexander's with a smile. "Here," she said. "Feel your son." She took her husband's hand and pressed it to the spot.

He grinned as the baby moved again. "And how are you sure it's a son?"

"He's already so full of life, Alexander. I can't imagine a sweet little girl causing such a ruckus."

"I know two other little girls who caused quite a ruckus, as I remember."

Ellie laughed. "Not so much until after they were born. No," she said decisively. "This child is definitely different. These are no butterfly wings. Not even from two butterflies."

The moon rose higher, and in the distance a harmonica player lifted a plaintive melody that carried on the wind. Alexander stood and pulled Ellie into his arms. She felt the rough warmth of his homespun shirt, the smooth softness of his buckskin vest against her cheek.

"I love you, Ellie," he murmured as he rested his chin on the top of her head. She could feel the deep resonance of his voice as he spoke and closed her eyes to cherish its sound. "Oh, how I love you!"

Ellie stepped back slightly so she could see into his eyes. Her deep love for this man welled up inside her to the point she thought she might suddenly weep. He cupped her chin and tilted her face upward, then he kissed her, gently at first, then more passionately. For a moment they looked into each other's eyes, the bittersweet sounds of the harmonica drifting toward them from the wagon camp.

Then they danced in the moonlight to the soft strains of "My Old Kentucky Home." To the northwest, the wagon train wound far beyond the distant moon-silvered trees until it became a gray ribbon disappearing into the horizon.

Somewhere a rooster crowed, then crowed again. Three or four dogs scuffled through camp, nosing first around one tent then another, a yip or a growl marking their trail. It wasn't long until the sounds of a waking camp began—folks calling out greetings as they laid wood for a breakfast cook fire or struck their tents and began loading bedding and blankets into the wagons.

Dawn started its stretch across the eastern sky, casting a pale light into the heavy canvas of Ellie and Alexander's tent. She lay quiet and watched her husband rise, watched him unwind his body from his pallet. Sensing her gaze, he looked down at her with a warm and sleepy smile. "It's time," he said simply, then stooped to give her a kiss.

She nodded, feeling the fast beat of her heart, from his closeness, from the day she knew was about to dawn. "It's really here," she said, throwing back her covers.

After a few minutes, Ellie pulled on her clothes and stepped out of the tent and into the morning. In the space between the tent and their covered wagon, Alexander's morning cook fire was already crackling, the coffeepot on the iron grate. Alexander had left to get the oxen. Ellie yawned then stepped toward the wagon to wake the girls.

She smiled to herself. This was like no other morning since the beginning of the rendezvous. Around her stirred the disorder of the first day's start, many of the folks already hitching unruly teams to rigs, others still packing or cooking.

Ellie was climbing up the rear of the wagon when she spotted Sarah and Meg, still in their nightclothes, chasing through camp with Becky and Louisa O'Donnell, falling over wagon tongues, getting up and running again. Dogs barked, sniffed the ground, barked again, jumping and running with Joey, Mary, and John Calvin Miller, who chased behind the squealing girls. Laughter and giggling and happy shouting seemed to rise from every corner of the camp.

She started after the girls, passing Alexander and his older sons driving the oxen teams into camp. Some of the men from neighboring wagons called out to each other as they prodded their teams into place. Whips cracked and flicked, and cattle bawled in the distance as the men closed them in for the drive.

Ellie put her hands on her hips and looked around camp, shaking her head at the cacophony of motion and sounds and smells. Mules brayed and chains jangled against the dull thud of wood yokes as teams were joined to wagon tongues. And mixed with it all, smoke from dozens of cook fires swirled into the dawn mist. Already it clung to the canvas of the wagons, the tents, and every piece of clothing packed or worn by the girls, Alexander, and herself. Ellie wondered if she would ever rid her skin and hair of it.

Within a few more minutes, she had reined in the unruly twins and headed them back to the wagon to get dressed and eat breakfast. But try as she might, the little girls wouldn't sit still for one bite of egg or one piece of bread. Not even for their father.

Alexander, after gulping down his own breakfast, gave them each a wink and a salute before riding out to check on the Mitchell and Prewitt boys, today's riders, and his newly appointed foreman, Silas Edwards, all readying to drive the herd.

The captain rode his Appaloosa around the back perimeter of the herd and spoke with Lawson Mitchell, today's point man. He nudged the horse up a nearby rise and watched Silas Edwards give the signal—a rifle shot—and the thundering nine hundred head of cattle moved out, bawling, as five hundred horses galloped to one side, kicking dust into the air.

Still mounted, Alexander threaded his way through camp back to Ellie and their wagon. Folks called out greetings to him as he passed, and he tipped his hat. Little Becky O'Donnell waved as she packed dishes in a flour barrel for her mother, and kind-faced Reverend Brown looked up with a smile as he hooked a cast-iron skillet to the wagon side. A couple more of the five little O'Donnell girls raced by. It seemed one or more of the brood turned up everywhere he looked.

He had known most of the families nearly all his life. They were solid folks, stouthearted and hardworking. Abe Barrett was yoking his team as Alexander passed, and as usual, Abe grinned and nodded as he called out a greeting. The two men had been friends since boyhood. It had been Abe who had talked him into being captain, then talked the company into electing him. He could see the excitement of the day's departure in Abe's eyes as he passed.

As the captain headed toward his and Ellie's wagon, he passed Hampton and Sadie, shoving barrels and boxes into the back of their rig. He dismounted to greet them.

"I'm glad you're along, son," he said, wondering if his pride showed in his face. "Your being here's a big help." Already his son was showing leadership abilities Alexander hadn't seen before.

Sadie grinned into Alexander's face. "Wild horses couldn't have kept us from comin'," she said. "Isn't that right, Ham?"

Hampton nodded and gave his father a mock salute. "It's all I ever remember our family talking about, Pa. Now, here we are on our way." His grin was as wide as Sadie's. He looked up at the clear sky. "I'd say it's a good day for heading out."

"Fair skies leavin' mean a fair journey," said Sadie, smiling confidently as if she knew this for certain. She pulled her poke bonnet forward and gave Alexander a nod. "We'll pray this is true."

Before he could answer, Billy and Bess stepped up from where they'd been checking their oxen team's yokes a few wagons back. "Hey, Pa," Billy said. "When do I get to ride point?"

"When your pa decides," Bess said, laughing. "Until then, mister, I want you back here eating dust with the rest of us."

They talked for a few minutes about the day's trek, then Alexander remounted and continued riding to his own wagon. Even from the distance of a few wagon outfits back, he could see the flame-haired Liza Barrett helping Ellie finish packing the breakfast dishes and iron pans. Though she was older than Ellie by some years, Abe's wife was Ellie's best friend and spirit kin. She was a woman of great joy and an easy companion. There was not a neighbor unwelcome by her fire, not a child in the company unwelcome in her lap. She loved to sing, and she loved to laugh. Her joy was contagious, and Alexander knew that Ellie loved her dearly.

Farrington touched his hat to Ellie and Liza, then dismounted. "Greetings, ladies. Ready to pull out?" He rubbed the neck of his faithful Appaloosa.

"Oh, my, yes," Liza said. "Abe and I've been awake most the night planning how to get our grandchildren ready and into the wagon by sunup." She squinted at the horizon. "And I think we'll just about accomplish our goal." Then she laughed and added, "Of course, the only reason we're up and moving so early is to get that coveted first place in line." She winked wryly at him. Everyone knew the first day out, at least, that coveted place belonged to the captain and his family.

Liza gave Ellie a quick embrace and headed across the circle to the Barrett wagon. Alexander turned his attention to Ellie. The strain that had been on her face during the long weeks of planning and rendezvous was still there. She was a fragile woman, and though she scoffed at his worry, it didn't stop him from thinking about what this trip might take from her. Since she'd been carrying this new baby, she hadn't been well. He knew she tried to keep her weariness from him, but he could sometimes see the pain in her face, and it troubled him.

He loved Ellie. Oh, how he loved her! She was as slim as a meadow reed, with a fragile beauty that sometimes took his breath away. Though he never told Ellie so, he took pleasure just watching her, especially at night by the fire. Maybe it was her gentle spirit that caused him to feel so protective. Many times he wanted to gather her into his arms to hold forever, safe from whatever it was that caused her weariness.

Alexander looked at his wife in the brightening of the morning. She smiled at him, and his heart lifted when he saw the light in her eyes. He swallowed the lump in his throat as he watched her settle onto the wagon bench. The twins were atop their ponies, Buttercup and Gingerbread, waiting to follow their father. His daughters watched him expectantly, the rising sun striking their rosy faces.

Ellie would be all right. They would all be all right. For he was leading his family to a golden land kissed by the setting sun.

The captain mounted his Appaloosa and made sure Meg and Sarah were following, and the three rode to the front of the company.

He lifted his rifle and fired once into the air. It was the signal to move out.

"California! Ho!" shouted the twins in unison at the top of their lungs. "California! Ho!" came the thundering reply from the rest of the Farrington train.

The long caravan of wagons stretched out across the grassy landscape, rows of canvas sails against the purple-blue sky. Rolling, creaking, dust billowing, children whining, cattle bawling, families laughing and talking, children whining some more.

Once they'd moved onto the trail, Ellie walked beside her oxen team, holding the long reins in one hand and wielding the goad or popping the whip in the other whenever the beasts stubbornly tried to go their own way. Meg and Sarah played under the shelter of the wagon cover, their ponies now tied behind.

The sun was already too warm, and a new, almost desperate weariness threatened to melt Ellie's limbs. But she couldn't stop to rest. None of the company could stop. Not today. Not for a hundred days.

There was still an eternity to go.

"Git up, there! Haw, come on, git up!" The cries echoed through the company then were repeated again and again.

Around Ellie dust stirred and billowed, blotting out the sun. The pounding of cattle and horses' hooves thundered and vibrated the ground.

"Push on. No rest now. This is it," she whispered in rhythm with the creaking wagon wheels. "It's just the first day, but this is it.

"Ho! for California! We've finally begun.

"Don't stop. Don't look back.

"Push on," she whispered. "Push on!"

TWELVE

Cherokee Trail
Spring 1857

The late-spring runoff filled the tributary to the Arkansas River as it hurried over bits of rock that had been tumbled smooth in the turbulent waters. Near shore, a rock-strewn sand bar was as visible as though seen through glass, but as it stretched to the center of the mighty river it disappeared into the dark churn of the water.

At the river's edge, the Appaloosa gelding stretched its neck to the water to drink. Captain Alexander Farrington leaned back in the saddle and surveyed the crossing. It had been nearly two weeks since the wagon train had pulled out of Crooked Creek, and the long caravan was making its way along the south bank of the sidewinding river, pushing northwest along a little-known trail that would eventually join up with the Oregon-California road. The guide for the company would be hired when they reached Fort Laramie; until then Alexander was both captain and scout.

He had ridden out early, ahead of the company, to find a suitable crossing. Now, with the caravan and its accompanying cattle herd less than a half-mile behind him, he looked out again across the river, his eyes measuring the distance to the sun-scorched grassland on the other side. The river was wide, certainly more than a stone's throw, but it didn't appear an impossible ford for the wagons. The slope of the bank and the lay of the river rock seemed right.

He urged the Appaloosa into the water. The rock gave the bottom a solid feel beneath the gelding's feet. Alexander glanced both upstream and downstream for signs of quicksand. Often it couldn't be seen until it was too late. But the rocky sand bar stretched in both directions. And where the current would lift the wagons and stock, mud wouldn't matter. The wagons would float easily enough with their watertight linings of rawhide and tallow.

Water covered the captain's boots now as he coaxed his horse farther out from shore. The current grew swifter as the Appaloosa moved with determined spirit toward the river's center. Alexander could feel the chill of the water now reaching his thighs and the strength of the river pushing hard against both him and the horse. Now the Appaloosa was swimming, its head up, its body a trembling ripple of muscle and resolve. He rubbed the gelding's neck, coaxing the horse on, and headed him into the current to avoid being swept downstream.

Suddenly the muddy river bottom dropped away, the churn of the water stirring up mud so thick the depth couldn't be told. The captain spoke to the Appaloosa, urging it on with the press of his thigh. The horse swam, then found its footing on the other shore. It climbed the bank and stopped to shake the water from its body.

Alexander let the horse rest, enjoying the heat of the sun on his shoulders for a moment as he looked back across the river. In the distance, the first of nearly a thousand head of livestock rounded the bend. The cattle moved along the river's edge, bawling and complaining as the cowhands cracked their whips and called out to keep them from stalling at the water.

Now the caravan was snaking down the long, gentle slope toward the river. Kicked-up dust clouds drifted toward the east, causing the folks who were walking to keep west of their wagons. The train was so distant Alexander couldn't make out faces, only shapes of bright color: the women in poke bonnets of reds and oranges and yellows with skirts of browns and greens billowing in the wind, and the men's shirts appearing white instead of gray in the sun's glare. Even the hooped canvas stretched above the wagons shimmered an unnatural white.

He was proud to be leading this company west. And for a moment he took in the beauty—patches of color below an azure sky—of the caravan moving slowly toward the green river, which sparkled in the sun.

As the wagon train wound its way toward the river, Alexander could see Ellie sitting in the front of the lead wagon. She'd asked for the place in line that would be first to cross the river. He had started to disagree until he saw the fierce determination in her eyes. Then he'd conceded.

It was time to get the Appaloosa to the other side to sound the signal for the crossing. "Come on, old boy," he said to the horse after a minute. "We've got some folks to move." He reined the gelding toward the water, and this time they hit it full bore.

"How deep you reckon it is?" Abe Barrett had asked when Alexander joined him at the river. He had ridden ahead of the train to join his friend at the crossing after the signal was fired.

"Deeper than it looks. We'll have to float the wagons. I'm afraid the current might take the teams and the whole works if we don't send them across separately." Alexander glanced at Abe, measuring his reaction. He had never known a man with better sense.

The captain went on, "How about tying a line to a wagon, having a rider take it across, then hitching the line's other end to a team—maybe three or four yoke—on the other side? If the team's on solid ground they'll pull a floating wagon easy, even with the current being what it is."

"Wheels off?" Abe looked skeptical.

"We'll just hoist them into each wagon—and rebolt them on the far bank. We'll need a crew on each side just for the taking off and putting on."

The sun still lay low in the eastern sky, but already it was taking on a white-hot shine. Nearby a ground bird skittered through the brush, and overhead the squawking of jays rose in the air. Grasshoppers sawed their legs in the tall grass while the heat lifted the smell of dirt from the earth.

Alexander took off his hat and pulled out his kerchief to wipe the sweat first from his forehead then from the inside band of the hat. He waited for Abe to speak. "Well, go on and say it, Abe," he finally goaded. "I can tell you've got more on your mind than wondering how we're going to pull off the wheels."

Abe grunted, still seeming lost in his thinking.

"I been noticing how the current changes," Abe finally said, squinting and looking across. "See there, underneath, Alexander. It's moving unpredictable and swift. Not a good combination." Abe took off his hat and scratched his head, then went on, "I'm wondering what'll happen if the rope hitched to the wagon breaks." He frowned, his eyes still on the river. "That'll leave folks with nothing between them and a swift float back to Fort Smith."

"You've got a better way?"

"First of all, I'd leave the wheels on. It'll be easier for the folks to get their rigs in and out of the river." Abe went on, explaining his plan.

When he'd finished, Alexander slapped his friend on the back. "You just got yourself into a job, friend. You're in charge. Forty wagons and 137 souls are in your keep. But don't let it worry you. Like you said, if any break loose they'll just float on back to Fort Smith—once they get through the falls."

Still laughing, Alexander mounted the Appaloosa and headed for the train. He looked back to see Abe galloping his horse along the water's edge. He reached down as he rode and scooped a hatful of water, drenching his head. After a few minutes, Abe was whooping and riding like lightning to catch up to Alexander.

But right now the captain had eyes only for the wagon train as he rode toward it. Ellie's outfit was still first in line. Directly behind her wagon was Hampton and Sadie's rig, and following them was the family's supply wagon, driven by Alexander's younger son, Billy. His plainspoken wife, Bess, was at his side, a wide smile on her freckled face.

Ellie raised her hand and waved then smiled as he rode up to her wagon. He pulled alongside to ride beside her the short distance to the crossing. The twins, leaning through the canvas opening at the front of the wagon, called out to their father, waving and giggling.

Ellie's red poke bonnet had fallen to rest on her shoulders, and strands of her dark hair lifted in the wind against her sun-browned cheek. Her face was unreadable, but her eyes shone with the challenge of crossing the river.

The sun shimmered hot above the landscape. From atop her wagon's front bench, Ellie shaded her eyes with her hand and squinted as she gazed across the river. Beside her, Alexander rode the gelding in comfortable silence, lost in his own thoughts.

She sighed as she popped the whip above the oxen and thought about the terrain on the far side of the river. Until now the wagon train had wound its way in and out of patches of pine and oak, mostly along the river. The forests brought a sense of home, smelling of dust and pine and decaying leaves. But after the crossing there would be nothing between her and that wide, blue expanse of sky.

Ellie looked forward to it. She drew in a deep breath, thinking it would bring her closer to heaven than she'd ever been. Even the thought of the tall prairie grasses brought her joy. She imagined how they would roll and bend in the wind, a silver-green ocean shimmering under the white-hot sun.

Oh yes! God's sweet earth, solid and warm and joyful, spreading all the way to eternity.

The wagon hit a rut and swayed a bit. Ellie caught her balance and cracked the whip to keep the oxen moving. But she needn't have bothered. The team was moving faster now, excited by the smell of water and pushing on without much prodding. Alexander caught her gaze and grinned. They were almost to the crossing.

Now only the river lay between her and that prairie. She wanted to be first across the river, first to see that magnificent open sky.

As if reading her mind, Alexander looked over and asked, "You sure you want to do this, Ellie?"

"Do what, Mommy?" Sarah asked from her place behind Ellie.

"What's Mommy want to do, Papa?" Meg called out at exactly the same time.

Ellie laughed. "One at a time, now, girls. We're going to be first to cross. And yes, Alexander, I'm sure." She tilted her chin toward him and smiled. "I wouldn't miss this chance for the world."

"Yeah, Papa, we wouldn't miss it for the world either!" Meg said, nearly jumping up and down in excitement.

"Phoebe thinks so too!" Sarah said, jumping her doll up and down on the back of the wagon bench.

"I believe I've got the bravest family in the company," he said. "I'm proud of you all." Then he reined the Appaloosa closer to the wagon. "But you girls need to mind your mama, you hear?"

They nodded solemnly.

"You must sit perfectly still."

"We will, Papa," Meg nodded. "We promise."

"Even if the wagon starts rocking and swaying in the river, I don't want to see you stand up or get excited. You must sit still and let your mama handle the team."

"Yes, Papa."

"And no screaming or giggling. The team'll be skittish. You might cause them to panic. Do you understand?"

"Yes, Papa."

"All right, then. There's one thing you can do."

"What?" Meg asked. They both smiled up at him, their dark braids gleaming in the sun.

"You can blow me a kiss when you pass me in the river."

Sarah wrinkled her nose. "You're gonna be in the river?"

"I'll be waiting out on a sand bar to help out if any wagoners need me. It's about halfway across."

"Here's one now," Meg said, blowing him a kiss. "In case we forget later."

He grinned at his daughters and gave them a small salute before turning the Appaloosa toward the river.

Ellie laughed suddenly. "Stop right there a minute, Alexander. I'm counting on you and Abe. I hope you have this thing figured out down to a gnat's whisker. Believe me, I'm not about to halt this team in the middle of the river while you two are scratching your heads wondering what to do next." She pulled her poke bonnet forward to shade her face then looked up at him and smiled.

From her wagon bench a few teams back, Liza Barrett called up to Ellie with a hoot, "That's the way to tell him, sweetie! Maybe you and I should be out there in the middle of the river, simply directing folks as they cross. Seems a bit of a lah-tee-dah kind of job to me, compared to driving these unruly beasts across!" Some of the other women joined in the laughter as Alexander and Abe rode off, shaking their heads.

A half-hour later, the captain stood facing the company at the top of the inclined riverbank. Ellie watched with pride as he called out for the families to gather around him.

The rear wagons had now pulled forward to join the rest, most of the oxen slowing to a halt without command. Downstream, the herd was nearly across; the few remaining head were swimming hard against the current, moaning and bellowing to the sky as they went. The sounds carried across the water and mixed with the shouts of trail hands and the cracking whips that kept the animals moving through the muddy water.

He explained how each rig would ford, then asked Abe to supply the details. The sun was straight overhead, and Ellie pulled her bonnet closer to her eyes. As Alexander and Abe talked, she noticed that most of the men seemed to listen without emotion, their dusty faces resolute. The women, on the other hand, openly showed their feelings ranging from fear to anticipation. The children, wading and splashing at the water's edge, seemed only to care about life's small joys, giggling with abandon, unaware of the dangers of the crossing.

After Abe finished, the captain headed the mare to the sand bar in midstream, where the current seemed to ebb. Abe stayed at the water's edge to help the families as their wagons plunged into the river.

By now most of the livestock had climbed up the bank on the far side and were taking their fill of grass in the fields beyond. Some of the cowhands, the Prewitt boys and the Mitchell brothers, began to make their way back to the other side of the river, where the wagons waited to ford.

Ellie moved her rig forward to the edge of the incline. Behind her, the remainder of the wagons pulled into their places in line. While they awaited their turn, they tied down trunks, furniture, and supplies, readying their belongings for the float.

Ellie met Alexander's gaze and gave him a nod that she was ready. She sat very still, whip in hand. The unusually quiet twins were sitting just behind her, watching through the front opening. As Joel and Lawson Mitchell tied tethers to each side of the wagon, she waited silently until the job was done.

Finally, Abe Barrett gave the signal.

Coming off the bluff without a hold-back rope, Ellie didn't let the oxen balk at the river. She stood up as they reached the water's edge and drove them straight in. The twins squealed, forgetting their father's warning, as the team splashed into the water.

The crossing began upstream from where the pull-out lay so the downward-sweeping current would work with the beasts instead of against them. Ellie remembered Abe's warning to pull out before that point, which was marked by a gnarled and crooked oak overhanging the river.

The water moved wildly after that, he'd said, and getting out would be almost impossible for a ways downstream.

Ellie kept her eyes on the backs of the oxen, their gray-white coats now shining wet in the sun. Their stocky legs were beginning to lose the feel of the river bottom, and with snouts in the air and loud bawls of protest, they began to swim.

Underneath, their hooves churned up silt and mud, hiding the river bottom from view. The wagon rocked, the upset animals and the swift power of the current playing with it like a toy. Ellie shouted out to calm the oxen then reached with one arm to steady the girls.

Meg looked up at her with a grin, happy for the ride.

"Yahoo!" shouted Sarah, then clasped her hand over her mouth dramatically.

The wagon swayed, and Ellie could feel it beginning to float. By now the lead oxen were nearly midstream to the sand bar. She had been warned that the feel of footing, then its immediate loss, might confuse the animals and make them even more giddy.

Joel and Lawson were now closing in on either side of the lead oxen. But just as they did, the current suddenly seemed rougher, and the wagon swayed violently and dipped. Though the tether ropes held, the belongings shifted and slid in back, tipping the wagon even farther.

The oxen were mostly over the bar and began to fight the water as they again lost their footing on the other side. The wagon evened out as it crossed the bar, though it still listed dangerously to the downstream side as it began to float again.

Team and rig began to move faster downstream, the sweep of the river harder now. Suddenly the upstream lead ox went under, and the one yoked to it fought for an instant then slipped under with its partner. Lawson Mitchell grabbed for the yoke, but it was too heavy to pull up. The rest of the oxen snorted and bawled as they felt themselves being sucked into the water.

Ellie stood and began to whip the beasts, urging them on with shouts and blows to their bony backs. She didn't think about the marks left by the whip. She didn't think about anything. She just shouted and whipped.

Alexander was suddenly beside the team, grabbing for the heavy wooden yoke. Tying ropes first to the yoke then around their saddle horns, the men pulled the animals' heads above water. The oxen were stunned and worn, but they began to swim again through the water. Within minutes, they had reached the riverbank and clambered out just yards upstream from the crooked oak.

Ellie popped the whip again. The tired team kept pulling, their feet unsure as they climbed the steep bank with its slippery mud, but the wagon finally pulled out of the water and up to solid, flat grassland.

As soon as Ellie halted the oxen, the twins jumped down and ran to meet Alexander, now galloping the Appaloosa toward the wagon. "Did you see us, Papa? That was something! Did you see how Mama drove the wagon?"

"That I did! That I did!" he said with pride. Then his eyes met Ellie's. "That was some fancy driving."

She nodded, accepting the compliment. He turned the Appaloosa back toward the sand bar, and the girls climbed into the wagon for shelter from the beating sun.

Just then Sarah let out a screech, followed immediately by another.

Alarmed, Alexander turned immediately back toward Ellie. By now the little girl was sobbing hysterically in her mother's arms.

"What is it?" he asked as he halted the Appaloosa by the wagon.

"Phoebe," Sarah sobbed inconsolably. "Phoebe's gone. I think she fell in the river."

Alexander met Ellie's gaze over the top of Sarah's head.

"You can have my dolly," offered Meg. "I'll give her to you."

"I want Phoebe," Sarah wailed. "I want Phoebe!" And the little girl dissolved once more into sobs.

"I must get back to the crossing," Alexander said to Ellie. His horse danced sideways and snorted. To Sarah he added gently, "I'll help you look for Phoebe later. When all the wagons have crossed, then you and I can go downriver and take a look."

She sniffled and nodded, then rubbed her eyes.

Alexander kicked the gelding in the flanks and headed back across the river, calling out more directions as he rode. Then he positioned himself again on the sand bar in midstream, and the next team started down the incline to the river. Rig after rig followed—his sons and their families, Pleasant and Cynthia Tackett and their children, Jesse and Polly O'Donnell with their five lively daughters, Abe's son George Barrett and his family, the captain's nephews James and Robert, and James's widowed mother, Jane, all plunging their teams into the water, nervously moving across, and then pulling out again just before the crooked oak.

He grinned as the signal was given for the next wagon to move into the water. It was the Barrett wagon with Liza at the helm. She flicked the backs of her oxen with her whip, and the beasts lumbered forward, pulling the rig into the water, steady and smooth.

He was struck by the woman's spirit. Her love of life showed on her face. She seemed aglow with it, even down to the gleam of her red hair.

The sun was straight overhead now, causing a glare on the patterns of fast-moving ripples. Liza's outfit continued on, and she half-stood, whip in hand, popping it just above the team, yelling out steady and even. Her gaze didn't move from the oxen and the river straight ahead. They progressed across the river, past Alexander and the sand bar and down to the crooked oak. Without mishap, the oxen climbed the steep bank and pulled the wagon to dry ground.

Within minutes, Liza had clambered from her wagon bench to join Ellie and the twins on the far riverbank. The next time he glanced back, Liza was holding Sarah in her arms, strolling along the river's edge, and he knew it was to console his brokenhearted daughter. He also knew how impossible it would be to find the wooden doll, even though he'd promised Sarah to look. He couldn't bear to think of her little disappointed face when she understood the certainty of her loss.

He turned back to help the few remaining wagons cross. By now, the wagoners seemed less fearful, and even the most timid drivers urged their teams into the water full bore. In time for the nooning, all had forded and were in place on the western side of the river.

While Ellie and Meg set out a meal of salt pork and johnnycake left from the previous night's supper, Alexander swept Sarah up to sit in front of him on the saddle. Still teary, she sighed and settled her back against him. He suddenly wished he could shelter Sarah from all heartaches she would ever face in her life, and he encircled her in his arms and kissed the top of her head. Then he clucked to the

Appaloosa and flicked the reins, urging the horse into a trot toward the riverbank. A moment later he reined the horse into a turn downstream from the crooked oak.

For nearly an hour they searched the tangles of grass and brush and driftwood along both sides of the river. But there was no sign of the doll. Finally, Alexander couldn't put off the inevitable any longer. They needed to eat their noon meal, and he could waste no more time getting the train on its way. He glanced up at the sun. They had miles to cover before sundown.

By the time they rode back into camp, Sarah was crying again. He helped the little girl dismount before swinging his leg over the saddle and stepping to the ground.

"I'm sorry, sweetheart," he said, kneeling and looking her in the face. "How about if I whittle another Phoebe for you? Or better yet—it can be her sister. A twin sister."

But Sarah shook her head slowly, her lower lip trembling. "The only baby I want is Phoebe," she said, her eyes watery. "The only one ever."

Thirteen

The days that followed were dry, raw, and wind warmed. As the wagon company moved slowly across the prairie, Ellie often walked beside the team, trying not to think about her aching muscles. She licked her sore lips, only to feel them dry and crack again in the windy heat.

The sun beat down on her head, seeming to sear right through the poke bonnet. The wind lifted her dark hair away from her sunburned face, bringing respite from the heat, only to settle then kick up again. Blisters and sores covered her feet. And her legs, though hard with new muscle, ached with weariness and bled from insect bites. Along the road, badger holes threatened to wrench an ankle, and she found herself nearly too weary to step over them.

The growing child in her belly caused the small of her back to burn with pain with each step she took. But she lifted her chin and whispered a prayer for her baby in rhythm with the turning of the creaking wagon wheels:

Beloved Savior, she would breathe,
Protect this your child.
You have knit him together
In my womb.
In my heart.
His days are in your hands.
Even as are all of ours . . . Alexander's and mine,
Meg's and Sarah's.
We are yours . . .

The twins skipped and ran and walked and complained and whined alongside Ellie part of the time and happily rode in the wagon the rest. Alexander had cautioned the company to walk as much as possible so as not to tire the already struggling teams of oxen and mules.

Each day the train rolled in a straight line across the flat land, a vista unbroken by mountain or tree as far as Ellie could see. The prairie grass rose tall, sometimes taller than a person on horseback. Fed by the late spring rains, it shone pale green in the sun. It stretched toward the horizon, shiny and wind-rippled like the sea Ellie imagined.

The families didn't call out to each other as much as they had at the start, and even the children seemed subdued, perhaps from the monotony, Ellie thought, or perhaps by the fear of being lost in the giant grass. At night the somber mood seemed to lift. In groups around the night fires, sounds of talking and laughter and singing again filled the air. They danced and sang and clapped to the fiddle player and listened to stories about Indians and mountain men and the pioneers who'd gone before them.

When the children were in bed and the men gathered to plan the next day's trek, Ellie sat with Liza Barrett, Polly O'Donnell, William Cameron's wife, and Jane Farrington, discussing womanly concerns such as how they could stretch their supplies. Hampton's wife, Sadie, and Billy's Bess sometimes joined them as well—though, because they were barely more than children themselves, the young women seemed to prefer the company of the unmarried girls, with their gossip and lighthearted chatter.

Ellie was already concerned about replenishing the food stock. Most wagon trains heading west couldn't carry enough for the entire journey, so they depended on settlements along the way where feed for the cattle and food for the families could be purchased. What they had packed in Crooked Creek would be depleted by the time they arrived at Fort Laramie.

Ellie wondered if there were places where supplies were so scare as to not be available. But when she voiced her concern in front of the other women, Liza chuckled and said, "We have enough to worry about today, Ellie. Let's not start worrying about tomorrow quite yet."

But Ellie couldn't let go of the notion. She thought maybe it was because she was feeling fiercely maternal as her babe moved and kicked inside her or because of her joy in watching Meg and Sarah thrive in the fresh air and prairie sunshine, seeming to grow taller and stronger each day.

One night after the girls were snuggled into bed as dusk settled on the grasslands, Ellie strolled from camp to be alone with her thoughts. The travelers had circled their wagons next to a small, winding creek, and its evensong of frogs croaking and crickets and katydids sawing beckoned her.

A breeze rustled the grasses, carrying with it a perfume of damp earth and grass and wildflowers. In the distance, the final rays of the sun slid from view, and a pale mist began to settle on the land. Ellie drew in a deep breath. The world had never seemed so alive.

God was with her in this place! His presence was so real, so comforting, that quick tears sprang to her eyes. She walked closer to the bubbling stream, delighting in its music, listening to the still, small voice that spoke to her heart.

Beloved, you are mine.

Your love for your children is a reflection of my own love . . . for them. For you.

Your journey is difficult, my child,
And the road ahead harder than you can know.
But I am with you, my beloved.
I will never leave you. I will never forsake you.

Ellie lifted her eyes toward the afterglow where the sun had slipped beneath the prairie. The grass stood tall, its tassels silhouetted against the darkening sky like sentinels. The heaviness she had carried in her heart for weeks seemed to lift with the night birds taking wing.

Later, as Ellie fixed her bedroll next to Alexander's, she looked up at the ink black sky with its pinpoints of dancing fire, and her heart leapt with joy at the knowledge that the God of creation, the God who ruled the universe, called her "beloved."

Alexander reached to take her hand. He lifted it to his lips in a gentle kiss, then turning on his side, he scooted his body close to her back, wrapping one arm around her waist. His hand now rested on the place where the baby would continue his butterfly antics throughout the night. Ellie smiled and placed her hand on top of Alexander's. Her love for this man, so often too weary to talk at the end of the long days, welled inside her.

Around them drifted the soft voices of families settling into wagons and onto pallets by their campfires. Once in a while, a child's sleepy voice drifted across the night circle, calling out to his or her mother. Then the voices stopped, and Ellie could hear only the distant bawling of cattle and the din of nearby creek frogs.

Pulling her quilt over her shoulders, Ellie watched the dying embers of the fire until she fell asleep.

It was mid-May when Alexander turned the company due north; they were just days from intersecting the California road. The bone-weary families seemed to take energy from the knowledge of its nearness. They would soon join hundreds of other travelers heading west, and they would welcome the company.

As the train lumbered forward, now and then they crossed Indian foot trails running east and west. The day they spotted the first trace, the morning draw had put Ellie's wagon at the head of the train. She had felt a new weariness and aching in her womb, so she decided to drive the team from the bench. The twins sat behind her in the wagon bed, leaning out of the canvas opening. Alexander rode beside her with Abe Barrett on the other side of the wagon and slightly ahead.

Ellie noticed they both seemed more watchful than usual.

"Pawnee," Abe Barrett said to Alexander as they crossed another trail. Her husband nodded in agreement.

"Indians?" shouted Sarah, nearly hopping up and down in her excitement. Her sister added a few whoops and hollers, her hand patting her mouth to create a wild warbling sound.

Alexander gave his daughter a frown, and Meg halted the noise.

"Will we see one, Papa?" Sarah asked. "I want to see a Pawnee."

"I'm sure we will," Alexander said absently as his eyes continued to search the trails through the grass. "Though I've told you, they're more of a nuisance than anything to fear."

"Still, I want to see one," she persisted.

"Me too," added Meg with two fingers lifted featherlike behind her head.

The girls disappeared inside to play as one wheel hit a rock and swayed the wagon. Ellie lifted the whip, popping it above the oxen's backs. They lumbered forward, jerking and rocking the wagon again. They rode onward.

Ellie was especially glad for her husband's watchful company today. She glanced over at him with pride, noting the changes in him since they had left Crooked Creek. He fit in the Appaloosa's worn saddle as if one with the powerful animal. His red-brown hair strung to his shoulders from beneath his hat, giving him more the look of a mountain man than the country farmer he had been.

The way he rode in the saddle, it was obvious he was where he was born to be . . . following his dream. Ellie marveled at how her husband seemed to be made for the width of the sky, the brilliance of the fine spring grasses, and the wildness of the unceasing wind.

Just as I am, she thought, raising her eyes to a sky so deep it made her dizzy. She ached with the wonder of it. How she loved God's creation! She wondered if when he made this land he'd used heaven as a pattern . . . just as she used a dress pattern for sewing.

Still smiling to herself at the notion, she looked west, where thunderheads were churning upward, brilliant and bold against the darkening sky. The sounds of distant thunder rumbled across the land, and a low, flat wind pressed the grasses eastward.

Suddenly, Ellie felt like singing. And so she did. Looking up at the sky in all its expanse, she started singing "Oh! Susanna." Alexander glanced at her with surprise, grinned, and then joined in with his rumbling bass.

The twins stuck their heads out of the canvas opening, wide-eyed in wonder, then they started singing and clapping in rhythm. Within minutes, up and down the long caravan, folks lifted joyous voices—melodic, raspy, deep, off-tune, or operatic—and the noise of it carried across the prairie.

Ellie chuckled, popped the whip at the oxen from time to time, and continued to sing, "Oh! Susanna, oh, don't you cry for me, for I've come from Alabama with a banjo on my knee . . ."

By that night, a small band of Indians, Pawnee and Kansa, according to Alexander and Abe, began tagging along behind the train, pestering the travelers to trade for food and trinkets.

When the company stopped for their nooning or circled the wagons for the night, the Pawnee women quickly spread tattered blankets on the flattened grasses and placed clay bowls, grass baskets, beads, and shells on the ground next to trinkets they had traded or stolen from other wagon trains.

Ellie wondered at the hunger that would cause the too-thin women to trade the useful items or the objects that had once struck their fancy. With watchful, dark eyes, the women beckoned the families from the Farrington train to come nearer. Through sign language they acted out their need for food and clothing for themselves and for their children. Their men stood silently behind, their arms folded across naked chests, their stares a challenge to deny their women's offers.

Alexander told Ellie and the others that it was better to trade than ignore the group. They would get what they came for anyway—by stealing or raiding if necessary. Though Ellie knew it was wise, she was still reluctant to give up their precious food supplies.

On the third night of the Pawnee presence, the band camped nearer to the company than before, almost within a stone's throw of Ellie's wagon. Alexander was out with Abe checking the herd, and she knew it was with good reason. The Pawnee had that day been joined by another group of braves on horseback. Both bands together now totaled maybe forty women, men, and children. They could easily run off with a hundred head of cattle or more.

Ellie, pulling out her cookware to start supper, tried to cover her nervousness and ordered Meg and Sarah to stay near the wagon inside the circle.

But the little girls, with their friends Prudence Angeline and Louisa O'Donnell, had grown more and more curious about the Indian children, and they sidled closer to the Pawnee camp. Ellie couldn't take her attention from them for a moment for fear they would draw too close.

The Indian encampment was a hubbub of activity. Babies squalled, and scrawny dogs nosed for scraps from both the wagon camp and their own. On one occasion, Ellie glanced up from her cooking fire to see a young woman watching her, a baby at her breast as she sat by her own fire. The woman stared with unblinking black eyes, looking hungry and sad. Around the Pawnee cook fire sat two tiny boys and a black-eyed little girl about the age of the twins.

Finally, Ellie could no longer look at the woman's hungering eyes. She pulled a fresh-baked johnnycake from the griddle, wrapped it in a dishcloth, and called the girls.

Meg's eyes danced when Ellie explained what she wanted them to do, and Sarah nodded vigorously.

She placed the warm bread in Meg's hands. "Now, I want you to take it to the woman feeding the baby then come right back, you hear?"

They nodded. "Yes ma'am." Then Ellie touched the little girls on the shoulders, indicating they needed to wait a moment.

The woman was watching Ellie carefully, her baby still suckling at her breast. Then she moved her dark-eyed gaze to a freshly washed calico skirt hanging from the back of Ellie's wagon. Ellie could see the hunger on her face, more for the dress than for food, so she stood and gathered it into her arms, folding it neatly.

She handed it to Sarah. "Take this, too, sweetie, and give it to the woman." Sarah nodded solemnly.

A few minutes later, the twins walked the short distance to the Indian camp. The woman stood as they approached and walked resolutely toward them, and her skinny baby boys and the black-eyed little girl remained by the fire.

Hands on hips, Ellie stood, carefully watching the proceedings. Meg and Sarah handed first the dress then the johnnycake to the woman. The woman took the calico and held it in the same arm with the baby. Then, with deerlike grace, she moved back to her fire as the twins turned their attention to the black-eyed little girl who was now coming toward them. The three girls stared at each other for a minute, then Meg took Sarah's hand to start back to the wagon camp.

Ellie let out a deep sigh as the girls began walking toward the wagon. Then she frowned. Sarah had stopped in her tracks, yanking her sister's arm to halt as well.

She appeared to be frowning at something the black-eyed Indian girl was holding in her arms. But before Ellie could even begin to comprehend what had caught her daughter's attention, Sarah let out a cry that stood Ellie's hair on end.

Suddenly Sarah grabbed for the Indian girl's bundle, but the child wouldn't release her hold. Around them, the Indians' dogs set in to a howling, yipping bark, growling, their neck fur standing tall.

Sarah squealed even louder and yanked harder.

By now the entire Indian encampment and half the wagon company, including Ellie, were rushing to the place of the fracas. Sarah cried and yanked and cried even louder than before.

Ellie pushed some Indian children aside, trying to get to her daughter. When she finally reached Sarah's side, her daughter was still trying to pull the small bundle from the black-eyed child. Tears were tracing down her dusty cheeks. "It's mine!" she yelled, sobbing. "It's mine!"

Meg, standing solemnly to one side, lifted a sad-eyed gaze to her mother. But she seemed too overwrought from the frightening commotion to speak.

"What is it?" Ellie breathed as she knelt beside Sarah, attempting to pull her away from the crowd. "What is it?" she repeated even as she saw the bedraggled bundle now secure in the black-eyed child's arms.

"It's Phoebe," Sarah sobbed. "It's Phoebe!"

FOURTEEN

Sarah cried herself to sleep that night, sobbing for Phoebe. Ellie, Alexander, and even stoic Meg tried to console the brokenhearted little girl. Finally she slipped into a troubled and restless sleep, crying out for her missing baby.

Ellie and Alexander looked at each other helplessly and discussed what they might barter to get the doll from the Pawnee.

"It's not right to do that to the little girl," Ellie concluded as they settled onto their pallets by the night fire. "If we bargained for the doll from her family, she would be just as sad as Sarah. Her parents would benefit from whatever we might give them, but the child would be left with empty arms."

"That's one of the reasons I love you so much, Ellie," Alexander said, sliding closer to his wife.

"Why?" Ellie asked, loving the sound of his voice as he spoke of his care for her.

He rested his head against hers. "The way you care about others, not just our family, your concern for the feelings of a little Pawnee child." He fell quiet a moment. "Actually, I agree with you. But I can't think of any other way to get Phoebe back. I know it seems small in the grand scheme of things, considering all we face ahead. But . . . " His voice faltered, and he let out a deep sigh.

"But your little girl's heart is broken."

"Yes," he said softly. "I won't always be around to comfort her when her heart breaks, but at a time when I am here—such as now—there should be something I can do."

Ellie turned to look at her husband in the starlight. "What a sorrowful thing to say—that you won't always be around."

He laughed lightly and pulled her close, and she settled her back against him as he circled his arm around her. "You know what I mean, Ellie. Once we're in California and Sarah grows up and falls in love, marries, and has babies of her own, I won't always be there. Not in the same way I am now . . . to kiss a skinned knee or wipe away a tear." He let out a deep sigh. "I know it's impossible, but I can't help wanting to protect Sarah and Meg from heartache."

"You can't protect them from life," Ellie murmured. "Heartache is part of living."

"I just don't want her to learn it now," he said quietly. "She's only six years old." His voice dropped sleepily. "I think about Amanda Roseanne and Rebecca, now married with families of their own. It doesn't seem that long ago that they were small enough to fit in my arms. And now, they're a thousand miles away."

They lay quietly, and soon Alexander's breathing became deep and even as he slept. Ellie listened to a sudden wind moaning through the prairie grasses, and she gazed up at the starry heavens that seemed more brilliant than ever tonight. She lifted Alexander, Sarah, and Meg before their heavenly Father, trusting them all into his care, before drifting off to sleep.

In the predawn darkness of the following morning, the Pawnee were striking camp and preparing to leave. Alexander was up and had already set out the dried cow patties for the fire when Ellie awoke.

"You need to look at the wagon bench," he said as Ellie stood and stretched her limbs.

"What is it?"

"Come look. I've got a lantern."

Ellie followed him to the yoke end of the wagon, where he lifted the lantern high.

There, on the bench, was Phoebe. Dirty and bedraggled, the doll's tattered and shredded clothes barely clung its worn-smooth body.

Ellie met her husband's eyes in wonder, and he smiled.

Smiling at its pungent and smoky odor, Ellie gently lifted the doll almost as if it held a life of its own. She stepped up the stairs at the rear of the wagon then slipped inside where the twins slept on the cornhusk mattress.

Moments later, she tucked Phoebe into Sarah's arms and whispered for her to wake.

Sarah's squeal of delight heralded the first joy of the morning. The second was when Meg, without their prompting, marched into the nearly dismantled Pawnee camp, holding her hatbox. In it lay her still-unnamed wooden doll with all its little doll clothes.

They watched as, solemnly, she presented her gift to the little black-eyed Pawnee girl. The two girls settled onto a nearby blanket that hadn't yet been folded and packed away. Wordlessly, Meg lifted the lid and took the doll from the box.

She placed it in the child's hands.

For a moment, the little girl sat as if stunned. Then she touched the doll's face in wonder, the still brightly painted blue eyes and pink lips, the hair made from a horse's mane. Then she looked up at Meg and smiled.

It was the first time Ellie, who still watched from a distance, had seen any of the Pawnee smile.

Then the girl pointed to herself and uttered a word Ellie couldn't understand. But it was obvious that her daughter did, for Meg smiled and pointed to herself.

"Meggie," she said slowly.

"May-gee," the black-eyed little girl repeated, then she pointed to her new doll. "May-gee," she said and smiled again.

Ellie felt her eyes smart with tears as Meg made her way back to the wagon. Meg's doll finally had been named.

The wagon company pulled out by dawn, and before the nooning it was obvious they were heading into a bank of quickly building clouds.

"Mommy, there's a storm coming. Over there." Meg, sitting next to Ellie on the wagon seat, pointed west at the billowing thunderheads. "I heard Papa tell the Barretts we're gonna have lightning and thunder like we've never seen before."

"He said it'll make our storms back home seem like steam from a kettle," Sarah added. She was rocking Phoebe, completely lost in the wonder of having her baby back in her arms.

Ellie glanced at the gathering clouds, awed by their living, breathing, building size, the omnipotent power they seemed to hold in their darkening forms. They were going to bring trouble; she could feel it in her bones.

Within the hour the wind kicked up, and the sky turned a gray-green then darkened to shades of twilight, though it was only midday. Abe rode to the rear of the train to tell the cattlehands to gather in the herd; they were stopping early to make night camp.

Alexander gave the signal to circle the wagons. There was no high ground, so the rigs pulled in one behind another on the flat, open land.

"Stay in your wagons!" he commanded, his voice rising because of the wind. "No one should be riding—or walking—in this."

Ellie watched him make the circle, stopping by each wagon and checking to see if folks needed help. Abe and some of the other men followed suit.

"Are you and the girls going to be all right here alone?" he asked as he rode up to their wagon and dismounted. "I'm going to have to be out with Abe and the hands. The herd's already spooked. We're worried they'll stampede"

"We'll be fine," Ellie shouted above the wind. A heavy gust whipped her hair around her face, and her skirt billowed and slapped against her legs. "Since Abe will be with you, Liza said she'd like to join the girls and me in our wagon."

Earlier Alexander had unhitched the team and driven them to mingle with the rest of the nervous herd. Now, their heads down against the driving wind, she and Alexander struggled to fasten the canvas flaps at the wagon's ends. He cinched the rope that tied the canvas to the wagon bed, and Ellie finished tying the rope into a square knot and wound the rope ends around the rig's tongue. Another heavy gust hit, and with it came the first damp feel of rain.

"You'd better take cover. It's about to break," Alexander shouted. He reined the horse to move on, hesitated a moment, then turned back again to Ellie. "Be careful, Ellie. Don't go out for any reason. Especially don't let the girls out. There may be some flooding."

Nervous and jittery, the Appaloosa stepped sideways then back again with each blowing gust and rumble of distant thunder. Alexander patted the horse's neck.

Ellie nodded and stepped up into the wagon. A lantern hung on a side peg, and the twins were examining Phoebe, completely unconcerned about the storm. They were busy discussing the doll's adventures after falling from the wagon on the river. Outside, the wind howled and whipped against the canvas wagon cover.

The rain started, fat drops that stirred the dust. To the west, the low rumble of thunder grew louder. Ellie could hear the sounds of the herd, the whinnying of the horses, the stomping and snorting of the cattle, the bawling of the oxen. There were "haws!" and "gees!" coming from the cattlehands trying to calm the nervous beasts.

Alexander had ordered most of the train's able-bodied men to the patrol. She knew that thousands of head of cattle had been lost in storms like this, bolting and running away in fright, never to be found.

Just as the rain began a steady beat on the canvas and the dust was turning to mud, Liza Barrett called out, "Anchors a-weigh in there!" in a cheerful voice.

Ellie grinned and opened the flap. "Come in, dear, or you'll catch your death," she said, stepping back as Liza climbed into the wagon and removed her oilcloth rain cape.

After she'd given each of the girls a vigorous hug, Liza settled into one of Ellie's two small farm chairs.

The wagon's cramped interior was filled with stacked barrels and trunks and a few pieces of furniture—a sideboard tipped on its side, a small hand-planked table with a gingham cloth, and the two farm chairs. Though crowded, the little room had a cheerful look to it, with a vase of wildflowers the children had picked that morning, a mandolin given to Ellie by her grandmother in one corner, and wood-carved blocks and toys strewn across the tiny patch of bare floor.

Ellie took pleasure in lighting her lantern each night when darkness fell. It was a symbol of warmth that spoke of enjoyable quiet, solitude, and well-earned rest. It was almost magical the way it transformed her wagon into a home. Today, its glow seemed more welcome than ever.

"The best way to while away a storm," Ellie said, "is to visit with a friend you love." It seemed they were often too busy with loading and unloading wagons, cooking and baking, washing clothes, and driving teams of unruly beasts to take time for a deep-heart talk.

Liza squeezed Ellie's hand. "All we need is a cup of tea." Then she chuckled. "Though I'd like to see you get a cook fire started in here." She shook her head slowly as the storm kicked up a howl again and the wagon rocked with the force of the wind.

The lantern swayed, and shadows danced across the canvas walls. A lightning strike landed close by, followed by an angry clap of thunder that shook the ground. The little girls squealed, then went back to making up stories about Phoebe's adventures.

Lightning struck again. The inside of the wagon turned brighter than daylight for an instant then dark as midnight outside again as the thunder rolled.

Through a break in the canvas, Ellie could see the lightning's jagged strikes in a macabre dance across the plains. It was beautiful, both in its might and its danger. But with each strike, she could see the wet, scraggly herd in the distance, and her awe of the storm's power quickly turned to worry about Alexander and Abe.

She glanced at Liza and saw the concern in her friend's face as well.

"God is with us all," Liza said gently. "We aren't alone in this horrible storm."

They turned the conversation to news of their families and friends, trying to keep their minds off the storm. But the rain continued to fall, a steady pounding on the canvas.

After a time, Ellie stood and made her way through the tangle of barrels and boxes to the rear of the wagon. Lifting the flap, she was surprised to see the deepening lake of mud that surrounded them. She turned again to Liza. "Even if it stopped right now, we wouldn't be able to leave until this mud dries. It's already up to the wheel hubs."

Liza joined her, lifting the other side of the canvas flap. "It looks bad," she agreed. "But we know how strong that prairie sun is. If it comes out full force, this will dry out in nothing flat."

Meg and Sarah had moved to the cornhusk mattress, plopped down, and were now making up a new version of Phoebe's travels with the Pawnee. The two women returned to the small table and settled again into the two farm chairs.

"How are you feeling, Ellie?" Liza asked, leaning forward and keeping her voice low so as not to worry the children. "I saw you rubbing your back the other day while you were walking beside the team."

"I'm feeling more early pangs than I did with the twins," Ellie admitted with a frown. "But it's at night when they're the worst. In my back."

"When is the baby due?" Liza asked.

"Not until the end of September."

"You'll have the baby before we get to California, then."

Ellie nodded. "Yes. I figure we'll be crossing the Sierra Nevadas about the time this wee one arrives." She patted her stomach. "I just hope it won't be in the snow."

"I'll be with you when your time comes, Ellie. I'm here to help in every way I can." Liza's expression softened. "But think of the joy! God is giving you this child when you thought there would be no more."

Ellie nodded. "He's a miracle baby. I know God's got a special purpose for him." She laughed lightly. "Or he wouldn't have given him to us at this worst possible time."

Outside, the storm continued to howl, and the rain sheeted off the canvas. Liza frowned. "I know you're worried. But don't fret about the snow in the Sierra Nevadas. I've heard most of the companies head through Utah Territory if there's a question about the snows hitting early. Abe said there's a well-marked California road called the Old Spanish Trail that heads off south from the Great Salt Lake."

"Through Mormon country?" Ellie said. Something unsettling about that route nagged her but she didn't know why, so she dismissed the thought.

Liza laughed. "I've heard they're good-hearted folks who've been treated miserably in some of the places they've lived. They've been persecuted and run clear out of towns in Missouri and Illinois. Homes burnt. Families killed. The Missourians still hold a special hatred for them."

"I wonder how they treat folks heading through their territory." Ellie said, settling against her chair and absently rubbing the small of her back.

"I suppose unless you're from Missouri, you'd be treated fairly," Liza said wryly. "Besides, Utah is a U.S. territory. We're not entering a foreign country. Mormons are good, law-abiding citizens who treat their visitors in a law-abiding manner. I've heard they're right hospitable." She smiled. "Even if this storm delays us and we have to take that route, I'm certain we'll find them gratified we've come their way, even more gratified to sell us their wares . . . though for a dear price."

Ellie shivered as a gust of wind hit the canvas sides of the wagon, causing it to quiver and creak. After a time, she pulled out some venison jerky and hardtack and berry preserves, and the little group ate their supper, listening as the winds howled and the unrelenting deluge continued.

Liza spent the night with them, insisting that Ellie sleep on the mattress with the twins while she curled up on a pallet of patchwork quilts.

But Ellie couldn't sleep. Again, she wondered about the unsettled feeling she had over the thought of heading into Utah Territory. Things had been so hectic as they were packing and readying to leave, she could've heard any tidbit of gossip and forgotten it three minutes later.

But what was it she'd heard about the Mormons? Who had she heard it from? A circuit preacher perhaps? A neighbor?

She supposed that at the time she heard it, Utah Territory seemed too far away to give much thought to, its people too foreign to identify with, so she hadn't dwelt on Utah or its people . . . until now.

Just as she was falling asleep, it came to her.

The twins were snoring lightly, so she pulled herself up on one elbow, resting her cheek on her palm, facing Liza's pallet. "Liza," she whispered, hoping her friend was still awake. "Liza!"

"I'm awake. What's wrong?" Liza whispered back.

"A circuit preacher came by a few weeks before we left. He'd just ridden from Van Buren." She leaned closer and dropped her voice to an even softer whisper. "He said there'd been a murder there."

Liza sat up on her pallet. "That's just down the road a piece from our home place."

Ellie nodded. "I can't remember the details. Only that it happened in Arkansas. Seems a Mormon was shot down in cold blood. The killer's wife had run off with the Mormon."

"I've heard of that happening before, but it doesn't have to lead to murder," Liza said sleepily, lying down again.

"Wait!" Ellie whispered loudly. "There's more."

"Hmmm?"

"It seems the Mormon already had several wives."

"What?" Liza was sitting up again. "You know for certain that's true?"

"The circuit preacher said Saints believe in polygamy. They don't believe people are married legally unless it's in their own ceremony."

"I always thought polygamy was a rumor," Liza whispered.

"The preacher is a good man. He doesn't repeat idle gossip. I'm sure he was telling the truth."

Liza was quiet for a moment. "I wonder why a woman would agree to take a husband who already has a wife. Nothing would ever make me agree to such a thing."

"Hmmm," Ellie mused in agreement, lowering her head back

onto her pillow. "I wonder why anyone would want to share the man she loves with someone else. I can't imagine it."

Several minutes ticked by, when she remembered something else. "Liza?"

"More news about the Saints?" Liza's tone was light but sleepy.

"I remember the reverend saying the man was a special agent of Brigham Young. I'm wondering how the Mormons would take to seeing folks from Arkansas," Ellie murmured, "if they place blame."

"How could they blame the entire state?" Liza asked sleepily. Then she chuckled. "Imagine such a thing."

Ellie didn't laugh with her but pulled her covers over her shoulders and closed her eyes, listening to the rain striking the canvas. She didn't fall asleep until it was nearly dawn.

It rained hard for three days without pause. The lightning and thunder and heavy winds moved on after the first night, but the rain continued from a leaden sky, relentless, dumping a damp and muddy misery on the travelers.

The morning of the fourth day, Alexander, worrying about falling behind schedule, ordered the wagoners to line up their wagons and start moving again.

It was a futile attempt. The rain-soaked wagons were heavier than usual, and the women and children had to ride inside because of the rain and mud. The oxen bleated, and the horses reared and snorted in protest as they strained to pull rigs that were sunk hub-deep in mud. Axles broke on four different wagons, causing further delays when the company was forced to stop for repairs. That day they made less than three miles.

The following day they were able to travel only one mile. And still the rain poured.

That afternoon Alexander called the men together in the center of the wagon circle. At the front of the group were Jesse O'Donnell, Josiah Miller, and Pleasant Tackett. Reverend Brown was a ways back, and Abe Barrett was at his side as usual. Just as they started talking, the Mitchell and Prewitt boys joined them, back from riding out to check the herd. They were followed by the foreman, Silas Edwards, on his high-stepping bay. Rain drizzled from their hat brims and their oilskin rain gear. The boys and Edwards quickly dismounted, and their horses whinnied and stamped impatiently.

Alexander wiped his face then explained to the men that with the delay it would be prudent to double back to where the Cherokee Trail joined the Santa Fe, follow it west as far as Bent's Fort, and then head due north up the eastern face of the Rockies, past Pike's Peak to Fort Laramie, where they would meet the California-Oregon road.

There were several reasons for this plan, he explained. The cattle would have better grazing land. The Santa Fe Trail was used for trade—it wouldn't be overgrazed, and the trail wouldn't be as taxing on the herd. "This way it's a greater distance in miles," he concluded. "But overall it will be the fastest. I figure we'd arrive at Laramie right on schedule—by mid-July, maybe earlier."

"Too dangerous," Silas Edwards countered, rain streaming from his hat. "It's not as well traveled. We're courting disaster to try it. If we're too late to cross the Sierras . . ." He didn't finish, but Alexander knew Edwards—and all the others—were thinking about the Donner company of '46, trapped in severe storms for months with no food.

"I see the stretch between Pike's Peak and Laramie being our only concern," Abe Barrett said. "That's Cheyenne and Arapaho country."

"The Santa Fe is heavily traveled. Also patrolled by government troops. But you're right, Abe, about the rest. We'd have to post guards of our own after we reach the Cherokee road cutoff."

The men discussed the idea for a few minutes, and Farrington could see some of the men weren't in agreement with his plan.

Edwards's face was set in a scowl. "If this is a better route, why didn't you plan on it from the beginning?" he grumbled. "Think where we'd be by now."

"The Santa Fe's a commerce trail. That means it was made for cargo wagons—Conestogas, the heaviest wagons made," Alexander explained patiently. "And for good reason. A wagon can get pretty beat up on that trail. Most of us have light farm wagons. That's why it wasn't my first choice."

"How much time do you suppose we'll lose by doubling back?" Abe asked.

"Maybe a week," the captain said. "More or less."

"Plus what we're losing because of the storm," Abe said.

Reverend Brown spoke up. "We'll lose more time if we continue on north. Any of you thought what the Smoky Hill River will be like? After a storm this size, we won't be able to cross for days."

The men spoke a few minutes more about their options, and Alexander could see some were discontent with his decision. A feeling of disquiet settled over him for the first time since they pulled out of Crooked Creek. This company of friends and family might not be so congenial toward him or each other by the time they struck Laramie.

He and Abe rode back to the wagons in the still-pouring rain. He couldn't shake the feeling of apprehension.

The deluge lasted four more days. Then it took three more days for the ground to harden enough to hold the weight of the teams and rigs. By the time they had doubled back to the Cherokee Trail, they had lost two more crucial weeks of travel time.

As the train rolled out once more, Alexander kept his fears to himself: It would be a hard push to make Laramie by mid-July. It would be harder still to cross the towering Sierra Nevada Mountains before the first snow.

Fifteen

During the first week of June, they turned west onto the Santa Fe Trail, discouraged because they still had nearly two thousand miles to go. A spirit of nervous disquiet settled on many; they knew they had fallen behind schedule, and time was a precious commodity they could ill afford to lose.

Ellie heard some in the company blaming Alexander for the blunder of starting north when they should have planned to head west on the Cherokee-Santa Fe from the beginning. Then they complained the outfit should have left earlier in the spring.

Others defended the captain, especially in Ellie's presence, saying the rain delay would have happened anyway. After all, it didn't just rain over that one spot where they'd camped in the mud in Kansas Territory. Ellie tried to ignore the scuttlebutt, but her heart ached for Alexander.

As soon as the train pulled onto the Santa Fe Trail, Ellie found herself wide-eyed at her first good look at the huge freight wagons and their drivers—the old mule skinners, or bullwhackers, as they called themselves. Just as she had read, their wagons were piled high with goods for trade in Santa Fe: hardware, cutlery, hats, shirting, linens, hosiery, and anything else the traders thought might bring a profit.

But soon the novelty of seeing the freighters wore off, and the long days melted into each other then repeated their white-hot rhythm as the days melted into weeks. The tall spring grasses turned gold then brown, becoming sparse and dry, until finally disappearing altogether.

The creaking of the wagon wheels became louder as the wood shrank and dried. The air turned hot, seeming to cause the ground to sizzle and making the horizon look liquid. The parching air burnt Ellie's lungs as the company moved across the flat, dry land that now seemed more desert than prairie. But Alexander kept the train moving, most days insisting on fifteen miles, some twelve, a few close to twenty.

The dust rose under the slow hooves of the cattle and horses. It settled on Ellie's skin and filled her nose, caught in the back of her throat, and gritted her teeth, making her wonder if she would ever be clean again. The sun seared through her bonnet, and her head throbbed with the nearly unbearable firelike burning of it. Sometimes she wondered how the babe inside her could survive the heat, but somehow he did survive—even thrived, as evident in the changes in her body.

At night, Ellie and the twins scrubbed in the nearby Arkansas River to rid themselves of the dust and grit. But by the next evening, they had to start all over again.

Sarah and Meg seemed content enough with the hard journey. They complained less often and, overall, had quieted somewhat.

They had plenty of water, following the Arkansas River as they did. And buffalo provided fresh meat, though sightings of the herds, once within eyeshot of the road, now grew scarcer. Alexander, Abe, Pleasant Tackett, and some of the cattlehands left the company to find herds north of the Arkansas where the grasses were more abundant and the herds still grazed.

More Indians, mostly Comanche and Kiowa, and once in a while some southern Cheyenne as they neared the Cimarron cutoff, tagged along, begging for food and trinkets. Alexander said it was better to feed them or give them small mirrors, trinkets, or jewelry to avoid conflict later. The Indians in the Southwest were far more aggressive, he added as a warning to all, than those they'd seen so far.

By mid-June, the party arrived at the Cimarron cutoff. They headed the lumbering train northwest onto the mountain road, toward Bent's Fort, now a few dusty days away, where they would replenish their supplies. Some mule skinners on the Santa Fe had warned them that the fort's reserves were meager, and though she didn't voice her worries to either Alexander or Liza, still Ellie worried.

"What's Bent's Fort like?" Ellie asked her husband the morning they were due to arrive. He had just finished lifting the box of iron cookware and plates and utensils into the back of the wagon. Though she felt strong enough to perform her usual chores, Alexander now insisted that he do all heavy lifting when possible.

He hoisted Meg up to the wagon bed then reached down and did the same for Sarah, who was holding the ever-present Phoebe. "Just one building," he said, answering Ellie's question. "One large, dusty, sun-parched adobe building," he laughed. "Hardly qualifies as a fort."

"And this is where we resupply?" Ellie didn't laugh with him, feeling suddenly vulnerable.

"That's it."

"We've still got quite a ways to go before we get to Laramie." She tried not to sound worried.

"The game we find will hold us. Then the Laramie supplies will last us to Bridger. And, of course, until we reach the Mormon settlements north of Utah."

Ellie had heard the rumors about taking the southern route to California. "Have you decided for sure, Alexander? I mean, to go through Utah Territory?"

"Actually, I was talking about the settlements along the trail—not those in the territory. But I see no reason not to take the Old Spanish Trail to California, if we need to. A lot depends on our timing. We'll know more once we get to Laramie."

"I worry about going through Utah," she said suddenly. "There's just something that doesn't set well with me about the idea."

She was surprised to see the concern in his face. Then he laughed as if to alleviate her fears. "I've heard the Saints will be more than happy to turn our desperation into dollars. Especially when they see a wealthy train like this one heading into their territory."

"Of course it depends on how desperate we are, doesn't it?" Ellie asked solemnly.

Her husband nodded. "If we do travel through Mormon country, it will be because we're desperate. And they'll have us over a barrel. The cost will be high. There's no doubt about that." Then he laughed. "Of course, the Saints aren't alone when it comes to driving a tough bargain. I think most folks would do the same in their place."

That afternoon the company halted at Bent's Fort, though only long enough to purchase a few supplies for a premium price then move on without delay. When they pulled out again, there was more talk about resupplying in Laramie.

That night by the fire, some voiced concerns that the cattle were thinning too fast because of grazing on the dry, sparse, spindly brush of the Santa Fe instead of the lush, taller grasses of the California-Oregon Trail. Some said they'd lose their shirts if they had to buy grain in Utah. Then the talk turned to the people who called themselves Saints. There was endless speculation about their beliefs and practices. Ellie and Liza exchanged looks as their theology was bantered about. Ellie suspected that some of the bizarre practices talked about were probably fabricated, though she didn't say so. They seemed too outrageous to be true.

The train snaked onward across the dry-grass plain, and it seemed to Ellie the entire company was ever mindful of the stark, clear sunrises at their backs and the blinding red sunsets heating their faces.

Even the eternal optimist Liza Barrett spoke up one night by the fire about the feeling that they'd covered no distance at all when they measured the span behind. She said that it seemed an eternity to go when they looked ahead.

Yet westward, ever westward, they trudged, finally leaving even the blessed waters of the Arkansas. And the days of white-hot sun beat down harder than before, stretching one after another into searing, still, and cloudless weeks.

Ellie tended to the twins' blistered lips, sunburned faces, and thin, bite-covered limbs; she did what she could with her own swollen feet and hands.

Wearily, so wearily, with Alexander riding by her side, she cracked the whip over the team again and again as the wagon wheels creaked and the oxen bawled and the mules brayed, heads down, methodically placing one sore hoof before another.

They turned off the Santa Fe, north onto the lonely Cherokee cutoff, the portion of the trail that would lead them along the eastern face of the Rockies. It was spoken of, sometimes in whispers, as the loneliest, bleakest, most danger-filled part of the journey they had yet faced.

By summer solstice they got their first glimpse of the mountains.

Polly O'Donnell was the first to spot Pike's Peak, and her pronouncement brought the first lighthearted touch to Ellie's life that she'd known in weeks. "We're almost halfway!" Polly shouted. "This is the place. Pike's Peak marks the spot!"

The others looked. Sure enough, barely visible in the afterglow of sunset, the peak's silhouette rose into the sky. Hats were thrown into the air as cheers and whoops and hollers sounded up and down the long train.

Later, at the night fire, a spirit of spontaneous celebration lightened hearts and feet. Abe Barrett pulled out his fiddle and started to play "Oh! Susanna." Hampton Farrington joined in with his harmonica as his wife, Sadie, watched with shining eyes. And to everyone's surprise, old Reverend Brown hobbled to his wagon and back with a washtub. Stringing a catgut from it to the top of a pole, he twanged along when Abe and Hampton swung into "Camptown Races."

Ellie caught Hampton and Alexander exchanging a look of pride, as if each recognized in the other the exhilaration of their shared adventure. *Father and son, so alike,* she thought. Though Hampton was leaner and darker than her husband, he was just as serious in his pursuits. There was also that fiery light in his gray eyes that spoke clearly of his love of family and life and God—just like the light in

Alexander's. And, of course, Hampton had that same burning in his gut for the grand trek west. But that burning wasn't limited to the Farrington men, she realized, looking at all the faces in the firelight. Each man here, and probably many of the women, had that same burning in their souls.

By now the singing and dancing were in full swing. Holding hands, Sarah and Meg whirled by. Alexander's nephew, James, danced by with Melissa Ann Beller. James's brother, Robert, swung Liza's granddaughter, Vinia, into his arms, and at the same time, the Prewitt and Mitchell boys each grabbed the hands of the older O'Donnell girls and began clapping and laughing and whirling around the night fire.

To one side, Ellie sat on a barrel tapping her foot to "Old Folks at Home" and watching Alexander, who was talking to Josiah Miller about tomorrow's trek. Josiah's wife, Mary, stood nearby, swaying and singing to the music, looking impatient to dance with her husband.

Alexander seemed to sense Ellie's gaze and looked up with a raised brow. Then, crossing over to where she sat on the flour barrel, he reached for her hand.

"I don't know that I should dance," she said. "Just look at me." She looked down at the evidence of the growing child within her.

"Do your feet feel like dancing, dearest?" he asked.

"Well, yes. But maybe it's not seemly."

He smiled into her eyes. "You've never looked more beautiful to me," he said softly. He turned her hand over, rubbed the calluses with his thumb, then lifted his gaze again to her eyes. "Never," he said. "And that's what's seemly to me."

She looked up at Alexander, his hair shining in the firelight, the love in his eyes glowing just as brightly. He pulled her into his arms as the musicians started "My Old Kentucky Home," and they began to move with the music.

Gradually, others joined in around them, children and old folks. Reverend Brown put down the washtub and asked Liza to dance. She consented, but Abe wanted to dance with her himself and handed his fiddle to Billy Farrington, who started sawing his bow to "Oh!

Susanna" again, one of the very few songs he could play. Billy's wife, Bess, stood nearby tapping her foot and clapping to the beat.

Around and around the circle they whirled, the captain and Ellie, Jesse and Polly O'Donnell, Liza and Abe Barrett, Pleasant and Cynthia Tackett, William and Martha Cameron. Even the Reverend asked Jane Farrington, Alexander's sister-in-law, to be his partner in a hoedown.

Now and then, barely heard above the sounds of laughter and singing, the coyotes' barking yips and the owls' lonely calls drifted from the distant hills. The fiddle and harmonica played on into the deep night, now sweet and playful, now sad and melancholy. When it was done, Alexander pulled his mandolin out of the wagon and strummed "O God, Our Help in Ages Past."

Soft voices joined him in chorus: mothers, young and old, holding babes in arms and fathers cuddling toddlers in their laps and older couples clinging to each other. All lifted their voices heavenward.

"Before the hills in order stood,
Or earth received her frame,
From everlasting thou art God,
Through endless years the same."

Above the huddled families stretched a canopy of stars, blazing pinpricks of shimmering fire in a velvet black sky. Ellie thought there'd never been a finer evening.

Long after the travelers had gone to their wagons for the night, two figures stole silently away from the circle. When they had reached a small embankment not far from the herd, Silas Edwards turned to Abe Barrett.

"Some of us have been talking," Silas said.

"About what?"

Silas cleared his throat. "We've been giving the captain the benefit of the doubt. Waiting for him to push us harder, to move us along faster, to make up for his blunder. Make up for the time we lost. But he's not doing it."

"Why come to me? What do you think I can do about it?"

"Talk to him. Tell him we're wasting time. That we need to be moving along from daylight to dusk. We should be doing twenty miles a day instead of fifteen. He'll listen to you."

"He's got his reasons for keeping the pace slow. Don't forget we've got old people along. Folks like Reverend Brown. And the captain's being careful of the livestock. He knows the toll moving too fast would take. It's not worth it. I've heard him say so."

"If our crossing's too late, skinny stock will be the least of our troubles."

Abe looked hard at the man standing next to him. "I'd be careful if I were you." Abe thought for a minute. "The captain's a tough man. Especially tough against those he might think are against him."

"I wish he'd get tougher about the time runnin' against him," Silas countered.

"He knows the dangers we face. I trust his judgment."

"Some of us've been talking about going to him with our complaints," Silas continued. "Give him a chance to prove himself."

"Or what? What're you talking about, man?" Abe was getting angry and wondering why he'd agreed to talk to Silas. It didn't matter that the man was Alexander's trusted foreman over the herd and cattlehands. He was hinting at mutiny.

"I'm talking about electing a new captain. Pure and simple. One who'd get us over the Sierras before it snows."

"You're going too far. I won't be party to it."

"Maybe you will when you find out what else he's got on his mind."

"What are you talking about?"

"There's talk he considering taking the Old Spanish Trail through Utah Territory."

"So what if he is? Many wagon trains head through the territory. Get charged an arm and a leg for supplies, but other than that . . ." He shrugged.

"He's considering his options because we're running so far behind schedule."

"Maybe they're good options."

"I didn't tell you what else I heard."

Abe stared at the man. "What?"

"When we were back on the Santa Fe, an old mule skinner told me on good authority that the president of the United States is about to send troops to Utah Territory to put down an uprising."

"A mule skinner told you that?"

Silas nodded.

"And who'd he hear it from?" Abe laughed. "Some lizard on the trail?" He shook his head. "Think about it, man. The Saints leading some kind of rebellion against the government of the United States? I've never heard anything so half-witted."

"He didn't say how he knew."

"Well, then, it sounds like a rumor to me," Abe said. "Someone's trying to embellish the truth." He paused, shaking his head. "Or telling a bald-faced lie. That's what I think."

Silas Edward stared at him, and when he spoke again his voice had lost its fire. "I hope you're right, Abe," he said with a deep sigh. "I hope you're right."

Sixteen

Dust billowed under the slow feet of the herd in the distance. The wind carried the dust backward, hot and thick, and it settled on the Farrington company, their teams, their wagons. By now the arched canvas covers, once as white and lofty as ships' sails, had turned a dingy brown-gray.

Northward they moved, the sounds of the bawling and complaining cattle carrying back to Ellie as she walked beside her team. She now kept a kerchief over her nose and mouth and smaller cloths over the twins' faces, but nothing kept their necks and hands from turning dark from the sun and coarse from the wind. The sun bore down as hot as fire, and with growing dismay, Ellie realized that the creeks for washing and drinking were now farther apart than before.

The days dragged by with the train winding slowly forward, the high wagon tops swaying as wheels hit ruts and bumps. Now the oxen were thinner, plodding along even more slowly with their massive heads down, and despite her own weariness Ellie walked beside them rather than giving them the added burden of her weight in the wagon. Meg and Sarah, with Phoebe tucked safely under her arm, still playful for all their tiring journey, climbed on and off the wagon, sometimes falling, sometimes laughing, sometimes crying.

To the sides of the trail, Ellie pointed out to her daughters various prairie dogs, slow-waddling porcupines, and owls. But she didn't show them the human bones, skulls and rib cages, parched white from the sun, sometimes close by the trail, other times scattered off in the distance, dragged there by wolves or coyotes. If Alexander was riding beside her as they passed the bones, their eyes would meet in silent acknowledgment.

Some of the more curious boys, especially Alexander's nephews, James and Robert, along with David Beller, tried to figure from bits of clothing which skeletons were those of Indians and which were those of white travelers. But the rest of the company spoke in hushed tones as they passed, as if they didn't want to know.

Sometimes Ellie spotted wolves in the early mornings and evenings, tails down, yellow eyes intelligent. But they kept their distance, their expressions watchful; she wondered if they somehow sensed the coming buffalo hunts.

Herds of buffalo covered more of the land now; great rolling shadows of them moved across the slopes and plains. And downing the beasts became more sport than necessity. Fresh meat was now plentiful, too plentiful, and Ellie watched carefully that Sarah and Meg didn't eat too much; many of the older folks and children suffered with diarrhea and dehydration because of it.

Weeks passed, and the train pushed closer to where the Cherokee Trail intersected the California-Oregon road near Laramie. The spirits of the people and teams seemed to rise knowing they were just days away. The country turned from flat to rolling hills, and trees hung gracefully over streams of water. The shade and the cool-water springs and good grass appeared more often now.

Wagons tipped and creaked and rattled as the terrain roughened. The oxen leaned into their yokes. Slower now they moved, careful of the swaying and tipping.

The captain was the first to spot Fort Laramie. He had ridden out ahead of the train and was on a rise above the slope leading down to the fort. There it lay below him, with its sun-bleached buildings and stands of trees casting welcome shadows on the grass, the first woods they'd seen in weeks—lush, verdant woods that promised cool shade and soft breezes.

Alexander was struck by how much it had changed since he'd been there years before. Then it had been a dusty group of buildings built by early fur trappers. Now, he figured, no self-respecting mountain man would darken its gates.

Since the California gold rush, it had become a way station for tens of thousands of emigrants heading west, a gathering place for ragtag tribes of Indians—mostly Dakota Sioux—dependent on government handouts, and a post for second-rate traders to sell buffalo skins.

Laramie Creek was at the base of the slope where Alexander stood, and beyond it he could see a scraggly group of Indians begging by the entrance to the fort. The captain remembered the magnificent and proud bronzed Dakota Sioux warriors who had once raised their tepees near the fort. It was sad to see the majestic people reduced to such measures. Glancing one last time at the fort, he reined the Appaloosa and returned to the wagon company.

One by one the wagons reached the crest of the hill overlooking the Laramie, then rumbled down the other side and splashed through the creek. With the pounding of hooves, the jangle of yoke chains, and the shouting of the teamsters as they moved, the families, little ones, and even the elderly hollered out in delight as they crested the hill and saw the fort.

It was their first sighting of civilization in months, and it was also the first time they had laid eyes on the California road.

As Ellie's rig crested the hill, she halted the team and stood with the twins beside her. Liza, whose wagon followed Ellie's, halted her oxen as well and walked forward to stand with the group. Ellie was glad to stop for the rest. She had kept her discomfort to herself, but since morning, pains stung her abdomen with each step. She rubbed her back anxiously.

Liza was looking down the hill at Laramie. "There're buildings. Think of it!" she laughed. "Real buildings, Ellie."

"And trees!" little Sarah added, as much in awe of the sight as Liza Barrett was.

"Look!" Meg shouted. "There's grass as green as tree frogs."

"How long will we stay here, Mommy?" Sarah asked.

"Just overnight, child," Ellie answered.

"I'd like to stay here forever," Meg said with a dramatic sigh. "My legs are so tired of walking."

Liza pulled the little girl into a hug. "So are mine, child," she said. "So are mine."

The oxen started down the slope on their own, the smell of water prodding them better than any whip could. Meg and Sarah took off after them, laughing and shouting, trying to get them to stop.

Ellie and Liza followed, picking their way among the rocks and low-growing shrubs.

Then Ellie felt another deep and searing pain in her lower abdomen. She gasped and doubled over. Liza was immediately by her side, supporting Ellie with her arm. Meg and Sarah, already by the creek bank, turned with worried expressions as the oxen lumbered to a halt beside them and stretched their necks to drink.

"Ellie, what is it?" Liza whispered just as another stabbing pang shuddered through Ellie's body. She slipped to the ground, and Liza knelt beside her, enfolding her in her arms. "Lean against me, Ellie," she said. "Close your eyes and breathe deeply."

Ellie nodded, unable to speak until the pain subsided, and Liza went on, her voice low and soothing. "It's going to be all right. Just relax."

Ellie did as Liza said and kept her eyes closed for another few minutes. She could hear the twins' worried voices coming closer, then little hands touched hers. She took another deep breath and felt the pain subside. Finally she opened her eyes. Meg and Sarah's faces had paled with worry.

"Easy now," Liza said, supporting Ellie as she stood. "Easy."

"I—I'm all right," she said shakily. "Just a bit weak, that's all." She leaned against Liza for a moment. Meg and Sarah put their arms around her on the other side, and slowly, very slowly, they walked down to the creek.

Ellie knelt and patted some cold water on her face then settled onto a flat boulder to rest. The children splashed and played in the water, and after about ten minutes, she felt her strength return.

"Do you want me to fetch Alexander?" Liza asked.

"No, don't bother him with this. I'm all right, really." She looked toward the Laramie gate, knowing that her husband was inside seeing the commander about the company's accommodations. "It's only a few hundred yards or so. I can make it."

"If you promise to lean on me," Liza said seriously, "and go to bed and rest for the remainder of the day, once we're inside."

Ellie smiled, trying to calm Liza's fears—and her own. "I promise," she said. "But I've got a strong hankerin' for a soak in a nice hot bath right after. I've been thinking about that since we left Crooked Creek."

Liza laughed. "I'll find the means to get you just that while you're resting. I might even try it out myself, though I might not ever get out again once I'm under those bubbles." She shouted for some nearby wagoners to take over moving their rigs across the creek, then she stood and circled her arm around Ellie's waist. Ellie leaned on her, and they slowly made their way across the creek and up the bank on the other side.

Moments later, with one twin skipping on either side, Ellie and Liza slowly walked through Laramie's tall, wooden gateway that was flanked by a dusty band of Sioux and a few scraggly traders. Their stacks of smelly buffalo skins covered with flies caused Ellie's stomach to lurch. She swayed slightly, and Liza helped her catch her balance. As they passed the Indians, Sarah clutched Phoebe close, hiding the doll in her arms.

Just as dusk settled over Laramie, in a makeshift saloon at the rear of the fort Alexander and Abe Barrett waited to meet with two men who had given their names as Matthias Graves and Red Jakes and hailed from Missouri. The men had seen the Farrington company arrive and asked for a meeting with the captain, saying it would be a time of mutual interest.

Alexander had agreed, figuring they wanted to connect up with the company. Wagon trains often joined up with others traveling the same direction, parted, then joined up with still others. It was considered to be mutually beneficial when it happened.

Farrington knew that the Missourians would gain from such an alliance, but when the unkempt men slumped into their chairs at his table, he wondered why he'd agreed to talk to them. Before they had even stated their case, something told him they were trouble.

The first man to speak, Matthias Graves, a lean, hard-muscled man with straw-colored hair, leaned forward, his expression earnest. "You all are running late," he began. "Not a good thing with what all's ahead." He worked his jaw as he waited for Farrington's response.

Alexander nodded but didn't speak.

"We're lookin' to find a company to hitch up with," Red Jakes said. His piercing pale eyes reminded Alexander of a hawk's. His hair, the little he had, hung in a greasy red fringe above his ears.

Farrington exchanged a look with Abe, but neither spoke. A half-smile curled Graves's lips, replacing the rippling of his jaw.

"We hear you all are headin' to California," Jakes said, grinning and scratching his head. "We're a small company—thirty-one members, headin' the same direction as you. We'd be much obliged to carry on with your train."

Graves leaned forward again. "We'll keep our herd separate. You'll never know we're trailin' along behind."

Farrington didn't like the looks of either of the men any better now than he had before. "Well, men, I hate to disappoint you. But we're running late, just as you said," he said. "We're a company of families, old folks, and younguns. We won't be traveling much faster now than before." He paused. "I don't think hitching up with us would do you much good."

"We thought you might be planning on picking up time by headin' through enemy territory."

"Enemy territory?" Abe asked, frowning. "What are you talking about?"

Graves laughed. "Mormon country. I think both of our parties are too late to cross the Sierra Nevadas. By necessity, we'll have to make our way through Utah Territory."

"I would hardly call the Mormons our enemies," Alexander said, shaking his head slightly.

Graves and Jakes exchanged a knowing look then laughed again loudly. "You don't know much then, Cap'n," Red Jakes said with a guffaw.

The cattlehands and traders at the bar and other patrons at tables scattered throughout the small room now turned to listen to the lively conversation.

"What are you talking about?" the captain asked, his impatience growing for these men and their rude manner.

"They're out to git us Gentiles," Red Jakes pronounced importantly. "I hear they're sworn to git even with all of the good ol' U.S.A. for killing their Prophet."

Before Alexander could even begin to understand what the men were talking about, Graves sat back, teetering on his chair legs, and narrowed his eyes. "What we're gettin' at, Cap'n," he said sardonically, "is that your company and mine are gonna be headin' south through Utah in just a few weeks. The disposition of those people toward us Gentiles ain't good, I tell you. Ain't good at all. I doubt we can git through Mormon country in one piece."

There was a burst of laughter from the rest of the room at the ridiculous statement. Though fiercely protective and prone to drive hard bargains, the Mormons had a well-known reputation as a peace-loving people. Even Alexander smiled when Abe Barrett rolled his eyes and slowly shook his head.

But the Missourians didn't laugh.

Alexander let out a deep breath and nodded slowly at the unkempt men. "First of all, I'm not certain we can't make it over the Sierra

Nevadas before winter sets in. Secondly, what you're saying about the Mormons simply is not true. I've been through Utah myself and found the people hospitable. Their beliefs may strike us as curious . . ." The minute he said it, Alexander knew he shouldn't have mentioned the Saints' beliefs.

Red Jakes hit the table. "A bit strange!" he hooted. "Why, these folks believe they can be gods! Did you know that? Gods!" he repeated incredulously.

By now the room had fallen deathly quiet, silent enough for each man to hear Jakes add in a clear voice, "That's why I'm proud I was in on the killing of their Prophet."

He paused dramatically, looking around at his audience. "I stood up for what I know to be right. Those lyin', thievin' Saints had robbed us of all that was decent back in Missouri. And me and my friends took the law into our own hands. I was in on the shootin' of Joseph Smith and his brother, Hyrum, myself."

He let out a colorful string of curse words. "You should've heard that Prophet of the Saints cuss as he tried to get off some shots. But we was too good for him. He could have begged for mercy, but it wouldn't have done him any good. He was a goner."

Alexander wanted to be rid of these men as quickly as possible. He cut into Jakes's tirade before the man could go on. "As I said," the captain repeated slowly, "we're traveling too slow for your group. We'll take our chances . . . alone."

Jakes set his lips into a hard, half-sided smile. "Well, Cap'n, you're probably right. We'll go our way, and you just go yours." He chuckled and pushed back his chair to stand. "You watch. We'll probably end up in the same place anyway." He laughed again as Graves also stood.

They had almost reached the door when Graves turned and looked back at Alexander and Abe. "You do know about the troops."

"What troops?" Abe Barrett asked with a frown.

Red Jakes lolled against the doorway, wearing a thin-lipped grin. "You haven't heard?"

"There's about to be a war," Jakes said. "With the Mormons."

Again there was laughter in the room.

Red Jakes rubbed his balding scalp and stared at Farrington. "Johnston's army's preparing to march to war. Two thousand troops. Goin' to war, I tell you. In Utah."

Farrington settled back in his chair. "We haven't heard of it." He glanced at some of the men in the room. "Anybody else in here heard of a Utah war?"

Several cowhands playing poker in a corner shrugged. One said, "Nah," without looking up from his hand. A bearded man who stood by the rough-hewn bar nodded. "I heard somethin' about it some weeks back, but I ain't heard nothin' since."

Alexander was surprised when Abe spoke up. "Someone in the train said he'd heard it on the Santa Fe. Heard it from an old mule skinner."

Then a young man dressed in black and sitting in the rear corner of the room spoke up. "I heard something about it not too long ago." He teetered on the back legs of his chair, leaning against the wall, his hat pulled low over his eyes. His eyes briefly met Farrington's.

"What'd you hear?" Alexander got the feeling the man knew more than he let on.

"That troops are on their way."

"Where'd you hear it?"

For a moment the man in black didn't speak. "From a ferry captain on the Weber River—back near Bridger." He sounded reluctant to give any more information, but he added, "It might've been rumor."

Jakes cleared his throat then cleaned something from his teeth with his tongue. He stared at the young man in black. "Strikes me as odd you'd be comin' from someplace so close to the enemy. You one of them thievin' Saints, boy?"

The young man simply returned the hard stare and didn't answer.

Finally, Jakes turned back to the captain. "Something tells me you all are poorly informed, wouldn't you say so, Matthias?"

Graves laughed, looking straight at the captain. "Seems to me that an outfit so far behind schedule is probably just as far behind on the news."

A few minutes later the two men meandered out the doorway. The sound of their boots clomping down the wooden walkway disappeared into the hubbub of people milling about the fort.

Lucas Knight, still teetering his chair against the wall, clasped his hands behind his head and looked across the room at the captain of the wagon company. The captain's suspicions were correct. Lucas did know more than he'd let on, much more. He'd already been to Fort Kearney and inquired about the troop movement west. The man who'd spoken earlier was right—two thousand troops were preparing to march to Utah. And Lucas was heading back with the news.

Lucas was watching the captain, trying to decide if he should speak to him privately, tell him to steer clear of the territory and why, when Red Jakes and Matthias Graves burst back through the saloon's swinging doors.

Jakes strode across the room to face Lucas.

"You know how to read?" He grinned wickedly.

Lucas nodded.

"You want to know why those so-called Saints . . ." He drew out the word as if it felt filthy in his mouth. ". . . those Saints are gonna catch what's comin to them?"

Lucas didn't take the bait. He kept his voice low and calm. "Why's that?"

Jakes scratched his greasy thatch of red hair then waved a folded yellowed newspaper page at Lucas. "This here's why. You just read this." And he handed the paper to Lucas.

"This here's from that highfalutin *New York Times.* It'll tell you why."

Lucas unfolded the paper and scanned the first few sentences.

"Where'd you get this?"

Jakes grinned. "Off a dead Saint." He spat on the floor. "He was headin' west in an awful hurry. Ran into one of my bullets." Jakes laughed at his own joke. "When I took this out of his pocket I knew why he was hurryin' along. He was riding to warn the Saints that a war's a-comin' to that place they call Deseret."

Lucas stared for a moment at Jakes then looked back at the article. It was dated May 20, 1857.

It was the account of a man named John Tobin, a soldier who had come to Utah Territory and embraced the Mormon faith. Lucas knew the man well, as did everyone in Deseret. Tobin had used his military experience to help train Brigham Young's private army. For a while he had been engaged to the Prophet's daughter Alice Young.

Then, the article stated, something happened that caused John to renounce the Mormon faith. He realized his life was in danger and he, in the company of three companions, fled south along the Old Spanish Trail—hoping to reach San Bernardino.

About seventy-five miles south of Parowan, they decided they would have better protection if they awaited the arrival of a mail train from the north.

"What's the matter. You can't read?" Jakes broke into Lucas's thoughts. "You're supposed to be readin' this to us all, not to yourself." Jakes grinned. There were murmurs of agreement from the card players in the corner.

"Yeah, read it." Two old wagoners at the bar chimed in.

Lucas shrugged. "You want to hear it, you'll hear it." Holding the paper to the dust-filled light near the window, he began to read. He started at the beginning, though he skipped through some of the details, reading aloud only those sections he wanted the group to hear.

The place Tobin and his company selected for their camp was on a ledge of rocks near some bushes. About four o'clock in the morning, the moon shining brightly at the time, the attacking party crept up and fired down from the top of a rock.

Tobin was shot in the head, a ball entering close under his eye, passing diagonally through the nose and cheek, and lodging in his neck. He was also shot in five other places and left for dead. The other men escaped into the bushes, one of them, however, having been shot in the back of the neck, and another having had two fingers shot off.

When the other men returned to camp after the attackers left they found that Tobin was still alive, and with the assistance of the mail party, who soon overtook them, they carried him along . . .

Quickly scanning the final paragraph, Lucas decided to leave it out. He looked up at the group watching him intently. He didn't realize his mistake until Jakes spoke.

"You forgot to read some parts," Jakes said. "I wonder why that is."

"Makes me wonder too," Graves, who until now had been silent, agreed. "I been noticin' while he was readin that there're other parts he left out."

"Who said I was finished?" Lucas said, his voice flat, controlled. Before anyone else could speak, he began to read the final paragraph:

There is no doubt but that the attack was planned in Salt Lake City and that orders were sent from here to execute it. It was said publicly by the Mormons, immediately after the Tobin party left the city, that they would not live to get through to California. The Mormons here, in speaking of this transaction, wink their eyes to each other and say, "The Indians are very bad on the lower road."

Lucas folded the yellowed paper, knowing he was going to have to do some fancy talking to get out of the place alive. He could see by their expressions that they thought he was hiding something—that they suspected he was a Mormon.

Feigning nonchalance, Lucas tossed the folded paper onto the table and settled back in his chair.

Red Jakes cleared his throat. "I hear tell an officer in Colonel Albert S. Johnston's army said that if the Mormons will only fight, their days are numbered. He said, 'We shall sweep them from the face of the earth, and Mormonism in Utah shall cease.' "

Lucas had heard enough. He thought of Hannah and Sophronia. And a deep anger began to boil inside him. Sweep them from the face of the earth? For what? For existing? He stood, and his chair tipped, then clattered noisily onto the floor behind him.

Every hard-eyed gaze in the room was aimed at him. Matthias Graves stood menacingly. Fighting to keep control of his actions, Lucas started to move to the doorway, but Red Jakes moved quickly to block him.

There was a murmur from the group, reminding Lucas of the sounds of wild animals before a fight. He moved his hand slowly to the bowie knife in its sheath on his belt.

"Gentlemen," the captain said suddenly, pushing back his chair and standing. "I'd like to have a word with this young man."

The room fell silent.

"Now, if you'll excuse us—" The captain looked to his friend, now standing beside him, then nodded at Lucas, a signal to head to the swinging doors of the saloon. Lucas, with the wagon captain on one side and the captain's friend on the other, moved toward the exit.

But before they reached the doorway, Lucas heard Red Jakes yell, "We're gonna kill every lousy varmint. Nits make lice!"

A roar of emotion filled Lucas's heart and mind, blotting out all reason. He whirled, and in one swift, smooth motion—just the way John Steele had so carefully taught him—he grabbed for his bowie and lunged toward the enemy.

Seventeen

Utah Territory
July 1857

On the morning of her wedding day, Hannah awoke to the sounds of a desert wind sweeping across the valley. It began shortly after dawn, low and murmuring. But by noon it gusted and screamed, bending trees and blowing sand. Hundreds of tiny new apples in Sophronia's orchard were stripped from their branches and hurled to the hot ground. The wind raked twigs and sand against the brick sides of the house, rattled the shutters, and shook the front swing.

Hannah sat at the kitchen table with her aunt. "It's a hard thing you're doing, child," Sophronia said, her eyes luminous with unshed tears.

"I can bear it," Hannah said. "It will be a marriage in name only. I may say the vows, but inside I'll be rejecting every one of them."

"Does John know that's what you're planning—I mean about not consummating the celestial vows?"

Hannah looked away. "No," she said, pausing. "I intend to keep it that way until we reach the ranch and can figure out a way to escape."

"To him those vows mean a higher place in the priesthood, in heaven. He'll not be easy with you, Hannah. He's got a mean spirit deep inside him. He's cruel. And I fear for you, child. I fear . . ."

More often now Sophronia's age showed in the deep worry lines in her face, in her frail voice, quivering now with emotion.

"I know." Hannah realized it was hard for Sophronia because she felt responsible for her outspoken ways, for shooting John Steele, for causing Hannah this present heartache.

"It's your spirit I'm worried about now, more than your body," Sophronia said. She stood and hobbled to the window, pulled back the lace curtain and stared out at the wind-bent apple trees and the broken sticks of plants remaining in her garden. "I can't help feeling you're going to some outlandish altar for sacrifice to save us both," she said. "Where is God in this, child? Once I thought I knew . . . now I'm wondering."

Hannah got up from the table, walked over to Sophronia, and circled her arm around the older woman's shoulders. She hugged her close. "You would do the same for me," she said quietly.

Sophronia nodded. "That I would, child. Seventy times seven if I could."

"Then let me do this for us both." For a moment they watched the wind gust noisily, blowing more sand into the yard, then Hannah turned again to Sophronia. "Besides, I wouldn't be going so willingly if I didn't know something you don't know." A hint of laughter had crept back into her voice.

"Whatever it is, it won't change what's happening to you today," Sophronia said.

"It might change how you see it, Sophie," Hannah said. "Listen to this . . . I found out John's ranch is near a meadow on the California Road. A heavily traveled road!" She tilted her chin upward and smiled, willing the older woman's spirits to lift. "At the meadows, companies often stop for days on end to rest their herds before starting across the California desert."

"The ranch where he's taking us tomorrow?"

"The same."

"And you're thinking what I'm thinking?" Sophronia asked. A glint of life had returned to her eyes.

Hannah nodded. "Exactly what you're thinking."

"That we may still be able to slip in among one of the companies."

"Yes," Hannah said. "That's what will get me through the ceremony today. Today is just the first step toward getting us away from John Steele, from all the rest."

The clock on the mantel struck noon, and Hannah and Sophronia looked at each other, both acknowledging the time had come.

Sophronia unwrapped the wedding gown she and Hannah had so reluctantly sewn. Before slipping it over her head, Hannah fingered the delicate fabric, thinking how they had hurried through each stitch, unwilling to consider what the finished garment would symbolize.

They had sewn the gown from yards of pale yellow satin and ivory lace that Harriet Steele purchased from the mercantile in town and presented one afternoon while calling on Hannah. Harriet tried to be pleasant, seeming to know how painful the union would be for the younger woman. She'd even brought a pattern she said was from the marriage of one of John's other wives.

Sophronia stood back after she had hooked the dozens of tiny buttons at Hannah's back. "You're beautiful, child." Hannah moved to stand in front of the long mirror. Sophronia's fingers trembled as she picked up a crown of dried wildflowers and greenery she'd gathered days ago: fronds of bleeding-heart fern, buttercups, wild roses, lupines, and bachelor's buttons.

She placed the delicate wreath on Hannah's head, arranging her curls around it, then considered her in silence. "It's your spirit I fear for, child. What you're giving up can never be again."

Hannah understood what Sophronia meant. As she gazed at herself in the mirror, she thought of her dream of marrying the young man she'd loved since childhood. "I had wanted my wedding day to be filled with joy, not a sham simply to be endured," she said.

"And you wanted your groom to be Lucas."

"Yes," Hannah whispered. "I really did." Then the moment passed, and she touched Sophronia's cheek gently. "I only wish you could be with me." It was unfair that her aunt wasn't allowed to attend the sealing. But being unmarried, Sophronia was unable to enter the sealing room where the ceremony would take place.

The wind howled, and the shutters banged against the windows, and Hannah shuddered, turning away from her image in the mirror.

By one o'clock the wind had settled down, and a short time later, John Steele arrived in a carriage drawn by two spirited bays. Hannah quickly embraced Sophronia, then walked with John to the street and moved inside as he held open the carriage door. A short time later, the carriage halted.

Hannah looked up at the stark, white building and shivered as John took her arm. He escorted her up the steps, through the entrance, and into a long, windowless room with an immense pitch to the ceiling. She stood mutely, suddenly feeling very small and insignificant. John tried to take her arm, whether in a gesture of comfort or possessiveness, Hannah didn't know. She stepped away from him as he gave her a puzzled look.

Before he could speak, a woman walked toward the couple, nodded to John, then whisked Hannah to the bride's room, a wide chamber with ornate mirrors covering two of its walls. The floor held the sheen of polished wood, and deeply upholstered chairs and benches flanked the mirror. The look of it was dark, strangely intimate in a frightening way. Again Hannah had the feeling that the building itself was closing in on her.

Then she followed the endowment worker through another door that led to a private cubicle.

"You will need to disrobe," the woman said quietly. Then, before Hannah could protest, the woman deftly began working the tiny satin-covered buttons at the back of Hannah's bridal gown. Hannah held her breath, feeling herself blush all over as her clothing spilled onto the floor around her.

"This is called a shield," the woman whispered. She lifted a thin cloth robe, let the folds fall out gently, then slipped it over Hannah's head. It was open at the sides, and Hannah was naked beneath it. Again she blushed and fought the urge to run from the room, from this holy place . . .

Next, the woman beckoned Hannah to follow her to another small room completely enshrouded with flowing white veils.

"Now you will be washed and anointed," the woman said, nodding to a small stool, indicating that Hannah should step onto it. She swallowed hard then did as she was bade.

An older woman dressed in a long white robe glided into the room. Hannah's heart pounded, and she found it increasingly difficult to breathe. Even the veils hanging at the walls seemed ready to enshroud her.

The woman's face was beatific, and Hannah searched her eyes for some sign that she knew what Hannah was feeling, some sort of kinship, of humanity, of sanity.

But the older woman held her blissful smile without a flicker of honest compassion. "Bless you, dear, on your special day," she said. Her hands touched Hannah beneath the gown. "I wash you so that you may be clean from the blood and sins of your youth." Then, moving her hands over Hannah's body, the woman blessed each part. From time to time she dipped her fingers in a basin of sacred water then touched Hannah again.

With her eyes closed, Hannah stood completely still during the ritual, trying to chase away the feeling of transgression against her body, against her very soul. Hot tears of anger filled her eyes, and she bit her lip to keep it from trembling.

She had told Sophronia she wouldn't believe her vows, wouldn't utter words from her heart. But this was almost more than she could tolerate—it wasn't something she could choose to ignore. It violated her to the core.

She fought the urge to slap away the hands that touched her and run from the living, breathing building that threatened to suffocate her. She tried to take a breath to calm herself, but her ribs felt as though they were made of iron; they wouldn't bend.

The endowment worker touched Hannah's forehead. "This is so your thoughts may be acceptable to heavenly Father," she said softly. Then she rested her fingertips on Hannah's lips. "This is so you may always speak godly words." She touched Hannah's arms, breasts, loins. "This will make you fruitful," she pronounced. Next her hands touched Hannah's legs and her feet. Her voice was nearly a chant as she blessed each part of Hannah's body.

When she finished with the water she began again, this time using oil, anointing Hannah from head to toe. All the while, the older woman watched her with a kind but distant smile.

"You have a new name now," the woman said when she was finished, her voice low. Taking Hannah's hands in hers, she drew her close and whispered in her ear, "Your new name is Naomi."

Hannah drew in a deep breath. So what she had heard about being given a secret name was true. She stood silently considering the new name and its implications. A sudden sting of tears filled her eyes.

Beloved child, I *have called you by name. You are mine.*

The woman misunderstood Hannah's tears. "It is a wonderful thing, and you'll understand its fullness a bit later." Then she reached to a shelf where, neatly stacked in three rows, lay folded, rough-looking holy garments.

She handed Hannah her garments. "You are to reveal your name to no one," she said solemnly, "except when it is asked of you during today's ceremony. You'll know, dear, when the time comes," she added with a smile.

Hannah unfolded the garment carefully then held it up. It was one piece and made from thick cotton. It had a high neck and reached to the ankles and wrists, with a generous opening at the crotch.

"You're to wear them always." The wrinkled corners of the woman's mouth still curved up, sweetly. "Next to your skin with nothing between." She went on to tell Hannah they represented the covering God gave Eve in the garden and that they would protect her until her work on earth was complete.

Sighing deeply, Hannah followed the worker back to the bride's room she had left earlier. There she covered the hideous undergarments with the ivory satin gown and looked at her odd reflection in the mirror.

A moment later, she followed the worker to another large room, called the Creation Room, at the end of the hall.

John stood with a group of young men, and he turned and smiled as she approached. There were at least twelve other couples waiting with John and Hannah.

A high priest dressed in flowing robes instructed the brides and grooms to be seated, then proceeded to teach them a special handshake. Next they were told to draw their thumbs across their jugulars, from ear to ear, as though they were cutting their throats for revealing the handshake to anyone on the outside.

Sophronia's words about sacrificing her spirit came back to her. Yet nothing could have prepared her for the acts of violence she was mutely assenting to carry out should she be unfaithful to John or to the Church. Was God in this? Could he be here participating, just as the man dressed as God was?

Come away, my beloved.

More rituals followed. And more symbolic signs of death. A darkness settled over her with each new sign and ritual. By the time she had finished learning the "sure sign of the nail"—a handclasp where she linked little fingers with the bride next to her, then pressed her other fingers into her pulse—she felt herself trembling inside, as if some force other than herself resided there.

She took a deep breath and closed her eyes, trying to rid herself of her fear as she pretended to cut out her heart and slashed her hand across her abdomen as if disemboweling herself.

For in acting it out, she was promising to submit to death at the hands of someone in authority wielding out justice. Blood atonement.

Next, a thick white veil with deep slits in its center dropped onto the stagelike platform. The grooms formed a queue behind it, and the brides did the same in front.

"The drape is a symbol of the veil that separates this life from the next," the high priest intoned.

Hannah faced the curtain alone. The endowment worker moved her closer until she stood directly in front of a pair of slits in the veil.

On the other side, John slipped his arms through the slits and reached for her. Hannah was told to place her arms beneath John's and then around him. They were then moved toward each other so that through the veil their bodies touched.

The high priest then asked that they press themselves together, foot to foot, knee to knee, breast to breast, hand to back, and mouth to ear.

John made the sign of the nail into Hannah's hand and asked her to identify the token and its penalty. She gave him the sign he required.

A moment of silence followed, then she could feel his hot breath in her ear. "Tell me your new name," he whispered.

"Naomi," she said.

I *have called you by name. You are* mine!

John Steele was about to call her into a symbolic heaven with her new name . . . when she released her hold on him and stepped backward, her heart thudding beneath her ribs.

I have called you by name. You are mine, *child. You are* mine.

If she believed what the Church and its leaders—the Prophet himself—said, it wouldn't matter how good she was, how she loved, or gave herself for others.

If she believed in Joseph Smith, Brigham Young, and the Jesus Christ they had shown to her, all that mattered was that she needed to please her husband.

It was John Steele who would have to whisper "Naomi," when she died.

He was her key to entering heaven's gates, entering eternity.

John Steele!

There was murmuring now among the other brides and grooms, and John was angrily whispering her name to get her to return to the curtain.

Behold, the veil of the temple was rent forever.

Come away, my beloved.

"Naomi!" John murmured low, so no one else could hear. "Naomi."

The endowment worker stepped close to Hannah, encircled her in her arms, and whispered, "All brides have second thoughts sooner or later, dear. Don't despair. But you must continue now. You're keeping the others waiting." She looked nervously back at her other charges, standing impatiently in line.

Hannah shook herself free of the woman's embrace and nodded grimly.

Come away, my beloved!

"Come along now, dear," the endowment worker said, gently pulling Hannah toward the curtain.

Hannah focused her thoughts on her plan to get to the south of the territory—her plan to escape. This ceremony was merely the first step in executing the plan. Breathing easier, she again stepped to the veil.

John, his voice low, began to whisper the rest of the ceremony, breathing heavily into her ear. "Health in the navel, marrow in the bones, strength in the loins and in the sinews," he chanted. He was talking about her health . . . her ability to procreate. She felt a blush creep over her again and held her breath as he continued to chant. "Power in the priesthood be upon me. Upon my posterity for generations of time and throughout all eternity."

Then his arms clasped her in a strong-as-iron embrace, and they stood perfectly still. Hannah could feel her heart—and his—pounding as one. That frightened her more than anything she'd experienced in the ceremony so far.

"Well done, thou good and faithful servant," he finally breathed. "Enter thou into the joy of the Lord."

Then they joined hands in one of the secret clasps, and John pulled Hannah through the slits in the veil.

At the bowery, the newlywed couples were feted all afternoon and into the night. Hannah refused to dance or eat or drink.

After the experience of the ceremony, she understood afresh John's need to procreate. Icy fingers crept up her spine, and she shuddered.

It was nearly midnight by the time John escorted Hannah to the carriage once again. He clucked the horses forward, and the sounds of their hooves on the stone streets echoed through the night.

Hannah's hands were frozen, and when John tried to take them in his, she pulled away.

This time, instead of giving her a puzzled expression, John Steele looked completely confident, lifted a brow, and smiled sardonically.

"I won't ask if I may carry you over the threshold," he said as they walked to the front door of his house. "I can see that you're going to need some time to adjust to the idea of my . . . how shall I put it? . . . my nearness."

Hannah hoped her sigh of relief wasn't audible as he opened the front door and let her pass in front of him. Perhaps it wasn't going to be as difficult as she thought to keep him from what he deemed his godly right.

The lard-oil lamps inside the house had been dimmed, and the presence of Harriet and his other wives was not apparent.

Taking a lamp from a stand in the entry, John led Hannah up the stairs to the first door on the right. The long, wide hallway was flanked by at least nine other tall, oak doors, and again, Hannah felt relieved. Obviously each wife had her own separate quarters. She hoped that meant she would also enjoy the privacy of her own room.

Watching her expectantly, John pushed back the bedroom door then held it open for Hannah to enter. The room was well-lit with two lamps burning on bedside tables that flanked a large, ornately carved, burled-oak bed. The covers had been turned back in an unspoken welcome, and nightclothes lay folded neatly at the foot of the bed.

One set was feminine, obviously newly sewn, of tulle and lace and ribbons. The other, a cotton nightshirt, had been placed just beside it.

Hannah felt fear, then rage, ignite someplace deep inside and spread through her body, soul, and spirit. She raised her gaze to John Steele, hoping to see there had been some mistake. She knew by his expression there hadn't been.

John closed the door behind him, his ice blue eyes never leaving hers.

EIGHTEEN

Fort Laramie
July 1857

In the gathering dusk of evening, Ellie sat on a stool by the cook fire mending a tear in Meg's pinafore. Two of the girls' calico dresses, one of Alexander's brown shirts, and her own cotton chemise had been hung to dry on a rope strung between the wagons. Liza had pinned them up earlier, after insisting that she include the Farrington wash with her own when she went to the creek, giving Ellie some time to rest.

Ellie was feeling better, though weak from her earlier discomfort. She drew in a deep breath, enjoying the rhythm of her needlework, the smoky fragrance of the air, and the rise and fall of voices around the fires talking over the day's events. The hum of cicadas had now given way to the racket of crickets and, from the Laramie Creek some yards away, to the croaking of frogs. Moths flitted about the fire, sometimes hurling themselves into the flames with a sizzling snap.

She looked up as Alexander walked toward the wagon. The children were in bed, and Ellie was trying to decide how best to tell Alexander that she needed rest before they moved on, hoping to convince him to stay one more day at the fort.

A younger dark-haired man followed her husband, and Abe Barrett limped along on the other side. Alexander's shirt was torn, and he was rubbing a scrape on his jaw. Abe, who didn't look much better, didn't speak, just gave Ellie a half-grin and hurried on to his wagon.

"My lands, Alexander!" Ellie frowned, setting aside the pinafore. "What's happened?"

Her husband smiled sheepishly, but before he could speak, the younger man spoke up. "Ma'am, I'm afraid it's my fault. Some folks over at the saloon were trying to pick a fight. Your husband and his friend came to my rescue."

"Ellie, this is Lucas Knight," Alexander said. "Lucas, my wife, Ellie."

Lucas removed his hat to give her a gentlemanly nod, and she noticed a swelling cut above his temple. "Ma'am, I'm pleased to make your acquaintance." He smiled, and Ellie noticed his eyes were kind, though wary.

Alexander rubbed his jaw again and grinned at the young man. "Fact is, I don't think you needed any help. Something tells me you could've handled that rowdy crowd single-handedly. You move as fast as greased lightning with that knife."

Lucas Knight gave him a steady look but didn't respond.

"Let me tend to those wounds," Ellie said. "You both just sit yourselves down, and I'll be right back." They pulled up a couple of farm chairs near the fire, and she went to the rear of the wagon for some strips of cloth, then returned with a pail of water the twins had earlier fetched from Laramie Creek. The men were speaking of Johnston's troop movement into Utah but stopped as she settled onto her stool, poured a ladleful of water onto a piece of cloth, then started to dab at Lucas Knight's temple. He lifted a hand in protest.

"You just sit still, now," Ellie said with a motherly tone. "You've taken a nasty blow here, young man." He let his hand fall feebly into his lap and gave her a grin as she gingerly dabbed at his wound. She could see he wasn't a man used to being fussed over. She rinsed the cloth, wrung it out, and folded it. "Now, hold this to your head to keep the swelling down," she commanded sternly, then turned to minister to Alexander.

Lucas Knight grinned at her as she worked. She noticed that he looked both surprised and grateful, as if he hadn't expected such treatment from a stranger.

When she finished, Ellie stood in front of the two men, hands on hips, shaking her head slowly. "My goodness," she said. "I do believe you boys better stay out of that saloon from now on. These Laramie folks aren't as friendly as some of the Indians we've met along the way."

"Believe me, Ellie, we didn't go in there hankering to fight," Alexander said. "Fact is, these ruffians came after us. Call themselves the Missouri Wildcats."

"I don't believe they wanted to let me out of there alive. Again, I'm much obliged to you for coming to my assistance."

Ellie pulled up another chair. "Why would they come after you?"

He gave her a long, assessing look before answering. "I don't know, ma'am," he said finally.

"Where you headed?" Alexander asked, sitting forward.

The young man looked wary, as if weighing how much to tell. He settled back, turning his hat brim in his hands thoughtfully. "I'm headed west, to Utah Territory."

"You're Mormon." There was no question in Alexander's tone; Ellie knew he must have decided before he spoke.

Ellie waited for Lucas to answer, but he sat still, turning his hat and watching her husband with that same wariness on his face she'd noted earlier.

"You saved my life back there," he said finally. "There's no need, I suppose, for me to beat around the bush with someone who'd lay his own life on the line to save my skin." He suddenly grinned. "You saved me once, and though some might disagree with your decision, I doubt you'd kill me just because I call myself a Saint."

Alexander nodded slowly. "You're safe here, son, no matter what your beliefs."

Lucas drew in a deep breath. "The thugs in the saloon were right. Troops are readying to march west out of Leavenworth. Some two thousand. I'm heading back to warn Brigham and the others."

"How soon do you think the troops will get to Utah?" Alexander asked.

"Surprisingly enough, the reports are that they're in no hurry. It'll probably take several months. Some say not until after the first of the year."

Alexander looked thoughtful. "Is there a rebellion? Is Buchanan right to have sent them?"

"There's no rebellion," Lucas Knight said, but Ellie thought he looked uncomfortable with the question. He shifted his eyes away from Alexander's, and glanced at Ellie. "Where're you folks headed?" he asked.

"We're going to California," Ellie told him with a warm smile. "Not sure north or south yet. But the captain promises me it'll be near the ocean."

Lucas frowned and leaned forward. He stared at the fire for a few minutes then looked back to Alexander. "You plan to bypass Utah," he said.

"You just got through saying there's no rebellion," Alexander reminded him. "And the coming war sounds like it's months away."

Lucas Knight glanced at Ellie then back to Alexander, as if it seemed he wanted to say more, but instead he remained silent.

"We're running late," the captain said. "It's nearly the end of July, and we should've passed Independence Rock on the fourth. If we can't recover some of that lost time, we'll need to take the southern route into California. Head south on the Old Spanish Trail."

Lucas Knight stood and walked over by the fire, then turned again to them, his hands clasped behind him. Above them now the stars were a canopy of spangled pinpoints in a deep navy blue sky. "It might be better to spend the winter at Fort Bridger—anywhere—then cross the Sierras in the spring."

"We don't have the supplies to do that," the captain said, shaking his head and thoughtfully assessing the young man. "We've got nine hundred head of cattle to feed, five hundred horses. They'll die unless we can get grain for the winter—or get them over the Sierras and into California. And the little children, the old folks . . . " he hesitated. "I fear they couldn't last through a winter of deprivation."

Lucas Knight didn't respond.

"Unless," Alexander went on, "unless we winter at Salt Lake, buy grain from your people."

"I would avoid wintering there," Lucas said quietly.

"Why the warning?"

Ellie broke in, "Does it have anything to do with our train being from Arkansas?"

Both men looked at her, puzzled.

She hurried to explain, "I heard that a man was murdered in Arkansas a few months back . . . "

The young man looked surprised.

"Do you know of it?" Ellie asked.

He shook his head. "I hadn't heard anything about it. Did you say he was murdered?"

Ellie nodded and told him the sketchy details of what she'd heard. She felt weary and troubled as she spoke.

"I don't know that one train is any safer than another in a time of war," he said finally. "And this is a time of war. Again, I beseech you to make your detour."

"I will mind your words, son," Alexander said thoughtfully. "But when we arrive at Fort Bridger, we may not have a choice."

The two men went on to discuss the trail ahead, and Alexander invited the young man to join up with them at least as far as South Pass. Ellie thought Lucas Knight was going to decline, but he surprised them both by saying yes, he'd be pleased to spend a few days on the road with them. After a few more minutes, he stood and shook hands with the captain then nodded to Ellie.

"Thank you for your kind ministrations," he said to her. "Your gentle spirit reminds me of those I've left back home."

"I'm glad you'll be spending more time with us," Ellie said, sensing some deep sadness in the young man's words. "The trail can be lonely, I would think, when you're riding alone."

"I'll see you at daybreak," Lucas Knight said as he turned and walked into the darkness.

"Good night," Alexander and Ellie called after him.

By the time Alexander laid out their pallets by the night fire, Ellie had decided to keep to herself the afternoon's bout of pain and her need for more rest. Her uneasiness about heading through Utah Territory far outweighed her concern about her pain and bone weariness.

"Alexander—?" she murmured as they were about to fall asleep.

"Hmmm?" he breathed.

She propped herself up on her elbow, watching him in the starlight and in the dying embers of the fire. His face was leaner than when they left Arkansas, and now even in his state of half-sleep, she could see him working his jaw. She touched his cheek gently, thinking of how she loved him. He opened his eyes and met her gaze.

"Alexander," she said, thinking of all she wanted to say about her fear of what lay ahead, of her pain and worry about having the baby in a safe place, of not wanting to head through Utah Territory. But Alexander felt the weight of his captaincy heavy these days, even heavier now, she knew, since tonight's conversation with the young Mormon man.

So she smiled, tracing her fingers lightly along his jaw. "I love you," she whispered finally. "That's what I wanted to tell you. I just wanted to say I love you, my dearest."

Alexander reached over, drawing her into his arms, and kissed her tenderly. Ellie snuggled up against him and closed her eyes, listening to the deep thud of his heart and taking comfort in his nearness.

The following morning, as usual, rifles were fired into the air well before dawn, signaling the group to begin preparations for another day. The sleepy camp came to life, the travelers pouring out of their tents and wagons, setting their breakfast fires, eating, packing, hitching teams to wagons, and pulling into line. By now there were few stragglers; most in the company had learned if they were late with their morning preparations, they would find themselves at the rear of the long, dusty caravan.

Alexander had just finished hitching the oxen team to the wagon and was riding to the front of the caravan several wagons forward when Lucas Knight rode up. He nodded to Ellie, seated on the bench, and to the twins hanging out of the canvas opening behind her.

"Ma'am," he said, tipping his hat.

"How's that head?" she asked, noticing the swelling had gone down somewhat.

"Much better," he said with a grin. His horse whinnied and danced sideways a few steps. "Thanks to you."

"Mommy, who's that man?" Meg asked, looking up at him, wrinkling her nose.

"Phoebe wants to know too," Sarah added, the tip of a dark braid in her mouth.

Before Ellie could answer, Lucas laughed and moved the horse closer to the wagon. "My name's Lucas Knight," he said and gave them each a gentlemanly nod. "And who, might I ask, are you beautiful ladies?"

Meg giggled. "Well, I'm Meg, and my sister's name is Sarah."

"Meg and Sarah, I'm pleased to make your acquaintance. Pleased indeed." He tipped his hat again.

"And this is Phoebe," Sarah said, thrusting the doll toward him. "She lived with the Indians for a while."

He looked surprised, and Ellie laughed. "Actually, it's true." And she told him the story about Phoebe's mishap in the Arkansas River and her surprising reappearance with the band of Indians. Lucas listened appreciatively, and Ellie sensed that his wariness was lessening. He seemed to have an immediate affection for the twins, and they for him. By the time he'd moved forward to ride with Alexander at the head of the train, the little girls were whining to get their ponies from the herd and ride with Lucas and their papa.

The sky was just turning silver-pink in the east when the caravan of wagons was ready to roll. The herd moved out first, then the wagons, one by one.

Lucas Knight rode with the Farrington train for nearly a week before he knew it was time to head on alone. On his last night with the group, he joined Ellie and the captain for supper.

"I'll be leaving in the morning," he said as Ellie filled his plate with beans and fresh-roasted buffalo steak.

"I figured we were probably moving too slow for you, son," Alexander said as Ellie filled his plate. He rested one booted foot on the wagon tongue, propping his plate on his knee as he ate.

Nearby, Becky, Louisa, and Prudence Angeline O'Donnell sat giggling with Sarah and Meg. Phoebe, the worn, dirt-smudged doll, was propped up beside Sarah with her own pretend plate of food.

Lucas looked around at the wagon camp, at the families now mostly sitting and eating in groups, the children talking and laughing as they ate. Later, the harmonicas and fiddles would appear, and there would be singing and dancing for them all, young and old.

In many ways, he hated to leave them. They were good people, surprising him that they had no feelings one way or the other about Mormons; they had accepted him without question about who he was, where he'd come from, or what he believed. The captain had shown him respect, and Ellie seemed ready to welcome him into their family.

Watching them together sometimes made him think of Hannah. The captain and Ellie seemed to have a courting kind of love after—what did they tell him?—nearly twenty years of marriage. He noticed it when their eyes met, sometimes over some silly word that one of their children uttered, or as they just exchanged a loving glance when they thought no one was watching.

He might not have noticed, except for the empty place in his heart that was meant for Hannah alone. And he wondered if he and Hannah would ever have a chance to marry and share the kind of love he'd seen in the Farringtons.

Lucas could see for all her brave spirit that Ellie Farrington wasn't well. Her ankles and wrists were heavy with swelling, and her breathing seemed labored when she walked. He often caught Alexander watching her tenderly, his anxiety apparent, but neither of them complained.

After supper that last night, Alexander got out his mandolin and started to play softly. Before long, the wagon company had fallen quiet, listening. A warm and gentle breeze carried through camp, bringing the lowing and soft bawling of the distant herd.

And as folks stood in twos and threes, and sometimes more, to dance, the sight etched itself into Lucas's soul. John Steele had taught him to believe that the Gentiles thought of the Mormons as vile objects of their hatred.

He looked over at Ellie, swaying to her husband's sweet music, arms folded protectively across the shelf created by the baby she carried, and he went over to her.

"Ellie—?"

She looked up.

"Would you care to dance?"

She smiled, and for a moment her weariness faded. "I would like nothing better, dear Lucas," she said as he swept her gently into his arms.

They moved to the music of Alexander playing "Jeanie with the Light Brown Hair."

"We'll miss you when you go," she said.

He turned her in time to the music. "You all have been good to let me join up with you."

"I can't believe that God didn't lead you to us," Ellie said, looking up at him.

He almost stopped dancing, meeting her calm gaze.

"Nothing happens by accident, you know," she went on. "He's got us all right in the center of his hand. It's his love that keeps us there."

"I don't think it's that easy," Lucas said, turning her gently as they danced.

She surprised him by laughing. "I agree. I would imagine there are times when God has a hard time loving us."

"That's not what I meant. He requires certain things of us to be accepted into his kingdom."

"You mean we have to work to earn his love?"

Lucas nodded thoughtfully. "I've never thought about his love being part of it. But, yes, we have to work to be accepted by him. Period. That's what I meant."

"To earn our place in his heart," she persisted.

"Yes," Lucas said.

"But God says he's loved us with an everlasting love," she said. "If it's everlasting, how can he put a condition on it? How can he make us earn it?"

"I believe God has certain requirements," he said. "Requirements that make us righteous and holy . . . acceptable in his sight."

"What are they, Lucas?"

He fell silent, knowing full well he couldn't tell a Gentile about vengeance and blood atonement. She wasn't one of God's chosen elite. She wasn't a Saint. She wouldn't understand.

"Christ's robe of righteousness wrapped around us—around the worst of who we are—is what makes us holy in God's sight," she said softly.

"There are parts of the Bible that weren't translated properly," he told her. "What you're saying about God's love and Christ's robe of righteousness is simply mankind's way of taking the easy way out. That removes responsibility for our actions."

"Easy way out?" She paused. "What I'm talking about isn't an easy road. It's about loving others the way God loves us. It's about forgiving others the way he's forgiven us. Yes, he does require something harsh from us, but he gives us something invaluable in return."

Lucas thought that perhaps she'd get around to seeing that nothing in life was free, especially from God. "What is it he requires, in your view?" he asked.

She smiled again. "Your life, Lucas."

"My life?" He'd heard that before . . . from John Steele and the Avenging Angels, the Church and its priesthood. All of them wanting to own him—body, soul, and spirit. "And God promises in return—?"

"His life in us. He gives to us from the abundance of all he is. Above and beyond anything the world has to offer. Love, peace, joy, grace, forgiveness." Her face seemed to glow with the thought of such gifts. "And we—because he is in us—obey his commandment about loving others as ourselves. We give to others from our heart's abundance."

Lucas stopped dancing. "I don't see how that's possible."

"I suppose it isn't, humanly, at least." Around them the music played on, the stars shone brightly, and the night fires by the wagons died to golden embers.

"A God of love," Lucas mused as he led Ellie back to her wagon. He stopped suddenly. "What about when men hate you, cause you pain and suffering? What then?" He was thinking of the persecution of the Saints, of Haun's Mill and his mother and father. His baby brother.

"Do you mean will I be able to forgive . . . to extend the same grace to others that God extends to me?"

He saw the earnestness in her face, and though his question had been for himself, he knew Ellie was thinking of her own circumstances. Perhaps considering her fears about the future of her children, her unborn infant.

"Yes," he said. "That's what I'm asking."

She looked up at the heavens for several moments then back to him. With a small smile, she said. "I don't know about tomorrow, Lucas. I only know that I—and my family, born and unborn—rest in God's hands. His loving hands. What he'll require of me I can't know. I only know where I rest right now."

He didn't respond, and after a moment, she said, "Will we see you in the morning before you leave?"

"I'll stop and say good-bye." Lucas started to leave, then turned to face her again. "Thank you, Ellie, for speaking forthrightly."

She nodded. "God be with you, Lucas Knight. You're already in my prayers, you know . . ." She gave him a quick smile. ". . . just as you are already in God's hand."

Away from the firelight, the stars shone even brighter than before. Lucas walked out into the grassy field beyond the camp, toward a small creek that fed into the wide and muddy North Platte a distance away. He stood there for a moment, considering the star-spangled sky . . . the God who created it all.

And he thought about Ellie's faith, a faith that his doctrine told him was false. He frowned. If he was so convinced it was false, then why was he drawn to such a God as she described?

Why did this God seem to be drawing Lucas to himself? And had been long before Lucas met up with the Farrington company?

What was it Ellie said . . . that God loved him with an everlasting love?

He looked deep into the heavens above him, almost becoming lost in its depths. Could there be but one God? What about the others? What about his own desire to become deity? Then it was as if a quiet presence joined his thoughts, and he almost stopped breathing as he listened.

I am the first, and I am the last.

I am the living God, the Savior, the everlasting King.

It is I who reveal the deep and secret things. It is I who know what is in the darkness, and the darkness does not hide you from me.

It is I who make the night shine as day, my beloved child.

It is I.

For a long time Lucas stared into the velvet darkness and listened to the voice of the stream and music of the night. In the distance, an owl cried out, and from the wagon camp the melancholy sounds of the captain's mandolin carried toward him.

NINETEEN

Lucas rose in the predawn darkness and, after packing up his bedroll, headed out to the herd for Spitfire, saddled the stallion, tied on his gear, then rode back into the wagon camp.

The families were just beginning to stir, getting ready to leave. Some of the men had gone to the herd to fetch their teams; others were laying the morning cook fires or greasing wagon wheels for the day's journey. He spotted the captain hitching the oxen team and then saw Ellie and the children packing bedding and cook pots into the rear of the wagon.

He dismounted to say his farewells, shook hands with the captain, and nodded to Ellie. Then he grinned at Meg and Sarah and stooped down to greet them at their level.

"I've been working on something for you," he said.

Meg's eyes grew wide, and she crowded in front of her sister. "What is it?" she demanded.

He chuckled as Ellie scolded Meg for her rude impatience, and Sarah stepped forward, giving him an angelic smile, clearly designed to show off her own exquisite manners. She had Phoebe, the raggedy doll, tucked under one arm. "Mister Knight, we shall miss you," she said with a small curtsey.

"And I'm going to miss you," Lucas said. He stood and rummaged through a saddlebag. "That's why I want you to have this." He handed her a miniature carved rocking horse.

"You made this for me?" Sarah asked, holding the toy in her hand and turning it over and rubbing the tiny whittle marks on the wood. "It's beautiful!" She drew out the word in awe.

"Just for you . . . and Phoebe, of course," he added.

Standing on one foot, then the other, Meg waited impatiently, trying not to ask what he'd made for her. Her eyes were bright in anticipation, and he winked at her as he reached into his saddlebag again. Spitfire shook his mane and danced sideways a few steps.

"And this, m'lady, is for you." Lucas presented the little girl with a wooden flute he'd carved from a willow branch.

Meg caught her breath audibly, and her mouth formed a perfect O. He showed her how to place her fingers over the holes on top and blow through the mouthpiece. A shrill whistle split through the morning air. Meg giggled and made the sound again.

"Now, next time we meet, I'll teach you how to play an Irish jig," he said, grinning at her obvious delight. "That's a promise."

"*Will* we meet again?" the captain said after the little girls had clambered into the rear of the wagon with their treasures.

"I hope so," said Lucas, meaning it. "But I'm thinking it may be in California, not Utah. Please consider what I've told you about taking the Old Spanish Road."

Ellie looked at him, her clear eyes seeming to pierce clear through to his soul. "You said you might see us in California?"

He nodded.

"Does that mean you might be going there on a mission . . . or are you thinking of leaving Utah, for good, I mean?"

He considered her silently for a moment, reluctant even now to say aloud the direction he'd been heading all along. "It's not a mission," he finally said with a heavy sigh. "But I can't tell you any more."

Alexander broke in. "Why not just keep riding? Head over the Sierras yourself. Better yet, join up with us."

"I've got to warn Brigham Young about the troops. He may know by now, but I've got to make sure." He paused.

Ellie touched his arm. "There's another reason, isn't there? I mean for going back?"

He smiled into this gentle, godly woman's eyes. "Yes," he said simply. "Two reasons. Sophronia and Hannah. Sophie's a woman who practically raised me from childhood, and Hannah's her grandniece.

I've got to get them out before I can leave." He frowned. "It's dangerous to leave the territory, you know." But he could see by their expressions that they didn't know, they couldn't begin to comprehend the danger apostates faced.

"And your Hannah . . . she's a special young woman?" Ellie asked.

"I've asked her to marry me." Then he chuckled. "Actually, she's asked me. Three times since she was ten years old."

Ellie and the captain laughed with him. Alexander patted him on the back. "Then I'd say you'd better hightail it back before she changes her mind."

They shook hands again, and Ellie kissed him on the cheek. "God be with you, Lucas," she said as he swung a leg over Spitfire's saddle.

"Until we meet again . . ." Alexander said. "Look us up in California."

"Somewhere near the ocean," Ellie added with a laugh. "Just follow the coast from Oregon to Mexico. Look for the grandest ranch in the state, the one Alexander's promised to build me."

Lucas laughed as Spitfire shook his head, sending his mane flopping and his bridle jingling. But before Lucas could leave, Meg and Sarah raced from the covered wagon. Alexander lifted one twin into his arms and Ellie the other so they could reach Lucas with a good-bye hug and a loud smack of a kiss on each of his cheeks.

Lucas felt more lighthearted than he had in weeks as he kicked Spitfire into a trot and headed toward the California road. Wagoneers and cattlehands he passed along the way called him by name and waved good-bye. He nodded, giving them a half-salute, until he'd reached the front of the forming caravan. The herd was commencing to leave, thundering hooves kicking up dust to the south of the road. The wide and sandy North Platte lay to the other side.

The sun had now risen and swept across the landscape, washing the grasses and rocks and river in sepia hues. By the time he craned around in his saddle to look back, the wagons had formed a single file. With the morning sunlight on the high, arched, canvas wagon tops, they took on a shimmering pale gold hue. From this distance, there was no sign of the worn and ragged gray from weeks on the trail.

Children played and skipped in and out of the wagon beds, and the women and men walked alongside their teams.

Faintly on the wind, he heard the "haws!" and "gees!" of the wagoneers as the caravan slowly moved forward, and the shouts of laughter and cries and whines and giggles of the children. Lucas smiled as he watched them. These were good people, and he would miss them. If it weren't for Hannah and Sophie, he might have considered staying with them to cross the Sierras into California.

He reined Spitfire around to face west, kicked him into a trot, and after a few minutes the stallion picked up to an easy canter. Within a short time, the sun hot on his back, Lucas had left the train miles behind, winding along the North Platte, more quicksand and mud than water.

A couple of hours later, Lucas headed up a rocky bluff that afforded him a view of the California-Oregon road, stretching into both east and west horizons. The North Platte snaked for as far as he could see. To the east he spotted the Farrington caravan, still beside the Platte, and to the southwest of the train, the herd of cattle and horses looking like a single rolling, living beast.

In the sun, Spitfire's hide gleamed, and Lucas rubbed the stallion's neck, letting him rest before starting back down the cliff to the trail. He was about to nudge the horse forward when he noticed a billowing cloud of dust a few miles behind the Farrington company. He stared for several minutes then realized it was another, smaller herd of cattle, and just beyond it, a smaller company of wagons.

He extended his small brass telescope and peered at the group. Two men rode point a distance ahead of the remainder of the company. Lucas squinted into the telescope, adjusted the focus, then looked again.

He could see neither of the men's features clearly from this distance, but there was something familiar about one of them as the man took off his hat and wiped his forehead with a kerchief. The balding head with its red fringe of hair reflecting the morning sun, the slope of his shoulders, told Lucas all he needed to know.

The small group was the Missouri Wildcats they'd encountered at

Fort Laramie, riding like the wind to catch the Farrington company, just as they'd threatened more than a week ago. Calculating the distance between the Wildcats and the Farringtons, Lucas decided the second company would overtake them by the time he galloped back to warn the captain.

He wondered briefly if his presence would help Alexander or further antagonize the Wildcats. He lifted the telescope again, watching the group for a several minutes, realizing his presence would only endanger the Farrington company. The smaller company didn't take long to join the Farrington train, pulling into place behind the last wagon as if one with them. Lucas reluctantly turned away from the sight and headed Spitfire back down the cliff. By high noon, he was again galloping west along the California road.

Ellie's wagon was midway in the long caravan. Today, as had become her pattern since the incident at Fort Laramie, she rode on the bench to drive the team. Though it was harder on the oxen, she knew that with each step she walked during the white-hot, weary and dust-filled days, the chances of a premature birth for her baby increased. The pain that struck her early on in the small of her back had now settled under her ribs, almost seeming to crush her heart. She had nearly three months to go before the infant could be born full-sized and healthy. And she worried daily that it wouldn't be so.

She prayed for him, just as she had when she had walked by the team earlier. Now, though, she rubbed the place where he kicked and turned in her belly, and she spoke to God in rhythm with creaking wheels.

Blessed Father,
This child is yours.
Be with him. Guide him.
Protect his ways.
I place him in your arms, dear Father.
And Meg and Sarah, too.
Your love for them is deeper and greater than mine.

Then she raised her eyes to the distant horizon. Thunder clouds were building to the southwest, towering in silver-white magnificence, and Ellie considered their harsh beauty against the deep purple sky.

There is a fear inside me, she breathed.

Oh, Lord! A dread fear that threatens to crush my bones.

Still she kept her eyes westward. A hush had fallen over the land, and the clouds had created patterns of darkness the travelers would pass through. Ellie shivered.

Oh, God, help me!

I fear so!

Then a ray of afternoon sun broke through the towering thunderheads, nearly blinding her with its intensity. The oxen bawled, the wagon swayed, and the wheels creaked onward in their ruts. And Ellie felt the babe move inside her. Smiling to herself, she lightly touched the little elbow or knee or fist, following its path across her belly.

Do not fear, my beloved.

When you pass through the waters,

I will be with you.

And, my child, when you walk through the fire,

The flames will not touch you.

You are precious in my sight,

And I love you . . .

The wagon wheels creaked as they rolled onward, and Ellie let her mind rest with thoughts of God and his tender mercies. A wind kicked up, lifting strands of hair from her hot face. She closed her eyes, letting the sun touch her face and the breeze caress it.

And I love you . . .

And I love you . . .

Soon the company entered the shadows cast by the thunderheads, and great drops of rain began to fall. The scorching air cooled, and Ellie breathed in the fragrance of dust mixed with rain.

And I love you . . .

All afternoon the caravan snaked in and out of the shadows of clouds. The rain never fell hard, and by the time the wagons circled for the evening, the massive thunderheads had drifted toward the eastern horizon.

"Ellie!" Liza Barrett ran across the night circle, lifting her skirts above her ankles so that she could move faster. Today, the Farrington and Barrett wagons had been a distance apart during the trek, and now they were parked across the circle from each other.

Ellie looked up from the dried-buffalo-dung cook fire, wiping the perspiration from her forehead with her sleeve. She'd been dredging buffalo steak in wheat flour, readying it for stewing. The fat sizzled in the Dutch oven, sending up the aroma of wild onions and bay leaves. The company had hunted the last of the buffalo a few days earlier, and this steak, which had been heavily packed in salt, was all that remained. Ellie was none too sorry. Neither were most others in the company. They'd all had their fill of buffalo cooked every way imaginable.

"Ellie!" Liza called out again as she drew closer.

Ellie waved, then dropped the last of the cut-up steak into the pot, gave it a stir to mix it with the onions, and placed the heavy iron lid on top. She wiped her hands on a nearby cloth as she stood to greet Liza.

"Have you heard about the Wildcats?" Liza asked when she was finally standing near Ellie.

"You mean bobcats?" Ellie glanced worriedly around the camp to find the children, relieved to see them playing with the little O'Donnell girls. "Or mountain lions?"

"No, no, that's not what I meant. It's a group that caught up with us today. They're camped back a ways, but they've sent their scout over to talk to Alexander and Abe about joining up."

"They call themselves Wildcats?" Ellie shook her head and frowned, still wiping the flour from her hands. "Sounds like some militia or secret fraternity or something." She shook out the cloth and hung it on a hook on the rear of the wagon.

Liza laughed with her. "They say they're called the Missouri Wildcats." She helped Ellie pull out the trunk with the eating utensils then climbed into the wagon to lift out the small farm table and chairs. When they were in place on the ground in the shade of the wagon, each of the women settled into a chair.

"How did you find out about them?" Ellie asked.

"One of them came looking for the captain. Just happened to stop by on our side of the circle. Abe took the man out to the herd. Said he thought the captain was there checking some lame horses." Liza looked worried, an unusual expression for her normally sunny disposition.

"I've heard it's a common thing for one company to join up with another," Ellie said. "I don't think it's out of the ordinary at all."

But Liza's expression didn't change. "Do you know who this group is?" she asked.

"Nothing more than what you've already told me."

"Do you remember back at Laramie, the fight in the saloon?"

Ellie nodded. "The night the men met Lucas Knight."

"Yes. The Missouri Wildcats are a bunch of ruffians and thugs." Liza shaded her eyes against the slant of the sun and looked out toward the grazing herd. "Abe told me that night," referring to how they jumped Lucas, "that these men don't know how to take no for an answer."

"Alexander never mentioned it," Ellie said. "He and Lucas only said that the ruffians took great offense to Lucas being Mormon. He mentioned it almost seemed the group was in some sort of blood feud with the Mormons, maybe from the Saints' days in Missouri or Illinois."

Liza leaned forward. "It doesn't bode well if they're with us and we have to make a detour through Utah."

"I doubt that Alexander, or any of the other men, will allow it, Liza. I just can't imagine them letting this group of scoundrels tag along with our families." She stood to busy her hands, feeling the dread fear welling up inside once again. Though her words were brave, she was as fearful of the outcome as Liza was. She stooped by the cook fire and, and with a pot holder, lifted the lid of the Dutch oven. The aroma filled her nostrils as she stirred the stew, but it only served to nauseate her. She quickly set the heavy lid back in place and turned again to her friend.

"Ellie, are you all right?" Liza moved to her side and took her arm. "You're pale as a full moon, child. Here, lean on me."

Ellie touched her forehead, closing her eyes for a moment as the ground seemed to sway. Liza circled her arm around Ellie's shoulders and led her again to the chair. "I'm all right," Ellie finally managed to whisper as she settled into it. "Really, I'll be fine." She drew in a deep and shaky breath. "I'm just tired. That's all."

The pounding of approaching hooves interrupted them a few minutes later. Ellie looked up to see her husband reining the Appaloosa to a halt near the wagon. Abe followed on his sorrel. They both dismounted and walked over to where Ellie and Liza sat at the table.

"Ladies," Alexander said, tipping his hat. His eyes met Ellie's with a worried look. He bent to give her a quick kiss.

"Smells good," Abe said, glancing at the steaming pot.

Ellie smiled, hoping she looked stronger than she felt. "How about the two of you joining us for supper? There's plenty."

The men exchanged glances. "We'll need to be riding out tonight for a while," Alexander said. "We just came by to let you know not to expect us until later."

"It'll keep," Ellie said. "I'll move it into the coals for you to have when you get back."

"Where're you heading?" Liza asked.

Alexander answered for them both. "There's a group camped a few miles back that's decided to attach itself to our company. That's what the rider who came by earlier wanted. We thought we'd made ourselves clear, but apparently not."

"You've already told them no?" Ellie asked.

Alexander nodded solemnly. "The first time they asked was in Laramie—before the altercation with Lucas Knight."

Ellie stood, touching her husband on the arm. "They sound dangerous, Alexander."

"There's safety in numbers. We've got several of the hands and some of the other men going." He gave her a kiss on the cheek. "We'll not be gone long, Ellie. You just keep that buffalo stew hot."

Minutes later, the two men mounted and kicked their horses to a trot. They joined the other riders—Silas Edwards, the Mitchell boys, the Prewitt brothers, Hampton and Billy Farrington, and Jesse O'Donnell—just outside the circle, and as the sun slipped beneath the horizon and an ashen dusk settled heavily onto the land, the company rode east.

It was well past dark by the time Alexander returned. An unnatural quiet had fallen over the normally lively company. Tonight there was no music or dancing, no laughter or singing. The word about the Missouri Wildcats had spread among the travelers, and a few groups of husbands and wives huddled together, speaking in hushed tones.

Something told Ellie that part of their discussion included criticism of Alexander. Every day she overheard talk about his leadership causing them to run late.

Alexander sat down heavily and pulled his chair to the table. Ellie spooned the stew into his bowl then sliced a wedge of cornbread. "What happened?" she asked, arranging the dishes before him on the table. She could see the worry on his face and figured she already knew the answer. "Did they agree to leave us alone?"

He shook his head as Ellie placed a fork and knife next to the bowl of stew. "No," he said, lifting his fork to take a bite of stew. "They're not of a mind to listen. We've warned them, though, to stay a good distance behind. We really can't do much more than that."

"Maybe they'll tire of trailing behind," Ellie said hopefully. "Their herd won't find much grass left for grazing once ours has moved through."

"I mentioned that fact to them, El," Alexander said. "They're stubborn. They've got it in mind that they're safer with us. Once we're west of Independence Rock, we may have Indian trouble ourselves."

"There haven't been attacks for years, Alexander. You said so yourself. I didn't think it was much of a worry."

"Not from attacks on the company—but on the horses and cattle. Nearly every company coming through here loses hundreds." He took another bite of stew then cut a second piece of cornbread.

"They won't be content to stay a few miles behind, then, will they, Alexander?" Ellie settled into the chair across from him at the little table.

"No," he said with a heavy sigh. "No, if it's safety they're looking for, they're going to get as close to us as they can."

The air was heavy. No hint of a breeze broke the feeling of sticky heat that had settled over the night camp. Alexander looked up at the sky. Even the stars were obscured by the moisture in the air. "I think tomorrow we may get our rain," he said.

"There's something else bothering you, Alexander." Ellie reached for his hand.

He smiled into her eyes. "You've always known me too well, Ellie."

"And you've always tried to protect me too well, Captain Farrington," she said with a small smile. "What is it?"

"There's another reason the Missouri Wildcats want our protection." He let his hand rest beside the bowl of stew.

"It's because of Utah, isn't it?" she asked.

He nodded slowly. "They've guessed correctly that we have no other choice but to take the Mormon road to the Old Spanish Trail and head across the desert into southern California."

Ellie moved her gaze to the fire's dying embers. "And the Wildcats think the Mormons are to be feared?"

He nodded again, still not finishing his stew. "They say the Mormons have a secret army called the Danites. They kill in the name of the Church. In the name of God."

"I have a hard time believing that, Alexander. It sounds to me like this group is simply trying to convince you there's a reason to stay together."

"I hope that's true," he said, once again picking up his fork and taking another bite of buffalo.

"I think our greatest worry," she said softly, "comes not from the Missouri Wildcats but from people in our company. There's talk about electing a new captain."

"I know, Ellie. I've heard. But it's only talk."

"There are those who say they'll leave the train if we head through Utah Territory," Ellie said.

"Then maybe they'll have to do just that," Alexander said, his face grim. "I can't make them stay with us. I can only point out their folly in crossing the Sierras this late."

"Then we'll be a smaller group than before," Ellie said. "A more defenseless company, followed by thugs and ruffians."

"Yes," Alexander said, staring at the dying fire. "But we won't know any of this as a certainty until we reach Fort Bridger."

"Suddenly, I'm afraid," she whispered. "Alexander, I'm so afraid."

He reached across the table and took her hands in his, then lifting them to his lips, he kissed them gently. His gray eyes met hers as if unable to release her gaze. She could see Alexander understood her fear. He didn't make light of it or tell her to ignore it. Instead, he gazed into Ellie's eyes, silently affirming a love that would never die, a love that would live on no matter what lay ahead.

Around them, most of the families were now in bed, and those still awake began putting out their oil lamps.

Soon the only light remaining in the night circle was from the dying embers of the dung cook fires. Smoke hung heavy in the air, and there was not a hint of a breeze to push it away.

TWENTY

Lucas reined Spitfire to a halt at the summit of Big Mountain. Through the pass before him spread his first far-off view of the Great Salt Lake. The sun was setting behind a high pile of clouds, casting crimson-and-purple shadows across the valley of the Saints.

For days he'd ridden the stallion hard, making good time along the trail—through Emigrant's Gap, Devil's Gate, South Pass along the Sweetwater, Fort Bridger—and finally into the Wasatch Mountains. The climb ahead would be difficult: through the southern end of East Canyon, up and over Little Mountain, and through Emigration Canyon, the last one before the valley itself. He planned to wait until morning to attempt it; the moon wasn't yet full enough for night riding, and Spitfire needed the rest.

He put the horse out to graze near a wooded spring, gathered some twigs, and started a small cook fire. He'd shot a small rabbit earlier in the afternoon, and now he proceeded to gut and skin it and skewer it for roasting. Pounding a couple of forked twigs into the ground on either side of the fire, he then set the rabbit in place. Soon it sizzled and popped as the juices splattered into the flames.

As he tended the rabbit, his thoughts turned to the difficult days he knew lay ahead. With each hour of his travels since leaving the Farrington train, he'd had a growing sense of trepidation. Now that he'd almost reached the valley, it was clearer to him than ever: He had but one mission, and that was to see Hannah and Sophronia safely out of the territory, no matter the cost. He would sacrifice his own life, if necessary.

He wondered why it had taken him so long to see the bitter truth of their circumstances. Through the years he'd been lulled into believing that the Saints were his only family, his protectors, his champions. And after what he'd seen done to his mother and father and baby brother by the Gentiles, he'd distrusted all people outside the valley, outside the confines of the Church.

Yet something, perhaps Someone, was drawing him away. Even his aborted mission to England had served to show him that there existed another truth worth considering. Perhaps it was because he'd spent hours alone on the trail, away from the doctrine preached by the Prophet, his elders and apostles, away from people who spoke the same words, repeated the same phrases they'd heard in services the Sunday before.

This mission had been Lucas's first alone, without the company of elders and bishops and apostles. And he'd relished the lack of intrusion into his innermost thoughts.

He turned the rabbit to brown on its other side and drew in a deep breath. Around him dusk had fallen, and the night music of the woods began to play, the voices of owls, the whistles of bats, the sawing of crickets' legs, now and then the soft whinny of Spitfire still grazing near the bubbling spring.

He thought about his chance meeting with the Farrington train, his talks with Alexander and Ellie. Especially Ellie. The entire encounter had served to pull away some covering that had blinded him for nearly all his life. Since his conversation with Ellie the night before he left the train, thoughts about God had been pouring into his heart and soul, thoughts he couldn't ignore. And he had pondered them as he rode, pondered a God different than he'd known before.

A God of love, not vengeance. A singular God, all-knowing, all-powerful, full of grace and glory. A God who had existed from everlasting to everlasting.

Lucas knew that such a God existed. He wasn't sure how he knew. He just did, feeling its certainty clear through to his soul.

But one thought still pierced his heart. He had committed brutal crimes on behalf of the Church. He hadn't actually held the knife when an apostate's throat was being slit. He hadn't actually held the knife when a young man was mutilated for not giving up his betrothed to an elder who wanted to marry her. But he'd been present during dozens of atrocities carried out in the name of God.

And he had done nothing. He had remained silent. And he knew his intimidating presence as a Danite, an Avenging Angel, kept the victims in check as surely as if Lucas had bound them with ropes. He knew he was just as guilty for the crimes as if he'd wielded the knife himself. Crimes against the innocent. Crimes against men who had been questioning the truth given to them by the Saints—just as he himself was now questioning. One by one their faces came to mind, and he heard their cries for mercy, their screams of pain. And he saw his face turning away from theirs, ashamed at what he'd witnessed.

Lucas stared into the fire, unable to bear the darkness inside him.

After a moment, he absently turned the rabbit again, and its juices splattered and smoked. In the distance a screech owl screamed, then was answered by another, farther away. A breeze kicked up, rustling the leaves and shifting the cook fire's ashes, sending sparks into the air.

How could God forgive him? Lucas couldn't even forgive himself. How could this God he was just beginning to understand accept a man so filled with darkness? He smiled grimly to himself. Maybe the Saints were right. It was easier to believe you could achieve God's favor through your own efforts, obedience, and good works. It was easier than considering the chasm between the darkness in a man's heart and the holiness of God.

He considered the Saints' recent teaching of blood atonement. Could it be possible that there were sins—such as his—that couldn't be forgiven in any other way except through the shedding of blood? Even the ancient Hebrews believed in the atonement of sins through blood sacrifice, though it was that of an unblemished lamb.

Lucas stood, making his way through a stand of aspen toward the spring to check on Spitfire. The stallion nuzzled his palm, and he patted the animal on its neck, feeling the velvet smoothness of its hide. Then, stooping near the water, swift moving and clear, Lucas scooped up a handful and drank of its sweetness.

It is not sacrifice I require, my beloved.

It is your heart.

Lucas looked up through the surrounding trees into the blackness of the night sky. A light breeze rustled the quaking aspen, carrying the fragrance of the roasting meat in a mix of fresh, pine-scented air and wood smoke. He bent to drink again from the stream.

The sacrifice has been made, my child.

It was I who was wounded, so that you might be healed.

Lucas slept restlessly that night; a dark and troubled awareness of his return to the Salt Lake valley kept pressing into his mind. Several times he awoke with a start only to fall again into a fitful sleep. Finally, an hour before dawn, he rose, saddled the stallion, and packed his gear. Before the first rays of sun spilled through the aspen, he kicked the horse to a trot along the winding trail that led down Big Mountain. Lucas rode Spitfire hard all day, camped that night at the mouth of Emigration Canyon, then late the following evening reined the stallion to a halt at the corral near his cabin.

The next day was Sunday, and Lucas—clean-shaven, bathed, and in fresh clothes for the first time in weeks—rode into town. He felt better than he had in days, and his anticipation of seeing Hannah mounted with Spitfire's every step.

He turned toward the meetinghouse a few minutes before the services were scheduled to begin, dismounted, and secured the stallion's reins to a hitching post. He figured he'd surprise Hannah and Sophie by his presence during the services as well as put in a needed appearance. He didn't want to alarm the Prophet, John Steele, or any of the others, and he planned to play out his role as a Saint in the highest standing until he could get the women safely transported from the territory.

Porter Roe, still sporting a full beard and a mane of stringy hair, was standing at the entrance. "Lucas!" he cried, striding down the stairs two at a time to meet him. "We weren't expecting you for some time. What's happened?" They shook hands as his piercing gaze flicked across Lucas's face.

"I've got news for Brother Brigham," Lucas said. "Got as far as Kearney before turning back. It was too important to ignore."

"When'd you get in?"

"Last night, late."

"And if your news came from Kearney," Roe began with a frown, "you might as well have continued on your mission. Your news is about Johnston's army?"

"So Brigham's already aware of it."

"I delivered the message myself. I was in Illinois when I heard about the troop movement. Hightailed it back here as fast as I could."

They were standing in front of the meetinghouse now. A few people milled about, some calling out greetings to Lucas, others making their way inside to be seated.

"I didn't know you were heading east last time I saw you," Lucas said. "You were here in the valley the night before I left." Images of Brother Hambleton's killing flashed through Lucas's mind. He briefly wondered if Roe had been ordered to follow him. "How was it you ended up in Illinois?"

Roe gave him a hard look but didn't respond to the question. "I was in Springfield June twelfth," he said simply. "Heard Senator Stephen Douglas make a speech. He said he had it on good authority that we Mormons are not loyal to the U.S. government." Porter lifted a brow sagaciously. "He charged that nine out of ten of Utah's inhabitants are aliens, that Mormons are bound to their leader by 'horrid oaths,' that the Church is inciting Indians to acts of hostility, and that the Danites, or Destroying Angels, as he called us, are robbing and killing American citizens."

Lucas couldn't help laughing. "Well, brother, I'd say he's right, wouldn't you?"

Roe gave him another piercing stare before continuing. "There was another speech, one I didn't hear, a few weeks later. It was reported by one of our brothers who stayed behind in Springfield after

I left. It was given by Abraham Lincoln, who said that Utah's territorial status should be repealed and that we should be placed under the judicial control of neighboring states. He said, 'The Mormons ought to be called into obedience.'"

"That's when President Buchanan stepped in and issued the order to attack," Lucas added.

Roe nodded. "Buchanan responded by calling the 'Mormon problem' one of civil disobedience. And soon after, General Scott dispatched the orders to Fort Leavenworth, instructing Johnston to outfit a detachment of twenty-six hundred men and officers for garrison service in Utah—specifically to restore order and support civil authority—no matter the cost."

"What's been the response here?"

This time Roe laughed. "You should've been here for Brigham's Independence Day sermon on the twenty-fourth of July. We had the usual gathering of hundreds of families from all over the territory—north and south. Celebration's been going on for a couple of weeks now. Fact is, most of the families are just now starting to leave." He looked toward the meeting room. "Standing room only inside. Today's the last day of the celebration."

Lucas knew all about the Saints' Independence Day. He and Hannah and Sophie had usually celebrated it together—starting on the anniversary of the day that the Saints had first entered the Salt Lake valley. Folks camped in parks around the city, sang and danced and thanked God for their blessings . . . and their blessed Zion, their Promised Land.

If the Prophet ever needed to get news to the whole territory about Church edicts or revelations, it was always a good time to present them. Lucas could only imagine the fiery speeches—by Brigham Young himself, his council, and his apostles.

Roe let his assessing gaze again flick across Lucas's face. "Not only the Prophet, but everyone who spoke told our people how they need to prepare for war. Our enemies will be overcome, Brother Knight, have no doubt about that."

"I have no doubt," Lucas agreed, wondering if Roe had reason to doubt his sincerity.

"I thought not," Roe said. "According to Brother Kimball, our enemies shall be annihilated before they reach Big Mountain. He said, 'And we shall have manna!'" Roe chuckled. "Which, of course, was looking at the bright side of the situation. But when you think about it, it's true. The U.S. government has seven hundred supply wagons heading our way. They're also bringing seven thousand head of cattle." He smiled. "Just suppose, Brother Knight, that the troops don't get here but all those goods and cattle do."

Lucas nodded. The Saints were always shrewd, turning the advantage their direction. "Manna from heaven," he agreed.

"The United States is sending troops to make desolation of our people," Roe said, his voice rising in passion. "We do not intend to let that happen. Brigham told our people to arm themselves—men and women alike. We will fight to the death. Every one of us."

Lucas frowned. "I thought you said the troops were ordered to Utah to restore civil obedience . . . not to make desolation of the Saints."

Again, Roe's piercing eyes met his. "Do you suppose for one minute, Lucas, that they will stop at deposing Brigham and taking over all we have worked for a decade to build? This land is ours. If the troops do happen to make it over Big Mountain, we already plan to burn everything in their path rather than to hand it over to the United States government."

Lucas said nothing. Through the doors of the meetinghouse he could heard the Saints singing what sounded like the final hymn before the sermon. He started to say something about going inside, when Roe spoke again.

"Gentiles are our enemies, Lucas; don't ever forget that. They march against us, God's chosen people, and it is our duty to kill them. The manna is simply God's thank you for carrying out His will."

"Blood atonement," murmured Lucas.

"Yes, son," agreed Porter Roe. "Blood atonement. Our enemies are marching toward salvation—they just don't know it." He chuckled. "We'll be doing them a favor by saving their eternal lives." With that, he draped his arm around Lucas's shoulders as the two men walked inside the meetinghouse.

Brigham Young was just standing and moving to the podium to introduce the first speaker, Heber Kimball, a member of the First Presidency, when Lucas and Roe took the two remaining seats in the back row. Lucas scanned the congregation for Hannah and Sophronia. He spotted them on a front bench on the women's side of the room, curiously seated between Harriet Steele and one of John's other wives. John Steele sat in the opposite bench on the men's side.

But Heber Kimball's fiery opening statement drew Lucas's attention away from Hannah. "The president of the United States be cursed!" Brother Kimball shouted, pounding his fist on the wooden podium. "In the name of Israel's God, curse them all! For the United States has sworn to destroy every Mormon man . . . to take every woman and child into captivity!" He leaned forward, narrowing his eyes. "It is even rumored that our women are to be used by the troops for their pleasure. And, my brothers and sisters, we will not—I repeat—*will not* let that happen."

Gasps, followed by murmurs of alarm, rose from the congregation. Lucas glanced around to see if anyone else doubted the truth of what Kimball said. But everyone appeared to be hanging on his words, alarmed and frightened. Lucas wanted to stand and calm the frenzy. Everything he'd heard about the coming troops had to do with occupation, not killing and pillaging and taking anyone captive. But if he dared oppose the speaker, or the general mood of the moment, he wouldn't make it to the back door without being taken captive himself—probably by Porter Roe. He settled back in his bench to listen.

Now Heber Kimball had finished; he turned to nod to Brigham Young as the leader took center stage. The man looked out over the congregation in silence for a moment. "During the past two weeks you have heard about the coming war. And as Brother Kimball has said, our people are in grave danger if we don't prepare for the coming invasion," he said, his voice rising in anger. "I say to each and every one of you, repair your firearms. Turn your scythes into bayonets. Burnish and sharpen your sabers. It is our duty to defend Zion against the Gentiles! Ready your swords, my brothers and sisters. March with me into battle!"

He paused, his impassioned gaze moving across the congregation. "God has given His chosen people this land, and let no man dare come against us. Let no government dare attempt to take away our valley! We will fight to the death to defend it."

His voice dropped to a whisper, and there was not a sound from the congregation as he continued. "Now, my beloved Saints," he began, "there is something else on my heart of which I must speak. Something far more troubling than the enemy from outside our gates. And that is the enemy within.

"I have knowledge of someone in our congregation who is that enemy!" He paused, his eyes searching the faces of the men and women before him. Lucas wondered if it was his imagination that the man's gaze seemed to hesitate briefly when it reached him. "This person has knowledge about being saved in the kingdom of our God and Father, and of being exalted. He has the beauty and excellency of the eternities before them—compared to the vain and foolish things of the world.

"Yet this young man has committed a sin that he knows will deprive him of that exaltation he desires." He paused, again dropping his voice. "But he cannot attain what he wants without the shedding of his blood to atone for that sin . . . to be saved and exalted with the gods!

"Is there anyone in this house, man or woman, who would not say, 'Shed my blood that I may be saved and exalted with the gods'?"

There were murmurs of agreement from across the congregation. Lucas could feel the sweat dripping down his back and an odd, tightening sensation of his collar. He swallowed and kept his eyes on the speaker.

"If you love yourselves, brothers and sisters, you should be glad to have your blood shed. In this way, you would be loving yourselves unto an eternal exaltation.

"And I ask you, will you love your brothers and sisters likewise when they have committed a sin that cannot be atoned for without the shedding of their blood?

"Will you love that man or woman well enough to shed his blood, her blood?"

The room was heavy with heat and silence, and Lucas felt he couldn't breathe. He glanced at Hannah in the front row, where she sat as still as death. He sensed the movement of her arm as if she were taking Sophronia's hand in hers.

"There are many instances where men have been righteously slain to atone for their sins. I have seen hundreds more for whom there would have been a chance for them to rise in the first resurrection if their lives had been taken, if their blood had been spilled on the ground . . . a smoking incense to the Almighty.

"But these are now angels of the devil. I have know a great many men who left this Church for whom there is no chance whatever for exaltation with the gods. But if their blood had been spilled, it would have been better for them.

"This, dear brothers and sisters, is loving our neighbor as ourselves. If he needs help, *help him.* If he desires exaltation and it is necessary to spill his blood on the earth in order that he may be saved, *spill it.*

"Any of you who understand the principles of eternity, if you have sinned a sin requiring the shedding of blood, you should not be satisfied until your blood is spilled, that you might gain exaltation." Again, Lucas thought the Prophet was looking straight at him.

"That, my brothers and sisters," concluded Brigham Young, "that is the way to love mankind! If we love our enemies as much as we love ourselves . . . we will shed their blood gladly! For through their shed blood shall they find life."

Another voice rose up in Lucas's mind, a quiet, gentle voice filled with compassion:

It was I who was led like a lamb to the slaughter, my son.
It was I who bore your iniquities, your pain, your sorrow.
It was my blood that was shed for you
So that you might enter through the gates of eternity.

Lucas kept his face straight forward and tried to breathe normally. He suspected that someone must surely know—how, he couldn't begin to guess—of his heart's turning. He fought the urge to run from this meetinghouse, this territory, and to keep running until he was free of his guilt and the iron bands that held him prisoner within his own soul.

He focused his gaze on Hannah, her curls the color of sunlight that poked out from beneath her frilly Sunday bonnet, the beautiful angle of her cheek, the long sweep of eyelashes he could see even from here. In just a few moments he would look into her eyes, and he would be ready to face anything.

By now Brigham Young had ended his discourse and had invited the congregation to stand for the final prayer. Shoes scuffled on the wood-plank floor, and the benches creaked as people got to their feet. A few minutes later, the congregation was dismissed, and Lucas moved to the aisle, letting people pass as he searched the crowd for a glimpse of Hannah.

Finally he saw her and smiled.

But Hannah, after meeting his gaze for a moment that seemed to hold all of eternity, turned away.

John Steele suddenly moved toward her, speaking briefly to Sophronia then to Hannah. She nodded, keeping her head down. Then Steele encircled her with his arm and ushered both Hannah and her aunt out the side exit.

By the time Lucas made his way through the crowd to the same exit and raced down the stairs to the street, the three had stepped into a carriage. Hannah faced straight ahead as Steele cracked his whip above the backs of the perfectly matched grays, and the carriage lurched forward.

"Son," a voice said behind him, "John wed your Hannah while you were away." He turned to see Harriet Steele standing, gazing up at him tenderly, her tired eyes full of sadness. She touched his arm as if to soften the blow.

"It can't be," Lucas finally managed, shaking his head in disbelief. "We were to become betrothed."

"It seems young Hannah changed her mind," Harriet said simply. "John didn't tell me how he convinced her. They've been wed some weeks now, and he's moved her to his ranch near Mountain Meadows. Sophronia Shannon lives with them."

"I know the place. He's taken me there." Lucas's voice was low, angry. "John said he was saving it for a wife who might not get along with the rest."

"Or for a pearl of great price," Harriet said quietly.

Lucas's simmering rage threatened to erupt. He struggled to contain it for Harriet's sake. It wasn't the poor woman's fault. "Was it against her will?" Harriet didn't answer. "Tell me, Harriet. What did he do to make her change her mind?" Hannah had been at the center of Lucas's world since he met her. And now that world had been destroyed, all in a matter of minutes. All that remained was a whirling, white-hot rage. "Tell me how it happened," he said one last time. "Please."

But Harriet Steele, the woman who'd raised him as her own, couldn't, or wouldn't, answer his question. Obedience to her husband was primary in her thinking. She stared into his eyes for one long moment then turned away as if she could no longer bear to acknowledge what she saw there.

Porter Roe suddenly stepped to his side, grasped his elbow gently, and pulled him a step away from the others. "I see John Steele's taken himself another bride," he said, watching the departing carriage.

Lucas stared at him, unseeing, for a moment. Finally, he nodded. "Yes, I just heard about it," he said.

"You're being summoned inside, Lucas," Roe said, changing the subject as if it held no significance to Lucas.

"Now?" Lucas asked.

"Yes, now. Our brother Phineas Potts was murdered in Arkansas—just a few months back. Shot down in cold blood. We're meeting today to discuss what's to be done."

"To avenge his blood?"

"Yes. And there's something else."

"What is it?"

Roe smiled. "We decided that upon your return you would take the oath. John Steele can't be here—he's heading to Cedar City today—but as captain of the Danites and as your patriarch, he's left this for you with his order to sign it." He handed the oath to Lucas.

Lucas unfolded it and began to read:

In the name of Jesus Christ, the Son of God, I now promise and swear, truly, faithfully, and without reserve, that I will serve the Lord with a perfect heart and a willing mind, dedicating myself, wholly and unreservedly, in my person and effects, to the upbuilding of his kingdom on earth, according to his revealed will. I furthermore promise and swear that I will regard the First President of the Church of Jesus Christ of Latter-day Saints as the supreme head of the Church on earth and will obey him the same as the supreme God in all written revelations under the solemnities of a "Thus saith the Lord," and that I will always uphold the Presidency. I furthermore promise and swear that I will assist the Danites, the Avenging Angels, in the utter destruction of apostates, and that I will assist in setting up the kingdom of Daniel in these last days, by the power of the Highest and the sword of his might. I furthermore promise and swear that I will never communicate the secrets of this decree to any person in the known world, except it be to a true and lawful brother, binding myself under no less a penalty than that of having my blood shed. So help me God and keep me faithful.

Lucas glanced up at Porter Roe after he had finished reading the oath. "My name has already been written at the bottom," he said. "With the year and day."

"Yes," said Roe. "You are to place your signature beneath it." He smiled again.

"And if I don't?"

"This directive is from God himself, son," he said. "You can't disobey your heavenly Father, now, can you?"

Twenty-One

Sitting straight in the saddle, Hannah nudged the big sorrel stallion in the flanks. John Steele rode beside her, and Sophronia rested inside the canvas-covered wagon rolling along slightly behind the horses and being driven by a friendly young Saint who had been assigned to a post near Cedar City. The small company had left immediately after the morning services, stopping only to trade the carriage for the already-packed wagon, and now they headed out of Salt Lake City under a sweltering sun hanging in a pale and hazy sky.

They'd been in the valley for two weeks during the Saints' Independence Day celebration, and now it was time for John to get back to his assignment as Indian agent to the Utes in the south of the territory.

As usual, Hannah did her best to ignore her husband, keeping her back as straight as a picket, holding the reins in one hand and keeping her eyes on the trail. In the daylight hours her behavior toward him was civil, but nothing more. At night she endured his advances only by keeping her mind focused on her eventual escape. Already, since their marriage, John had been gone from home more often than he was there. His travels as Brigham's Indian agent and his captaincy of the Danites kept him on the road to all ends of the Mormon kingdom, and of course, his wives in the posts along the way needed overseeing.

Hannah prayed for the day that a new young virgin would capture his fancy and he would tire of coming home to their ranch in the mountains. But her very indifference seemed to provide an irresistible challenge to him, so that day hadn't come.

Wanting to be alone, she kicked the tall sorrel stallion to a trot and rode off the trail as soon as they were clear of the city. John had often complimented her on her excellent horsemanship and, as during their previous treks up and down the trail, didn't try to stop her.

Her thoughts turned to Lucas and the shock of seeing him after the morning service. Confusion and pain had squeezed her heart in that moment of recognition, almost as if her very life had been wrung out of it. She was actually glad when John—who'd also noticed Lucas's presence—whisked her immediately away. It was good Lucas hadn't come any closer, for she couldn't have borne the hurt and rage in his face when he discovered what had happened.

What could she say to him? How could she explain? There were no words. No matter the reason for the sham of the marriage, the girl Hannah once was—spirited, innocent, and so filled with love for her young man—no longer existed. All that was pure had been defiled. Body, soul, and spirit.

She no longer had any claim to Lucas, nor he to her. Their love, their plans for the future, had been destroyed. Hot tears stung her eyes, and she swallowed hard as she looked out over the heat-shimmering terrain. She had made two promises to herself, however, for both her sake and Sophronia's. The first was her ironclad commitment to get them out of the territory on the first California-bound train that neared the ranch. And the second? She would never succumb to feeling sorry for herself. Never. Her tears dried, the feel of them tight and salty on her sun-warmed face.

She reined the sorrel sharply to the left to miss a jackrabbit then headed the stallion toward a nearby creek and rode alongside it for a half mile or so. It was bone dry from the August heat, and even the leaves of some dusty cottonwoods at its banks were turning brittle and yellow. The sorrel kicked up puffs of red-colored dust as she rode.

After a few minutes, Hannah noticed Sophronia peering through the front of the canvas wagon cover, so she turned the horse back to the wagon to keep her aunt company. The white-hot hours passed slowly as they rode. Other groups in wagons and on horseback passed by, calling out greetings. A band of Utes rode by on an adjacent trail, kicking up a fine dust that carried for miles. The shadows had grown long in the late-afternoon sun by the time John reined his horse to a halt.

He pointed out a campsite near a natural spring and, with the help of the young Saint, pitched tents and started a cook fire. As soon as supper was over, as had become his habit while they sat around the campfire, John spoke long and eloquently of God's will for them all—particularly as it related to the sacrifices they must all make to bring about God's kingdom.

Tonight as his bright, pale eyes watched Hannah, he spoke of the honor of Mormon women. "You, my dear," he said with a fervent tone, "will eventually become a queen and priestess to me, your husband, just as I am working to become a king and a priest to God. I am directly linked to him, just as you are directly linked to me."

Hannah tried to keep her lips from curving into a smile when Sophronia rolled her eyes heavenward.

John didn't notice and continued. "And our kingdom is more than this temporal kingdom on earth. In heaven, where our spirits were born, there are many gods, each having his own numerous wives." He drew in a deep breath and rose to stoke the fire. "You see, Hannah," he went on, "your obedience is a necessary step toward your own progression to godhood."

"My obedience to you, or to God?" Hannah asked, already knowing what he would say.

He nodded. "To me, of course. That was explained in our marriage ceremony. I know you find the idea of plural marriage distasteful, but if you consider the logic of it, you can see why God has ordained it. It is necessary to people other worlds." He frowned. "And you see, dear, the more wives I take, the greater the population that will follow and the sooner we will have our own world to rule."

"You then, become a heavenly father of your own world," she said. "People will pray to you."

"Yes. And you, dear Hannah, will be a heavenly mother."

There was a choking sound from Sophronia, which she turned into a coughing fit.

"And will people pray to me as well?" Hannah asked, suppressing her own smile.

"Oh no. Only to the heavenly Father."

"I see," said Hannah. "But if I am your queen and priestess . . ."

"You aren't yet, my dear," he said with a raised brow. "Remember I said you would *eventually* be my priestess, just as I am a priest."

"How do I achieve this . . . honor?" Hannah asked.

"It is earned," he said. "And I am the one to decide when you're ready."

This time, Hannah stood and stoked the fire then watched as the sparks flew into the black sky.

At sunrise the following day, Hannah and Sophronia walked to the spring to fill their canteens.

"Sophie, you must be careful with the looks you give John. I still worry that he'll accuse you of apostasy."

Sophronia patted Hannah's hand and sighed. "Dear child, don't worry about me. I think he's accepted me as some old crazy woman. He doesn't seem to pay much attention."

"Still, I worry," Hannah said.

"It was good to see you smile last night, child."

Hannah grinned. "It's just that his words about my becoming some kind of heavenly mother—or a priestess, of all things—struck me funny. Can you imagine such an idea?"

"For you, or for all Mormon women?"

"Both," she said, dropping her voice in case they might be overheard. "If you look at it clearly, a woman can't reach God except through her husband. Doesn't it seem to you that a man then holds the keys to much more than her salvation?"

Sophronia nodded slowly. "I've thought about that for some time, especially after you told me what went on in the endowment house."

Hannah's countenance fell with its mention.

"Child, what's happened?" Sophronia asked. "Though I saw your face light in a smile or two last night, I know your spirit is heavy—more than usual."

"Lucas was at morning services yesterday."

Sophronia stopped abruptly. "I didn't see him."

"He was at the back of the room—just before we left."

"He saw us?"

"Yes, he did."

"So he must know . . . about John, about your marriage." Sophronia reached for Hannah's hand and squeezed it.

"Probably not when he first saw us, but I'm sure someone's told him by now." They had reached the spring, and Hannah knelt to fill the first container. "I'm glad I didn't see his face when he found out."

"We will get away," Sophronia said, standing behind her. "And then . . ." Her voice faltered.

"And then . . . ?" Hannah looked back over her shoulder. "If you're thinking about Lucas and me being together again, don't, Aunt Sophie. There's no longer such a thing, and can never be—whether I'm here or out of the territory completely."

Around them the early morning sunlight was now spilling across the rushes, cattails, and clumps of cactus that framed the small pond. It sparkled on the ripples and reflected off the slender stems of the reeds that twisted in the morning breeze.

Hannah handed Sophronia the full canteen then plunged the second one under the water as her aunt twisted the cap on the first.

"What's happened to you couldn't be avoided," Sophronia said as Hannah stood. "You mustn't carry the guilt for what John's done to you—to us." She touched Hannah's cheek affectionately. "I'll never forget what you've sacrificed, because you did it to save me."

"I keep thinking there should have been another way, Sophie. If we'd left sooner or covered our trail better . . ." Her voice dropped, and she shook her head slowly.

"There was nothing to be done—especially by you."

"I love you, Sophie," Hannah said softly. "I don't know how I'd make it through this without you."

"Speaking of love, Hannah, I've been thinking about something during my hours in the wagon."

Hannah smiled. "I hope it's detailed plans for the day we leave, Sophie."

"No, this is something different. A long time ago before I joined up with the Saints, I read someplace in the Holy Bible that God doesn't want our sacrifice, he only wants our hearts."

Hannah nodded. "There are parts of the Holy Bible that aren't properly translated."

"That's what we've been told . . . by the same men who say they are gods in the making and say that our only way into heaven is by their calling our names.

"But what if we've been told wrong?" Sophronia went on. "All this killing has bothered me for a long while. I've told you that plenty of times. I used to think it was necessary—back in our early days when folks were persecuting us. But now? The very idea of blood atonement, punishing people for their doubts about the Church or for criticizing the Prophet . . ." She sighed heavily and shook her head. "I just don't believe it's right, Hannah."

A thoughtful frown creased Sophronia's forehead. "Yet God is real. I know he is. And I was thinking that if it's not sacrifice he wants, then that means there's no way to *earn* our way into heaven through pleasing our husbands, as John would have us believe. Or even on our own.

"If you think about it . . . if it's our hearts God wants, they're filled with everything we've ever done in our lives—good and evil all mixed together."

"Yet if that's what he wants," Hannah mused, "we would have to give him our hearts just as they are. There's not a way for *us* to make them acceptable."

"Or pure," Sophronia added, raising a brow.

Hannah knew her aunt's meaning. "You're trying to tell me that it wouldn't matter to God that I've been defiled."

"That's a strong word, honey." Sophronia must have seen the pain on Hannah's face, for she wrapped her arms around her grandniece and held her close for a moment. "Oh, child, I'm sorry. I'm so sorry for what you're enduring."

"I don't think God or anyone else can ever take it away or its memory," Hannah said bitterly. She looked into her aunt's careworn face. "Aunt Sophie, do you mind if I stay here alone for a few minutes?"

Sophronia smiled softly. "No, child. You stay. I'll make an excuse for you to John."

"Thank you," Hannah said, kissing her aunt's downy cheek. Then she settled onto a sandstone rock beside the spring. A breeze rippled the waters, and they moved in the sunlight, almost as if thousands of tiny diamonds had been tossed across the surface.

Then an odd calm came over her, as if someone had brought a candle into the pitch black room that made up her soul.

My child, I have loved you with an everlasting love.

You are precious in my sight.

I betroth you to me forever . . . in lovingkindness . . . in mercy.

The small company moved southward for three more days. The August sun beat down with an almost unbearable scorching heat. The mules and horses plodded along, slower now. By the fourth day, a wind kicked up in the late morning, and to the west, great piles of thunderheads began to build.

John decided to stop early and take shelter on high ground. After camp was made, Hannah approached her husband. She'd increasingly felt the smothering confines of riding near him, being with him day and night, especially in this searing heat. She needed some relief.

"I'm going to take the sorrel out for a ride," she told him as the sky was darkening with rain-laden clouds. Sophronia was resting in the wagon, and it was a perfect opportunity for a short ride across the mesa.

"It's not a good time to go riding," he said.

"It may not be, but I've decided to go anyway," she said, knowing it was indeed foolish with the impending storm but feeling she would suffocate if she didn't get away, at least for a few minutes.

"I'll come along, then. It's not safe for you to go out alone," he said.

"I intend to go alone," she countered, turning from him. "Please, don't try to stop me."

He reached for her shoulder, but she shrugged off his hand and hurried to the makeshift corral near the wagon. She let out a sigh of relief when he didn't follow.

Moments later, she'd saddled the stallion, mounted, and was galloping across the red-rock country far from camp, away from John's ever-watchful eyes. The air was cooler now because of the coming storm; now and then she felt a light touch of raindrops on her face. She'd loosened her hair, and it caught in the breeze, lifting off her neck as she rode. Closing her eyes, she tilted her face as the stallion thundered across the mesa, enjoying the rhythm of his pounding hooves, the freedom of release.

Finally slowing the horse to a walk, she wound through some alders toward an outcropping of black lava that she figured would overlook the road they'd been traveling on. They would soon intersect the Sevier River, and she thought the lookout point might afford her a pleasant view. So she drew to a halt, tied the reins to a nearby shrub, and moved through the slender trees to the outcropping.

She'd taken only a few steps, however, when she heard the sounds of hoofbeats pounding the earth. John Steele! She was certain. Fighting waves of sickening anger, she walked farther into the forest of trees, searching for a place to hide. The brush was thick—buckeye, spent wild lilac, buckthorn—and she moved quickly into some large clumps and knelt down, out of sight.

She heard the heavy boots moving through the brush and held her breath.

"Hannah," called a voice. It wasn't John Steele; it was a voice she would have known anywhere, even in her dreams. "Hannah," it came again, and she felt a flood of tears sting her eyes.

It was Lucas, but she couldn't face him.

"Hannah," he said again. "I need to talk to you. I won't force you, but please, let's at least talk."

By now her tears were spilling down her cheeks, and she covered her face with her hands.

"I've been following the wagon," he called to her, "hoping to catch you alone. This is the first time. I must know what happened. Please, talk to me. I promise to leave you then if you want me to."

For a moment, the only sounds Hannah could hear were those of the wind crying through the trees, the distant thunder rolling across the mesa, and the thudding of her heart.

Finally she stood, her face still wet with tears, to face Lucas, who was still sitting atop Spitfire. Neither of them spoke. Lucas was the first to move, dismounting then taking a step toward her. Hannah was still surrounded by the buckthorn and wild lilacs, so she made her way through the brush to meet him in a small clearing among the alders.

"Hannah," he whispered hoarsely. "First, tell me, are you all right?" His gaze was caring, breaking Hannah's heart all the more. She knew how his expression would change once he heard everything that had happened with John Steele.

She couldn't speak. Not yet. As she looked into his beloved face, her eyes filled with tears once more, obscuring his image. She blinked and wiped her eyes with her fingertips. He reached for her hand, but she pulled it away from him.

"Tell me, Hannah."

Hannah bit her lip and turned away, unwilling to see the pain in his eyes as she told the story. Her voice was low, controlled, when at last she spoke. "After you left," she began, "John came to me and said that you were going to England to fetch yourself a wife."

"You believed him?"

She shook her head. "No. I knew that if it was planned you didn't know it."

"Then why—how did he get you to agree to marry him?"

"So you know."

"Yes, Harriet told me."

The skies were grayer now, and large drops of rain had begun to dampen the soil, splashing off the alder leaves and rustling the dry brush. A clap of thunder rolled, crashing closer than before.

"Let's take cover," Lucas said gently and reached for Hannah's arm to lead her farther into the stand of trees, under the canopy of branches. He went back for the horses and led them to shelter near where Hannah stood waiting.

"Did you want to marry John, Hannah?" he asked when he returned. "Is that why you agreed?"

His hair was damp from the rain, and Hannah fought the urge to brush it from his forehead, feel its texture as she combed it with her fingers. "You know me better than that, Lucas. I wouldn't have done it."

"Then why?"

She told him how they'd tried to flee, about their capture, and how her aunt had shot at John with her Hawken. "He was going to try her for apostasy, Lucas. When he said that I could save her, I agreed to the marriage. He told me we'd be living in the south of the territory, near Mountain Meadows." She gave him a wry smile. "Probably the best hope for getting out of the territory. That's what gives me the only glimmer of sanity in this madness."

"So you've not abandoned plans for leaving."

Hannah searched his face. "Are you still riding with the Danites?"

"You're afraid I might turn you in?" He let out a short, bitter laugh, shaking his head. "Oh, Hannah, if you only knew . . ." He reached for her hand, and this time she didn't pull away. "I came back for you—and for Sophie. I got as far as Fort Kearney and knew I couldn't leave you. I heard about the troop movement out of Leavenworth, and it gave me the excuse I needed to return without suspicion."

"You were coming back for me?" She bit her lip, feeling the threat of tears again. "Oh, Lucas . . . no!" Her voice was a ragged whisper.

"I'd decided to get you and Sophie out to safety. Completely away from here. But I had no idea what had happened. I trusted John."

"What will you do now?" Hannah asked, her voice barely a whisper. "Are you still going to leave?"

"I would never leave you, Hannah. I'll get you to safety. I swear it. Both you and Sophronia."

Hannah moved away from him. Around them now sheets of rain

were falling, and the faraway rumble of thunder seemed to cause a steady shaking of the ground. But the canopy of leaves protected them except for when gusts of wind slanted the rain toward them. In the distance, jagged flashes of lightning brightened the dark sky.

"I can't leave with you," she said.

"I don't mean right now," he said, misunderstanding. "You're worried about Sophie being able to travel at her age. I've thought of little else on my way here. I've made plans . . ."

"No," she said firmly. "I've heard that women who leave their husbands, or the Church, face dangers. But I've also heard that when a man takes another's wife—especially the wife of a man as powerful as John Steele—it's death or unspeakable horrors worse than death." She paused, looking into his eyes. "What I've heard is true, isn't it, Lucas?" His eyes didn't lie, and she knew without his speaking a word that she was correct. "I won't let you face that, Lucas."

"I'd give my life for you, Hannah. Gladly."

"And I for you, Lucas," she said. "But I can't leave with you."

"There's something more . . . another reason . . . beyond what you've told me." He paused, but when she didn't comment, he went on as if trying to understand her feelings. "You are the same to me now as you've always been—"

"No!" she interrupted. "I'm not the same. And please, speak no more of rescue or of going away with me. What has happened has changed us both. It can't be undone, Lucas. Ever."

"I'll do my best to convince you you're wrong, Hannah. I'm going to return to your camp and travel with you. John is expecting me." Lucas laughed bitterly. "I had quite a welcome waiting for me when I returned to the valley. First, finding I'd lost you to him, then that he'd arranged for me to take my oath as a Danite against my will. John left word that he personally will oversee my first mission alone. I believe my loyalty is being tested."

"Oh, Lucas! What will happen if you don't agree to do it?"

He didn't answer, and Hannah met his anguished gaze. She knew Lucas well. If he was forced to kill for the Church, his soul would be just as ravaged as hers had been by John Steele.

"Leave right now, Lucas. Ride on without us. Get out of the territory before it's too late. Please," she entreated. "John won't know you've been here. Just ride on, quickly. You know the territory better than most. You can make it out."

"I won't leave you, Hannah."

"We'll join up with the next suitable wagon company that nears John's ranch. We've already planned it. We'll get out."

"I won't leave the territory without you," he repeated. Then he pulled her into his arms.

"God help us," she whispered.

Twenty-Two

Fort Bridger
Early August

Ellie cracked her whip over the oxen's scrawny backs, heading her wagon into the night circle just outside Fort Bridger. The outpost wasn't a military fort as she had expected but more of a supply depot surrounded by pines and scrub brush. At least it would provide them a place to buy grain and ammunition.

She worried now that the company was noticeably smaller. Weeks before, seven families had formed their own company and had taken the Sublette cutoff, or as many called it, the Parting of the Ways, desperately and stubbornly seeking to make up for lost time through a dangerous shortcut to California. They had become vehemently opposed to Alexander's captaincy and had caused trouble nearly from the first day the train pulled out of Fort Laramie.

It seemed to Ellie that every time an iron tire rolled off and wobbled in the dust like a coin, Alexander was blamed for not insisting on better-built wheels. Or when they traveled through dust as fine as flour, rising so the wagoners couldn't see, they blamed the captain for not getting them nearer water. Or when oxen hooves split, the shoes fell off, and there was no hot tar for curing the animals' feet, her husband was blamed for not telling them to bring a greater supply of whatever was needed.

The final straw came when the company was attacked by a roving band of Cheyenne braves near Devil's Gate. No one was hurt, but they lost several hundred head of cattle and a small *remuda* of their best horses, including Meg's and Sarah's ponies. Alexander was blamed for the attack by the dissenters, who said more men should have been stationed to guard the herd.

The first time mutiny was mentioned was at Independence Rock on the Sweetwater, when folks began pointing out that they were at least a full month behind schedule. By the time they reached South Pass—immediately following the incident at Devil's Gate—insurrection was imminent, openly led by Silas Edwards. Alexander's solution was to simply order Edwards and his followers to take the trail of their choice—as long as it was not the same road taken by the Farrington company.

By the time the wagons pulled into the Green River Campground, the travelers' spirits were low. They'd trudged hundreds of miles along the California road, a trail lined by hundreds of ox carcasses and furniture and tools unloaded by earlier wagon caravans. As their own teams wearied, some in the Farrington party had lightened their own rigs as well, leaving beside the trail such treasures as spinet pianos, bedsteads, and chests. Ellie had stubbornly held on to her family heirlooms—the cradle Alexander had made for the new baby, the hand-painted trunk filled with a set of blue willow dishes, a stout and sturdy rocking chair made of Arkansas pine—refusing to let anything of hers be left alongside the trail.

Now, here they were at Fort Bridger. They'd made it this far, Ellie thought proudly as she halted the team. It hadn't been easy, but they'd made it. But they had a thousand miles to go, and she tried not to think about what lay ahead.

She gingerly climbed from the front of the wagon, her growing girth making her movements more awkward by the day. She had just stepped to the ground when she heard the beat of horses' hooves and Alexander rode up on the Appaloosa. The horse shook its head and whinnied softly, tossing its mane and jangling the bridle.

She smiled up at her husband, the sight of him still quickening her heart. His gaze met hers from beneath his hat brim, pulled low over his forehead. His concern for her was etched on his sun-leathered face.

"How are you feeling, El?" he asked as he dismounted. He removed his hat and raked his fingers through his sand-colored hair.

"Don't you be worrying about me, Alexander," she replied, not willing to add to his worries by complaining about her discomforts. "You've got plenty enough to think about just getting us on the Salt Lake Road."

He unharnessed the team and prepared to drive them out to the herd for grazing. "Nonetheless," he said, "I want you to spend time napping before supper."

"I intend to, Alexander," she said, giving him a smile that she hoped would relieve his anxious thoughts about her health. "But mainly because I don't want to fall asleep before the night-fire council is over." Tonight Alexander planned to tell the entire company about their coming travels into Utah Territory, mapping out the route and the dangers along the way. He would also be discussing the growing irritation from the Missourians still trailing the train.

He left with the oxen, who now obeyed with just a word to turn them left or right. Ellie watched them go, feeling sorry for the poor beasts with their dull coats, spindly legs, and bony backs. They bawled and complained as they moved, heads down, lifting one heavy hoof after another.

"Mommy," Meg called, clambering from the back of the wagon. "Mommy!"

"I'm here, child," Ellie said quietly to her daughter. "You needn't shout."

Meg rounded the wagon, braids flying. She was followed by Sarah, who held Phoebe tenderly in her arms. "Mommy! Prudence Angeline said that her mommy's gonna let her stay up tonight for the night fire. I want to too!"

"Me too!" declared Sarah, her bottom lip already starting to protrude. "I want to dance and sing with everybody else." She started to sing "Sweet Betsy from Pike" at the top of her lungs and turned in circles, arms wide out.

Laughing, Ellie drew her daughters to her, enjoying the feel of her arms around them. "I'd already decided to let you stay up a little later tonight, girls. Prudence Angeline's mama and I had already discussed it."

"You did?" Meg's eyes were wide.

"The Reverend Brown has a special story planned just for the children."

"He does?" Sarah asked.

Ellie nodded. "We'll all gather in the circle right at sundown for some singing and dancing—" She smiled at Sarah. "—and storytelling. Then you'll be off to bed while the older folks meet."

The twins started to race off with their news, but Ellie firmly held onto their little arms. "There's a catch to staying up late, however," she said.

Meg let out an exaggerated sigh. "I suppose we have to take a nap," she said. Sarah stuck out her bottom lip in a pout.

"That's right," Ellie said, and she hugged them close again. "The three of us are going to lie down together right now, and I don't want to hear a peep out of any of us for an hour."

"Peep!" said Meg, hopping along beside Ellie as they headed to the back of the wagon.

"Peep!" mimicked Sarah, then scolded Phoebe for making the sound.

A few minutes later the three were resting quietly on the cornhusk mattress in the shade of the wagon. The twins cuddled close, one on either side of Ellie, and she sighed contentedly, drinking in the puppylike fragrance of children who'd been playing in the sun. She was suddenly overwhelmed with a mix of emotions, feeling protective and proud and filled with her love for them.

She rested on one elbow, gazing down at Sarah, whose sun-browned cheek was resting on love-worn Phoebe. Sarah's little turned-up nose now had a darker dusting of freckles than when they'd left home, and her sun-blistered lips had turned the color of spent roses. Ellie brushed a stray wisp of hair away from Sarah's forehead then turned to look at Meg. She couldn't help smiling. The child seemed full of mischief and energy even when sleeping. Just the curve of her lips suggested she might be dreaming about her next escapade or a trick to play on her sister. Ellie planted a soft kiss on her daughter's cheek then settled back against her pillow.

She rested her hand on the baby in her womb and frowned, wishing he'd kick or scoot an elbow or heel across her stomach. He'd been so active early on that it worried her that he'd become so still. Her ankles and wrists had nearly disappeared with swelling, and so often now, she couldn't catch her breath when walking. Ellie didn't care so much about her own discomfort as she did about bearing a healthy baby.

She gazed up at the arched canvas ceiling above her, relaxing in its soft light, the dappled play of shadows caused by some cottonwood leaves dancing in the breeze outside the wagon.

"Be with my children, Father," she prayed. "All three of them. They are life's promise and hope. I suppose it's natural to worry about our future when it seems so uncertain. And Lord, I try not to worry or fret—and I don't for myself. Or even Alexander. But it's for my children I pray.

"Protect them, Father," she breathed, feeling a flutter of movement in her womb. "Keep them close to you." As she closed her eyes in sleep, words of comfort settled into her soul.

Their names are engraved on the palms of my hands.
Precious child, fear not; they are my lambs.
Even now, I carry them close to my heart.

That night after supper, Reverend Brown called the littlest children—all those six years and under—into a circle. They ran and skipped and giggled and poked each other as they gathered close.

Ellie watched the excited faces of the little ones sitting in front of the reverend. His face was kind, the lines around his eyes crinkling upward. He was old, so old that many doubted in the beginning that he could pull his own weight. But not only had he taken care of his own rig, but he'd become invaluable in his support of Alexander's captaincy. He was a voice of calm in the midst of the storm, a voice that even disgruntled travelers would listen to, even if they wouldn't listen to Alexander.

"Little ones," Reverend Brown said, "I want to tell you a story about three boys named Shadrach, Meshach, and Abednego."

Meg turned to catch Ellie's gaze, wrinkling her nose at the sound of the strange names. Ellie signaled for her daughter to turn around and face the storyteller, which she did.

"These young men were living in a foreign land. They loved God very much, but the people in the land where they were living worshiped idols. Who can tell me what an idol is?"

Meg jumped up and down, holding her arm up as straight as a picket. "I can. I can!" she shouted.

Smiling, Reverend Brown nodded toward her. "Meg?"

"It's a big thing that's supposed to be God—but isn't," she said with a smug smile, looking back to see if Ellie was watching. Ellie and Alexander had told the little girls this Bible story before.

"Uh-huhh," said Prudence Angeline. "There's no such thing. It's a statue . . . or something."

"What's a statue?" Nancy Huff said, wrinkling her nose.

Reverend Brown smiled. "Well, let me see if I can explain. Imagine if someone carved a big cow out of stone, covered it with gold, then told everyone it was God."

"That's an idol?" asked Prudence Angeline, wide-eyed. "A cow?"

"It can be anything that people worship instead of God," said the Reverend. "But let me tell you what happened when these three young men were commanded to bow down and worship an idol in this foreign land."

"Was it a gold cow?" Felix Jones asked.

"No one knows for sure what this idol looked like exactly. But I think it might have been made to look like a very tall, very big man, maybe like the king himself."

"Was it gold?" Meg wanted to know.

"Yes, it was covered with gold." Reverend Brown paused. "What do you think Shadrach, Meshach, and Abednego did when the king told them to fall down on their knees and pray to this golden idol?"

"They didn't do it," the children chorused.

"They did not," said Reverend Brown, "because they loved the one true God with all their hearts. There was no room in their hearts for another god, a false god."

"Besides," said Sarah, looking smug, "God told them it was bad to worship any other god besides him."

"The king told Shadrach, Meshach, and Abednego that if they didn't worship the golden image, he was going to throw them into a blazing hot furnace. And what do you think the young men said to him?"

"Maybe they should've run away," said Meg, totally caught up in the drama, not remembering she'd heard the Bible story before. "That's what I'd do. I'd run away."

"Remember, Meg, they were in a foreign land. They were captives of the king of this land. They couldn't leave." He smiled at the children. "Shadrach, Meshach, and Abednego said to the king, 'If we are thrown into that fiery furnace, the God we serve is able to save us from it. He is able to rescue us. But even if he chooses not to rescue us, we want you to know that we still will not worship your golden idol.'

"The king was furious. He wanted these boys to obey him—not God. He ordered the furnace heated to seven times its normal heat. And he tied up the young men and threw them into the furnace."

There was a gasp from the children, and a few of them looked over at the nearby campfire and its long tongues of hot, orange flames.

The reverend's voice was gentle as he continued. "But something very unusual happened."

"What?" the children cried in chorus.

"The king jumped up and looked into the furnace. 'There are four people in the fire!' he shouted. 'I thought only three were thrown in.'"

There were murmurs of awe from the children. "Who was the extra person? What happened then?" asked little Felix Jones.

"It was Jesus!" Reverend Brown exclaimed. "The same Jesus who's with us today! He was suddenly in that fiery furnace—right in the middle of the flames—with the three young men who loved him. He had untied them, and they were all four walking in the furnace."

"What did the king do then?" Sarah whispered.

"He shouted, 'Servants of the Most High God, come out!' and they did. Shadrach, Meshach, and Abednego walked out of that furnace, and their hair and clothes didn't even smell like smoke."

"Mine do," said Felix. "My ma said she'll never be able to rid me of the smell of cook smoke."

Reverend Brown chuckled. "I think all of us feel that way," he said. "Now I have a Bible verse for you to tuck away in your heart. Will you do that for me?"

They nodded, and he pulled out his worn, leather Bible, flipping through its pages to a place that, as soon as he began reading, Ellie knew was from Isaiah 43, one of her most beloved passages.

"Fear not, for I am with thee." The children repeated it several times. "I want you to always remember those words. Because no matter what happens—good or bad—God is with you. Even if you can't see him, he's there—just as he was in the blazing furnace with Shadrach, Meshach, and Abednego."

Ellie thought about the rest of the passage as he continued talking to the children. "I have called thee by thy name; thou art mine. When thou passest through the waters, I will be with thee; and through the rivers, they shall not overflow thee; when thou walkest through the fire, thou shalt not be burned; neither shall the flame kindle upon thee. . . . Fear not: for I am with thee."

Reverend Brown smiled at the children. "God doesn't promise us that life will be easy. But he does promise that he will be with us." He paused.

"Like the time I fell out of the wagon and split open my head," said Prudence Angeline, rubbing the spot for emphasis.

"Or when I got bit by millions of skeeters from the Sweetwater willows," added her sister, Becky.

"Or me, when that big rattler jumped at my horse and he bucked me off," said Billy Tackett.

All the children were now adding their own list of maladies, injustices, and discomforts endured on the trek. "God is with us no matter what happens," the reverend said when they'd finished. "Let's say the verse one more time, remembering that it's God speaking these words to you."

"Fear not, for I am with thee," chorused the children again.

"Now, how about a song or two before you head off to bed?" the reverend said, pulling out his fiddle.

"I've got one!" Meg shouted. "'Sweet Betsy from Pike!' It's my sister's favorite song!"

The reverend began to play, and the children sang and danced and clapped their hands. Ellie and Alexander looked at each other over their heads and smiled.

When the little ones had been put to bed in the wagons, Ellie and the other mothers met back at the night circle for the discussion about the trail ahead.

Alexander stood and walked to the center of the group. "As you know," he began, "we've made the decision to take the southern route into California."

There were a few worried murmurs among the listeners.

"We've lost a number of our company in the last several days, and that's what we need to discuss," he said. "That leaves us more vulnerable than before."

There were nods of agreement.

Jesse O'Donnell stood near the back of the group. "There's that contingent of Missourians—the ones that call themselves the Wildcats—following not far behind us," he said. "Pretty tough characters. Maybe we ought to let them join up with us."

"They been tryin' to anyway all the way from Laramie," said Alexander's son Hampton.

Abe Barrett stepped forward. "I'm inclined to agree with the captain on this. He's held them off all this way because they're uncouth ruffians. We both think they'd be more trouble than they're worth."

Alexander nodded. "Another problem is that they're openly hostile to Mormons. My fear is that instead of giving us strength against the

Saints, should there be any trouble, they would cause a greater disturbance. Back in Laramie they were set to kill Lucas Knight just because they suspected he was Mormon."

"I still say the Mormons aren't gonna give us any grief," Jesse O'Donnell added thoughtfully. "They're known throughout the States as being pleased to offer assistance to wagoners, selling grain and supplies to folks heading out of the Great Salt Lake for the Hastings cutoff or the Old Spanish Trail."

Several men chuckled. "For a steep price," someone called out.

Abe shrugged. "We're a wealthy train. We can afford it. We'll need supplies desperately by the time we get there—grain for our herd, food for ourselves."

Liza stepped up to stand beside Ellie. "I remember what you told me about that fellow who was killed in Arkansas," she whispered, a frown furrowing her brow.

Ellie sighed heavily. She'd been thinking of the same incident. "The man who was killed by an irate husband for wife-stealing."

"Do you want to say something, or shall I?"

"Go ahead," Ellie said.

Liza stepped forward to stand by her husband. Abe smiled as she approached. "Folks," she said, "just before we left Arkansas, a Mormon man was killed. Ellie Farrington, who told me the story, says she heard on good authority that the man was a special agent of Brigham Young.

"I don't know about you all, but I worry about going through Mormon country because we're from Arkansas . . ."

"No reasonable person would blame the entire state for the actions of one man," Jesse O'Donnell interrupted. "We may think these Latter-day Saints practice a strange religion. But I believe they're reasonable people."

Other voices spoke up, some agreeing, others disagreeing. Finally, Alexander held up a hand, taking charge of the meeting. "I recommend we head, as planned, into the Salt Lake valley. If we sense danger, we can still take the Hastings cutoff."

"That's the route of the Donner party," Liza said quietly. Beside her, Abe circled his arm around her shoulders and pulled her close. The whole country had heard the tale of the wagon train finally reduced to cannibalism.

Alexander nodded. "We'll have to decide which is the greater danger," he said. "Tomorrow morning, we'll wait to strike camp until every family's had a chance to enter the fort and buy enough supplies to get to the valley. Then we'll replenish there.

"And while you ladies are buying supplies, some of us men will go over to the Missourians' camp and have a talk. They've stayed a few miles behind us since Laramie—at least, since we last told them to keep their distance. They're not part of our company, by any stretch, and we want it to stay that way."

"We'll just hope the Mormons don't think they're part of our train," said Liza. Her voice carried into the quiet of the night, and Ellie saw the worried expressions cross the company members' faces, young and old. No one spoke, and after a minute, they all quietly made their way back to their wagons and tents. Later, when Hampton picked up his fiddle to play, the songs sounded mournful.

At ten o'clock the following morning, the new supplies were packed, the rigs were hitched, and the train moved away from the rough-hewn buildings at Fort Bridger. Ellie looked back, thinking this might be the last friendly place they'd see until they were out of Utah Territory. She quickly brushed the thought from her mind, popped the whip, yelled "Haw!" to the team, and the wheels began to roll forward, creaking and bouncing across the rocky soil.

Alexander was riding point today with Abe by his side. Ellie saw them in the distance, leading the long line of wagons southwest onto the Salt Lake road.

Twenty-Three

The Road to Cedar City

To protect Hannah from suspicion and to keep John from knowing that they'd already met, Lucas waited to arrive at camp until well after Hannah had ridden in. John was indeed expecting him and greeted him warmly.

Hannah treated him with feigned indifference, but Sophronia ran to him and rocked him in her arms as if she would never let him go. John introduced him to the young Saint who was traveling with them, and after exchanging news of the trail and the latest reports about Johnston's troops, John and Lucas walked some distance from camp to talk out of earshot of the others. By now the summer thunderstorm had moved to the east, and a bright, round moon lit their path.

"I'm glad to see that you've agreed to take the oath," John said. "I figured you would."

Lucas leaned against a tall outcropping of boulders, crossing one ankle over the other. "You didn't leave me a choice," he said.

"I figured it was for your own good, son," John said. "You're either for us or against us. And I think you're aware by now that your orders come straight from God. You're right about having no choice. The elders and apostles—Brigham himself—are merely God's messengers."

"With that thinking," countered Lucas, "it would seem that the priests cannot give a wrong order."

"They've been spoken to by God, son," John said, his tone still conciliatory. "And it's high time you started listening to their wisdom."

Lucas decided not to challenge the man's words. He wanted to give no cause for suspicion. "Brother Roe said that you would tell me about my first mission," he said. "I'm assuming I'll be riding with you."

John shook his head slowly, watching Lucas as if assessing his sincerity. "No, you'll not be coming along with us—though it's no wonder you want to."

"What do you mean?"

"Hannah," John said simply, his ice blue eyes flicking across Lucas's face.

Lucas's hands fisted at his sides, and he fought the urge to tear John Steele limb from limb. He could feel his jaw tensing, and his breath coming fast and shallow. One more word about Hannah, and he would not be able to stop himself from hurting the man. Hurting him. And getting nowhere. Certainly not getting Hannah and Sophronia safely beyond Utah's borders. He steadied his breathing and simply returned John's stare.

"I'm talking about my mission," he said, finally. "Not a holiday ride down the Old Spanish Trail."

John seemed satisfied that he wouldn't be challenged about his new bride. "There are rumors about a train heading into the territory—a company from Arkansas."

Lucas figured he was talking about the Farringtons and was surprised anyone knew about the train. "There are many trains coming through this time of year."

"Not this wealthy. Not from Arkansas."

"I assume you're referring to Phineas Potts . . . and you're talking about blood atonement."

John looked pleased that Lucas had already guessed the general intent of his mission. "Why yes, I am indeed, son. You see, we're aware that you rode along with that particular train for some time—made friends with their captain. Seems that you even had an altercation with a group in Laramie. Some hateful folks called the Missouri Wildcats."

Lucas's jaw was working in anger, and again he fought to keep his voice controlled. "You had me followed?"

John didn't respond, and Lucas wondered who might have been in the saloon that night or who had trailed him and reported back on his whereabouts, his actions.

"So that's why you had the oath waiting for my return. You'd even dated it." He narrowed his eyes. "You even knew the day I would return."

Again, John didn't respond to his statement. "The important thing here, Lucas, is that you've gained the trust of the captain of this train . . . Farrington, is that it?"

Lucas nodded. "Alexander Farrington."

"We can use that."

"How?"

"Your mission is to ride back to meet them. They will be arriving in the valley within days. Meet them and find out their intentions."

"That's all?"

John chuckled. "You were expecting more?"

Lucas was relieved. Perhaps John understood his reluctance and wouldn't push him toward a mission of atonement after all.

"If you want me to warn them to stay clear of the territory, I've already done that. I told them it wasn't safe—that they needed to take another route."

John didn't comment. "Our scouts tell us they must not have listened to your advice. Just ride with them, Lucas, find out what you can. I want to know everything, from where they've hidden their trunks of gold—which we hear are considerable—to the number of chests of silver eating utensils. We already know the size of their herd." He chuckled. "In fact, you could say some of the cattle and a few horses got to the valley ahead of the train."

"You attacked them?" Lucas asked, already guessing the answer. He himself had been on "Indian" raids with the Avenging Angels.

John laughed again. "Not me personally, no. But it's surprising what good luck war paint can bring a Saint." Then his expression sobered. "We're preparing for war. Our coffers must be full if we're going to drive off the U.S. troops."

Lucas said nothing, and John continued thoughtfully, "The U.S. forces are hoping to kill Brigham Young. Even now they march toward our Deseret, declaring they will destroy every man, woman, and child in order to wipe us out of existence."

"That information isn't correct," Lucas interjected. "I heard they're coming to depose him, not kill him."

John dismissed his words with a wave of the hand. Lucas knew he didn't believe him. He also knew that if he pursued the line of thought, it would merely be considered another reason to believe he was softening toward the Gentiles.

John's voice was now rising with passion. "Brigham himself has cursed President Buchanan, saying he will fight until there's not a drop of blood left in his veins." John stood and moved toward Lucas, his eyes cold and unblinking. "Now tell me, son. Is it too much to ask any one of us to defend ourselves however we can . . . by taking gold or silver, cattle, or even wagons from our enemy?"

"And blood atonement?" Lucas said. "Is it also part of this mission?"

Again, John seemed to study Lucas's face as if looking inside his soul for some sign of commitment. He didn't answer the question. Finally, he said, "Porter Roe will be contacting you once you return to the valley. For now, you are to leave immediately for Salt Lake." He looked up at the full moon. "You might as well leave now; it's a good night for traveling."

"One more thing, John," Lucas said, before they started walking back to camp. "Why did you want to tell me about the mission? Couldn't Roe have done the same?"

"I raised you as my son, Lucas," John said, throwing his arm around the younger man's shoulders as they walked. "Though you've ridden with the Angels countless times, I know how you've evaded killing. And now I'm sure it's no surprise to you to know you are being tested. I think you're at a crossroads. I'd always planned for you to someday take my place. But now, I think you've got some devils you're wrestling inside—devils of doubt and skepticism. You could go either way."

Lucas dared not even swallow, afraid he would give himself away. He merely nodded.

"There are those—Porter Roe is among them—who think you've already made your decision. They wanted to ask you on the spot when you returned, 'Whom do you serve, God or mammon?' But I wanted to see you, son, give you a chance to redeem yourself." He looked grim. "But it's going to be up to you. And there will be no second chances."

"I understand," Lucas said, finally.

They had almost reached camp, and Lucas could see the flicker of the small night fire through the trees. Hannah sat on the far side, facing Lucas, her head tilted downward. Sophronia was by her side, mending something by the firelight. Hannah seemed lost in thought, and instead of looking small and fragile, she seemed cloaked in a new strength. Her pale, wild curls glistened in the firelight, and it struck him suddenly that the strength that had always been within Hannah was also being tested and found not wanting.

Instead, God was with her. God was giving her strength. In the instant their eyes met when he stepped into the compound, he recognized in her the same fresh hope that God was giving him. Hope and love beyond human understanding, beyond what two people could give each other.

He looked at her in wonder, and she gave him the briefest smile as if understanding his thoughts.

"There's something else." John, still at his side, broke into his thoughts. He turned Lucas away from the group, dropping his voice so as not to be overheard. "You're my adopted son."

"Everyone knows that."

"The crossroads we talked about?"

"Yes," Lucas said.

"Just because of your relationship to me, don't expect they'll go easy on you . . . should you choose the wrong road."

"I know that, sir."

"If anything, you'd be set up as an example. It could be very bad."

"I know that too." Lucas started to turn away.

"One more word of instruction."

"Yes, what is it?"

"You will be watched."

"Are you worried my actions will make you look bad?" He wondered about the real reason for John's warning, for his concern.

For a moment, the older man didn't answer. "You're my adopted son, Lucas." But Lucas said nothing in response. John Steele obviously knew his bitter thoughts, because he said, "God's ways are mysterious, son. Mysterious indeed." And that was the end of the discussion.

Lucas said his good-bye to Hannah and Sophronia, and then John called Lucas to kneel in front of him, with the other young Mormon at his side.

John bowed his head and began to speak, his hands pressing heavily on Lucas's head: "Father God, bless this your servant as he sets forth on his journey. Bring success to your servant's mission. I speak with all the authority and power of the priesthood when I say, Bring down a curse upon the heads of our enemies, their children, and their nation.

"Go with this thy servant," John intoned. "Make him as quick as a serpent and as wise as a fox. May he strike our enemies dead, and may the blood that pours from their veins avenge the deaths of our Prophet, Joseph Smith, and his brother, Hyrum, and atone for the sins of these cursed enemies of yours, Father God, and of your chosen people."

John Steele solemnly nodded at Lucas. "Go, now, my son. And may our God be with you."

Minutes later, Lucas saddled Spitfire and swung onto the stallion's saddle. He looked back at the small band of travelers, and Hannah met his gaze. Then he kicked the stallion into a trot, and they headed back up the trail to Salt Lake City.

It took less than two weeks for Lucas to intercept the Farrington train. He had just reached Emigrant's Gap when he first spotted the dust from their herd, then trailing behind as the winding caravan of high-topped wagons jerked along the narrow, rocky valley. He kicked Spitfire to a gallop, and threading his way along the winding trail, hurried to greet them.

He had no intention of carrying out his mission. His only concern was to get the train to head as quickly as possible out of the territory. He'd already devised a route that would take them on a little-known trail to the east of Salt Lake that intersected with the Oregon road.

Lucas spotted Alexander Farrington on the Appaloosa riding at the front of the caravan, and he held up his hand in greeting as he galloped toward the captain.

"Lucas Knight!" the captain called out, recognizing him. "Good to see a friendly face, man!"

Lucas chuckled, riding closer then reining Spitfire to the left to pull up beside the Appaloosa. "Those you'll soon encounter won't be, though, my friend."

Farrington nodded, his sun-worn face showing his concern. "We're running so late, we really didn't have much choice. We've had trouble along the trail that's delayed us even more since we last met."

"You're still planning on taking the southern route?" Spitfire danced sideways on the trail a few steps, and Lucas nudged him in the flanks to settle him down.

"There's always the Hastings," the captain said, pulling his hat down against the sun and looking west.

"I wouldn't recommend it," Lucas said. "Crossing on that trail in August might be worse than facing the Mormons."

The captain shook his head slowly, his eyes still on the western horizon. "We've seemed ill-fated somehow from the beginning. Delay upon delay," he said quietly. "Sometimes I think I'm simply not fit for the job. You won't find me volunteering again."

"You told me this is your third trip across."

Farrington grinned. "I always traveled with smaller groups. Trappers and settlers mostly. These folks, however, are a different sort.

More stubborn than trappers' mules." He craned a bit in the saddle, looking back at the winding caravan of wagons slowly making their way through the pass. "We've lost some in a mutiny back at Devil's Gate. Good riddance. They'd become troublemakers. A couple of wagons from Ohio joined us at Bridger. But we're still smaller than we were when we left Arkansas."

"How about the Missourians?"

"The ones I kept you from killing?"

It was Lucas's turn to grin. "The same."

"They're still a ways behind us. I wouldn't let them catch you in their sights, Lucas."

"I'm not worried." He reined the stallion around some loose rocks. "Have they given you any trouble?"

Farrington shook his head. "Not really. They keep to themselves. A few of us talked pretty straight to them back at Bridger. Told them that where we're headed we didn't want to hear a word against the Mormons." He pulled his hat down against the slanting sun. "They agreed. But then, we're not in Mormon country yet."

"You hit Mormon country the minute you rolled out of Bridger."

"That right?"

"You're being watched. They've known your every move since you left Laramie."

Farrington slowed the Appaloosa, frowning. "Now, how's that?"

Lucas wondered if the captain suspected him of reporting their actions. "If it makes you feel any better, they've known about every move I've made too—from the fight in the saloon to my leaving your company a week later."

Still sitting tall in the saddle, the captain pulled back on the reins a bit as they headed around a steep curve in the mountainside trail. Rocks spilled down the side of the mountain, and a cloud of dust lifted. "That doesn't make me feel better, son." After a minute, he added, "And now they've sent you to check on our progress."

Lucas nodded. "Those were my orders."

"And you're to report back?"

"Yes. But my intentions differ from my orders."

"Isn't that dangerous?"

"Might be."

"What is it they want from us, Lucas?"

"Your cash, gold, silver, firearms, and ammunition."

"Sounds like they're preparing for war."

"They are." Lucas gave the captain a steady look. "I think there may be another way around this."

"How's that?" Farrington peered at him from beneath the rim of his hat.

"I'll negotiate on your behalf. If you're willing to buy your way out of this." Lucas drew the stallion to a halt, and Farrington did the same with his horse. "You've put yourself in great danger by heading into Utah right now. News of Johnston's troops got here before I did. Also news of the murder of one of our apostles in Arkansas."

Farrington nodded slowly. "We know about both."

"But you don't know the frenzy you're heading into." Lucas drew in a deep breath. "And the Missourians following you . . . if they can't keep their mouths shut . . ." He shrugged.

"They may be as thick-headed as mules, but even they know better than to throw out barbs in hostile territory."

"There's a campsite just outside the city. You can let your herd rest while I see if I can get some of the leaders to talk to you. I'm hoping that if they will agree—and if you're willing to pay for safe passage—they'll give you an escort through to Mountain Meadows. That's at the south of the territory. Beyond that point you'll be safe."

Farrington, now riding again, kept his gaze straight forward as if weighing Lucas's proposition. "How do we know they won't want it all—and we'll still not be guaranteed safe passage?"

"It might be your only hope of getting through alive."

Farrington glanced at Lucas sharply. It was the first time that physical danger had been mentioned. "We're not the enemy," he said.

"Most people think the enemy is any Gentile."

They rode in silence for a few minutes. "I'm not going to give up what is rightfully ours," the captain finally said. "Not gold or silver or arms. You can ride back and report what I've said."

"Sir, you're making a mistake. They plan to take whatever wealth you've got anyway. I was sent here to find out how much you've got and where it's hidden."

"We're well armed, and we're prepared to fight, if necessary." Farrington looked at him, puzzled. "I've been through Utah Territory before and found the people peaceful and hospitable. How can that have changed?"

"You're still not convinced of the danger, are you?"

"Your people are made up of families—children and couples and old folks—just as we are. Some were probably born in our hometowns. Your war is with the United States government, not with us."

Lucas knew he wasn't going to convince the captain. Finally, he nodded. "I promise to try to negotiate on your behalf—without the gold or silver."

"Do what you can, son," the captain replied. "But we have no choice. We must take this route."

Lucas stayed with the Farrington company as the caravan continued making its way through Emigrant's Gap and snaked across the valley to a campsite just east of Salt Lake. That night after the wagoners had moved their rigs into place and supper was finished, Lucas spotted Ellie and the children.

Ellie greeted him warmly. "Alexander told me you'd joined us, Lucas. I'm glad to see you." The twins wrapped their arms around him then ran off to find the wooden flute he'd carved for Meg. He walked with Ellie to a chair so she could sit. Her breathing seemed labored, and he noticed she didn't look well.

She settled her back against the chair, closed her eyes for a minute, then gave him a weary smile. "I didn't think I'd see you again until we got to California."

"Things didn't work out quite as I had planned."

She smiled. "Right now, it seems to me they never do."

He knew she spoke of their trek through Utah. "I remember your telling me that because God's got us in his hand . . . nothing's an accident."

"He allows things to happen," Ellie agreed. "Things beyond our control." She frowned and reached for Lucas's hand, held it gently, and patted it. "You went back to get your Hannah and her aunt—is that what didn't work out?"

He told Ellie about John Steele, explained how the man had saved his life and how he and Harriet had adopted him years before. He concluded by saying, "John Steele took Hannah as his wife while I was away."

"But you said he and his wife raised you?"

"He has more than one."

"Oh, Lucas!" Ellie said. "Then it was against Hannah's will."

"Yes."

Before she could comment further, Meg and Sarah ran up with the flute. Lucas grinned and sat a girl on either side of him. "All right, now watch carefully." He lifted the flute to his lips and began to play an Irish jig. Soon some of the other children had gathered around him and were clapping and dancing.

Then Lucas showed Meg how to do the fingering for "Twinkle, Twinkle, Little Star." She followed his lead and very slowly played the little tune.

"I want to try. Let me!" Sarah cried, reaching for the toy.

"Huh-uh, it's mine," Meg said, twisting her shoulders away from her sister.

Ellie scolded Meg for her selfishness, and Meg reluctantly handed the flute to Sarah. But before she could play one note, Lucas pulled another small flute from his pocket.

"I thought you might want to play together," he said.

Sarah caught her hand to her mouth. "The rocking horse belongs to Phoebe, you know," she said sweetly. "And Phoebe doesn't share."

"Then this will be yours and only yours," he said, placing the wooden instrument in her hand. After a few more minutes, both girls were playing "Twinkle, Twinkle, Little Star" and leading the rest of the children out to play like little pied pipers.

"You're so good with them—you should have a dozen of your own, you know," Ellie said.

"Children?" Lucas laughed. Then he sobered, thinking of Hannah.

"You must still try to get her out."

"I won't leave without her." He frowned, and Ellie seemed to read his mind. "But she says she won't leave with me."

"She's afraid you won't love her after what's happened."

He nodded, comforted somehow by her quick understanding. "Hannah hasn't said that. She wouldn't. But I know her well. It's in her mind."

Ellie looked thoughtful for a moment. "Lucas, could we help get her out—get you both out?"

"It would be dangerous for you." He paused. "But I've been thinking the same thing. Hannah and Sophronia are at John Steele's ranch near where you're heading in the south of the territory. Not far from there, wagon companies rest and prepare for their journey across the desert. It's called Mountain Meadows."

"Can you get them to us?"

"I'm going to speak to the Church authorities to see if I can escort you through the territory. If they agree, I'll be with you—at least long enough to see that Hannah and Sophie are safely among your numbers."

"Maybe that's why God has led us this way," Ellie said softly. "The more I ponder the strange reasons for life's twists and turns, the more I think that God's direction has more to do with the miracle of changed lives than with anything else."

"You've taught me a lot already about your God."

"He's your God, too, Lucas," Ellie said. When he didn't answer, she went on. "I'm looking forward to making Hannah's acquaintance. I feel I know her already."

Later that night, Lucas rode into the valley and headed straight to Porter Roe's house. The moon was still bright enough to travel by, and as Lucas approached the house, he was struck by its elegance. It was an imposing two-story, not nearly the size of the Prophet's mansions, but impressive nonetheless. One of Roe's wives met him at the door and ushered him inside. The place smelled of fresh-baked bread and was filled with the commotion of a lively group of women and their multitude of children.

"Did you get the information we need?" Roe said after they were seated in his lavish front parlor. It was the one place in the house where the children weren't allowed.

"No," he said, "I didn't. I spoke at length with Captain Farrington, and he's clearly stated that they have nothing to do with the coming war. They're merely a group of families—children . . ." Lucas gestured toward the rest of Porter's house, still alive with children's voices and laughter. "They want nothing more than to travel safely through as quickly as possible."

"You've warned them that they're entering hostile territory?"

"Of course."

"That wasn't your mission, Lucas."

Lucas ignored his statement. "I'm here to plead with you on their behalf. Let them travel safely through. I'll escort the train if you're concerned with the actions of the settlements along the way."

"That is a concern. Brother Brigham has already sent a messenger along the route, saying that no one is to provide grain or food of any kind to this group. No assistance whatsoever." His cold gaze flicked across Lucas's face. "Brigham feels strongly about this, son. The order couldn't be clearer: Anyone found trading with or selling to this train will be severely punished. That tells you what Brigham thinks of this particular Arkansas train."

"They need supplies to make it to California. We've always been more than willing to sell to emigrants."

"We are at war."

"These people are not the enemy."

"All Gentiles are our enemy."

"Let this train go through peaceably," he said. "They have done nothing to us . . . against us."

Roe stood and moved to the front window. He pulled back the heavy velvet curtain and peered out. Lucas could hear the distant sound of hoofbeats approaching. From the sound of it, there were several riders. The horsemen dismounted, then approached the Roe house, and Lucas recognized their voices. He knew them well. He had heard them many times as he rode with them through the midnight darkness.

By now Roe had turned back to Lucas. "It's clear tonight that you've softened toward the Gentiles. Do you remember the vows of priesthood you took—long before your Danite oath?"

Lucas nodded, and with a sinking feeling, knew he'd walked into a trap. He glanced to the open doorway, calculating his chances for escape. But he was too late; it was now filled with the men who'd come to discover the outcome of his mission.

"You have taken both the vows of holy priesthood and the Danite oath." He paused, and a mantel clock ticked loudly. The only other sound was that of quiet breathing from the Avenging Angels, now circling him like wild animals watching their prey.

"I have," answered Lucas.

"Then what has turned you into a Judas, son?" When Lucas started to speak to defend himself, Roe held up a hand to stop him, and his voice dropped menacingly. "You cannot plead ignorance. You know that Judases are trodden under the feet of the Church and trampled until their bowels spill.

"Are you a Judas, Lucas Knight?" he asked again. "There are those of us here who believe you are."

Lucas stared silently at the men.

"Are you willing to stand up with your Church against our enemies?" Roe continued. "Are you willing to avenge the deaths of our Prophet, Joseph Smith, and the apostle Phineas Potts?"

Still, Lucas didn't answer.

"Are you willing to carry out acts of vengeance against this train?"

"You speak of blood atonement?" Lucas asked quietly. The images of Alexander and Ellie, feisty Meg and sweet Sarah suddenly appeared before him. The coming baby. The families that made up the company. He pictured them all. They danced under the starlit skies, singing, playing banjos, fiddles, and harmonicas. The twins whistled through their flutes and giggled and played with Phoebe, the doll that had once lived with the Indians.

"Yes," Porter Roe said. "That's exactly what I speak of." And the men stared at Lucas, awaiting his answer.

"No," Lucas said quietly. "I cannot take vengeance on this train. These people are not our enemy."

"Take him," said Roe bitterly to the men. "Get him out of my sight. He is Judas himself, an abomination before God."

TWENTY-FOUR

Salt Lake Valley

At sunrise, Alexander, Abe Barrett, and most of the men in the company rode out toward the herd to hold council about the coming days on the trail. The cowhands waited as the herd grazed in the distance.

"Men," the captain began, "there's some hard riding ahead. But before we move out, we've got to get into town for supplies. From what I've heard, these folks may not think too kindly of us because of the coming war. I don't think it's as bad as our young Lucas makes it out to be, but nonetheless, we'll need to be cautious. I suggest we send families, so we don't appear too threatening. And a few at a time, so as not to overwhelm them with our numbers."

The men nodded in agreement, and a few commented about who should go first. Some were skeptical about letting the women and children go in alone.

"Ellie's planning to go in this morning. And Liza said she'd go with her." He looked at Abe, who confirmed it with a nod. "My children will go with them. Abe, you're going along as well?"

Abe nodded. "I'll be driving. And providing protection," he said, patting the rifle at his side.

"I must stay in camp. Lucas Knight said he'd arrange for me to speak to some of the Church leaders today—perhaps Brigham Young himself. He says maybe if we can show ourselves as peaceable we'll be able to get through the territory without assault."

Abe nodded toward the eastern horizon. "Looks like we got company," he said.

Alexander turned to watch the riders heading toward them. "Jakes and Graves. They must be getting nervous now that we're among the Mormons. They've made no bones about how they feel."

A few minutes later, Red Jakes and Matthias Graves reined their horses to a halt by the group and dismounted.

"You've kept your distance," Alexander said. "Appreciate you folks paying mind to our request."

Red Jakes grunted a reply, and Graves stepped forward to do the talking. "We been talkin' about what we're up against," he said, kicking some mud off his boot. "I know you wanted no part of it when we talked in Laramie, but now that we're here—both parties of us in the same predicament—we're thinkin' we oughta join forces."

Abe and Alexander exchanged glances. "As I recall, you were quite free-spoken about your hatred of the Saints," Alexander said. "My worry is that if any of your group dares to mention—even in jest—that they were in on the killing of Joseph Smith, you'll put the nails in all our coffins."

"We was just havin' some fun. Fact is, we never had anything to do with their Prophet's killin'. Besides, we spoke the way we did because we know the evil that lurks in some of these so-called Saints," said Jakes. "A body'd have to be pretty dull-witted to say such a thing here. Far as we see it, we're in enemy territory, and we're outnumbered. There ain't one in our party who'd disagree."

"No sir," added Graves. "We got people among us who've seen firsthand the skill of a Mormon who can scalp. Dress him up in war paint, and he's as mean as any Apache you'd ever wanna see."

"Mormons aren't the only white men to scalp," said Alexander. "It's white men who taught it to the Indians."

"Never mind who taught who what," said Jakes, removing his hat and scratching his fringe of hair. "It's the fact of it that matters. We're sayin' we'd all be better off joinin' up," said Jakes. "Protectin' each other."

"You're sure you can control your party?" Alexander asked.

Around him he could hear the men discussing the proposal. He glanced at Abe, who gave him an imperceptible shrug.

Reverend Brown moved to the front of the group. "We can't bring added danger to our company just to provide you with protection," he said, frowning. "You did nothing but cause trouble back at Laramie. We've heard how you carry on at the night fire. You're anything but quiet. You say the wrong thing in the wrong place, and you'll be getting more than yourselves killed."

Alexander nodded in agreement. "You tried to kill that young man back at Laramie. What're you going to do if you run into him—or someone like him—along the trail? Can you keep your mouths shut?"

"My friend here said it best," Graves said solemnly. "We seen firsthand the brutality of the Saints. Believe me, none of us will say a word till we're outa the territory." He cleared his throat and took off his hat. "We're askin' you, pure and simple: Please, allow us to join up. We'll circle with you at night for protection, but the rest of the time, we'll keep our distance."

Alexander finally agreed. "We'll allow you to pull up into the circle, and you can ride closer during the day." He narrowed his eyes at the men. "But the first time anyone in your group utters a derogatory remark to or about a Mormon man, woman, or child, we'll toss you to the wolves. You understand?"

"Yes sir," said Graves, echoed by Jakes. "Yes sir, we do. And thank you. We'll not be a minute's trouble."

The men mounted and rode back to their party.

"I don't know if you made the right decision," Reverend Brown said to Alexander on their return ride to the wagons. "Something tells me those Missourians have the right intentions, but . . . " His voice dropped off as he shrugged.

"The spirit's willing, but the flesh is weak," Abe finished for him, riding on Alexander's other side.

Reverend Brown grinned. "Something like that." Then he sobered. "But I mean what I said. I think we're heading into some difficult days. There's a spirit of darkness here."

Alexander slowed the Appaloosa to a walk, glancing over at him. "What do you mean?"

"As we came by some of the smaller settlements, women were watching us through closed curtains. I could tell they were afraid to come out and have a real look at us. I saw little children with terrified looks on their faces, scurrying into the houses. Now, why would that be?"

"They're expecting troops to come in and take over their land. They're afraid of being kicked out of their kingdom, the same as happened before," Abe said, drawing his horse up even with theirs.

"But surely they could see we're not an army. Anything but, with our squalling babies and laughing children and barking dogs," Reverend Brown said.

Alexander chuckled. "I'm hoping those laughing children and barking dogs will get us through the territory." *Alive*, he didn't add aloud, but it was in his mind. He glanced at the other men's sober faces and wondered if they were thinking the same thing.

When Alexander rode into the wagon camp a few minutes later, Ellie and Liza were readying to head into the valley. Hampton had hitched the team and loaded empty grain barrels and sacks into the wagon. Riding up behind the captain, Abe quickly dismounted and stepped up into the driver's seat of the wagon. The twins were already playing in the rear, and the shrill, wavering sounds of "Twinkle, Twinkle Little Star" carried into the balmy morning air.

Alexander gave Ellie a quick kiss just before she climbed up to sit on the bench next to Abe. Liza hollered brightly from around the corner then, picking up her skirts, clambered aboard and settled down beside Ellie.

"Be careful," Alexander said to them all. "If you suspect the slightest danger, leave immediately. We'll get our supplies someplace else."

"I'll take good care of them," Abe said. "Don't worry, Captain. We'll be back soon, and the next group can go." He flicked the whip over the team, and the beasts lumbered forward. Behind the wagon, five other families pulled out at the same time, and soon the small party was heading onto the Salt Lake road.

Ellie was in awe at the size of the beautiful city. It seemed to gleam in the morning sun. And green! There were trees and gardens, fruit trees, and berry vines winding over arbors. It rose from the desert like an oasis, a lush, beautiful garden oasis.

She looked from one brick storybook house to the next, each framed by beds of roses and sunflowers waving bright against the desert sky.

"Just look at it!" exclaimed Liza, grasping Ellie's hand. "My lands, I've never seen anything like this. Wide streets. As wide as I've ever seen in a city. Irrigation canals running here and there like rivers. And they're all laid out in precise order—the way I'd cut a cake!"

"Liza, look at the peaches! They're as big as saucers." She pointed to a side yard where an orchard's multitude of branches were bending nearly to the ground with the weight of the fruit.

"Oh, my sakes," breathed Ellie, her mouth watering. "Do you know how long it's been since I tasted a peach? I don't know about you, but I don't care what they charge for a bushel of peaches—I'm ready to pay any price!"

"I believe I'm ready to do the same. I wonder if there'd be enough time when we get back to camp to bake up a cobbler?"

The women laughed and talked, planning the items they'd buy first, the fruit and vegetables, flour and grain. Then they began to notice that the streets were emptying. Women and children were being hustled from the sidewalks, through doors that quickly closed.

A pall seemed to hang over the city as it emptied. Carriages disappeared. The people in those vehicles that remained turned neither to the right nor to the left but kept their eyes straight forward, as if not daring to look at the strangers.

As they drove along, shop after shop closed. Liza and Ellie exchanged glances, and Abe shook his head slowly in dismay.

"Stop here," Ellie suddenly said to Abe. There was a mercantile on the corner that hadn't yet closed, and people milled about inside. "Meg! Sarah!" she called out. "Come with me. Quickly, before it closes!"

Abe glanced over at Ellie and started to say something about it being too dangerous. But she put her hand on his shoulder. "We need to at least try. It will be all right. You stay here and watch the wagon. Liza, do you want to come along?"

Liza nodded and climbed from the wagon; then she reached up to help Ellie step down. The twins skipped around from the rear and joined the two women. The foursome crossed the street and entered the mercantile.

"I'm sorry, we're closed," the shopkeeper said immediately, stepping from behind the counter.

"But you have customers," Ellie said, stating the obvious.

"I said, we're closed," he repeated.

"We need food and supplies," she entreated, pulling her girls forward so they could be seen. "Please, we don't have long. And we have the means to pay you—"

"I said, lady, we're closed," he repeated.

"Pay you well," Liza said. "If you'll simply allow us a few minutes to gather some staples." She smiled. "We promise. We won't be long."

But the clerk ushered them to the door, his face closed to all emotion. "Good day," he said firmly as they stepped to the sidewalk.

Ellie held her head high. "We'll keep trying," she said as they stepped up to the wagon bench. "They can't all be so stubborn."

But as they drove through the city, there was not a shop that would open its door to them, not a friendly face among the few who roamed the sidewalks, not a friendly word spoken. Disheartened, the wagoners drove back to the train.

That afternoon another brief council was held, this time with the entire company, including the Missourians who'd now driven their wagons closer to the Farrington company. The Ohioans and the Missourians now made up for the number they'd lost when Silas Edwards left with his outfit of mutineers.

Alexander stepped onto the back of an open farm wagon so he could be seen. He looked out at the sea of faces, sunburned, tanned, and freckled, the women's heads covered with capotes for shade, the men in western hats curled slightly on the sides. The faces had changed since they'd left. Harder, leaner, wiser. There was now a wariness about them, especially after hearing the news about the people in town being unwilling to sell them supplies. Even the children, normally feisty with boundless energy, were subdued and stood silently near their parents.

"Folks," he said, "it appears that the Mormons are preparing for war against the States. I can think of no other reason for their lack of willingness to sell us the goods we need. At sunup we will head south to the Old Spanish Trail and make our way as quickly as possible to the territory boundary.

"You must take the order very seriously to keep to yourselves along the way. We will attempt to buy supplies from some of the outlying settlements. It could be that some of the more isolated farmers and ranchers will not have heard about what appears to be an order from the Church leaders not to sell to foreigners."

"Foreigners?" called out one of the Missourians. "This here's United States territory."

Alexander and Abe exchanged glances, then Alexander looked hard at the man. "We may know that to be legally true. But the fact is we're outnumbered—as one of your group earlier pointed out—by people who would disagree. And that kind of a comment called out in the wrong place could get us killed." The man grumbled for a minute then slipped back in among the Missouri outfit.

Farrington went on to describe the trail ahead. "It's mostly desert terrain between here and a place called Mountain Meadows. We'll find little grass for the herd this time of year. The best we can do is to move as quickly as we can from water hole to water hole. There are a few natural springs along the way, so we'll have water.

"At the least, we'll find granaries near Cedar City. If we haven't found a farmer to sell us supplies, we'll hope to buy feed for the cattle there."

"Or steal it," shouted a Missourian.

"That would be a big mistake, sir," Alexander said, giving him a cold stare. "If the Mormons didn't use you to decorate a cottonwood, I believe I would myself."

A silence fell over the group, and Alexander said a few more words about conserving their remaining supplies. "It will be a difficult trek," he concluded. "But there's a resting place on the trail ahead. We'll push through as hard and as fast as we can then spend a week or so at the Meadows, where there's plenty of grass and water, before the crossing to California."

Before he dismissed the company to return to their wagons, Jesse O'Donnell spoke up, "What happened to Lucas Knight? I thought he was arranging a meeting for us with Brigham Young."

Alexander nodded. "That had been his plan." He paused, again noticing the wary expressions. "But he didn't return."

"You never heard anything from him?"

"Not a word," Alexander said. "But we can't wait. We'll pull out in the morning."

Before sunup the following day, the caravan was snaking across the desert and onto the Spanish Trail. The first day they made good progress; the second day was even better. The third day they could only travel until noon because of thunderstorms and flash floods.

The monotony of the days was broken only by the dots of settlements along the way, none of which would welcome the weary travelers with their bawling, dusty, and hungry herd. So the company marched southward, their days blending together, blistering hot and dry.

Alexander had been wrong, he realized very soon. It seemed that some sort of order *had* been given throughout the territory. The company was met with open hostility. There was no food for sale, even for the children, no grain for the herd. Nothing.

People appeared afraid of the company and most often said nothing when spoken to, or else they ran into their houses and watched the travelers, looking out cracked-open doors or from behind veiled windows. Taunts were called out from the men, mostly in the larger settlements. Once in a while, the Missourians forgot Farrington's orders and yelled back uncouth remarks, but mostly the travelers felt intimidated by the ill will and kept to themselves.

After more than a week on the road, a band of Indians rode their ponies close to the train's ranks. They slowly inspected each wagon and its teamsters as they rode by, then followed a short distance behind the caravan. They were Utes, Alexander knew, having encountered them on earlier treks West. They didn't beg for food or trinkets but seemed content to sullenly watch the group as they made their way south.

Wagon wheels had dried out worse than ever now from the hot, dusty climate. Wood cracked and shrank, and the iron rims rolled off most of the wagons along the way, causing the loss of precious traveling time as the wagoners chased and replaced them. By the time the rigs rolled through Cedar City on the first of September, they creaked and groaned and rattled loudly along the road.

The setting was majestic, Farrington thought, admiring the red rock cliffs rising into a clear, blue sky. Trees were starting to turn fall colors and appeared liquid gold as they shimmered in the sun. The houses were the same English-style cottages they'd seen in the Salt Lake valley, made of brick and trimmed with bright shutters and roofs. Trees and gardens and flowers were abundant, and healthy cattle grazed in fenced grasslands fed by an intricate series of irrigation canals from mountain streams.

But again, in this place that seemed a beehive of happy activity, no one would sell to or trade with the company. They were met with icy stares and sullen or fearful looks.

Alexander was riding the Appaloosa alongside the wagon today, and Ellie drove the team from her bench. She noticed him watching and looked up.

"Are you going to the granary today?" she asked quietly.

He nodded.

"Do you have any hopes at all that we'll be sold grain?"

He smiled at her. "There's always that hope."

She gave him a quick smile. "It's my thinking, Alexander, that we might as well just head on to the Meadows. If the folks at the granary aren't inclined to sell, I worry that the Missourians might take matters into their own hands."

"It's bad business, Ellie," he said. "Whether they sell or not, it's bad business." He sighed heavily. "I'll just be glad when we can move out of the territory completely."

"We'll be safe at the Meadows," she said, watching his face.

"I've stayed there myself. It's frequented by many travelers."

"But you're no longer saying it's safe."

He met her worried look with a weary smile. "As I said, Ellie, I'll just be happy to get the company out of the territory." He didn't want to tell her about his growing uneasiness about not being able to replenish the food supplies for the desert they still must cross.

A short time later, with the train camped southwest of Cedar City, Alexander, Abe, Hampton, and Jesse rode back into town to see about buying grain.

Ellie and Liza gathered sticks for the cook fire and headed back to camp to start their meager meal. Some of the men had shot some rabbits and ground squirrels during the day's trek, but there weren't nearly enough for the entire company, so families were sharing their ingredients to make thin stews. Flour was now depleted, so there were no longer biscuits or flatbread. Even the cornmeal was nearly gone, and most of the families had put away what little supply they had for the journey across the desert.

Liza stood at the rear of the wagon, using the tailgate as a worktable to cut up a couple of small, skinned squirrels. In the shade of a nearby cottonwood, Meg and Sarah sat on a stump, making up new songs on their flutes. A few scrub jays were squawking in the top branches, fluttering and hopping from limb to limb then squawking again at the girls' flutes. Giggling, the girls imitated the squawks, and more jays arrived to add their voices to the chorus.

Ellie had pulled up a bunch of wild onions when they'd gone for wood, and now she chopped them into tiny pieces then dropped them into the Dutch oven a few at a time. The onions sizzled as they hit the small spoonful of lard at the bottom, their pleasant aroma rising in the balmy desert air.

She shook out a bright cloth to cover the small table and added a vase full of wildflowers Sarah had picked. Ellie hummed to herself as she worked then smiled across at her friend.

"I declare," said Liza with a grin. "You can be happy doing the simplest chores. Here we are, preparing a supper made of wild varmints, and you're acting as if it's a meal fit for royalty."

"There's a particular reason I'm happy tonight," Ellie said.

Liza carried the pieces of squirrel to the big iron pot and dropped them into the sizzling onions. Ellie stirred the pot as the squirrel meat browned.

"And what is the reason, if it's not the stew?" Liza asked, lifting a brow as she dropped another few pieces of squirrel into the pot.

"Our trek might not be over, dear," she said. "But there's another journey that's almost done."

"What are you talking about?"

Ellie gave her friend a knowing smile and patted her stomach. "I believe it's nearly time for this young man to make his appearance."

Liza quickly wiped her hands and rushed to Ellie's side. "Have they started? The birth pangs, I mean?"

Ellie laughed quickly, patting Liza on the arm. "Oh no. You'll be the first to know, believe me." She took a deep breath. "The baby's dropped, for one thing. And the other? Well, I can feel it in my bones. He's ready."

Liza laughed and dropped into a chair, fanning herself. "I thought you meant you were ready right now." She laughed again. "And you're still convinced it's a boy?"

"It would please Alexander."

"And how about you, Ellie? What do you want?"

Ellie glanced at the twins, still giggling and playing under the canopy of cottonwood branches. "There's nothing like little girls—sweet and sassy and full of fun." Then she looked back to Liza. "After those two, it's hard to imagine what rearing up a little boy would be like."

"You're frowning. Why's that?"

Ellie smiled softly. "I've had it in mind that I'd like to name this child Faith. And that's not much of a name for a boy. Besides I haven't mentioned it to Alexander. Naming babies is the last thing on his mind right now."

"Might toughen him up to be named such a name." She laughed. "He'd have to fight every little boy who teased him."

Ellie chuckled. "Well, maybe it's a girl after all. I do believe, though, we won't have long to wait to find out."

Liza reached for her hand. "You rest now, Ellie, and let me finish fixing supper."

"Works every time," she teased. But she gratefully settled onto a chair and put her feet up on an empty grain barrel.

Just before supper, the men returned with bad news—the owners of the granary refused to sell. Alexander, shaking his head in disbelief, said he'd offered an entire chest of gold in exchange for enough grain to see them across the desert. Even that offer was refused.

The company spent another glum evening around their night fires. Reverend Brown played a few songs on his harmonica, but no one felt like singing or dancing, and he soon put it back in his pocket. The company quieted earlier than usual that night and soon settled into their beds and tents.

It seemed to Ellie that she had just closed her eyes when the sounds of shouting and gunfire erupted in the distance. But surprisingly, dawn's pearl light had just begun to crown the eastern horizon when Ellie sat up on her pallet and looked over at Alexander.

He was already scrambling to find his shirt in the predawn darkness. Someone across the circle lit a lantern, followed by a few others around the camp.

"What's happened?" Ellie murmured sleepily. Her heart thudded in alarm.

"I've got a pretty good idea it has something to do with the Missourians," he muttered, jamming his foot into a boot.

He had just grabbed his hat when Red Jakes rode into camp, shouting, "They got Graves! We went to get ourselves some grain.

They wouldn't sell. We thought we'd help ourselves anyway. We'd just loaded the barrels when they came after us with rifles. Matthias was in the wagon, and we got separated when we were ridin' away. I think they got him."

Ellie figured Jakes had probably taken off to save his own hide. She could see her husband's hands fisting at his sides. "You did what?" he roared.

"Cap'n, we gotta have grain, or we're gonna die anyway," Jakes said shakily. "If our cattle don't make it, we don't make it. It's a matter of survival. That's what we all decided."

By now the men in both companies had gathered around. "We better go after him," Abe said. "No matter how we feel about what he did." Several of the Missourians agreed loudly.

But before Alexander had decided whether to risk sending anyone after the renegade, the sounds of a horse-drawn wagon rattling down the desert trail carried toward them. Seconds later, Matthias Graves drove up, looking sheepish.

"We'd better hightail it outa here," he said. "It's nearly dawn anyway. But no matter, we'd better go."

"Tell us what happened," Farrington said, his voice low and controlled.

Graves grinned and glanced at the back of the wagon. "Well, first of all, we got us some barrels of grain for the herd. Second of all, them Mormons ain't too pleased that we got away. I was hidin' when my friend here left me in the lurch." He glared at Jakes. "But as it turned out, they followed him for a bit instead of me then turned north to someplace called Parowan to gather up a posse." He paused. "Heard them discussin' it before they left. But I'm sure they'll be showing up before too long."

"You've put us all in danger, Graves," the captain said. Even in the dim light, Ellie could see his jaw working. "I've a mind to split up our outfits—you go one direction. We'll go the other."

"They wouldn't believe you didn't have anything to do with it anyhow, Cap'n. One of us is just like the other to these Mormons. We're all the enemy—whether we're from Missouri or Ohio or Arkansas."

He looked hard at Alexander. "My suggestion is that we get out of here before those folks from Cedar get back with that posse."

Reluctantly, Alexander agreed, though Ellie could clearly see his pained expression. "Wagons, ho!" he shouted, and the command was repeated throughout the camp. Within minutes, the teamsters were hitching wagons, and the point men and flank riders were herding the cattle. Families' sleepy voices could be heard as they quickly rolled bedding and packed away the dishes and pots from the previous night's supper.

Ellie woke Meg and Sarah. They dressed quickly, not even complaining about the lack of breakfast, and helped her load the wagon. Alexander had no time to do much more than hitch the team. His attention was taken with getting the company under way before the posse caught up with them.

Finally the signal was given, and Ellie flicked the whip above the team. The beasts stepped forward, straining under the yoke, weak-kneed from their miles of heavy labor. The wagon lurched and groaned as it rolled onto the rutted trail.

They moved through sagebrush and cactus and gold-colored weeds, just now brightening in the morning dawn and catching the glint of the sun's earliest rays. In time for the nooning, the company would have climbed into the cool mountain air, making their way on a good road through piñon pines and cedars. By the time the sun sank into the western sky, Alexander had told her, they would be in Mountain Meadows.

Strangely, they were not followed.

Twenty-Five

The wagon caravan wound through the long valley leading to Mountain Meadows. The high-arched canvas covers swayed as the wheels hit ruts and bumps and stones along the way. But the cool mountain air seemed straight out of heaven, Ellie thought as they moved along. She closed her eyes and breathed in the scent of pines and dusty, iron red earth.

They passed ranches along the way, and the people they saw standing in their fields or near the houses didn't seem as openly hostile to the group. Ellie's wagon was near the rear of the caravan, a place she normally disliked because of the kicked-up dust from the outfits ahead. But today she was glad, because she'd already decided that if she found a friendly appearing family, she would pull her rig out of the caravan and attempt to buy food for the children.

As the company climbed higher, Ellie worried that even the gentle upward slope would be too much for the oxen. They hobbled along, mostly bones and hide now, and she watched them carefully, aware of the affection she'd developed for the beasts. They'd faithfully carried her family hundreds of miles, and tonight, at least, they would have some reward. The meadow, it was said, was filled to overflowing with good water and tall grasses, even this time of year.

Everyone seemed to be in better spirits, and she smiled, listening to their voices carrying up and down the long line of wagons. Children laughing and singing, the older folks calling out merrily.

Ellie let her gaze travel across the mountains, beyond the thick forests of small pines that flanked the trail. Ranches and log cabins dotted the hillsides, friendly looking with colorful gingham curtains at the windows and children playing in the yards. Each one seemed to be flanked by gardens and apple orchards filled with heavy-laden trees.

They had nearly reached the mountain's summit when a sapphire blue pond caught Ellie's attention. It was so still, so brilliant in the sun, that the trees and willows and cattails that framed it produced images as if in a mirror. A squat red barn was to one side and, just beyond it, the lush grassland of a small corral where several horses stood grazing contentedly.

Ellie was so busy admiring the beauty of the place that she almost missed the small ranch house that stood in a clearing just visible through the pines. She flicked her whip to move the team forward faster, for in her reverie she'd fallen slightly behind the rest of the train.

Then two women stepped onto the porch of the small ranch house, and to Ellie's amazement, they waved.

She halted the team abruptly and sat as still as could be. No one in the caravan looked back to see that she wasn't following.

Now the women were walking toward her, almost shyly, Ellie thought. She smiled, though they were still some distance away.

"Mommy!" Meg yelled from the back of the wagon. "Why'd we stop?"

"You can get out for a stretch," she called back through the opening. "I want to talk to these ladies. See if they'll sell us some food."

Both Meg and Sarah climbed quickly down from the rear of the wagon, noisily stretching their legs and arms. "Oooh," Sarah complained. "Phoebe is so tired!"

By now, the two women were standing near the wagon, and Ellie stood to step down. She swayed a bit and caught herself.

"Here, let me help you," said the younger of the two as she reached up to support Ellie's arm.

"Thank you," Ellie said, nodding to her stomach. "I'm not quite as spry as I was." Once on the ground, she stuck out her hand. "My name is Ellie Farrington, and these are my daughters, Meg and Sarah."

The twins skipped over and smiled at the ladies.

"I'm Hannah," said the young woman. Ellie was struck by her wide, clear eyes, reminding her of the light-reflecting pond she'd noticed earlier. A few light freckles graced her nose. But it was her hair that caught Ellie's attention—it was pale and curly, almost wild. The young woman had attempted to tie it back, but it sprung out of its ribbons as if defying being bound.

"And I'm Sophronia Shannon," the older woman said, taking Ellie's hand. She had the same eyes and wild hair, only her hair was pure white.

"I'm pleased to meet you," Ellie said pleasantly. "I'm with the Farrington train, just now heading up to Mountain Meadows. We'll be resting there for a week or so before traveling on to California."

"There are many who rest their herds and companies there," said Sophronia Shannon. "Though lately, there've been fewer."

Ellie decided to plunge right into mentioning the needs of the company for food and supplies. These ladies seemed friendly enough to possibly help. "We've not been able to buy food since we arrived in Salt Lake City," she said, carefully watching their expressions.

They looked genuinely sorry. "We have food you can have," Hannah said quietly. "We were told not to sell to you." She grinned. "But no one said anything about giving away food and supplies."

Ellie reached for her hand in her exuberance. "Give us food?" she repeated, unable to believe what she'd heard.

"How much can you carry?" Sophronia asked. "We'll load your wagon with all the fresh fruits and vegetables we've got."

Ellie threw back her head and laughed with joy. On either side of her, Meg and Sarah clapped their hands. "Are you sure?" she said, tears in her eyes. "You've been ordered not to help us—I wouldn't want either of you to find yourselves short or in trouble because of us."

Sophronia took Ellie's hand, and the three women walked toward the little ranch house. They had bushel baskets on the porch as if they'd been waiting for her. There were baskets of peaches, berries, corn, potatoes, and beans.

Ellie's eyes could scarcely take it in. "Could I . . . would you mind, that is . . . if my daughters and I tasted a peach right here?"

Sophronia, laughing merrily, stepped inside the house. Within minutes, she returned with fresh-washed peaches, sliced just right for eating.

Ellie's fingers trembled as she held a piece out to each of the girls. "We're so hungry," she whispered, "all of us." And she bit into the juicy, yellow-pink fruit.

After they'd loaded the wagon with the baskets and bushels, Hannah said, "We have something we'd like to ask you."

"After this—?" Ellie glanced at the abundance in her wagon. "After this, anything!"

"We want to leave with you," Hannah said solemnly. "We've got to get out of the territory. No one knows we're planning this, and should they find out, your company could be in grave danger."

Ellie looked at Hannah suddenly, studying the young woman's lovely face, then Sophronia, noting her age. Their resemblance. And she remembered hearing of them before, hearing their names before. Of course! Why hadn't she realized it when she first met them? Her mind had been so transfixed on their friendliness, the prospect of buying food, she hadn't really paid attention. *Hannah and Sophronia, Great-Aunt Sophronia.*

"Lucas Knight," she whispered thoughtfully. "You know Lucas Knight, don't you?"

Hannah's wide eyes brightened, almost as if with tears. Then she tilted her head, quizzically watching Ellie. "Yes," she finally said. "But how did you know?"

"Lucas joined our company for a short while—out of Laramie. Then we met up with him a second time near the Salt Lake Valley." Again, she reached for Hannah's hand. "He spoke lovingly of you—of you both," she said, smiling at the older woman. "He told me what you've been through," she said gently to Hannah, "and that he wanted to get you away from here. He was making plans for getting you out when we met in Laramie."

Hannah's face seemed to light up with love. "You said you saw him back at Salt Lake?"

"Yes," Ellie said. "For just a short time."

"Tell me," Hannah said, her voice almost a whisper. "How was he?"

"He was trying his best to help us get through the territory unharmed. I don't know what he was able to do for us with the Church leaders. He rode into the city to set it up—a meeting with Governor Young, if he could manage it. But he didn't return to tell of the time and place, and we didn't see him after that."

Hannah frowned and exchanged an alarmed glance with her aunt.

"I'm sorry," Ellie said. "I didn't mean to worry you."

"He's probably trying to steer clear of danger," Sophronia said. "For your outfit and for himself. If our Lucas thought he was attracting too much attention, he may not have felt he could return."

"Alexander—my husband—said that Lucas told him he'd hoped to get permission to escort us through the territory. Then he'd planned to travel with us, and with you, to safety."

"Maybe he'll still manage to meet us in the Meadows," Hannah said, but her voice didn't sound hopeful.

Ellie glanced up the trail; the rear of the caravan was no longer in sight. "I'd better be going before my husband sends out the cavalry to find me." She climbed to the wagon seat and called for the girls, who'd gone to look at some ducks by the pond. They skipped toward her, braids flying. "I will talk to Alexander about when the best time would be for you to join us," she said. "If you don't have a wagon, you can ride with us. We'd count it a privilege to have you."

"I've been preparing our supplies," Sophronia said proudly. "I've got dried fruit enough for the whole company. And dried venison too."

"I'll return tomorrow with Alexander's direction on how to proceed."

"Bring another wagon," said Hannah with a smile. "We'll fill it with more supplies."

Ellie started to flick the whip then looked back down at the women. "Are you safe doing this?" She frowned. "I assume your . . ." She couldn't bring herself to say the word "husband" under the circumstances. She started over again. "What I mean is, are you being watched? Are you safe having me return?"

Hannah seemed to understand Ellie's reluctance, and her own fear showed in her eyes. "He's away right now, caught up in a council with the Utes or some such thing. He's not due to ride back to our ranch until the end of the week. Whatever plans we make will have to happen before then."

"I'll tell Alexander," Ellie said, popping the whip over the oxen's bony backs. Slowly, the team started plodding up the hill. Ellie and the twins waved until they'd rounded the curve and Hannah and Sophronia were no longer in sight.

She drove the team another long and difficult hour before finally reaching the summit. "Girls, come look," she called to them. They scrambled to the front of the wagon and poked their faces through the opening.

"Look, there! Ahead," she said again, halting the team. The little girls climbed onto the bench seat, one on either side. She circled them in her arms and hugged them close. "That's the most beautiful sunset I've ever seen," she said in awe.

"It's *gorgeous,*" whispered Sarah reverently, and Ellie smiled at her daughter, wondering where she'd heard the word.

"It makes the flowers look like they're on fire," said Meg.

Ellie followed her daughter's gaze across the meadow. It was covered with a carpet of late-blooming summer wildflowers, mostly goldenrod, or so it appeared from this distance. With the angle of the setting sun, its brilliant, fiery colors, and a slight breeze, Meg was right. The meadow did appear to be in flames, beautiful, shimmering, liquid-gold flames.

As the three watched the sun melt into the western horizon, a rider rounded the corner, galloping full-speed toward them. Ellie smiled. It was Alexander. As he reined the Appaloosa to a halt, she could see his strained expression.

"I'm sorry I worried you," she said. "I'll explain, but first, look at the sunset with us."

Alexander dismounted, and Ellie and the girls stepped from the wagon. The four stood together in the quiet of the evening. The sky was now crimson above the dark, silhouetted mountains on the far side of the meadow. The goldenrod had faded from gold to dark orange and, as they watched, seemed to take on the color of embers and ashes. The breeze picked up and sang across the valley.

"It's peaceful here," Ellie said, looking up at her husband. "In a way, I feel I've come home. It's the first time I've felt that way since we left."

Alexander pulled her closer. "Maybe here, we'll finally be safe," he said, but the worry lines still etched his face. Beside them, Meg and Sarah, who had tired of looking at the sunset, played hopscotch. Sarah held Phoebe with both hands, making the doll jump into the squares the little girls had drawn with a stick in the red soil of the trail.

Alexander helped Ellie step back up to the driver's seat then tethered the Appaloosa to the rear of the wagon. The little girls played in back as the family headed up the trail toward camp, and Ellie told her husband about the wonder of finding Hannah and Sophronia.

That night the wagons were haphazardly circled. Everyone seemed to feel the dangers they'd faced during the previous weeks were now behind them. The herd grazed peacefully at the south end of the meadow in the tall, golden grasses.

Lying on her side, her back to Alexander, Ellie snuggled close to her husband, sighing contentedly as he wrapped his arm around her shoulders. The baby turned over, and she laughed, drawing her husband's hand to the place on her stomach.

Alexander chuckled. "You're still convinced it's a boy?" he asked sleepily.

She looked up at the star-spangled sky, and thought of God's tender mercies. "I want to name this child Faith," she said softly.

"Then we'd better hope this baby's a girl," he said, still chuckling to himself.

"That's what Liza said." She snuggled closer, feeling the beat of his heart.

"My beloved Ellie . . ." Alexander murmured. He raised up slightly and kissed her ear. She could feel him gazing at her in the starlight.

She turned slightly and smiled into his eyes then reached up to touch his jaw, tracing her fingers along it. "Alexander," she whispered. "I love you. How I love you!"

A short distance away from the night circle, sounds from the creek carried toward them, bubbling, rushing water and the sweet racket of frogs. Crickets sawed their legs in the willows, and a soft moaning wind blew down from the mountains.

The next morning dawned sunny and warm. The twins skipped off to play with the O'Donnell children, and Alexander prepared the wagon for Ellie's return to Hannah's and Sophronia's ranch. He'd distributed yesterday's bounty, and now there were more empty barrels and baskets in the rear of the wagon. Folks gathered round to send words of gratitude back to the ranch. The word had also spread that the two Mormon women would be joining the company for the trek to California. So, many words of welcome were sent along as well.

"Tell them it will be safer to wait until the end of the week to join us," Alexander said as he hitched the team. "We'll plan to rest here five days. We can't wait any longer."

"I'll tell them," Ellie said as Liza rounded the corner of the wagon to join her. Her friend grinned and gave Ellie a hug.

"I'm going to get that peach cobbler made yet," she said. Then, looking up at Alexander, she winked. "That's why I'll have your wife back here by midday—no matter how much she wants to stay and visit. I've got work to do to get my cobbler put together and baked by suppertime."

"As long as you save some for me," Alexander laughed. Then he gave Ellie a quick kiss and helped her onto the wagon bench. Liza stepped up beside her.

"Keep Meg and Sarah from eating too many peaches while I'm gone," she said. "After all these weeks without fresh fruit, they will be very sorry."

"I'll take good care of them," he promised. She followed his glance to the creek bed where the girls had gone to catch frogs with the O'Donnells. The sounds of the little girls squealing and splashing in the shallow water carried on the breeze.

Ellie turned back to Alexander. "We usually circle the wagons closer to the water," she commented.

He nodded. "It's not too far to keep them in sight." He smiled. "Don't worry, Ellie. I'll take good care of them." He slapped the rump of the lead ox, and the beasts moved forward, the creaking wagon following.

Ellie smiled at her husband and blew him a kiss. He stood watching as the rig moved up the trail from the meadow, and when they reached the top of the incline she craned around in the seat again.

From the golden meadow with its circle of high-arched wagons, its groups of playing children and busy families, Alexander still watched. Ellie waved, and he gave her a salute and a grin before turning away.

An hour later, Ellie and Liza halted the team in front of the ranch. The introductions were made as Liza clambered down from the bench.

Liza reached up to help Ellie descend. But Ellie frowned as she stood, then put her hand on her stomach. A stabbing pain made her catch her breath, and she sank again to the wagon bench, waiting for it to subside.

Hannah and Sophronia were beside the women in a heartbeat. Sophronia took Ellie's hand. "It's time, isn't it, child?"

"We'd better get right back to the train," Liza said, stepping back to the driver's seat.

Ellie nodded weakly, then she looked down at the dark circle staining the wood beneath her feet. "I don't know that we have time, Liza," she said, glancing back to her friend. "I believe my water just broke."

"We'd better get you inside, dear," Sophronia said, taking charge. Hannah nodded in agreement.

Liza frowned, as if considering their choices. "Yes," she finally agreed. "Ellie, I don't think this baby's going to wait for us to get back to the train."

But Ellie couldn't answer; she doubled over again in pain. When it had passed, the women helped her from the wagon and into the house.

As she settled onto a comfortable bed, she smiled up at Liza. "I know you said you'd be with me every minute of this child's birth. And I made you promise you would be. But I need something else even more."

"Anything, Ellie," Liza said, laying her cool hand on Ellie's forehead.

"Go for Alexander please, dear?"

Liza looked worried. "I don't want to leave you, Ellie."

Ellie grasped her friend's hand, squeezing it gently. "I'll be all right. But I want my husband. Can you fetch him?"

Finally Liza agreed and left immediately for Mountain Meadows, driving the wagon alone. Even before the oxen had taken their first steps, though, another pang pulled Ellie nearly to unconsciousness, and Hannah and Sophronia hurried to boil water and gather clean cloths. It passed, and Ellie smiled weakly as Hannah struggled into the bedroom, carrying a heavy pine cradle.

"I found it in the barn," she said as she started scrubbing it with soap and water.

She'd just folded a small blanket to pad the bottom when another white-hot burst of pain enveloped Ellie. She clinched her teeth and turned on the bed, praying for it to pass quickly. She called out for Alexander, not realizing that Liza had left only minutes before.

Only an hour had passed when soft cloths were laid into place beneath her. The pangs were coming fast now, and she could barely catch her breath between them.

Sophronia took up her position at the foot of the bed, and though it was not yet midday, Hannah illumined the room by lighting an oil lamp. Then she pulled a chair close to Ellie and held her hand during the worst of it, murmuring words of comfort and strength.

"I can see the crowning," Sophronia said triumphantly. "You can push now, child. When you feel the next pang begin, push with all your might. Push!"

Hannah wiped Ellie's forehead with a cool cloth, and Ellie took a deep breath. The next pang started deep within, and she squeezed her eyes shut, clinching her jaws. She pushed, again feeling pulled into a whirl of white-hot pain.

Suddenly there was a mewing cry, and Sophronia's lined face lighted with a smile. "Child," she said to Hannah, "bring me the basin of water. This little girl needs a bath."

"Girl?" Ellie whispered.

"Yes, you've got yourself a fine baby daughter. Pretty as a picture. In fact, I do believe she's got the sweetest crown of dark hair. Just like yours, child." Sophronia met Ellie's gaze with a look that said she shared her wonder, then she went back to tying and cutting the umbilical cord.

When she'd finished, Hannah carried the basin and a small blanket to the side of the bed, placing them near the infant. After a few minutes, she placed the tiny, wrapped bundle in Ellie's arms.

"Faith," Ellie said, touching a miniature pink fist. "Faith is her name." She brought the baby to her breast and lightly rubbed Faith's cheek with the back of her fingers. The baby turned and suckled, and Ellie closed her eyes. "This is the child of your promise," she murmured. "I give her to you, Lord. She is yours."

Twenty-Six

Alexander looked up as Liza headed into camp. She'd already halted the team just outside the circle, and now she ran, skirts gathered above her ankles, through the tall meadow grass.

Her cheeks were flushed, and she was shouting as she hurried toward him. "It's Ellie! She's back at the ranch house. The baby's on its way!"

He caught both her arms. "You left her there alone?"

Liza struggled to catch her breath. "She wanted me to. She asked me to come for you."

Alexander looked wildly around the camp, suddenly filled with joy and fear at the same time. "The twins?"

"I'll find them," Liza said. "You just go."

"No, I told Ellie I'd watch the girls. Maybe I should take them with me. But where are they?" He looked toward the creek, his gaze scanning the place where the children had been playing earlier. There was no sign of the little girls.

Liza grinned. "For a man who's used to making quick decisions and giving decisive orders, you sure are having a time with this one."

He shook his head slightly and grinned back. "Heaven knows, I've been through this before. But Ellie's had such a time carrying this one, it's different. Almost like it's the first."

"Just go!" Liza gave him a good-natured push. "Take the wagon—there's plenty of bedding and supplies for bringing Ellie back when it's time."

Alexander was striding toward the wagon just outside the circle when he heard one of the children cry out from one of the distant hills. He turned to see the twins and the O'Donnell girls all running toward him. He frowned, chiding himself for not paying better attention. None of them should have ventured so far from the wagons.

"Where have you been?" he demanded.

The children's eyes were wide with fear. "There're Indians out there!" cried Meg. "Real Indians."

"Of course," he said in a comforting voice. "This is Indian country. They're Utes, and they're no different than any of the others we've seen since we left home. They're probably coming to beg—just like all the others."

"But these are different," said Sarah, swallowing hard, her eyes still the size of saucers. "They're wearing paint on their faces."

"And there's lots of them," added Prudence Angeline. "More'n we've ever seen at once."

"They're coming 'round the mountains on their ponies."

Alexander scanned the horizon, anxious to be on his way but feeling he needed to first ease the children's fears. "Well, I don't see any now," he said. "They're probably on their way someplace else."

"They're hidden behind those hills," Prudence Angeline insisted. She pointed to some nearby rolling hills to the east of the meadows. "And some of them were already crossing the creek way down there," she said, pointing south.

Now he was concerned. "Which way were they going?"

The little girl pointed to the rolling hills on the west side of the meadow. Alexander followed her gaze, realizing for the first time that Mountain Meadows was in the shape of a perfect bowl surrounded by hilly mounds that would allow any hostile group—white or Indian—to see and not be seen. To shoot arrows or rifles with no fear of being shot in return.

If the children were correct and Indians were moving into position around the meadows, there would be no means of escape. He glanced at the wagon circle, noting how unprepared they were. How vulnerable. Folks were milling about, the men working on wagon repairs for the desert trek, the women starting to fix the noontime meal. Children were scampering around, and dogs were barking and chasing after them.

Then he noticed how carelessly the company had circled their rigs the previous night. He hadn't overseen it because he'd been so worried about Ellie disappearing when she pulled her wagon out of the caravan. He'd left to go back to find her, leaving the teamsters to form the night circle. They'd all been so relieved to get out of the openly hostile countryside between the Salt Lake valley and Cedar City they hadn't thought about any dangers that might still exist.

And now he realized how foolish they had been. Their only source of water lay yards from the circled wagons. If they came under siege, they would have no water supply. Plenty of ammunition, tough teamsters and wagoners and cattlehands to protect the train—but no water.

"Let's get back inside the circle," he said firmly. "I'll get some of our scouts to take a look." The small group headed into the circle, and Alexander scanned the hillsides. He could neither see nor hear anything unusual.

But there was an unnatural hush. The birds that earlier had been singing were now silent. The cicadas had stopped their buzzing racket. And even the earlier breeze from the mountainsides had stilled. It suddenly seemed strange to Alexander that he hadn't noticed it before.

The children followed him into the circle, and Alexander raised his rifle and fired off one shot, a signal for everyone to gather inside. People stopped their conversations and looked up in surprise. Several cattlehands, who were just leaving to go out to check on the herd, instead turned back and walked toward Alexander. One of the Mitchell brothers, walking with William and John Prewitt, was the first to reach him.

"I want you to ride out and take a look behind these mountains. It's probably a false alarm," he said to the three. "But we may have some unwelcome visitors. If we do, it's probably the cattle they're after, and we'd better get some extra guards out to the herd."

They nodded and started for their horses.

By now Liza had made her way to the front of the crowd, a worried look on her face. "You've not left yet?" she asked, puzzled.

He shook his head and explained. "The children spotted some Indians moving around in the nearby hills. I'll stay until we get this cleared up."

"Do you want me to go back to be with Ellie?"

"No," he said quickly. "I don't want anyone leaving the circle until we know what's out there."

The families had gathered around him now, silently waiting for him to speak. Some looked worried; they all looked puzzled.

"Folks," he said, "I don't want to cause any undue alarm, but some of the children have spotted Indians who've come to have a closer look at us."

There was a worried murmur, and he held up his hand. "Just to take some extra precautions, I want to go over our plans if we are attacked. First of all, we have ammunition enough for a small army, so I don't want you to worry on that account.

"Second, we are a disciplined group. We have planned for this, hoping it would never happen, but we're well prepared to handle it if it does. In this setting, we would put our plan into action immediately. Each family is responsible for the digouts beneath your wagons. If necessary, dig ruts beneath your wheels so that the wagons rest flat on the ground. As we do that, we'll tighten the circle, where necessary, so that no invader can enter.

"We will also dig trenches in the center of the circle, deeper than we are tall. This is for the women and children, so they will have some measure of protection from injury."

Everyone nodded in agreement, and Farrington smiled. "I know we've gone over our plans many times and never had occasion to put them into action. And today may be no different. Now, are there any questions?"

Jesse O'Donnell spoke up from the rear of the crowd. "We're a ways from the creek. Shouldn't we move the circle closer?"

Others joined him in agreement, and Farrington nodded. "We'll have to hitch up the teams to do it, but yes, I agree. It's the one way we're vulnerable right now." The crowd fell silent again, and Alexander's neck prickled with the feeling they were being watched. "As soon as we hear back from the scouts," he concluded, "we'll make a decision whether it's safe to go after the teams.

"Until then, stay inside the wagon circle. Families, keep together."

The groups had just dispersed when the Prewitts and Lawson Mitchell could be seen riding across the meadow as fast as the wind. Alexander could read the fear on their faces even from this distance. They rode in and quickly dismounted.

But before the three could utter a word, someone on the far side of the circle screamed. Another scream followed, then cries of dismay and fear; arrows as thick as horizontal rain flooded the circle.

To the north, shrill war cries split the air, and a thunder of hoofbeats vibrated the ground as the herd was rounded up by dozens of Utes and headed out of the meadow. A couple of the braves rode close enough for all to see the color of their eyes as they whipped the Farrington oxen into motion, and the beasts lumbered, moaning and bawling, across the meadow, pulling the wagon that Alexander had planned to take to fetch Ellie.

"Sir, we're hemmed in on all sides. That's what we came to tell you," said Lawson Mitchell.

The siege had begun.

Alexander shouted orders. Amid the cries and screams, women grabbed their children, and men grabbed rifles and ammunition, taking up positions behind the wagons.

The first attack lasted until evening, ending in a standoff. Three men in the company died from their wounds, and seven more were injured. As far as Alexander could tell, none of the Indians had been shot. As he had earlier noticed, they had complete protection because of the layout of the land. His only hope was that the Utes would quickly give up and move on.

At nightfall, graves were dug for the fallen men. The Reverend Brown spoke a few hurried words because of the work at hand, then he prayed over the bodies. Immediately, the shoveling began on the wagon trenches. It was well past midnight when they were finished, and Alexander again called the families together in the center of the circle.

"We've got to go for water," he said. "There's been no sign of movement outside since sundown. I'm going to try to get down to the creek."

"It's too dangerous," said Abe, who was standing closest to him. "I think we should wait them out. This can't last. What else could they want besides the herd?"

"I say wait them out," agreed Jesse O'Donnell.

"I don't think we have a choice," Alexander argued. "I'll go if you'll cover me with your rifle." He looked at Abe, who nodded. But even as Alexander spoke, he knew it would be impossible for Abe to give him cover: The Utes held the advantage with their unobstructed view of the wagon camp.

He took two buckets, one in each hand, and stepped from between the two wagons closest to the creek. He'd walked less than three yards when a barrage of arrows sliced through the air. Quickly, Alexander moved back into the corral.

"Maybe we could send out a child," said one of the men. "Maybe they wouldn't harm a child merely going to the creek for water."

"No," Alexander said firmly. "We'll wait them out—and pray they'll tire of this soon."

But the Indians didn't tire of the attack. For a couple of days it continued. No more lives had been lost, but Alexander grew more agitated by the hour. Just as he had worried, water was now dear.

"We must send someone for help," he said that night at council. "Are there any volunteers?"

Hampton said he would go, though Sadie begged him with her eyes not to. He gave her a quick kiss on the cheek, and a moment later was joined by Lawson Mitchell and John Prewitt. They were all young and perhaps stood a good chance of getting out of the meadow.

"I want you to go to one of the ranches we saw along the way. There's the one where Ellie's staying. The people there will be sympathetic to our plight, I'm sure, and will get word out that we need help."

The young men nodded solemnly. After they'd gathered some

supplies, Alexander walked with them to the edge of the circle. Abe and several of the other men stood with them, giving last-minute directions for how they felt they should proceed from the meadow to the trail.

The *remuda* had been run off with the herd, so the men didn't even have horses to ride from the meadow. Hampton met his worried gaze, and Alexander could see both fear and determination in his son's eyes. "God be with you, son," he said, and the two men fell into a rough embrace.

That night an eerie silence again fell over the meadow. Alexander lay awake, thinking about Ellie, hoping she was safe, that their baby was healthy. Perhaps Hampton was already with her. Perhaps help was on its way and he would soon be reunited with Ellie. Meg and Sarah were sleeping in the center trench with their little friends. With the usual resilience of children, they'd gotten over their initial fear and now seemed to look upon the whole affair as part of their adventure in moving west.

Alexander looked up at the starry heavens and prayed for them. "Father," he breathed, "care for the little ones. I worry at the outcome of all this, and I sometimes wonder if we'll get out at all. There's something wrong here that I can't identify, can't know. Please . . . take care of them," he prayed. He thought of a Bible verse that Ellie once mentioned. She said it was important to her because of her condition. He couldn't remember the exact words, but it had to do with Christ tending his sheep like a shepherd, gathering the lambs in his arms, and leading those with little ones in tow. "Carry them close to your heart, Lord," he prayed, picturing Jesus holding Meg and Sarah, one in each arm. "Carry them . . ." And he fell into a restless sleep.

The following day, the Indians attacked only once, early in the morning, and hopes were raised that they were indeed giving up. There was still worry about the diminishing water supply, but if indeed the siege was nearly over, they would soon have access to the creek.

There was not really a spirit of rejoicing in camp, but the children were allowed to come above ground for a while and play. The women fixed a noon meal, and afterward, Reverend Brown called the children together for a story. Alexander stood off to one side, watching for any sign of movement in the hills.

"One day long ago," Reverend Brown said when the children were seated around his chair, "Jesus asked for all the children to be brought to him."

"Suffer the little children to come unto me," recited Meg proudly.

"Ah, yes," he said with a smile. "You've heard the story."

The children nodded.

"Well, this time, it's going to be a bit different," he said, and he proceeded to explain. "I want you to close your eyes and pretend that you are a little child on the day Jesus blessed the children."

There were several murmurs of assent, and each little head was bowed and all eyes were squeezed shut.

"Now, think about how Jesus was sitting by the seaside, or maybe in a meadow just as we are. Some children wanted to come up to him, but some big men stood in their way. They said he was too busy. They said to go away."

"Ooooh," Sarah said sadly.

"But then Jesus reached out for each little child, each little baby, and he drew that child to himself. He put his arms around all of them and held them close—so close they could hear his heartbeat."

"I can hear my mommy's heart thud when she's holding me," Meg volunteered.

The reverend smiled. "That's right. Now think about Jesus holding you the same way.

"Keep your eyes closed, now. No peeking, Louisa. You either, Becky. Now, all of you, think about someone loving you more than even your mommy or papa."

"That's a lot," said Prudence Angeline.

"It is," agreed the reverend. "And there's something I want you to remember about this story. No matter what happens around you—no matter how bad and scary the world can be—Jesus is holding you, just as he held the children that day. And he'll never let go. Ever."

That night Alexander's son Hampton returned, alone. He was badly injured, and he stumbled into camp long after the families had retired to bed. Only the guards and Alexander had stayed on watch.

Alexander knelt at his son's side. Hampton's breathing was shallow, and he was bleeding from where he'd been shot in the chest and leg.

"Son—?"

Hampton looked up at his father, trying to focus. "I'm sorry. I didn't . . . I couldn't . . ."

"Don't worry about that now. All that's important is that you are alive. What happened to the others?"

"We were ambushed. They . . . they didn't make it. We got as far as a spring on the other side of the summit. We were so thirsty . . . we shouldn't have stopped. Should've been more careful . . ." His eyes fluttered closed for a moment.

"Rest, son. Get your strength back."

"Pa," he said, then grimaced in pain. He closed his eyes again and swallowed hard. "Pa," he whispered, "this isn't what it appears, you know."

"What do you mean?"

"There are Indians out there, all right. But the men who ambushed us were Mormons. They said now that we'd seen them, they'd have to finish off what the Indians started. They plan to kill us, Pa," he said, letting out a ragged breath. "Kill us all. It's the Mormons. Can you imagine that?"

Alexander sent for Sadie, who crept across the compound to kneel by her husband's side. Her face wet with tears, she gently laid her cheek on Hampton's uninjured shoulder. He moved his arm to cradle her gently.

Alexander, Billy, and Bess stood watch with Sadie, knowing by the sounds of Hampton's breathing that the end was near.

"Pa?" Hampton whispered suddenly, just past midnight.

Alexander knelt beside him. "I'm here, son." Sadie was still on the opposite side, holding Hampton's hand, with Billy and Bess beside her.

"Pa, I keep thinking about something Amanda Roseanne said once. It was a long time ago."

"What was it, son?"

"Something about lambs." He smiled. "Do you remember?"

Alexander thought of his own prayer and Ellie's oft-mentioned verse, but what had lambs to do with Amanda Roseanne? "No, son," he said. "I don't remember."

Hampton shook his head. "No matter," he whispered, his face peaceful. "Tell Amanda . . . ," he began, a swift light crossing his face, visible even in the darkness. He tried to speak again, only to have his words come out a gurgling cough. Finally he fell silent.

Alexander took his son's callous hand in his and held it, unable to bear the impact of his loss. He closed his eyes and prayed for strength.

When Hampton breathed his final breath, Billy put his arm around his father's shoulders. "The lambs," he said. "I remember."

Alexander looked up at him quizzically.

"It was what Amanda Roseanne told us on the day you and Miss Ellie were betrothed. The day we found out Miss Ellie was to become our new ma—that Jesus holds us like he holds his little lambs."

Alexander remembered. He bowed his head and wept.

Twenty-Seven

Ellie opened her eyes, blinking against the harsh morning sun that blazed through the bedroom window. As if she'd been awaiting the moment, Hannah Steele was instantly at her side, laying a cool hand against her forehead. She frowned in worry.

Ellie swallowed hard. "What happened?"

"You've been sick," Hannah said, settling onto the side of the bed.

Suddenly Ellie remembered the baby, and her eyes opened wide as she glanced about the room. Spotting the small cradle by her bed, she reached her hand down and gently rocked it with her fingertips.

"The baby's sleeping. And it's a good thing. She had us up most of the night, taking turns rocking her," Hannah smiled. "Your daughter doesn't like goat's milk."

"My . . . daughter?"

Hannah smiled. "You had a beautiful little girl. You named her Faith."

Ellie settled deep into her pillows, closing her eyes for a moment. She felt weary, so weary. "Faith," she whispered, "yes, I remember." Then she looked up at Hannah again. "How long have I been here?"

"This is the morning of the fourth day."

"I—I don't remember . . ."

"You lost too much blood, Ellie. And you've had a high fever—and chills. You had us worried."

Hannah poured a cup of water from a pitcher on the small pine table near the bed and placed it in her hands. Ellie sipped the refreshing liquid, and as she did, her mind began to clear. She frowned, glancing about the room in worry. "Four days?"

"Yes."

"Where's Alexander?" Worry settled on her like a shroud. "Did he come?"

Hannah drew in a sharp breath. "No," she said. "They haven't been here at all. No one's been able to leave the meadows."

"Why not?'

Hannah frowned, and for a moment she didn't answer. "Something's happened there," she said finally.

"What do you mean?"

"The Indians . . . the Utes . . . have attacked the train. That's all we know right now."

"No!" Ellie threw back the blankets and attempted to swing her legs to the floor. She swayed, grabbing for the headboard to steady herself. "That can't be," she murmured, leaning her head back against the pillows once more. "You said I've been out for four days. Since no one came, the company's been under siege all this time?"

Hannah nodded, reaching for her hand again. "From the last we heard, it's a standoff. Your company's well fortified."

Ellie drew in a shuddering breath as if still trying to take it all in. "Alexander . . . my daughters . . ." she said with a sob. "I must go to them!" She tried to get out of bed again.

"It would be too dangerous, Ellie," Hannah said, her expressive face full of sorrow. "You must stay here and keep little Faith safe." She lifted the infant from the cradle, placing her gently in Ellie's arms.

Ellie gazed down at her tiny daughter, who had now opened her still-unfocusing eyes. "Faith," she whispered, "Precious Faith." She touched the baby's dark, silky hair and cuddled her close.

"Oh, Father," she prayed when Hannah had left the room. "Protect my children. Put your arms around my family."

The following morning Ellie woke feeling stronger. "I'd like to try to walk now," she told Hannah. "I need to regain my strength."

The young woman wrapped her arm around Ellie for support and helped her take a few steps around the bedroom. They repeated the effort several times during the day, and by evening, Ellie felt strong enough to walk into the kitchen and sit by the fire, rocking Faith and visiting with Sophronia and Hannah for a few hours.

They spoke about the Indian siege and the latest news from the neighbors about the standoff. Ellie wondered if it was her imagination that Hannah and Sophronia seemed to exchange worried glances when they spoke of the attack. Their discomfort was especially evident when Ellie asked why the Mormon men in the region hadn't called out their forces to help the wagon company. They seemed to hem and haw, never quite answering her directly.

On the fifth day, Ellie was strong enough to walk slowly through the yard and around the pond.

"I need to go to Mountain Meadows," she said. "I know the lay of the land. I could hide behind one of the high ridges. I wouldn't be seen, but I would be able to see what's happening to my family."

"The danger would be too great, Ellie. Besides, you are still weak. The danger of losing more blood isn't past," Hannah said firmly. "Please don't think about going. It might only cause greater heartache . . ."

"My love for Alexander, Meg, and Sarah is stronger than any fear I feel for myself."

"Don't attempt it, Ellie," Hannah said. "It's better to wait until we hear that the siege is over."

That night Ellie couldn't sleep. Long after the house was quiet and tiny Faith had been fed, diapered, and was sleeping peacefully in her cradle, Ellie rose from her bed and went to stand at the lace-curtained window. The pond was barely visible across the grassy yard, and beyond it she could see the barn, standing squat and deep crimson red in the moonlight.

Ellie was far too restless to sleep, and now that she was feeling stronger, the urge was even greater to go to her family and friends at Mountain Meadows. She had prayed until she felt depleted of words. She knew God held them all in his hand, but she couldn't shake the feeling that whatever happened, she should be there.

Hannah was right about the risks, but still, Ellie considered it. She thought of Meg and Sarah, their sweet heart-shaped faces, the way their braids shone after a bath in the creek, the way they smelled of puppy dogs after they'd played in the sun. She closed her eyes, her arms aching for the feel of their little bodies pressed up against hers.

And Alexander. Oh, how she had prayed for her husband. He needed God's grace and strength to carry him through. She had loved him all of her life. And he had cherished her. No matter how misshapen she'd become bearing children, he'd made her feel she was the most beautiful woman God ever created.

God had given them greater gifts in their marriage than either had thought possible. She thought back to that long-ago day back at Drake's Creek when Alexander asked her to marry him. She'd been so young, it seemed now. Not much more than a child.

Yet God had brought them together—planned their union from time's beginning, she'd always thought. And their journey west that they'd plotted from the first day after their wedding, even that seemed part and parcel of their life's journey together.

God had led them this far. He'd taught them lessons along the way, the greatest of which was to wait on him for their needs. She'd always thought that life's journey was God's way of readying a person for heaven.

And really, this world was only a likeness of what heaven would be like. A sunflower-and-lupine-covered meadow, a waterfall tumbling and spraying in white-silver thundering power, or horses gleaming in the sunlight as they stood in a grassy field . . . all were but images of the real thing in heaven.

It was the same with people. All that was good in a child of God was but a likeness of the Father himself. And if God was perfecting that person through her life's journey, Ellie wondered how that person would appear in heaven reflecting all God's perfect glory.

Then another thought occurred to her. Perhaps if God's children were to see God's real beauty—either of heaven or a person's perfected soul—they might be blinded by its brilliance and purity.

As she held the lace curtains aside to look at the moon-silvered pond in the distance, she wondered if maybe all life's journey was but a veil between God's children and himself.

She smiled at the thought, wondering why it should strike her now, especially in the midst of all her worry and troubles. Nonetheless, the thought comforted her, and she hugged it close.

Ellie was about to return to bed when she noticed a glow coming from within the barn, the glow of lantern light.

She watched for several minutes as dark figures arrived silently. She could see some horses tethered a distance away. Hannah had confided in her about John Steele, the man she'd been forced to marry, and Ellie's first thought was that he'd returned.

A surge of hope rose in her. Hannah had said that John Steele was Brigham Young's agent to the Indians. If that were the case, then he might be able to convince the Utes to stop their attack at Mountain Meadows.

She reached for a wrap, tucked it around the long, white gown Hannah had given her, and hurried from the house. The night was cool, and a slight breeze lifted strands of her hair as she stepped toward the barn.

She had almost reached the door when the sounds of voices carried toward her.

Ellie stopped and, sensing danger, stepped into the shadows. She heard the words "wagon company" and held her breath, listening intently. The voices were muffled. She needed to get closer.

She crept around the barn's front corner to an open window and crouched beneath it. Now she could plainly hear the voices.

"It's gotta be completed," said one. "Especially now that they know."

"You should've never shot any of 'em—or at least not let any get away," said a deep, older voice. "If the attack should end today, they'd head to California, telling everyone they met that the Saints attacked them at Mountain Meadows."

Ellie frowned. Surely they weren't talking about the Farrington train. She couldn't comprehend that anyone other than the Utes might be involved. She stepped closer, thinking she'd misunderstood.

"Well, they'd not be too wrong, now, would they?" the first speaker said.

"My point is that there's no other solution. They cannot leave that place," the older voice said. "We have no choice."

"You didn't think there was a choice when you brought it up Sunday, John. Even then you said it was a matter of honor, considering what all they did coming through the territory. What they've been callin' our women, words worse than the devil himself would say. How they been whippin' their mules and callin' them Joseph and Brigham."

There were grunts of anger, and Ellie caught her hand to her mouth. Nothing remotely close to these accusations had happened in their company, not even with the ruffians from Missouri. Again, she decided they must be referring to another wagon train.

"You said yourself," the voice continued, "that we were bound by the holy priesthood to avenge the deaths of the Prophet and his brother. That God had sent us this wagon train from Arkansas for us to save their immortal souls through the atonement of their blood spilt on the soil at Mountain Meadows."

There were low murmurs that Ellie couldn't understand. But she knew now they were talking about the Farrington train. Her heart was thudding beneath her ribs in anger, dismay, and betrayal. How could any reasonable human beings plan such devastation on a group of families—God-fearing, God-loving families?

She bit her lip to keep from crying out and continued listening.

The deeper and older, more resonant voice was speaking again. "We wanted the Indians to finish the job, but it appears the company is too well fortified. I'd wanted us not to have any innocent blood on our hands."

A younger voice that Ellie hadn't heard before now spoke up. "Innocent? You never said there was *any* innocent blood in the train."

"Children's blood is innocent. And the women. But vengeance is vengeance, and I suppose the loss of the innocents is part of the price God requires."

Ellie thought she was going to be sick, and she wrapped her arms around her stomach, fighting the waves of nausea that swept over her. The blood of innocents? What were they talking about? *Oh, God,* she breathed, *what is this? What have we gotten into?*

"I have a plan," said a deep voice. The speaker was the man someone had called John. "It will keep us from soiling our hands with innocent blood. But it will require the cooperation of every able-bodied man in the territory. And of every tribe of Indians we have dealings with. I want you each to ride out and let the word be known. Every Danite brother is to meet at the meadow tomorrow to help. Every Indian who's not already here is to be told that the Big Mormon Chief has called upon them to help in this holy war.

"Tell them that these Americans—these hated 'Mericats' in the meadow—have promised to return with soldiers from California to kill every last Indian they see. Tell them my words." He chuckled. "I expect all of them at Mountain Meadows by high noon tomorrow. I think they'll be there." He went on to describe, in cold military terms, the details of how his plan would be carried out.

Ellie was now on her knees in the sandy soil by the barn, clutching her arms to her chest and rocking herself in silent sobs. She could scarcely take in the horror, the treachery, that she'd just overheard.

She drew in a shaky breath, forcing herself to be silent as the council broke up and the men made their way from the barn.

"You're coming back with us?" a younger man asked.

"This was just a meeting place," said a voice that was obviously Steele's. "Not a stop for a social call—even to see my wife. We've got a meadow full of trouble waiting. I'd say there's no time to think of anything but what's ahead . . . for any of us." He paused, and the others fell silent. "Now, brothers," he said quietly, "let me bless you before our mission begins."

The men knelt before John Steele in a circle, hands folded, heads bowed, and one by one, he pressed his palms to their heads. Bowing his head, Steele kept his voice low when he began to pray his blessing on the men. His voice faded into an unintelligible murmur. Ellie could hear only the soft intonation of religious-sounding words.

Ellie dared not breathe for fear of being heard. When the blessing was over, the men stood, shook hands, then mounted and rode into the darkness. She gathered her thin nightclothes above her ankles and slipped back down the path and into the house.

Once inside the bedroom, she stooped by Faith's cradle, kissed the baby softly, then pulled on the clothes she'd arrived in days earlier. She lit the lamp, keeping the light dim so Faith wouldn't awaken. Then she hurriedly scribbled a note for Hannah and Sophronia, asking them to watch over her child.

She didn't tell them where she was headed or what she'd heard. The man named John was surely John Steele, and she didn't want to place the young woman in any greater danger.

But Ellie knew that now she really didn't have any other choice. She had to get to Mountain Meadows without being seen by any of the men who were now combing the territory to call out their brothers.

She had to warn Alexander, because she knew how John Steele was going to trick the entire Farrington company into surrendering . . . a promise of safe passage to Cedar City and protection from the attacking Utes. Alexander and the others wouldn't recognize the real enemy.

TWENTY-EIGHT

The night he was tried for apostasy, Lucas Knight was found guilty. But John Steele had been wrong—the only reason he hadn't been put to death at once was because of his relationship to the Danite leader. No one was willing to slit the throat of John's adopted son. So a compromise had been struck, and Lucas was imprisoned in a house outside the valley to await John's return so that he himself could carry out the act of blood atonement.

"You better keep up your strength for diggin' your own grave," the first of his guards had taunted one night when bringing Lucas his supper. "And for lettin' your own blood." He'd laughed the evil laugh of those Danites Lucas knew to be young and inexperienced. They were always exhilarated with new power.

"Spare me the details," Lucas replied, assessing the man's weaknesses. "I've witnessed blood atonement more times than I care to remember. I know exactly how it's carried out."

The young guard shrugged and went about his business. But as days slipped by, it was obvious John Steele was in no hurry to make the journey north. And Lucas planned his escape while studying his series of guards. Some he knew, some he didn't. None were as young or naive as the first.

One night when he was guarded by the same young Danite, he moaned as if with a bellyache, carrying on until the young man rushed into Lucas's room.

He waited until the young guard bent over him, then he reached up and clamped the boy's neck in a choke hold, twisting his arm behind him. Lucas could have broken the thin neck, but he didn't. The young man seemed to expect the worst from the evil apostate and looked up at Lucas in mute surprise as he was bound and gagged and thrown onto the bed unharmed.

"Now you may be the one executed for failure of duty," Lucas said with a mock salute as he left. Though it wasn't true, he thought he'd give the Danite something to consider until his rescue.

Spitfire was corralled nearby, and within minutes Lucas had mounted and was riding deep into the mountains.

He had been riding south now for days, staying away from settlements and ranches where he might be identified. He kept off the trail, listening for bands of Indians and whites, both equally dangerous to him. The Indians were controlled by John Steele. They knew Lucas as his son and wouldn't hesitate to report back to John that they'd sighted him. And he was certain the white settlers throughout the territory would by now have been warned about his escape.

He watched for signs of the Farrington wagon train as he rode, though he knew it was unlikely he'd spot anything, being so distant from the trail. He figured he was one week or so behind the company. A single rider could travel much faster than a caravan of wagons with several hundred head of cattle, so he hoped he could get to Mountain Meadows before they pulled out.

As always, his thoughts turned to Hannah as he rode. His rage had lessened somewhat, but only because he knew his energy would be better spent planning their escape.

Spitfire slowed now, and patting the horse's neck, Lucas let him take his lead along a forested ridge.

Lucas drew in a deep breath, gazing up at the moonlit sky through the branches of some spindly pines. He looked forward to seeing the Farringtons again, getting to know the family better on the trail to California.

He smiled, thinking of Ellie's words about God the time they had danced in the night circle near Laramie. She said that God had brought Lucas to them. He remembered how, afterward, he'd looked up at the sky, considering a God of forgiveness and love, a God who required his life in exchange for what Ellie had called "an abundance of all he is, living in us."

And she had spoken about her tomorrows—Alexander's and her children's—all resting in God's hands. He'd seen the trust in her face, and he knew when she spoke the words that she meant them from the very depths of her being. Her expression when she spoke of God now suddenly reminded him of little Meg's when he'd placed the whittled flute in her hands. The look on the child's face had been one of pure joy, a delight that the giver of such a wonderful gift had chosen her to give it to. Ellie's face had been so like her daughter's when she spoke of the abundance of all God is, living in her.

Spitfire danced sideways on the trail as a fat raccoon sauntered by in the brush. Lucas reined the stallion away from the creature and steadied him with another pat on the neck and some soothing words.

He thought again of Ellie, the glow of love on her face, her child-like trust and her strong yet gentle ways. If God was living in her, it followed that it was God Lucas recognized within her spirit . . . and had from the beginning.

He understood that what she'd said that night was true: God had drawn Lucas there for a purpose. And that purpose was to meet the only true, living God.

He felt like shouting or at least throwing his head back and laughing aloud. While he had been held captive by the Avenging Angels, he'd had lofty thoughts that God had led him to the Farringtons to be their Moses—to take them safely through the territory.

Now he knew that wasn't it at all.

He halted the stallion as the truth soaked into his soul.

No, he'd been led to Ellie and Alexander so that he would see God . . . the true God behind the veil of the Saints . . . the veil of deceit.

He looked heavenward, feeling an inexpressible depth of emotion. He wanted to weep and shout and laugh. Instead, he remained silent, staring up at the velvet sky. At the eastern horizon the silver crown of dawn outlined the mountains. Lucas held up his arms and said simply. "Here I am, Lord. I'm yours." And a voice answered deep in his soul:

I am the true God, the living God, the everlasting King.
I have drawn you with lovingkindness.
And you are mine, my son.

As the sun rose, Lucas rode on instead of halting for the day. Suddenly, it seemed more important than ever to get to Hannah and Sophronia . . . to get all three of them into the Farrington company as quickly as possible.

He rode all day and by sundown could see the red cliffs of Cedar City glowing in the last rays of the sun. He skirted the town and headed straight for the mountain pass to the southwest. He was within a few miles of Hannah and Sophronia, but exhausted, he now stopped to camp for the night. He chose a small canyon, protected by a screen of cedars and scrub pines, knowing that the closer he got to the Steele ranch, the more dangerous it was for him. John Steele commanded a militia numbering in the hundreds at this end of the territory.

Lucas slept soundly then rose in the ashen light of predawn, saddled Spitfire, and headed toward the Steele ranch. He kept well off the trail, only stopping from time to time to listen for other riders. But the nearby trail remained strangely vacant.

Just as the sun rose over the eastern ridge of the mountains, Lucas spotted first the pond and then the rough-hewn ranch house belonging to John Steele. He had been there with John on some of their travels through the territory.

As Lucas rode closer to the ranch, he could see smoke curling from the chimney, disappearing into the clear morning sky. That meant that Hannah and Sophronia were home. His gaze took in the grassland beyond the barn. The distinctive bay that John Steele usually rode was not among the other horses. He hoped that meant the man wasn't home.

He rode a ways into the brush, tethered Spitfire to a low oak, then made his way to the front of the house. He listened for voices, still worried about John Steele being present, but was surprised to hear nothing except an infant's cry.

Lucas knocked and waited as he heard footsteps approaching. Sophronia answered the door. At first she stood perfectly still, her eyes full of love and welcome. Then she held open her arms, and Lucas fell into them.

"My child," she whispered. "You've come back to us."

He had just stepped into the house, his arm encircling Sophronia, when Hannah appeared in the kitchen doorway, holding a small bundled baby.

"Lucas!" she whispered. "You've come . . ." She moved toward him, her eyes never leaving his face.

"Hannah," he said meeting her gaze. For a heartbeat neither of them spoke, then he looked down at the infant.

Hannah noticed his puzzled expression and smiled gently at the child in her arms. "This is Faith—Ellie's baby."

"Ellie?" he said. "Ellie Farrington? How—?" Ellie had somehow found Hannah and Sophronia. He tried to take in the wonder of it. "Is she here?"

Hannah and Sophronia exchanged a glance, their expressions worried. "No," Hannah said. "She had come here for supplies when this little angel decided it was time to come into the world." Her voice dropped. "But something terrible's happened at Mountain Meadows, Lucas. She found out, and I'm sure that's where she's gone."

He was instantly alarmed, and all the fears he'd had for the group in Salt Lake City returned full force. "What's happened?"

"There's been an Indian attack. The Utes began a siege some six days ago now. The last we heard, though, it's a standoff."

"Are you sure it's the Indians?"

Again the worried looks. "I've been afraid to consider anything else, Lucas."

"I've thought of it plenty, though," said Sophronia, her eyes snapping. "I think it's some white Indians. It's been done before, you know."

Lucas nodded. It was no secret. "And you think Ellie left to go there?"

"I kept her from leaving for two days. But she took one of the mares during the night. Left us a note." The baby started to fuss, and Hannah lifted her to her shoulder. "I told her of the danger, but I didn't tell her the Mormons might be carrying it out. I didn't want to consider it myself."

"I'll go for her," Lucas said immediately.

"I think John's involved in this, Lucas," Hannah said. "He's been gone from here for a week, though some of the neighbors said they've seen him out riding."

Lucas nodded. "I'll watch for him," he said.

"Be careful, Lucas," Hannah said. She handed the baby to Sophronia and walked with Lucas to the door.

He took her hands in his. "Hannah, I'll find Ellie and be back. There's so much we need to talk about . . ." His words faltered.

"I know," she said, touching his cheek. "There will be time later, Lucas. God be with you. I fear for what you'll find."

He turned and headed quickly for the stallion. Within minutes the horse was galloping down the trail toward Mountain Meadows. If he could keep to the trail he would arrive there within the hour.

At daybreak, Ellie Farrington, riding one of the Steeles' mares, arrived at the pass that led into Mountain Meadows. She'd stayed a distance from the trail, though keeping it in sight so she wouldn't lose her way in the dim moonlight. Riders had passed her from time to time, but she'd remained behind the thick cover of piñons and cedars. She needn't have worried. They hadn't so much as glanced in her direction but rather had seemed lost in discussion, some arguing loudly, others speaking favorably about the activities at the meadows.

Ellie was feeling weak now from the ride and knew she could start bleeding again. But she ignored any thought of herself and kept her mind on getting to Alexander in time to save the company.

She had remembered the setting of the meadow well, its bowl-like shape framed by low mountains. She figured that if she could get to a vantage point where she could see without being seen, she might find an opportunity to slip into the wagon circle. Her chances were probably next to none, but she had to try.

Rounding a corner, she heard voices carrying toward her from ahead on the trail. She nudged the mare deeper into the brush then reined her to a halt until the riders passed.

One of the voices, deep and resonant, sounded familiar. It was one of those she'd heard last night. John Steele. She tried to make out his form through the thicket of brush but could see only brief glimpses of his silver-gray hair and stocky build. He rode a high-stepping deep red bay.

He spoke for a few minutes to a couple of men who were with him, calling one "Roe" and the other "Isaac." She caught only snatches of the conversation, then one of the men began to pray, offering what sounded like a blessing on John Steele's mission.

Ellie fought the waves of fear and nausea that threatened to overwhelm her. She drew in a deep breath and closed her eyes for a minute to calm herself, holding on to the saddle horn to keep from swaying. The men had now ridden toward the meadow, and she waited until they had moved a distance ahead of her on the trail before kicking the mare forward again.

As soon as she came over another rise, agony and realization cut through her heart like a knife.

She was too late. Too late!

The circle of wagons was surrounded by men. Not Indians in the hills, but white men with rifles—members of the Mormon militia she'd heard being discussed last night—standing within yards of each wagon.

Ellie covered her face with her hands and prayed for courage . . . for those in the wagon circle . . . for herself.

Dismounting, she tethered the mare's bridle to a small cedar a distance into the forest. She leaned against a tree for a minute, closing her eyes and trying to steady herself. She was weak, nearly too weak to step toward the shelter of rocks she'd spotted.

But she bit her lips together in sheer determination and moved slowly from the cover of trees to the outcropping of granite. She had just moved into position when John Steele, riding on the blood red bay, made his way to the Farrington company, waving a white flag.

Alexander met him, and Steele dismounted as some of the other men gathered round. She could see Billy Farrington, Jesse O'Donnell, and Abe Barrett standing nearby; behind them others began to crowd around. Reverend Brown stood off to one side. And she could barely make out Liza Barrett speaking with him. Alexander spoke to John Steele, and the conversation seemed animated. She hoped that her husband would see through Steele's plan, but she noticed that there seemed to be no wariness among any of the Farrington party.

She wanted to run down to them, risk an arrow in the back or a bullet through the chest, just for the chance to cry out to her husband, to tell him not to listen. Then Faith's tiny face slipped into her mind, and she knew she had to stay out of sight. No matter what happened, she wouldn't walk from this place only to face certain death.

The sun was higher now, beating hot and harsh on her face and head. She felt so weak. Unbidden, her eyes fluttered closed for a moment. She was beginning to see shimmering lights across the meadow grasses, and she blinked to clear her mind and vision. Her thirst was terrible, and as she looked down she knew the bleeding had started again, worse than before.

There was a commotion in the meadow, and she tried to focus again on the train. The shimmering was more pronounced now, and she couldn't quite make out the high-arched wagons. Wildly, her gaze flicked among the people, all standing in the train's center corral. She searched for her friends, Liza Barrett, Polly O'Donnell, Mary Farrington. They were there, holding on to their children and grandchildren.

She blinked again, trying to send away the awful shimmering, trying to see her precious Meg and Sarah. Her babies. Her sweet babies. There they were! First skipping to stand beside Alexander. Then no, he'd sent them away. Sent them to stand by Liza.

Ellie was pleased. Liza was more precious to her than a sister. It was fitting that the children each held one of her hands. Meg—

Margaret Elizabeth—had been named for her, Ellie's precious friend.

She should be with her friends, her husband, her babies. She started to rise to walk down the mountain then remembered she couldn't . . . She couldn't because the grass was on fire. She had first noticed it the other night. Even Meg and Sarah had seen it. That must be why it was shimmering so, shimmering golden in the sun.

Her weakness was worse now, nearly to the point where her head sagged against the warm stone. But wait. She had to see her babies. She tried once more.

There . . . there they were . . . all of them. Walking out in single file. That seemed strange, but why should she question it?

All the children, the tiniest children, were being loaded into wagons. There was Sarah holding Phoebe and Meg whistling through her flute, playing "Oh! Susanna" as they climbed into the wagon together. No, maybe the song was merely in her head. Stuck in there with the shimmering fields of goldenrod.

She struggled to raise her head to see what would happen next. She knew something was wrong, but she couldn't remember exactly what. She licked her lips to rid them of their dryness. But it didn't help, just like when she was crossing the prairie and they'd blistered in the sun. All those days her lips had bled and blistered as she'd walked next to the wagon, gazing into Alexander's eyes of love.

The same eyes that had shown her everything in his heart on the day they were wed back at Drake's Creek. She'd worn a crown of flowers that day, goldenrod, and she and Alexander had danced in a meadow like this. Whirled and danced. And Ellie's veil had caught in the breeze. Alexander had laughed, saying she might fly off like an angel if he didn't hold her tight in his arms.

And, oh! He had held her. For all those years he'd held her. She looked at him now, walking so proud and tall as he led this long line of men. Her captain. Her wonderful, strong, and loving captain.

But why had they laid down their weapons? Why were they walking single file, each next to a Mormon man? There was something dangerous about what they were doing, but she couldn't remember what.

And the women . . . why had their babies been taken from their arms? Their children ripped from them? She squinted as the women marched north through the goldenrod, the sunflowers, the lupines. They walked single file, just like the men.

The meadow grasses were burning, though not consumed. They shimmered again, pale amber and liquid gold. But still the wagon company marched side by side with their captors.

Her eyes searched for Meg and Sarah, but they were facing away from her. She longed to look in their sweet faces one more time, and her heart nearly broke in two because of the ache inside her.

Then she noticed that there was someone with the children in the wagon. Someone she hadn't noticed before. The little ones were gathered around Him, some on His lap, others nestled in His arms.

The wagon drove on, not stopping, even after the shimmering field had turned red with blood and was filled with the screams of the dying.

Ellie covered her ears with her hands, and she hardly knew her face glistened wet with tears. She kept her gaze on the figure in the wagon with the children, praying for Him to keep the little ones from turning to see the carnage behind them . . . their fallen mothers and fathers and grandmothers and grandfathers . . . their brothers and sisters and playmates.

The figure in the wagon turned toward Ellie, as if He'd known she was there all along. He seemed to beckon, and she wanted to go with Him, though somehow she knew she could stay with Him but not with the children.

At the same time, the meadow seemed filled with music and light. There was laughter and singing as friends greeted each other. She looked up to see Alexander striding toward her.

He held her wedding veil, and when she stood, he placed its crown of goldenrod on her head. The veil floated on a breath of wind sweeping across the meadow. They laughed at the joy of it. Then he gathered her into his arms, and she felt so light that even earth seemed no longer able to hold her.

"Ellie—?" a voice said in a hoarse whisper. "Ellie!" Her eyes fluttered open, but the pain of keeping them open was too great. She shut them again but not before she'd seen Lucas Knight kneeling beside her, his face filled with the tragedy of what they'd just witnessed. He lifted her head with his hand. "I've got to get you out of here," he said, his voice ragged.

"I don't want to leave," she breathed. "Alexander . . ." Her hand fluttered helplessly. "Don't you see? I can't leave."

Lucas tenderly wiped her face with a cool, wet cloth. "Ellie, I'm going to take you to Hannah's, to Sophronia's. They're caring for Faith. You must return."

She knew he didn't want her to think about what had happened in the meadow. But he didn't understand. She would rest, she thought, as he lifted her into his arms. She would rest and then tell him, tell them all what had happened.

As he carried her into the forest to where his horse stood waiting, Ellie kept her face turned from the meadow. When he'd mounted and lifted her onto the saddle in front of him, she asked, "Did you see?"

He nodded grimly as she leaned against his chest. "Not everything, but enough to know what happened."

"They have my children."

He looked into her face. "They saved the children? You saw them?"

"Yes," she whispered weakly. "Two wagons."

"Meg and Sarah?" he asked, his voice choking. "Did you see them?"

"Yes," she said. "They were in the first wagon with maybe six or seven others. And I saw three of the O'Donnell girls in the same wagon." She closed her eyes a moment. "I counted the children carefully, so I could tell who was saved."

"You must rest now, Ellie. You need your strength."

She closed her eyes. She'd been spared for a reason, and it wasn't to rest. "You must find them . . . every one. Promise me."

He met her gaze and nodded. "I promise."

When she opened her eyes again, Lucas was heading around the last curve before the Steele ranch. She trembled, remembering John Steele's role in the massacre. Lucas must have understood, because he held her more tightly.

"You're safe here," he said. "John Steele is still at the meadows. I would think he'll remain there for quite some time."

The next thing she knew, Hannah and Sophronia were bending over her at the sides of the bed where she'd borne little Faith. "My baby . . . ," she whispered, feeling weaker now than before.

"She's fine. Healthy and beautiful," Hannah whispered. She held a cup of water to Ellie's lips, and she sipped as Lucas supported her head. He helped her settle back into the pillows.

"I need to tell you everything that happened," she said. "But most of all I need to tell you about the children. You need to write down every name, so they're not forgotten."

White-faced, Hannah sat on the side of the bed and took Ellie's hand. "I promise you that the three of us will not ever forget the events that happened here today."

"I have a little journal," Ellie said, "that I've kept since we started our journey across. I carry it with me always, usually in my skirt pocket. It was with me the day Faith was born."

"I found it," Hannah said, standing to retrieve it from a lamp table near the window. She returned and placed it in Ellie's hands.

Ellie felt its worn leather cover, its ribbon marker, and brought it to her heart. "This is for my children," she whispered. "It's all I can give them of myself."

Hannah touched her arm. "Please don't say that, Ellie. You must live."

Ellie knew better. She'd known at the meadow. Even though Lucas had helped her stanch the bleeding at the meadow, she'd known. "Would you write down the names for me? Write them in this little book." She handed it to Hannah.

Sophronia went for the inkwell and a pen, and Hannah settled into a chair near the lamp table. She folded back the cover and dipped the pen in the ink.

"The children's names are Martha Elizabeth Barrett, Sarah Frances Barrett, and William Twitty Barrett. And there are the five little O'Donnell girls: Rebecca, Louisa, Sarah, Prudence Angeline, and Georgiana."

Ellie's eyes filled with tears as she thought of each child, how each represented a family of friends she loved. She continued, praying for strength. "And there were Alexander's grandchildren Kit and Triphenia Farrington. And little Nancy Huff, Felix Jones, and the Miller children: John Calvin, Mary, and Joseph. I saw Emerson and Billy Tackett."

Her voice dropped to a whisper. "And I saw Meg and Sarah, my precious little girls . . . my babies. They were in one of the two wagons filled with the children." She frowned and slowly turned her head to look up at Lucas. "Why do you suppose they saved the children?"

For a moment, only the scratching sound of the pen on paper could be heard. Finally, Lucas answered. "Their blood is considered innocent," he said, turning to look out the window, as if her pain was too much for him to bear.

"Lucas," Ellie said suddenly, "would you read something for me?"

"Of course."

"It's in my journal, toward the end. I wrote down something that always gives me comfort. Would you read it now?"

From the wooden cradle in the corner, a tiny cry sounded, and Ellie moved her head to look over at Faith. Sophronia, knowing it was time, stooped to lift the child into her arms, crossed to the bed, and placed Faith in Ellie's arms.

The shimmering had started again, and Ellie whispered, "Help me hold her, will you?"

Sophronia pulled a chair nearer, placing her arms around the baby and Ellie.

Ellie closed her eyes, feeling the warmth and security of the older woman's embrace and Faith's soft breathing as she stopped her crying. "Read, Lucas," she whispered. "Now, please?"

Hannah handed Lucas the journal.

"Fear not: for I have redeemed thee, I have called thee by thy name; thou art mine.

"When thou passest through the waters, I will be with thee; and through the rivers, they shall not overflow thee:

"When thou walkest through the fire, thou shalt not be burned; neither shall the flame kindle upon thee."

Ellie held up her hand for Lucas to stop reading. She smiled weakly, then looked down one last time at the precious baby in her arms. "Jesus was there, you know," she murmured. "He was there with the children, holding them in his arms."

The shimmering was now so bright that she couldn't make out their faces. "Take care of my children," Ellie said, though she wasn't sure it was with her voice or her thoughts.

Twenty-Nine

Three days later, Hannah knelt to place wildflowers on Ellie Farrington's grave. Lucas had dug it on a hillside near the pond, and from here the morning sunlight seemed especially brilliant. They had chosen the spot, knowing how Ellie would like it and also thinking that someday little Faith and the twins, Meg and Sarah, might want to visit the place and know that special care was given their mother.

"Hannah—?" Lucas called out, striding up the hillside behind her.

Hannah brushed her hands and stood to greet him. "You're ready to go?"

"Sophronia's packing me some provisions." He was now standing in front of her and took her hands in his. "I hate leaving you here, Hannah. It's something I swore I would never do."

She swallowed hard and touched his lips. "Don't say it, Lucas. We're doing what is right. If it weren't for the children . . ." Her voice faltered.

He turned her gently with his arm, and they began to walk down the pathway to the pond. "I'll come back as soon as I can get a government agent to come with me."

"I know it may take a couple of years for you to get back, Lucas. But even then I don't know that it will be safe for you to return. Not after what's happened. If it ever comes out that you know anything about what really happened . . ." Her voice faltered.

"Justice has to be seen to, Hannah. One way or another."

"The deception has already begun. A neighbor stopped by to check on me last night. He told me in great detail how the Indians annihilated the entire train."

"He still has no idea that there was a witness?"

Hannah shook her head. "No one knew Ellie was here. And now that the children have been given out to families all over the territory, it's assumed that Faith was brought here by one of the Danites. The neighbor never even asked where she came from."

Lucas looked across the pond. "I am ashamed that I was ever part of the Avenging Angels, that I ever thought there was a reason for vengeance."

She took his hand. "We were brought up in an atmosphere of hatred and fear. We knew no other way."

"Ellie said something to me once about Christ's robe of righteousness. I was trying to convince her that we have to earn God's favor. Of course, I was thinking about my own unworthiness, my own terrible wrongs."

Hannah smiled. "She told me that it's Christ's atonement for our sins that makes the difference—not anything we can do on our own. Certainly not giving our own lives or causing someone else to lose theirs."

"How strange that we pursue blood atonement so fervently when Christ was the One who made the sacrifice," Lucas mused.

"The robe Ellie mentioned—?" He nodded. "Ellie said that when we accept that sacrifice—his blood shed on our account—that's when his robe of righteousness is draped around our shoulders. All our sin, no matter how terrible, is removed from God's sight. We stand blameless and pure before him."

"Are you talking about what I've done," he asked gently, "or what's happened to you?"

"We both have much to overcome, Lucas. I wanted to come to you as pure and innocent as I was the day I met you. Instead, John Steele took me . . ." She couldn't go on. She merely stood, looking into Lucas's face, trembling and pressing her lips together to keep from crying.

He reached out and gently touched her cheek. "Oh, Hannah—" His voice broke. "If you only knew the things I've witnessed. Things I didn't try to prevent."

"If what Ellie says is true, then we can stand blameless before God through his Son," she whispered.

"I feel I've already met her God . . ."

"Our God," Hannah corrected gently.

He nodded. "But it's Christ's sacrifice I'm just beginning to understand." He hesitated, frowning in wonder. "When did you begin to believe that Christ lives in us?"

She smiled. "I think I saw him in Ellie from the moment I met her. But when she said that she'd seen him with her children, I couldn't doubt her words. I saw his love, his life, in her face. I believed her."

"It was the same for me," he mused, glancing at the small mound up the hill from the pond. "She told me back in Laramie that God never makes mistakes, that he'd led me to their train for a purpose. I know now what that purpose was. It was so she could introduce me to the living, holy God."

They turned to walk back down the hillside to the ranch house. "I'll find the location of every child while you're gone," she said when they were standing by Spitfire. "If you can't come back into the territory, have your agent—or that of the government—come see me. I'll have all the information he'll need. All of the children will be accounted for—and watched over by Sophronia and me—until they're returned home to relatives in the East."

Lucas cupped her face in his hands. "It takes courage to stay here."

She smiled gently. "Both of us are doing what we must for the children."

Sophronia stepped to the doorway of the house, holding tiny Faith in her arms. Lucas walked over to tell her good-bye.

He took the child and held her for a minute, gazing into her eyes. "Such a beautiful baby, born of such tragedy." His voice caught, and he said no more.

Sophronia wrapped her arms around Lucas and gathered him and the baby into her arms.

Hannah, tears now streaming down her face, went over to join the embrace. "I thought I would be braver than this," she whispered. She pulled back slightly, looking from Lucas to Sophronia and attempting to smile through her tears. "The only thing that helps is to think about what Ellie said, that God doesn't let anything happen by accident. He's had his hand on us all since the beginning, and he's not going to let go now."

For a moment Lucas didn't speak, then he said, "I leave you all in God's hands." Without another word, he placed the child again in Sophronia's arms and turned back to the stallion. With a nod to them all, he swung a leg over the saddle then headed down the trail.

Hannah watched him go, wondering how long it would be until she saw him again. Or if she would see him again.

"Lucas!" she cried, running after him. "Lucas!"

He craned around in the saddle, saw her running, and dismounted in time to catch her up in his arms.

"Oh, Lucas!" she cried again, her arms circling his neck as he twirled her around and pressed her close. "My darling, I love you. I've always loved you."

Then he stopped and held her tightly in his arms. "Hannah," he said his voice husky. "My beloved . . . my beloved Hannah! I promise I'll come back for you."

"Don't promise what you can't know," she said, kissing his palm when he'd released her. "Just promise me you'll think of me every day—just as I'm keeping you in my heart forever."

He brushed her lips with his, then again swung into the saddle. He pulled his hat down low and smiled tenderly at her from under its brim.

"Good-bye, my love," he said. Then he kicked Spitfire to a trot, waved once more, and was gone.

That evening, John Steele rode into the ranch, dismounted, and strode toward the house, the heavy thud of his boots reverberating across the wood-slat porch and announcing his arrival before he threw open the door.

Hannah had been humming as she held little Faith in her arms. She stopped abruptly, gazing up at him as he entered the room.

His face was haggard, his eyes circled by a bruise-colored darkness, and he stared into the room without speaking. Then he walked toward her and pulled back the corner of the blanket to peer at the sleeping baby.

"How did you get this child?" he demanded.

"It's one of those from the Meadows," she said simply.

"Someone must have brought it here," he shrugged as if there were too many details to keep track of. "The Indians, you know, killed so many . . ." He spoke in a false, halting way. "There were survivors. Young children. We had to see to their disposition. They've been taken in by families in the area." His voice was hoarse with fatigue, yet still held the familiar tone of arrogance. "So many details to attend to, bodies to bury, cattle to round up . . ." He shook his head.

"So I understand," she said.

He threw down his coat and moved toward the kitchen. She could hear the squeak of the hand pump as he drew himself some water. "Where's Sophronia?" he called to Hannah.

"She's in the barn, seeing to the horses," Hannah said, willing her voice to remain calm. Surely he was not about to demand his rights as her husband. Not now! She clutched the baby closer.

"And I see the child sleeps," he said as he walked back into the great room. Hannah stared at his boots. They were covered with splatters of blood mixed with dried mud.

He had reached her now, and he cupped her chin with rough fingers, forcing her gaze upward until her eyes met his. "Why don't you put it in its bed?" he said. His expression was frenzied, red-eyed, and wild. Images of the Farrington party came to her mind, and she caught her breath in fear.

"I want to rest," he continued. "And I want you beside me. You are my wife." He paused, one brow arched. "Need I say more?"

Hannah glanced down at Faith, sleeping so peacefully in her arms. She would do whatever was necessary to keep her safe. Before she acted against this man who dared to call himself her husband, she would first steer him as far as possible from the child.

"No, John, your words are as eloquent as usual," she said. "I understand perfectly." Swallowing hard, she stood and carried Faith to her cradle. She laid the still-sleeping baby on the soft quilted pad and tucked the blanket around her tiny shoulders.

John moved toward her. Hannah glanced at the rack where Sophronia's Hawken usually hung. It was empty. Her blood pulsed painfully up the side of her neck and into her temple, and she touched her forehead, thinking she might faint.

John's boots thudded across the wood floor as he stepped still closer. His arms were open to her. But Hannah couldn't stop staring at his boots. The mud. The dark spatters of blood. The blood of mothers with their children, their husbands and fathers and grandfathers . . . their families . . . who'd been slaughtered . . . by the hand of this man who stood before her. The man wanting to draw her into his embrace.

Hannah covered her mouth, knowing she was about to be sick.

Just then, Sophronia's voice carried toward them from the front door. "I think it's high time you headed down the road, Mister Steele," she said, her voice low and calm. "I don't care where. Or how. Just get."

John turned, seeming confused in his fatigue. The barrel of her Hawken was pointed dead center at John's chest. Before the surprised man could grab Hannah for protection, she quickly stepped away from him.

He rubbed his head, staring dumbfounded at the older woman, confused in his fatigue. "Have you lost your senses, woman?"

"Never had a clearer thought in my life," she answered, the rifle still aimed at his heart. "And nothing would do me more pleasure than pulling this trigger. As I said, you better be on your way before my finger itches any more than it does right now. You've got plenty of places to go where your welcome will be much warmer, I'm sure."

He shook his head slowly, edged a menacing glance at Hannah, then reached for his coat. Sophronia stepped back from the door, her aim unchanged, as he strode through and headed toward his horse. He mounted slowly, looking back, a dark expression on his face. Moments later, he rode from the ranch and headed down the road to Cedar City . . . the same direction Lucas had ridden just hours before.

Hannah gazed at her aunt, her wild white hair, her fierce eyes. She didn't think she'd ever loved her more than she did that moment.

"Thank you," she whispered hoarsely.

"Thank our heavenly Father, child," Sophronia answered with a smile. "He was the one helping me hold this thing steady."

"You've never had trouble taking aim before," Hannah said. "I had full confidence—"

Sophronia interrupted. "Always before, I've had time to load it with ball and powder." She smiled. "I took it down to clean it last night. This thing's as empty as a church pew on Monday morning. Knowing something like that can give a person quite a case of the shakes."

"You're a wonder, Sophie."

"The wonder will be if John Steele keeps away for good, child."

"I don't think I can bear it if he returns, Sophie." She glanced at little Faith, who was stirring in her sleep. "It would be worse than ever before. Now—" Her voice faltered. "—now that there's even more to protect."

Understanding her meaning, Sophronia walked across the room to the cradle and knelt beside it, adjusting the blanket. She planted a soft kiss on the baby's head, gazed at her a moment, then stood and smoothed her skirt. "It's in our favor that most of John's work is with the Prophet," she said. "I think there will be a lot of explaining to do as the tale spreads about the 'Indian' massacre. The Prophet's going to need all the help he can get. Maybe that'll keep John in Salt Lake valley."

"Especially after Lucas tells the truth outside the territory," Hannah added, feeling more hopeful.

Sophronia smiled gently. "I liked what Lucas said when he left . . . his words about leaving us in God's hands. I saw you watching the road John took, likely worried about him catching up to Lucas." She paused thoughtfully. "You know, child, we're placing our Lucas in God's hands—just where he said he was leaving us."

"And there we'll all remain," Hannah said, grateful for the reminder, "until we meet again."

"And after," said Sophronia with a knowing smile. "Forever after."

THIRTY

Utah Territory
May 1860

Hannah climbed up onto the driver's bench of the carriage. Sophronia had just settled into the back, and tiny, elfin Faith, whom they now called Fae, cuddled in her arms. They made quite a picture, Sophronia with her wild white curls, Fae with her dark, silken hair and round, happy face.

Hannah craned to look at the two and smiled. Fae had become so much a part of their world she couldn't imagine life without her. For nearly three years now, Hannah had been the only mother Fae had known. And of course, Sophronia had more than willingly filled the place of Fae's grandmother, or "Nanny," as she called her.

Fae gave Hannah a big smile and sighed as she leaned back into Sophronia's arms. "How long this time, Mommy?" Fae asked. Hannah thought she would never tire of the sound of Fae's sweet lisping voice. She now asked endless questions, and of course, whenever they started on one of their journeys to visit the wagon train children, she always wanted to know how long they'd be on the road.

Hannah grinned. "We're going to see your sisters. You'll like that. And it's not far."

"Sarah and Meggie?"

"Yes, Sarah and Meggie. They'll be so happy to see you. We're going to take them on a picnic. Won't that be fun?"

Fae looked up at Sophronia. "Nanny, make Mommy go faster. I

wanna have the picnic." Then she popped her thumb into her mouth and sucked noisily.

Hannah laughed as she turned to flick the reins over the backs of the two-horse team, and the carriage rocked as it moved forward. She knew they spoiled Fae terribly, but it couldn't be helped. Hannah's love for the little girl filled her heart to overflowing. Even tough Sophronia fussed over her like a true grandmother. They both worried about the inevitable; Farrington relatives from Arkansas would someday arrive to claim Fae as their own. Even now there were rumors flying through the territory that a government agent had finally come to gather the children and take them home.

Of course Fae would go with them. Ellie and Alexander would have wanted her safe in the arms of grandparents or aunts and uncles. The knowledge that she would lose little Fae sliced through Hannah's heart, and she tried to put it from her mind.

So she took one day at a time, visiting at least two of the children each week, keeping records of who they were with, where the families lived, which children had had their names changed through legal adoption. After the 1860 census, Hannah had even visited the courthouse in Salt Lake, poring over census records to make sure that not one of the Farrington train children had been overlooked.

She kept special watch over the children as they grew older and came of an age to be worked too hard. She'd worried that some of the families might have taken them in just to have extra farmhands to help with chores. But she found that the children had been welcomed into the families and were treated well.

Hannah tried not to mention the massacre, not wanting to cause any further sadness, but in the early months some of the older children brought it up anyway. They would wait until out of earshot of the family then mention such things as, "I saw Mrs. Rutherford wearing my mama's dress," or, "Did you know that when some bad men asked Nancy Huff what she remembered, and she told them—they shot her?"

Near Parowan, Hannah reined the horses onto a dusty road leading to the Rutherford ranch. The house lay up against the mountains, a sprawling dormitory filled with wives and children who lived under the tight rule of Luther Rutherford. He'd been at Mountain Meadows and had claimed Meg and Sarah for one of his barren wives. They now called Eliza Anne Rutherford "mother," but Hannah wanted them to never forget Ellie. She'd sworn to herself she'd keep their real mother's image alive for the little girls.

The twins, dressed in identical pinafores, saw her heading up the road and ran to meet the carriage almost before she'd halted the horses.

She stepped down, and both girls threw their arms around her, then Meg reached up to help Sophronia, and Sarah took Fae into her arms. Hannah smiled at the three little girls. Fae's smile was identical to her sisters', her hair the same mahogany color.

Eliza Anne Rutherford stepped out on the porch and waved as the small troop headed toward a grassy field shaded by cottonwoods and sycamores. She was a pale, tired-looking woman who seemed not to mind the days that Hannah came to visit the twins. In fact, most of the women didn't give it much thought that Hannah seemed to hold such interest in the welfare of the children. Hannah often thought it was ironic: Though he seldom spent time with her at their mountain ranch, her status as John Steele's wife gave them no cause to question her motives.

Hannah carried a worn quilt for sitting on, and beside her, Meg carried a basket of fried chicken and cornbread. Around them butterflies flitted in the sunlight, and spring birds twittered their songs. Fae wiggled and squirmed and said she wanted to walk, then, when Sarah put her down, said she wanted to be carried.

After a few minutes they found just the right spot for a picnic, and Meg and Hannah spread the quilt. Sarah sat Fae in its center, and they all settled around her.

"I have a surprise for you," said Sarah to Fae as Hannah reached into the basket for the chicken.

"What is it?" Fae asked, wrinkling her little nose.

Meg scooted closer on the quilt. She wore a knowing smile as if she'd been in on the idea. "Hurry," she said to her sister. "I can't wait for Fae to see it."

"Well, first," Sarah said dramatically, "Fae, you need to know how special my present is." Little Fae bobbed her head up and down excitedly as Sarah continued. "This is something I would not give to just anyone. Only you . . . because you're special."

Fae was up on her knees now, her eyes wide with excitement. Sarah reached into her pinafore pocket and drew out a worn wooden doll, though its clothes looked new.

"This is Phoebe," said Sarah softly. She placed the doll in Fae's arms. "Our papa carved it with his own hands."

"And Mama helped us make the clothes," added Meg.

"It's a baby," said Fae examining the painted face with her finger.

"Phoebe. Her name is Phoebe."

"Phoebe," repeated Fae, frowning at the sound of the new word. "Pretty Phoebe."

Hannah handed out napkins and cold fried chicken legs to everyone while Sarah and Meg told the story of Phoebe's adventures, from falling into the river to returning in the arms of a little Indian girl. The twins laughed about how Sarah had nearly caused an Indian war by fighting the little girl for the doll, then how it was found miraculously one morning on the wagon bench. They told how Meg had given her own doll, whom she'd never bothered to name, to the girl in return.

Hannah and Sophronia delighted in the story, asking questions about the Indians. But the twins abruptly stopped talking about the adventures, both of them turning somber. Hannah knew it was the memory of the wagon train that had caused it. She and Sophronia glanced at each other in silent agreement to ask no more questions.

"Phoebe's so you'll never forget me," Sarah said suddenly to Fae.

"What do you mean, honey?" Hannah asked, noticing the child's worried look. "Why would she ever forget you?"

Meg and Sarah exchanged glances, then Meg answered for her. "Mother told us that she heard someone's come for us. Someone from the government is in Salt Lake City right now. They've got some relatives with them. Mother also said that we can't expect to stay together—not even Sarah and me." Tears filled her eyes as she spoke. Eyes that had seen too much tragedy.

Hannah's heart went out to the little girl. "Meggie," she said, reaching over to hug her, "we don't know anything for a fact. Do you remember any of your aunts and uncles or your grandparents?"

Meg shook her head. "No," she whispered.

"I know that everyone back home is praying for your safekeeping. They're going to do the very best they can to give you a home. All three of you. They love you with all their hearts."

Meggie suddenly threw her arms around Hannah's neck. "But I don't want to leave you!" she sobbed. "You're the only one who loves us."

By now Sarah had moved across the quilt to Hannah's other side. She snuggled up close. "And you knew our mommy," she whispered. Fae sensed her sisters' sadness and went to Sophronia's lap, sucking her thumb and holding on to Phoebe.

Hannah prayed silently for the right words. Still holding the twins in her arms, she said, "We don't always know what's ahead for us, but God does. He knows, and he's got us in his hands. He is with us now—all of us. And he'll be with us when the time comes for you to leave."

"Can't you come with us?" Meg asked, looking up into Hannah's face. She gave Sophronia a teary and loving look. "And, Nanny, you too?"

Hannah saw a glimpse of Ellie in her expression, and it nearly broke her heart. "I don't know what the future holds for us either, honey." She smiled and gave them a big hug. "But God does."

On a sunny afternoon two weeks later, Hannah was planting squash and beans in her garden just beyond the pond when the sounds of distant hoofbeats and the creak of carriage wheels carried toward her. Sophronia and Fae were both napping, and she looked up, wondering if she should get the Hawken from its high rack just inside the door.

But before she could do more than stand and dust off her gardening pinafore, the carriage rolled into view followed by a small regiment of soldiers.

She walked down the hillside, around the pond, and to the front of the house. The carriage had now halted, and the driver stepped down and opened the door for a young couple and a leathery-faced man in uniform. All three looked hot and tired. The soldiers had halted their horses and dismounted.

"Mrs. Steele?" the officer inquired before Hannah could say hello.

She gave him a curt nod.

"We would like to ask you some questions," the officer said.

"Would you mind telling me what this is all about?" countered Hannah, growing irritated with his brusque demeanor and lack of manners.

The young woman stepped forward. She was pretty, with dark mahogany hair and pale skin, and when she spoke, her voice was soothing. "You'll have to forgive us," she said. "We've not had the most pleasant of stays—or receptions—in your territory. It makes us a bit out of sorts when we meet someone new."

She looked pointedly at the officer then back to Hannah. "My name is Amanda Roseanne, and this is my husband, Matthew. And this is Major Middleton, who's been sent by the president to help us. We've come about the children."

Major Middleton stepped forward and shook Hannah's hand. "We were given your name as someone who will help us find them all."

Hannah's heart caught. "Lucas? Lucas Knight gave you my name?" She gave them all a wide smile.

He nodded. "He's been instrumental in getting attention brought to this crime. He would have come with us, but he cannot safely enter the territory."

"I know," she said. "Do you know where he is now?"

"When we left he was still working on getting charges brought against the people involved here. His plan, however, was to meet us at Fort Bridger."

"Fort Bridger?" Hannah smiled again, feeling her heart skip. That was as close as Lucas dared come to Utah. Then she turned to the young couple. "You're related to some of the children from the train?"

"Yes," she said. "My father was the wagon master, Alexander Farrington."

"The captain? But, I thought," Hannah began, confused, "that there were only three Farrington children."

Amanda Roseanne's husband had stepped forward to stand near his wife, and Hannah noticed for the first time his clear wide eyes and pale wiry hair. His expression told her he was a good man, a man a person could trust. He smiled at her kindly. "The captain's first wife was Charity Anne Farrington. She died when Mandy was a child," he explained.

"Mandy?"

Amanda Roseanne smiled. "That's what Matthew calls me." She glanced at her husband affectionately. "He thinks Amanda Roseanne is terribly long." She laughed lightly before going on. "Ellie Farrington was a wonderful mother to me and my brothers and sisters," she said. "I was eight when she married my father, but she's the only mother I remember." She swallowed hard. "My two brothers, Hampton and Billy, and their wives were on the wagon train. Also my Aunt Jane and her sons, my cousins James and Robert. But it was my papa—" Her voice broke, and she couldn't go on.

"Your loss has been great," Hannah said softly. "So many . . ." Her voice faltered. She couldn't imagine the depths of the young woman's grief.

"Hearing about the twins and the baby gave us a reason for getting through the tragedy," Amanda Roseanne said. "We couldn't rest until they were found."

Hannah nodded, understanding, but now she worried that each child would go to a different family. "Will the children be kept together?" she asked.

Amanda Roseanne and her husband exchanged a loving look. "Yes," the young woman said. "We plan to take all three."

Hannah was glad, knowing the twins' fears, but the deep sadness in her heart about losing Fae caused a sting at the back of her throat. She looked away quickly so that no one would see the tears threatening to spill.

"Please," she said after a moment, "come in for a cool drink. I'll give you the list of names and the locations of each child. You'll, of course, want to see our little Fae."

They started to walk to the front door. "Fae?" mused Matthew as Hannah opened the door. "We were told the baby's name is Faith." They stepped inside and followed Hannah to the kitchen.

As her visitors settled into heavy wooden chairs, she answered. "Her given name is Faith; Ellie Farrington insisted on that." She paused a minute, laughing lightly. "But she's so tiny and angelic, almost pixielike, that I nicknamed her Fae."

She glanced at Amanda Roseanne. Little Fae would soon be hers, and Hannah hoped the name wouldn't be changed back to Faith. The young woman seemed to understand Hannah's heartache and gave her a gentle smile.

Hannah continued, "My brother called me Fae when I was a child, telling me it was because I reminded him of wee Kentucky fairies." She felt her cheeks flush, and she wondered at herself for revealing something so personal to strangers.

Then she noticed Amanda Roseanne's husband watching her intently. "That sounds a bit like Irish lore," he said.

"We Kentucky mountain folk revel in our roots," she said. "Irish, Scottish . . ." She shrugged. ". . . English."

"Were you born in Kentucky?"

"Wolf Pen Creek," she said, feeling proud of her heritage. "Though I'm sure you've never heard of it." She laughed. "Most people have no idea what's in our hills and hollers."

His gaze was fixed on Hannah's face. "Actually, I *have* heard of Wolf Pen Creek. And I know its hollers well."

She tilted her head, narrowing her eyes in thought. "And wee Kentucky fairies?" She noticed something in his face that caused her heart to pound.

"Yes," he said.

"And tales of Daniel Boone?" she breathed. Around the table, silence reigned except for the sounds of Hannah's and Matthew's voices. "And traces that were thought to be his trails?"

He nodded slowly. "Yes, Hannah," he said. "I often followed those trails."

"And once you followed them away from Wolf Pen Creek, never again to return?"

This time he didn't answer but kept staring at Hannah, his eyes luminous. He gave her an imperceptible nod.

Hannah tore her gaze from his, almost afraid to breathe, afraid to believe. She looked at Amanda Roseanne. "You and your husband didn't give me your last name," she said, swallowing hard.

"McClary," Matthew's wife said. "We're the McClarys."

Hannah turned back to the young man. "Mattie?" The word came out more like a croak.

Amanda Roseanne and the major exchanged puzzled glances.

"Mattie McClary," she whispered again, her voice trembling. "Mattie?"

He didn't answer, but a wide smile, so like Hannah's, spread across his face. For a moment, they stared at each other in wonder, then Matthew jumped up and grabbed her into a fierce embrace. "Hannah!" he cried. "Hannah!" He held her back and gazed into her face, touching her hair. "Look at you! All grown up. Oh, my little Fae!"

Hannah couldn't speak she was so beset with questions and tears and laughter bubbling up together from someplace deep inside.

"You've no idea how I've tried to find you! I visited Nauvoo again and again, trying to find someone who knew you, who knew where you'd gone."

Hannah touched her brother's face. "And you, standing here almost as if not one day had passed between our days in Kentucky and now! Oh, Mattie, I've missed you so!" She threw her arms around him once more.

Matthew finally drew back to look at his wife. "Amanda Roseanne, meet my sister Hannah." Then he turned back to Hannah. "Is Aunt Sophronia still with you?" he asked.

Hannah smiled and started to answer when Sophronia came around the corner, leading Fae by the hand. "Did I hear my name?" she asked as Fae lifted her arms to Hannah.

Matthew stood facing his elderly aunt, and Sophronia looked him up and down. "What is this good-looking young man doing in my kitchen?" There was a twinkle in her eye, and Hannah suspected that she'd overheard the ruckus and had waited to make her entrance, giving Hannah and Mattie some time to savor their reunion.

"It's Mattie," Hannah said in awe, now holding Fae in her arms. "Our Mattie McClary."

For a moment Sophronia just stood staring at Mattie. "I'd have known you anywhere," she said. "You look just like me, son." And she gathered him into her arms. "The hair's a dead giveaway," she laughed, reaching up to give his wiry hair a playful ruffle.

When the excitement had settled, everyone again gathered around the table. Fae snuggled onto Hannah's lap, staring wide-eyed at the strangers, her thumb in her mouth. After a bit of coaxing, she went to Amanda Roseanne and smiled up into her face.

The major finally cleared his throat to get their attention. His voice was much kinder now, and Hannah appreciated how he had slipped into the background during their reunion, allowing them time to rejoice and speak of the wonder of it all.

"We were told that you have a list of the children."

Hannah nodded. "I've been watching over them carefully, keeping track of name changes and moves. There are seventeen—spread out through the territory."

Major Middleton nodded. "I tried to get information along the way, but no one is volunteering anything."

"They won't," Hannah said. "People are afraid to talk. The dangers are greater than you can imagine."

"We got nothing from the investigation last year. And now, with all the talk of secession, the United States has other problems to attend to. Utah is at the bottom of the list—no matter what happened at Mountain Meadows. That's part of the reason it's taken us so long to get started on this mission."

Hannah was appalled. "You mean they don't care?"

"It's not that they don't care. There's a presidential election coming up. And the country is ready to split. It's a matter of priorities." His weathered face softened. "We understand you might want to come out with the children," he said. "There's room in the wagons—for you both. I know a certain young man who's waiting at Fort Bridger for you and your aunt to join him."

Hannah met Sophronia's hopeful look.

Her aunt answered for them both. "Yes," she declared. "We've been waiting for this day. God bless you for coming at last!"

Major Middleton gave them each a curt nod, though it was more military than unkind. "We will take your information and gather the children. We'll return by the end of the week. Can you be ready?"

"We're ready now," Hannah said with a smile, then paused. "But maybe I should accompany you. The children know me. They won't be so frightened if I'm with you."

"I agree," said the major. "An excellent solution."

Then Hannah glanced across the table at Amanda Roseanne. "If you would like to stay here with Sophronia and little Fae, you would have a chance to rest from your journey—and also to become acquainted with your new daughter." She smiled, trying to cover the hurt those three words—"your new daughter"—brought to her heart.

Amanda Roseanne seemed to understand her pain. "I would like that very much," she said softly. "Thank you."

Within the hour, Major Middleton, Matthew McClary, and Hannah drove off in the carriage, followed by the soldiers. One week later, all seventeen children had been found and brought to the ranch. Belongings were packed into two supply wagons that waited outside, horses and teams were rounded up, and early the following morning, five ox-drawn, high-arched outfits awaited their passengers.

Mattie helped Hannah into the lead rig. As they awaited Sophronia, Amanda Roseanne, and little Fae, he followed her gaze to the house by the meadow. "You've never told me what you think will happen to John Steele. You said only that he's gone into hiding on order of Brigham Young."

"No one outside the territory knows the part he played . . . knows that he was the Danite leader who planned and led the attack," she mused. "As long as no one talks, he's safe. As soon as word spreads, as I'm sure it will with all that Lucas is doing, the whole Church will be brought to trial. Dozens of Mormon men were in on the killings, and they must be held accountable for the murders." She spoke with fervor, just as she always did when the subject was raised.

"Will the Church protect him?"

For a moment Hannah didn't speak. "It's rumored the orders to kill the Farrington party may have come from Brigham himself. And now the Prophet has to protect John in order to protect the Church. Either that or he must let John be the scapegoat for the Church . . . for them all.

"Meantime, Brigham has given John a post to keep him from talking to any government official who might come here to investigate. He's been sent about as far from civilization as a body could get. And I've heard he's taken Harriet, his first wife, to live with him. They're on a desolate farm out by the Green River."

Her voice grew quiet. "It is a comfort to know that, in the eyes of the United States government, I was never John Steele's wife, if only because he was already married to Harriet."

"So, he didn't come back here—I mean, after the massacre?"

Hannah was touched by the concern in Mattie's face. She shook her head. "Only once, and Sophronia chased him off with her rifle." She smiled. "I don't know if the reason John never returned was because of God's intervention . . . or his fear of Aunt Sophie."

"Maybe both," Mattie said with a grin. By now Amanda Roseanne, with Fae in her arms and Sophronia by her side, had joined them. Mattie helped them into the wagon then turned to mount his horse.

Soon the caravan pulled on to the trail to begin the long journey north and east. The troops accompanied them, and two long lines of horsemen flanked the small company.

Fae reached her arms up to be held by Hannah, and she scooped the child close to her heart. Across from them sat Sophronia, Amanda Roseanne, and the twins, Sarah and Meg.

Fae, who bounced Phoebe on her lap, had already begun her endless litany of questions. Sarah and Meg moved closer and, with serious expressions, tried to answer each one. Hannah met Amanda Roseanne's gaze across their bent heads. The young woman seemed to be lost in some serious consideration. Hannah figured that the duties of taking on three children might be weighing heavy.

The wagon rattled along, swaying in the ruts, and Hannah thought about Ellie's final plea, that Lucas and Hannah find her children, find all the children. Though separated by a continent, together they'd done it. Lucas had remained in her heart and prayers during those years apart, and now the prospect of seeing him again at Bridger caused her heart to soar.

She looked out the rear opening of the wagon. Dust rose in billows, almost obscuring the view of the John Steele ranch. The pond sparkled in the sunlight, and in the shadows of the trees lay Ellie Farrington's grave. But Hannah was leaving it now—her life with John Steele and the Saints—and the past was as dead as that grave. A new life, a new beginning, lay ahead, as bright as God's promises.

She touched the small leather journal in her pocket. She'd brought it to give to Amanda Roseanne and Mattie to save for the Farrington girls.

As the house she'd shared with John Steele disappeared from sight, Hannah thought of one of the entries she'd read so many times in recent months that it seemed printed indelibly on her heart:

"Remember ye not the former things, neither consider the things of old. Behold I will do a new thing; now it shall spring forth; shall ye not know it? I will even make a way in the wilderness, and rivers in the desert."

Then Ellie had added beneath the Scripture verse: "Each new day begins afresh with God at my side. He is my constancy in an ever-changing landscape. I don't know about my tomorrows, but I know they belong to him. And all I know of my yesterdays is that he tells me not to remember them. They are his as well, to heal, to redeem."

The wagon swayed, and Hannah caught her balance. Around her the children were chattering about the journey ahead, and Sophronia and Amanda Roseanne were talking amiably about life in California and how it wasn't too late to cross the Sierra Nevada Mountains. The sounds of horses' hoofbeats pounding the trail, the creaking of wagon wheels, and Mattie's voice as he bantered with the troops mixed together into what Hannah thought was the most beautiful music in the world.

Thirty-One

Fort Bridger
June 1860

The small wagon company wound through the mountains leading into Fort Bridger. Hannah wasn't surprised when she saw how it had changed during the years since she'd last seen it. The original outpost had been destroyed by the Mormons during the months they had waged war against the United States. All that remained now were a few half-built, rough-hewn log cabins and a sprinkling of tents. It was still early in the season for most westward travelers, but a few trains of settlers circled in some nearby grassy fields, resting before continuing on the California-Oregon road.

As the small outfit pulled into their night circle, Hannah watched for signs of Lucas Knight. There were none. Leaving Fae in Amanda Roseanne's care, she mounted one of the mares she and Sophronia had brought along and rode through the other wagon camps, asking at the tents and cabins if anyone had seen Lucas. The answer was always the same: No one had seen someone of his description pass through.

Heavy-hearted, Hannah turned back to camp. A big moon now hung in a black velvet sky. She walked a distance from camp, near a small creek, trying to sort out her feelings. She had some decisions to make, and she'd hoped that once united with Lucas, they could consider them together.

Matthew and Amanda Roseanne had just that afternoon made a surprise announcement. They planned to leave the small company the following morning and strike out for California. They told her it had been their plan a few years back, before the massacre. Now that they were this far west, it seemed the perfect time to go. They'd asked Hannah and Sophronia to come with them. Hannah saw a new spark of life in her aunt's eyes at the mere mention of California, and she knew the trip would be a new beginning for her as well.

So as Hannah looked up at the moon, drank in the fragrance of the pine smoke, and listened to the now-sleepy voices of the children readying for bed, she considered the trip to California. Mattie and Amanda Roseanne were family, and though the twins had readily flown into their arms, little Fae had no intention of accepting anyone else but Hannah as her mother. How could Hannah possibly think of letting Fae go to California without her?

The crunch of footsteps on the pebbly ground drew her attention to the path. "Hannah—?" Amanda Roseanne said her name softly.

Hannah turned, smiling as the dark-haired woman walked closer, pretty even in the moonlight. Already she loved her as the sister she'd never had.

"Hannah, I need to talk with you about Fae," Amanda Roseanne said solemnly.

Hannah let out a deep sigh. She'd tried very hard to let the young woman mother Fae, knowing she was rightfully Mattie and Amanda Roseanne's.

Amanda Roseanne smiled, almost as if reading Hannah's thoughts. "I've watched you with Fae. She's enough your child to have been born of your womb. I can see the love between you."

"I love her with all my heart."

"That's why you must continue as her mother. If I took her from you now, she would be confused. I don't know that she would ever get over it."

"But we can't separate the girls. They need to be together—"

"She belongs to you, whether or not you say yes to this. But, Hannah, please come to California with us. We can live near each other. The children can be together every day. Fae will be yours. Besides," she said, "you and Mattie have just found each other. Please come with us. You, Aunt Sophronia . . . and Fae."

"Let me consider it . . . pray about it . . . tonight," she said softly. "I'll let you know in the morning." Amanda Roseanne turned to leave, but Hannah caught her hand to stop her. "You have given me the most precious gift in the world," she said. "Thank you."

That night as she lay on her pallet under the stars, she tried not to think that Lucas could be half a continent away. If she went to California, it might be months, perhaps years, before they met again. If she returned east to join Lucas in his fight for justice, she would be taking little Fae away from her sisters, her family.

She knew, even as she breathed a prayer asking for wisdom, what her answer needed to be. She would go to California to begin a new life, and though Lucas Knight had been in her heart for nearly as long as she could remember, she needed to let go of him and let God take care of her tomorrows. And his.

But as she turned her head away from the canopy of stars, she wondered how long the sadness of missing him would last. Forever, seemed the only answer to her bleak question.

The following morning, the McClary party readied to pull out of Fort Bridger. There were solemn good-byes among the children from the Farrington train, and Hannah spent a moment with each of them, assuring them of her love. They would remain in her heart always, she told them.

Matthew gave the signal and led the way on his horse, hurrying them this first day out. He said there was news of a California-bound company just a day or so ahead that he wanted to catch.

Hannah drove the lead wagon, and Amanda Roseanne drove the second team with Sarah at her side. Fae sat on Meg's lap next to Hannah while Sophronia rested under the canvas cover of the wagon bed.

They had traveled a distance from Fort Bridger when Meg pointed to a knoll up ahead. "Look!" she said. "There's somebody up there!"

Hannah followed Meg's gaze. The morning sun was streaking

toward the west, and the rider and his horse gleamed in the bright light.

The horse was tall, and its black hide shone in the sun. The rider wore a hat, pulled low over his forehead, but there was no mistaking his identity. The horseman and his stallion stood perfectly still, watching the small wagon outfit creak and sway its way up the hill.

Hannah popped the whip over her team's backs. She hoped the animals knew where they were going, because she wasn't watching. Her eyes were locked on the man astride the tall black horse she knew was Spitfire.

Finally Hannah halted the team and climbed off the bench. At the same time Lucas kicked Spitfire to a trot, reining the horse to a halt as he neared her. He slid from the saddle, and with a small cry, Hannah ran to his arms. He held her so close she could feel the thudding of his heart and feel his cheek on her head.

After a moment, Hannah pulled back slightly and looked up at him, her eyes watery. "Oh, Lucas!" She bit her lip to keep from crying.

He took her hand and lifted it to his lips. "I don't intend to ever let you go again, Hannah. Ever."

She settled into his arms, feeling the rough cloth of his shirt against her cheek. Then she thought about the crossroads she'd earlier pondered, and looked up at him. "Do you mind if our forever begins in California?"

He raised a brow and smiled into her eyes. "Anywhere, my darling. Just as long as we're together."

"Then let's go to California," she said, feeling she could dance all the way there if necessary.

He circled his arm around her shoulders, and they turned back to the wagon.

"Mommy!" shouted Fae as Hannah approached.

Hannah stopped and turned to Lucas. "There's something else I need to tell you," she said as she took her daughter into her arms.

He grinned. "I thought there might be." And he touched little Fae's dark hair with the back of his fingers.

Just then Sophronia looked out the canvas opening. "I see our family's complete," she sighed happily. "God bless us, each and every one." Her gaze took in everyone from Matthew, still astride his horse, to Amanda Roseanne, from Sarah to Meggie, then back to Lucas, Hannah, and baby Fae. "Now," she said sternly, "let's get these wagons moving to California! I want to get there while I'm still spry enough to enjoy bathing in that big ocean!"

Mattie McClary chuckled at his aunt's words and shouted the order to move out. The dust kicked up, and the oxen bawled and complained as they pulled the heavy wagons forward. Wheels creaked, and the jangle of yokes and chains carried toward him.

They had gone just a short way when Mattie craned around in the saddle to look back. Hannah, her hair filled with the light of the morning sun, her face shining with love, caught his gaze and smiled.

He remembered their mother's prayer of blessing on that long-ago day back at Wolf Pen Creek. She'd said she was placing Hannah in God's hands because she would be safe there, safer even than in a mother's heart.

Sometimes, she'd said, folks don't know they belong to God. They don't know they are in his big hand . . . where even their names are written forever. And when Mattie had asked if Hannah would ever know, his ma had said someday he would need to tell her.

He glanced back again at Hannah, driving the team with little Fae at her side and Lucas Knight riding next to her wagon on the tall stallion. Hannah was looking heavenward, a look of joy spreading across her face.

Hannah knew! Oh yes, she knew.

AUTHOR'S NOTES

The Mountain Meadows Massacre is a historical event, though historians have yet to agree on the true reasons behind the unprovoked killing of the wagon train families. In this work I have attempted to tell the story with as much historical integrity as possible.

The Veil's characters are largely fictional; however, many are based on actual participants of the massacre, both the victims and their executioners. Names have been changed, and in some cases the characters are compilations of historical figures. Lucas Knight and Hannah McClary are entirely the author's creations, but many of their experiences in *The Veil* are taken from accounts of Latter-day Saints who lived during this fascinating yet brutal era.

Many quotes in *The Veil* that are attributed to Brigham Young and other Mormon leaders are taken from actual sermons and writings. These are documented quotations, many of which were printed in newspapers and Church records of the day. Those quotes dealing with the practice of blood atonement are particularly significant in the unfolding of events leading to the massacre.

A number of books were helpful in developing the historical foundation for the novel, these in particular: Juanita Brooks, *Mountain Meadows Massacre*; Arthur King Peters, *Seven Trails West*; Irving Stone, *Men to Match My Mountains*; Sandra L. Myres (editor) *Ho for California! Women's Overland Diaries from the Huntington Library*; Francis Parkman, *The Oregon Trail*; Fawn M. Brodie, *No Man Knows My History: The Life of Joseph Smith*; Anna Jean Backus, *Mountain Meadows Witness*; Harold Schindler, *Orrin Porter Rockwell: Man of God/Son of Thunder*; Fanny Stenhouse (for more than twenty years the wife of a Mormon missionary and elder) *Tell It All: The Story of a Life's Experience in Mormonism* (foreword by Harriet Beecher Stowe); John D. Lee, *Confessions of John D. Lee.*

The latter reference, *Confessions of John D. Lee,* was especially helpful in researching the events leading to the Mountain Meadows Massacre. John D. Lee (on whom the character John Steele is loosely based) was executed for his role nearly two decades after the massacre. Historians agree that Brigham Young and church elders set up John Lee as a scapegoat after a first trial failed to convict and an enraged nation clamored for justice. After his second trial, Lee was indeed convicted, then executed by firing squad at the massacre site. None of the other Danites who participated in the massacre were ever brought to trial, though many are listed by name in Lee's *Confessions.*

Some 120 people lost their lives at Mountain Meadows in September 1857. The story of *The Veil* ultimately belongs to them, especially to the children . . . those who died and those who lived to tell what they had witnessed. Their names are engraved on a granite monument at the massacre site in southern Utah, just outside Cedar City.